Praise for *The New Voices of Fantasy*

★"This excellent anthology showcases up-and-coming speculative fiction writers, many of whom have received award nominations and critical attention to support their status as future influencers of the genre. The anthology opens with Alyssa Wong's Nebula-winning 'Hungry Daughters of Starving Mothers,' a gripping story of creatures who walk among humans and feed on ugliness. The stories vary in tone: Amal El-Mohtar's 'Wing' is lyrical, A.C. Wise's 'The Practical Witch's Guide to Acquiring Real Estate' is gently humorous, and Carmen Maria Machado's 'The Husband Stitch' is haunting. Some, such as E. Lily Yu's beautiful 'The Cartographer Wasps and the Anarchist Bees,' eschew the well-worn Western setting that is the English-language-fantasy default; others, such as Brooke Bolander's 'Tornado's Siren,' thoughtfully embrace their American and European settings. Fantasy legend Beagle and Tachyon publisher Weisman have provided a valuable snapshot of SF/F's newest generation of writers."
—*Publishers Weekly*, starred review

★"A companion piece of sorts to Beagle's critically acclaimed anthology, *The Secret History of Fantasy* (2010)—a collection of stories that transcended the conventions and clichés of contemporary fantasy—Beagle and Weisman's latest contains 19 comparable stories from some of the genre's most innovative and exciting new voices. . . . A stellar anthology that proves not only that fantasy is alive and well, but that it will be for years to come."
—*Kirkus*, starred review

★"This anthology represents some of the most exciting and interesting work in the fantasy field today, and anyone interested in the genre should read it immediately."
—*Booklist*, starred review

"Delightful and discomforting, indelible and self-assured, the stories of *New Voices of Fantasy* take our familiar old world and imagine it anew. In amongst the dancing buildings, lovelorn tornadoes, and domesticated vampires, we find our deepest truths dressed in fresh and unexpected garments. Rest easy, lovers of the genre: the future is in excellent hands."
— Helene Wecker, author of *The Golem and the Jinni*

"*The New Voices of Fantasy* is a fabulous collection of vivid, surprising, and remarkable stories. Highly recommended."
—Kate Elliott, author of *Poisoned Blade* and *The Very Best of Kate Elliott*

"These stories give me hope."
—Michael Swanwick, author of *Bones of the Earth* and *Not So Much, Said the Cat*

"The key word in this anthology's title is *new*, and if that doesn't quicken your heart, a sampling of the impressively diverse voices will."
—*See the Elephant*

"What Beagle does with this anthology is an elegant passing of the writing pen to a younger generation of fantasy writers."
—*Infinite Text*

Praise for the Editors

Anthologies edited by Peter S. Beagle
The Secret History of Fantasy

"All 17 stories eschew all or most of the conventions of commercial fantasy. . . . Start reading and expect to enjoy."
—*Booklist*

"Set[s] out to rewrite our concept of fantasy, and with the help of some of the world's best writers, succeeds admirably."
—*The Agony Column*

The Urban Fantasy Anthology (with Joe R. Lansdale)

"An essential book not only for longtime followers of such intriguing stories but those who thought fantasy only took place in the completely imagined worlds of J. R. R. Tolkien."
—*Bookgasm*

"An excellent collection of stories that showcases the best of urban fantasy (however you define it). Definitely a must-read!"
—*Interzone*

Anthologies edited by Jacob Weisman

Invaders: 22 Tales from the Outer Limits of Literature

★ "Superlative."
—*Publishers Weekly*, starred review

"Playful and imaginative."
—*AV Club*

"A superb batch of stories by literary authors who have invaded science fiction."
—*Black Gate*

The Sword & Sorcery Anthology (with David G. Hartwell)

★ "This is an unbeatable selection from classic to modern, and each story brings its A game."
—*Publishers Weekly*, starred review

"Hard and fast-paced fantasy that's strong from the first piece right through to the last."
—*Shades of Sentience*

The Treasury of the Fantastic (with David Sandner)

"A treasury in every sense and a treasure!"
—Connie Willis, author of *Doomsday Book* and *To Say Nothing of the Dog*

"This is an important collection for all lovers of fantasy and literature."
—*Library Journal*

Also Edited by Peter S. Beagle

Peter S. Beagle's Immortal Unicorn (with Janet Berliner, 1995)
The Secret History of Fantasy (2010)
The Urban Fantasy Anthology (with Joe R. Lansdale, 2011)

Also Edited by Jacob Weisman

The Treasury of the Fantastic (with David Sandner, 2001, 2013)
The Sword & Sorcery Anthology (with David G. Hartwell, 2012)
Invaders: 22 Tales from the Outer Limits of Literature (2016)

THE NEW VOICES OF FANTASY
PETER S. BEAGLE & JACOB WEISMAN

THE
NEW VOICES
OF
FANTASY

EDITED BY
PETER S. BEAGLE
AND JACOB WEISMAN

TACHYON
SAN FRANCISCO

Interior and cover design by Elizabeth Story
Cover art "The Tree Child" copyright © 2011 by Camille André

Tachyon Publications LLC
1459 18th Street #139
San Francisco, CA 94107
www.tachyonpublications.com
tachyon@tachyonpublications.com

Series Editor: Jacob Weisman
Project Editor: James DeMaiolo

ISBN 13: 978-1-61696-257-9

Printed in the United States by Worzalla

First Edition: 2017
9 8 7 6 5 4 3 2 1

CONTENTS

INTRODUCTION
Jacob Weisman

The New Voices of Fantasy collects the work of nineteen authors of fantasy who Peter S. Beagle and I firmly believe will soon be much better known. These writers are producing an important body of work. All of the stories in this book are recent, published after 2010. The authors included are still very much in the early stages of their careers. Some of them have already made the transition from writing short stories to writing the novels that will allow them to move forward in their careers. For some of these authors, that transition is still in their near future. A few, like the enigmatic Ben Loory, may decide to forgo novels entirely and go where their writing takes them.

Fantasy fiction has grown over the years, coming to dominate much of the commercial market of what was formally science fiction. Peter S. Beagle's groundbreaking 2010 anthology, *The Secret History of Fantasy*, explored the merging of genre fantasy and so called mainstream markets into a new form of literary fantasy. This anthology constitutes something of a sequel, leaping ahead to examine the work of a brand-new generation of writers working along similar lines.

For new writers to succeed requires both opportunity and exposure. Peter S. Beagle's own career took root when publishers were desperately struggling to find ways to capitalize on the sudden and unexpected interest in fantasy fiction in the 1960s following the republication of The Lord of the Rings in affordable paperback editions. Ballantine Books would produce a line of reprints of classic fantasy novels that ultimately led to the reprinting of Peter's first novel, A Fine & Private Place, and the original publication of his best known work, The Last Unicorn. Terry Carr's New Worlds of Fantasy anthologies ran to three volumes between 1967 and 1971 and would republish two more of Peter's stories. The boom in fantasy publishing would eventually lead to new works by Patricia A. McKillip, Stephen R. Donaldson, and Evangeline Walton, among others.

The sheer number of writers entering the field over the last decade, with new markets online and in print, has created a hothouse for new writers in science fiction and fantasy to experiment and find their voices. Just as Peter S. Beagle imagined a Yiddish magician in The Last Unicorn and Patricia A. McKillip imagined a woman as a powerful sorcerer in The Forgotten Beasts of Eld, the writers in The New Voices of Fantasy are very much a product of their own times, too.

Here you'll find Usman T. Malik's Pakistani professor who becomes obsessed with his grandfather's childhood stories; Alyssa Wong's serial killer facing ancient terrors far deadlier than himself; Sofia Samatar's reflection on the nature of fantasy and abandonment; and Eugene Fischer warning of the ease of cultural influence and appropriation. And you'll find other nontraditional stories, too. Ben Loory's tale of love and ducks; Maria Dahvana Headley's waitstaff serving inside a building come alive; Ursula Vernon's story of the mating habits of magical creatures very much like ourselves; and Max Gladstone's updating of the Dracula mythos.

What is certain is that The New Voices of Fantasy collects stories by amazing authors who are ready to expand the definition of what fantasy can be, and what fantasy will be. Even as Peter and I compiled this volume, the authors and stories we included were winning awards and accolades almost as fast we could keep track of them. The success of these writers can hardly be contained a moment longer.

BACK THEN
Peter S. Beagle

Jules Verne, who always considered himself a scientist, was distinctly put out by the work of the younger writer H. G. Wells. "Il a inventé!" the author of From the Earth to the Moon *sniffed at the author of* The War of the Worlds. *"He makes things up!"*

"Another damn fairytale. I can't abide fairytales."

Those were the words of Frank O'Connor, one of the great short-story writers of the twentieth century, back in 1960 when I was a member of the legendary Wallace Stegner writing class at Stanford University, which included people like Larry McMurtry, Ken Kesey, Gurney Norman, James Baker Hall, Chris Koch, Joanna Ostrow, and Judith Rascoe. O'Connor had succeeded Malcolm Cowley, who was as warmly tolerant of a student's variations from officially recognized realism as O'Connor was dogmatic. As far as Malcolm was concerned, all that mattered was whether or not the story *worked.* His ego was never tied up with his opinions.

One of the many styles of storytelling that O'Connor let the class know early on that he despised on principle (including D. H. Lawrence, old-country memoirs and folktales, and anything set in another century) was fantasy of any sort. Consequently he loudly trashed—not for its quality or execution, but clearly for what it was—a small, gently charming tale by one of the notably few women in the class. (It might have been Judy Rascoe, but I can't be sure.) It was a fantasy, so it *couldn't* be any good, and that was the end of *that*.

I was outraged at O'Connor's rigidity, and I holed up in Berkeley for a day and a half at a friend's apartment and returned for the next meeting of the writing class with a short story called "Come Lady Death." O'Connor gave it a grand dramatic reading (he had been a director of the Abbey Theatre at one time), looked around at the class, and announced firmly, "This is a beautifully written story. I don't like it."

Fifty-five years later, I think of "Come Lady Death" as little more than my Isak Dinesen imitation, but it's certainly the only good work I produced during that Stanford year. The rest of the time I spent in writing a dutifully realistic second novel about a young musician in France, which has nothing but—fair's fair—a *couple* of goodish scenes to recommend it. I rewrote it three times, but I knew when I was done that it wasn't much.

But "Come Lady Death" was published in the *Atlantic Monthly*, won an O'Henry Award in 1963, has been reprinted in many anthologies, and became an opera, with music by David Carlson, in 1993. And by then I was long since set—with an unintentional assist from Frank O'Connor—on an artistic path I'd truly never visualized as mine. I read Hemingway and Fitzgerald, and Wolfe as I was supposed to do, and wrote my dutiful papers on Mailer and Styron. But the ones I apprenticed myself to, and tried to imitate, and wanted to *be*, were Lord Dunsany (the master, *yes*, and he was still publishing when I was in college), James Stephens, Dinesen, Flann O'Brien, and John Collier. They still are.

The fantastic literature of my youth was consigned, with rare exceptions (most of those European or Latin), to a ghetto of pulp magazines and B or C movies, and even the most successful of its practitioners were well aware of this. Hence the following mini-memoir.

Years ago, knowing that I was scheduled to speak at an annual meeting of the Science Fiction Writers of America—which now includes *and Fantasy* in its designation—Ursula Le Guin, wisest of us all, warned me as follows: "Remember that most of your audience will be drunk by the time you get up to speak, and remember always that all of us feel, to one degree or another, that mainstream fiction has been stealing our ideas—and even our classic clichés—for generations, and selling them back to us as 'Magic Realism.' Tell them that, loudly and repeatedly, and the ones who can still stand up will be buying you drinks all night. And never forget that this is a small, highly incestuous group, and a lot of people here have been married to, or sleeping with, other members of the group—so watch what you say."

I followed her advice, and survived the evening. Even got asked back the next year, which tells you *something. . . .*

The group of remarkable young writers included in this book aren't at all likely to undergo either the intellectual snobbery or the commercial exclusion that my generation had to withstand, to one degree or another. Some of them have been accepted at the Iowa State writing program; all have published stories before appearing in this collection. That doesn't mean that they'll all make money—which is, however you slice it, still the hallmark of American success—or that they'll all be short-listed for Booker Prizes and be offered the kind of prestigious teaching post where you don't actually have to teach. They'll still be gambling, as we all do, on being noticed at all. Comes with the territory.

I envy them all, in one way: To be at the very beginning of their own careers, with so much ahead to be discovered, invented—and reinvented—to be attempted and flat-out screwed up (speaking for myself, I've never learned a damn thing—any damn thing—without first doing it wrong, usually a lot of times). And then, one midnight, to surprise themselves with a completely unexpected triumph. Learning what comes effortlessly, and with natural delight . . . and chancing the frustration of what does *not*, and still persists in dancing tauntingly on the horizon. And knowing, *knowing* that you'll never get it right. That there *is* no right: just the Thing in one's head—entirely real, eminently visible to the writer (and the painter, and the sculptor, and the musician)—that emerges as *it* chooses, and never quite as *you* choose.

That's the part I don't envy them for at all because, judging from the quality of their work, they'll all keep trying. As will I. Even though I know better, being an old guy.

HUNGRY DAUGHTERS
OF STARVING MOTHERS
Alyssa Wong

Alyssa Wong's considerable reputation rests on only the handful of stories. Still in her mid-twenties, she is the youngest author to appear in this collection. Her work has appeared in *Fantasy & Science Fiction, Strange Horizons, Black Static, Tor.com,* and *Lightspeed: Queers Destroy Science Fiction.* Her first published story, "The Fisher Queen," earned immediate acclaim and was nominated for the Nebula, World Fantasy, and Shirley Jackson awards. Wong's fourth story, "Hungry Daughters of Starving Mothers," was published the following year to even stronger acclaim, winning the Nebula and World Fantasy awards, and was nominated for the Shirley Jackson and the Bram Stoker awards, and was a finalist for the Locus Award. She was nominated for the John W. Campbell Award for Best New Writer in 2016. She lives in Raleigh.

"Hungry Daughters of Starving Mothers" is a warning about compulsion and the corrupting powers of negative emotions.

As my date—Harvey? Harvard?—brags about his alma mater and Manhattan penthouse, I take a bite of overpriced kale and watch his ugly thoughts swirl overhead. It's hard to pay attention to him with my stomach growling and my body ajitter, for all he's easy on the eyes. Harvey doesn't look much older than I am, but his thoughts, covered in spines and centipede feet, glisten with ancient grudges and carry an entitled, Ivy League stink.

"My apartment has the most amazing view of the city," he's saying, his thoughts sliding long over each other like dark, bristling snakes. Each one is as thick around as his Rolex-draped wrist. "I just installed a Jacuzzi along the west wall so that I can watch the sun set while I relax after getting back from the gym."

I nod, half-listening to the words coming out of his mouth. I'm much more interested in the ones hissing through the teeth of the thoughts above him.

She's got perfect tits, li'l handfuls just waiting to be squeezed. I love me some perky tits.

I'm gonna fuck this bitch so hard she'll never walk straight again.

Gross. "That sounds wonderful," I say as I sip champagne and gaze at him through my false eyelashes, hoping the dimmed screen of my iPhone isn't visible through the tablecloth below. This dude is boring as hell, and I'm already back on Tindr, thumbing through next week's prospective dinner dates.

She's so into me, she'll be begging for it by the end of the night.

I can't wait to cut her up.

My eyes flick up sharply. "I'm sorry?" I say.

Harvey blinks. "I said, Argentina is a beautiful country."

Pretty little thing. She'll look so good spread out all over the floor.

"Right," I say. "Of course." Blood's pulsing through my head so hard it probably looks like I've got a wicked blush.

I'm so excited, I'm half hard already.

You and me both, I think, turning my iPhone off and smiling my prettiest smile.

The waiter swings by with another bottle of champagne and a dessert menu burned into a wooden card, but I wave him off. "Dinner's been lovely," I whisper to Harvey, leaning in and kissing his cheek, "but I've got a different kind of dessert in mind."

Ahhh, go the ugly thoughts, settling into a gentle, rippling wave across his shoulders. *I'm going to take her home and split her all the way from top to bottom. Like a fucking fruit tart.*

That is not the way I normally eat fruit tarts, but who am I to judge? I passed on dessert, after all.

When he pays the bill, he can't stop grinning at me. Neither can the ugly thoughts hissing and cackling behind his ear.

"What's got you so happy?" I ask coyly.

"I'm just excited to spend the rest of the evening with you," he replies.

The fucker has his own parking spot! No taxis for us; he's even brought the Tesla. The leather seats smell buttery and sweet, and as I slide in and make myself comfortable, the rankness of his thoughts leaves a stain in the air. It's enough to leave me light-headed, almost purring. As we cruise uptown toward his fancy-ass penthouse, I ask him to pull over near the Queensboro Bridge for a second.

Annoyance flashes across his face, but he parks the Tesla in a side street. I lurch into an alley, tottering over empty cans and discarded cigarettes in my four-inch heels, and puke a trail of champagne and kale over to the dumpster shoved up against the apartment building.

"Are you all right?" Harvey calls.

"I'm fine," I slur. Not a single curious window opens overhead.

His steps echo down the alley. He's gotten out of the car, and he's walking toward me like I'm an animal that he needs to approach carefully.

Maybe I should do it now.

Yes! Now, now, while the bitch is occupied.

But what about the method? I won't get to see her insides all pretty everywhere—

I launch myself at him, fingers digging sharp into his body, and bite down hard on his mouth. He tries to shout, but I swallow the sound and shove my tongue inside. There, just behind his teeth, is what I'm looking for: ugly thoughts, viscous as boiled tendon. I suck them howling and fighting into my throat as Harvey's body shudders, little mewling noises escaping from his nose.

I feel decadent and filthy, swollen with the cruelest dreams I've ever tasted. I can barely feel Harvey's feeble struggles; in this state, with the darkest parts of himself drained from his mouth into mine, he's no match for me.

They're never as strong as they think they are.

By the time he finally goes limp, the last of the thoughts disappearing down my throat, my body's already changing. My limbs elongate, growing thicker, and my dress feels too tight as my ribs expand. I'll have to work quickly. I strip off my clothes with practiced ease, struggling a little to work the bodice free of the gym-toned musculature swelling under my skin.

It doesn't take much time to wrestle Harvey out of his clothes, either. My hands are shaking but strong, and as I button up his shirt around me and shrug on his jacket, my jaw has creaked into an approximation of his and the ridges of my fingerprints have reshaped themselves completely. Harvey is so much bigger than me, and the expansion of space eases the pressure on my boiling belly, stuffed with ugly thoughts as it is. I stuff my discarded outfit into my purse, my high heels clicking against the empty glass jar at its bottom, and sling the strap over my now-broad shoulder.

I kneel to check Harvey's pulse—slow but steady—before rolling his unconscious body up against the dumpster, covering him with trash bags. Maybe he'll wake up, maybe he won't. Not my problem, as long as he doesn't wake in the next ten seconds to see his doppelganger strolling out of the alley, wearing his clothes and fingering his wallet and the keys to his Tesla.

There's a cluster of drunk college kids gawking at Harvey's car. I level an arrogant stare at them—oh, but do I wear this body so much better than he did!—and they scatter.

I might not have a license, but Harvey's body remembers how to drive.

––––––––––

The Tesla revs sweetly under me, but I ditch it in a parking garage in Bedford, stripping in the relative privacy of the second-to-highest level, edged behind a pillar. After laying the keys on the driver's seat over Harvey's neatly folded clothes and shutting the car door, I pull the glass jar from my purse and vomit into it as quietly as I can. Black liquid, thick and viscous, hits the bottom of the jar, hissing and snarling Harvey's words. My body shudders, limbs retracting, spine reshaping itself, as I empty myself of him.

It takes a few more minutes to ease back into an approximation of myself, at least enough to slip my dress and heels back on, pocket the jar, and comb my tangled hair out with my fingers. The parking attendant nods at me as I walk out of the garage, his eyes sliding disinterested over me, his thoughts a gray, indistinct murmur.

The L train takes me back home to Bushwick, and when I push open the apartment door, Aiko is in the kitchen, rolling mochi paste out on the counter.

"You're here," I say stupidly. I'm still a little foggy from shaking off Harvey's form, and strains of his thoughts linger in me, setting my blood humming uncomfortably hot.

"I'd hope so. You invited me over." She hasn't changed out of her catering company clothes, and her short, sleek hair frames her face, aglow in the kitchen light. Not a single ugly thought casts its shadow across the stove behind her. "Did you forget again?"

"No," I lie, kicking my shoes off at the door. "I totally would never do something like that. Have you been here long?"

"About an hour, nothing unusual. The doorman let me in, and I kept your spare key." She smiles briefly, soft compared to the brusque movements of her hands. She's got flour on her rolled-up sleeves, and my heart flutters the way it never does when I'm out hunting. "I'm guessing your date was pretty shit. You probably wouldn't have come home at all if it had gone well."

"You could say that." I reach into my purse and stash the snarling jar in the fridge, where it clatters against the others, nearly a dozen bottles of malignant leftovers labeled as health drinks.

Aiko nods to her right. "I brought you some pastries from the event tonight. They're in the paper bag on the counter."

"You're an angel." I edge past her so I don't make bodily contact. Aiko thinks I have touch issues, but the truth is, she smells like everything good in the world, solid and familiar, both light and heavy at the same time, and it's enough to drive a person mad.

"He should have bought you a cab back, at least," says Aiko, reaching for a bowl of red bean paste. I fiddle with the bag of pastries, pretending to select something from its contents. "I swear, it's like you're a magnet for terrible dates."

She's not wrong; I'm very careful about who I court. After all, that's how I stay fed. But no one in the past has been as delicious, as hideously depraved as Harvey. No one else has been a killer.

I'm going to take her home and split her all the way from top to bottom.

"Maybe I'm too weird," I say.

"You're probably too normal. Only socially maladjusted creeps use Tindr."

"Gee, thanks," I complain.

She grins, flicking a bit of red bean paste at me. I lick it off of my arm. "You know what I mean. Come visit my church with me sometime, yeah? There are plenty of nice boys there."

"The dating scene in this city depresses me," I mutter, flicking open my Tindr app with my thumb. "I'll pass."

"Come on, Jen, put that away." Aiko hesitates. "Your mom called while you were out. She wants you to move back to Flushing."

I bark out a short, sharp laugh, my good mood evaporating. "What else is new?"

"She's getting old," Aiko says. "And she's lonely."

"I bet. All her mahjong partners are dead, pretty much." I can imagine her in her little apartment in Flushing, huddled over her laptop, floral curtains pulled tight over the windows to shut out the rest of the world. My ma, whose apartment walls are alive with hissing, covered in the ugly, bottled remains of her paramours.

Aiko sighs, joining me at the counter and leaning back against me. For once, I don't move away. Every muscle in my body is tense, straining. I'm afraid I might catch fire, but I don't want her to leave. "Would it kill you to be kind to her?"

I think about my baba evaporating into thin air when I was five years old, what was left of him coiled in my ma's stomach. "Are you telling me to go back?"

She doesn't say anything for a bit. "No," she says at last. "That place isn't good for you. That house isn't good for anyone."

Just a few inches away, an army of jars full of black, viscous liquid wait in the fridge, their contents muttering to themselves. Aiko can't hear them, but each slosh against the glass is a low, nasty hiss:

who does she think she is, the fucking cunt
should've got her when I had the chance

I can still feel Harvey, his malice and ugly joy, on my tongue. I'm already full of things my ma gave me. "I'm glad we agree."

Over the next few weeks, I gorge myself on the pickup artists and grad students populating the St. Marks hipster bars, but nothing tastes good after Harvey. Their watery essences, squeezed from their owners with barely a whimper of protest, barely coat my stomach. Sometimes I take too much. I scrape them dry and leave them empty, shaking their forms off like rainwater when I'm done.

I tell Aiko I've been partying when she says I look haggard. She tells me to quit drinking so much, her face impassive, her thoughts clouded with concern. She starts coming over more often, even cooking dinner for me, and her presence both grounds me and drives me mad.

"I'm worried about you," she says as I lie on the floor, flipping listlessly through pages of online dating profiles, looking for the emptiness, the rot, that made Harvey so appealing. She's cooking my mom's lo mein recipe, the oily smell making my skin itch. "You've lost so much weight and there's nothing in your fridge, just a bunch of empty jam jars."

I don't tell her that Harvey's lies under my bed, that I lick its remnants every night to send my nerves back into euphoria. I don't tell her how often I dream about my ma's place, the shelves of jars she never let me touch. "Is it really okay for you to spend so much time away from your catering business?" I say instead. "Time is money, and Jimmy gets pissy when he has to make all the desserts without you."

Aiko sets a bowl of lo mein in front of me and joins me on the ground. "There's nowhere I'd rather be than here," she says, and a dangerous, luminous sweetness blooms in my chest.

But the hunger grows worse every day, and soon I can't trust myself around her. I deadbolt the door, and when she stops by my apartment to check on me, I refuse to let her in. Texts light up my phone like a fleet of fireworks as I huddle under a blanket on the other side, my face pressed against the wood, my fingers twitching.

"Please, Jen, I don't understand," she says from behind the door. "Did I do something wrong?"

I can't wait to cut her up, I think, and hate myself even more.

By the time Aiko leaves, her footsteps echoing down the hallway, I've dug deep gouges in the door's paint with my nails and teeth, my mouth full of her intoxicating scent.

My ma's apartment in Flushing still smells the same. She's never been a clean person, and the sheer amount of junk stacked up everywhere has increased since I left home for good. Piles of newspapers, old food containers, and stuffed toys make it hard to push the door open, and the stench makes me cough. Her hoard is up to my shoulders, even higher in some places, and as I pick my way through it, the sounds that colored my childhood grow louder: the constant whine of a Taiwanese soap opera bleeding past mountains of trash, and the cruel cacophony of many familiar voices:

Touch me again and I swear I'll kill you—

How many times have I told you not to wash the clothes like that, open your mouth—

Hope her ugly chink daughter isn't home tonight—

Under the refuse she's hoarded the walls are honeycombed with shelves, lined with what's left of my ma's lovers. She keeps them like disgusting, mouthwatering trophies, desires pickling in stomach acid and bile. I could probably call them by name if I wanted to; when I was a kid, I used to lie on the couch and watch my baba's ghost flicker across their surfaces.

My ma's huddled in the kitchen, the screen of her laptop casting a sickly blue glow on her face. Her thoughts cover her quietly like a blanket. "I made some niu ro mien," she says. "It's on the stove. Your baba's in there."

My stomach curls, but whether it's from revulsion or hunger I can't tell. "Thanks, Ma," I say. I find a bowl that's almost clean and wash it out, ladling a generous portion of thick noodles for myself. The broth smells faintly of Hongtashan tobacco, and as I force it down almost faster than I can swallow, someone else's memories of my childhood flash before my eyes: pushing a small girl on a swing set at the park; laughing as she chases pigeons down the street; raising a hand for a second blow as her mother launches herself toward us, between us, teeth bared—

"How is it?" she says.

Foul. "Great," I say. It settles my stomach, at least for a little while. But my baba was no Harvey, and I can already feel the hunger creeping back, waiting for the perfect moment to strike.

"You ate something you shouldn't have, didn't you, Meimei." My ma looks up at me for the first time since I walked in, and she looks almost as tired as I feel. "Why didn't you learn from me? I taught you to stick to petty criminals. I taught you to stay invisible."

She'd tried to teach me to disappear into myself, the way she'd disappeared into this apartment. "I know I messed up," I tell her. "Nothing tastes good anymore, and I'm always hungry. But I don't know what to do."

My ma sighs. "Once you've tasted a killer, there's no turning back. You'll crave that intensity until you die. And it can take a long time for someone like us to die, Meimei."

It occurs to me that I don't actually know how old my ma is. Her thoughts are old and covered in knots, stitched together from the remnants of other people's experiences. How long has she been fighting this condition, these overwhelming, gnawing desires?

"Move back in," she's saying. "There's so much tong activity here, the streets leak with food. You barely even have to go outside, just crack open a window and you can smell it brewing. The malice, the knives and bullets. . . ."

The picture she paints makes me shudder, my mouth itching. "I can't just leave everything, Ma," I say. "I have my own life now." And I can't live in this apartment, with its lack of sunlight and fresh air, its thick stench of regret and malice.

"So what happens if you go back? You lose control, you take a bite out of Aiko?" She sees me stiffen. "That girl cares about you so much. The best thing you can do for her is keep away. Don't let what happened to your father happen to Aiko." She reaches for my hand, and I pull away. "Stay here, Meimei. We only have each other."

"This isn't what I want." I'm backing up, and my shoulder bumps into the trash, threatening to bury us both in rotting stuffed animals. "This isn't *safe*, Ma. You shouldn't even stay here."

My ma coughs, her eyes glinting in the dark. The cackling from her jar collection swells in a vicious tide, former lovers rocking back and forth on their shelves. "Someday you'll learn that there's more to life than being selfish, Meimei."

That's when I turn my back on her, pushing past the debris and bullshit her apartment's stuffed with. I don't want to die, but as far as I'm concerned, living like my ma, sequestered away from the rest of the world, her doors barricaded with heaps of useless trinkets and soured memories, is worse than being dead.

The jars leer and cackle as I go, and she doesn't try to follow me.

The scent of Flushing clings to my skin, and I can't wait to shake it off. I get on the train as soon as I can, and I'm back on Tindr as soon as the M passes aboveground. Tears blur my eyes, rattling free with the movement of the train. I scrub them away angrily, and when my vision clears, I glance back at the screen. A woman with sleek, dark hair, slim tortoiseshell glasses, and a smile that seems a little shy, but strangely handsome, glows up at me. In the picture, she's framed by the downtown cityscape. She has rounded cheeks, but there's a strange flat quality to her face. And then, of course, there are the dreams shadowing her, so strong they leak from the screen in a thick, heady miasma. Every one of those myriad eyes is staring straight at me, and my skin prickles.

I scan the information on her profile page, my blood beating so hard I can feel my fingertips pulsing: relatively young-looking, but old enough to be my mother's cousin. Likes: exploring good food, spending rainy days at the Cloisters, browsing used book stores. Location: Manhattan.

She looks a little like Aiko.

She's quick to message me back. As we flirt, cold sweat and adrenaline send uncomfortable shivers through my body. Everything is sharper, and I can almost hear Harvey's jar laughing. Finally, the words I'm waiting for pop up:

I'd love to meet you. Are you free tonight?

I make a quick stop-off back home, and my heart hammers as I get on the train bound for the Lower East Side, red lipstick immaculate and arms shaking beneath my crisp designer coat, a pair of Mom's glass jars tucked in my purse.

Her name is Seo-yun, and as she watches me eat, her eyes flickering from my mouth to my throat, her smile is so sharp I could cut myself on it. "I love places like this," she says. "Little authentic spots with only twelve seats. Have you been to Haru before?"

"I haven't," I murmur. My fingers are clumsy with my chopsticks, tremors clicking them together, making it hard to pick up my food. God, she smells delectable. I've never met someone whose mind is so twisted, so rich; a malignancy as well developed and finely crafted as the most elegant dessert.

I'm going to take her home and split her open like a—

I can already taste her on my tongue, the best meal I've never had.

"You're in for a treat," Seo-yun says as the waiter—the only other staff beside the chef behind the counter—brings us another pot of tea. "This restaurant started as a stall in a subway station back in Japan."

"Oh wow," I say. "That's . . . amazing."

"I think so, too. I'm glad they expanded into Manhattan."

Behind her kind eyes, a gnarled mess of ancient, ugly thoughts writhes like the tails of a rat king. I've never seen so many in one place. They crawl from her mouth and ears, creeping through the air on deep-scaled legs, their voices like the drone of descending locusts.

I'm not her first. I can tell that already. But then, she isn't mine, either.

I spend the evening sweating through my dress, nearly dropping my chopsticks. I can't stop staring at the ugly thoughts, dropping from her lips like swollen beetles. They skitter over the tablecloth toward me, whispering obscenities at odds with Seo-yun's gentle voice, hissing what they'd like to do to me. It takes everything in me not to pluck them from the table and crunch them deep between my teeth right then and there, to pour into her lap and rip her mind clean.

Seo-yun is too much for me, but I'm in too far, too hard; I *need* to have her.

She smiles at me. "Not hungry?"

I glance down at my plate. I've barely managed a couple of nigiri. "I'm on a diet," I mutter.

"I understand," she says earnestly. The ugly thoughts crawl over the tops of her hands, iridescent drops spilling into her soy sauce dish.

When the waiter finally disappears into the kitchen, I move in to kiss her across the table. She makes a startled noise, gentle pink spreading across her face, but she doesn't pull away. My elbow sinks into the exoskeleton of one of the thought-beetles, crushing it into black, moist paste against my skin.

I open my mouth to take the first bite.

"So, I'm curious," murmurs Seo-yun, her breath brushing my lips. "Who's Aiko?"

My eyes snap open. Seo-yun smiles, her voice warm and tender, all her edges dark. "She seems sweet, that's all. I'm surprised you haven't had a taste of her yet."

I back up so fast that I knock over my teacup, spilling scalding tea over everything. But Seo-yun doesn't move, just keeps smiling that kind, gentle smile as her monstrous thoughts lap delicately at the tablecloth.

"She smells so ripe," she whispers. "But you're afraid you'll ruin her, aren't you? Eat her up, and for what? Just like your mum did your dad."

No, no, no. I've miscalculated so badly. But I'm so hungry, and I'm

33

too young, and she smells like ancient power. There's no way I'll be able to outrun her. "Get out of my head," I manage to say.

"I'm not in your head, love. Your thoughts are spilling out everywhere around you, for everyone to see." She leans in, propping her chin on her hand. The thoughts twisted around her head like a living crown let out a dry, rattling laugh. "I like you, Jenny. You're ambitious. A little careless, but we can fix that." Seo-yun taps on the table, and the waiter reappears, folding up the tablecloth deftly and sliding a single dish onto the now-bare table. An array of thin, translucent slices fan out across the plate, pale and glistening with malice. Bisected eyes glint, mouths caught mid-snarl, from every piece. "All it takes is a little practice and discipline, and no one will know what you're really thinking."

"On the house, of course, ma'am," the waiter murmurs. Before he disappears again, I catch a glimpse of dark, many-legged thoughts braided like a bracelet around his wrist.

Seo-yun takes the first bite, glancing up at me from behind her glasses. "Your mum was wrong," she says. "She thought you were alone, just the two of you. So she taught you to only eat when you needed to, so you didn't get caught, biding your time between meals like a snake."

"You don't know anything about me," I say. The heady, rotten perfume from the dish in front of me makes my head spin with hunger.

"My mum was much the same. Eat for survival, not for pleasure." She gestures at the plate with her chopsticks. "Please, have some."

As the food disappears, I can only hold out for a few more slices before my chopsticks dart out, catching a piece for myself. It's so acidic it makes my tongue burn and eyes itch, the aftertaste strangely sweet.

"Do you like it?"

I respond by wolfing down another two slices, and Seo-yun chuckles. Harvey is bland compared to this, this strangely distilled pairing of emotions—

I gasp as my body starts to warp, hands withering, burn scars twisting their way around my arms. Gasoline, malice, childish joy rush through me, a heady mix of memory and sensory overstimulation. And then Seo-yun's lips are on mine, teeth tugging gently, swallowing, drawing it out of me. The burns fade, but the tingle of cruel euphoria lingers.

She wipes her mouth delicately. "Ate a little too fast, I think, dear," she says. "My point, Jenny, is that I believe in eating for pleasure, not just survival. And communally, of course. There are a number of us who get together for dinner or drinks at my place, every so often, and I would love it if you would join us tonight. An eating club, of sorts."

My gaze flickers up at her thoughts, but they're sitting still as stones, just watching me with unblinking eyes. My mouth stings with the imprint of hers.

"Let me introduce you soon. You don't have to be alone anymore." As the waiter clears the plate and nods at her—no check, no receipt, nothing—Seo-yun adds, "And tonight doesn't have to be over until we want it to be." She offers me her hand. After a moment's hesitation, I take it. It's smaller than mine, and warm.

"Yes, please," I say, watching her thoughts instead of her face.

As we leave the restaurant, she presses her lips to my forehead. Her lips sear into my skin, nerves singing white-hot with ecstasy. "They're going to love you," she says.

We'll have so much fun, say the thoughts curling through her dark hair.

She hails a cab from the fleet circling the street like wolves, and we get inside.

I run into Aiko two months later in front of my apartment, as I'm carrying the last box of my stuff out. She's got a startled look on her face, and she's carrying a bag stuffed with ramps, kaffir limes, hearts of palm—all ingredients I wouldn't have known two months ago, before meeting Seo-yun. "You're moving?"

I shrug, staring over her head, avoiding her eyes. "Yeah, uh. I'm seeing someone now, and she's got a really nice place."

"Oh." She swallows, shifts the bag of groceries higher on her hip. "That's great. I didn't know you were dating anybody." I can hear her shaky smile. "She must be feeding you well. You look healthier."

"Thanks," I say, though I wonder. It's true, I'm sleeker, more confident now. I'm barely home anymore, spending most of my time in Seo-yun's Chelsea apartment, learning to cook with the array of salts and spices infused with ugly dreams, drinking wine distilled from deathbed confessions. My time stalking the streets for small-time criminals is done. But why has my confidence evaporated the moment I see Aiko? And if that ravenous hunger from Harvey is gone, why am I holding my breath to keep from breathing in her scent?

"So what's she like?"

"Older, kind of—" *kind of looks like you* "—short. Likes to cook, right." I start to edge past her. "Listen, this box is heavy and the van's waiting for me downstairs. I should go."

"Wait," Aiko says, grabbing my arm. "Your mom keeps calling me. She still has my number from . . . before. She's worried about you. Plus I haven't seen you in ages, and you're just gonna take off?"

Aiko, small and humble. Her hands smell like home, like rice flour and bad memories. How could I ever have found that appealing?

"We don't need to say goodbye. I'm sure I'll see you later," I lie, shrugging her off.

"Let's get dinner sometime," says Aiko, but I'm already walking away.

Caterers flit like blackbirds through the apartment, dark uniforms neatly pressed, their own ugly thoughts braided and pinned out of the way. It's a two-story affair, and well-dressed people flock together everywhere there's space, Seo-yun's library upstairs to the living room on the ground floor. She's even asked the caterers to prepare some of my recipes, which makes my heart glow. "You're the best," I say, kneeling on the bed beside her and pecking her on the cheek.

Seo-yun smiles, fixing my hair. She wears a sleek, deep blue dress, and today, her murderous thoughts are draped over her shoulders like a stole, a living, writhing cape. Their teeth glitter like tiny diamonds. I've never seen her so beautiful. "They're good recipes. My friends will be so excited to taste them."

I've already met many of them, all much older than I am. They make me nervous. "I'll go check on the food," I say.

She brushes her thumb over my cheek. "Whatever you'd like, love."

I escape into the kitchen, murmuring brief greetings to the guests I encounter on the way. Their hideous dreams adorn them like jewels, glimmering and snatching at me as I slip past. As I walk past some of the cooks, I notice a man who looks vaguely familiar. "Hey," I say.

"Yes, ma'am?" The caterer turns around, and I realize where I've seen him; there's a picture of him and Aiko on her cellphone, the pair of them posing in front of a display at a big event they'd cooked for. My heartbeat slows.

"Aren't you Aiko's coworker?"

He grins and nods. "Yes, I'm Jimmy. Aiko's my business partner. Are you looking for her?"

"Wait, she's here?"

He frowns. "She should be. She never misses one of Ms. Sun's parties." He smiles. "Ms. Sun lets us take home whatever's left when the party winds down. She's so generous."

I turn abruptly and head for the staircase to the bedroom, shouldering my way through the crowd. Thoughts pelt me as I go: Has Aiko known about me, my ma, what we can do? How long has she known? And worse—Seo-yun's known all along about Aiko, and played me for a fool.

I bang the bedroom door open to find Aiko sprawled out across the carpet, her jacket torn open. Seo-yun crouches on the floor above her in her glorious dress, her mouth dark and glittering. She doesn't look at all surprised to see me.

"Jenny, love. I hope you don't mind we started without you." Seo-yun smiles. Her lipstick is smeared over her chin, over Aiko's blank face. I can't tell if Aiko's still breathing.

"Get away from her," I say in a low voice.

"As you wish." She rises gracefully, crossing the room in fluid strides. "I was done with that particular morsel, anyway." The sounds of the party leak into the room behind me, and I know I can't run and grab Aiko at the same time.

So I shut the door, locking it, and mellow my voice to a sweet purr. "Why didn't you tell me about Aiko? We could have shared her together."

But Seo-yun just laughs at me. "You can't fool me, Jenny. I can smell your rage from across the room." She reaches out, catches my face, and I recoil into the door. "It makes you so beautiful. The last seasoning in a dish almost ready."

"You're insane, and I'm going to kill you," I say. She kisses my neck, her teeth scraping my throat, and the scent of her is so heady my knees almost bend.

"I saw you in her head, delicious as anything," she whispers. Her ugly thoughts hiss up my arms, twining around my waist. There's a sharp sting at my wrist, and I look down to discover that one of them is already gnawing at my skin. "And I knew I just had to have you."

There's a crash, and Seo-yun screams as a porcelain lamp shatters against the back of her head. Aiko's on her feet, swaying unsteadily, face grim. "Back the fuck away from her," she growls, her voice barely above a whisper.

"You little bitch—" snarls Seo-yun.

But I seize my chance and pounce, fastening my teeth into the hollow of Seo-yun's throat, right where her mantle of thoughts gathers and folds inward. I chew and swallow, chew and swallow, gorging myself on this woman. Her thoughts are mine now, thrashing as I seize them from her, and I catch glimpses of myself, of Aiko, and of many others just like us, in various states of disarray, of preparation.

Ma once told me that this was how Baba went; she'd accidentally drained him until he'd faded completely out of existence. For the first time in my life, I understand her completely.

Seo-yun's bracelets clatter to the floor, her empty gown fluttering soundlessly after. Aiko collapses too, folding like paper.

It hurts to take in that much. My stomach hurts so bad, my entire body swollen with hideous thoughts. At the same time, I've never felt so alive, abuzz with possibility and untamable rage.

I lurch over to Aiko on the floor, malice leaking from her mouth, staining the carpet. "Aiko, wake up!" But she feels hollow, lighter, empty. She doesn't even smell like herself anymore.

A knock at the door jolts me. "Ma'am," says a voice I recognize as the head caterer. "The first of the main courses is ready. Mr. Goldberg wants to know if you'll come down and give a toast."

Fuck. "I—" I start to say, but the voice isn't mine. I glance over at the mirror; sure enough, it's Seo-yun staring back at me, her dark, terrible dreams tangled around her body in a knotted mess. "I'll be right there," I say, and lay Aiko gently on the bed. Then I dress and leave, my heart pounding in my mouth.

I walk Seo-yun's shape down the stairs to the dining room, where guests are milling about, plates in hand, and smile Seo-yun's smile. And if I look a little too much like myself, well—according to what I'd seen while swallowing Seo-yun's thoughts, I wouldn't be the first would-be inductee to disappear at a party like this. Someone hands me a glass of wine, and when I take it, my hand doesn't tremble, even though I'm screaming inside.

Fifty pairs of eyes on me, the caterers' glittering cold in the shadows. Do any of them know? Can any of them tell?

"To your continued health, and to a fabulous dinner," I say, raising my glass. As one, they drink.

Seo-yun's apartment is dark, cleared of guests and waitstaff alike. Every door is locked, every curtain yanked closed.

I've pulled every jar, every container, every pot and pan out of the kitchen, and now they cover the floor of the bedroom, trailing into the hallway, down the stairs. Many are full, their malignant contents hissing and whispering hideous promises at me as I stuff my hand in my mouth, retching into the pot in my lap.

Aiko lies on the bed, pale and still. There's flour and bile on the front of her jacket. "Hang in there," I whisper, but she doesn't respond. I swirl the pot, searching its contents for any hint of Aiko, but Seo-yun's face grins out at me from the patterns of light glimmering across the liquid's surface. I shove it away from me, spilling some on the carpet.

I grab another one of the myriad crawling thoughts tangled about me, sinking my teeth into its body, tearing it into pieces as it screams and howls terrible promises, promises it won't be able to keep. I eat it raw, its scales scraping the roof of my mouth, chewing it thoroughly. The more broken down it is, the easier it will be to sort through the pieces that are left when it comes back up.

How long did you know? Did you always know?

I'll find her, I think as viscous black liquid pours from my mouth, over my hands, burning my throat. The field of containers pools around me like a storm of malicious stars, all whispering my name. She's in here somewhere, I can see her reflection darting across their surfaces. If I have to rip through every piece of Seo-yun I have, from her dreams to the soft, freckled skin wrapped around my body, I will. I'll wring every vile drop of Seo-yun out of me until I find Aiko, and then I'll fill her back up, pour her mouth full of herself.

How could I ever forget her? How could I forget her taste, her scent, something as awful and beautiful as home?

SELKIE STORIES
ARE FOR LOSERS
Sofia Samatar

Sofia Samatar is an assistant professor of English at James Madison University.

Her first novel, *A Stranger in Olondria*, was published in 2013 and won the World Fantasy, Crawford, and British Fantasy awards. A sequel, *The Winged Histories*, followed in 2016. Her short story-collection *Tender* and a poetry chapbook, *Monster Portraits*, illustrated by her brother Del Samatar, are scheduled for publication in 2018. Samatar won the John W. Campbell Award for Best New Writer in 2014. Her short work has appeared in *Clarkesworld*, *Strange Horizons*, *Lightspeed*, and *Lady Churchill's Rosebud Wristlet* as well as in numerous anthologies. She lives in Harrisburg, Virginia.

"Selkie Stories Are for Losers" was nominated for the Nebula, Hugo, British Science Fiction Association, and World Fantasy awards. It is a heartrending story about love and loss.

I hate selkie stories. They're always about how you went up to the attic to look for a book, and you found a disgusting old coat and brought it downstairs between finger and thumb and said "What's this?", and you never saw your mom again.

I work at a restaurant called Le Pacha. I got the job after my mom left, to help with the bills. On my first night at work I got yelled at twice by the head server, burnt my fingers on a hot dish, spilled lentil-parsley soup all over my apron, and left my keys in the kitchen.

I didn't realize at first I'd forgotten my keys. I stood in the parking lot, breathing slowly and letting the oil-smell lift away from my hair, and when all the other cars had started up and driven away I put my hand in my jacket pocket. Then I knew.

I ran back to the restaurant and banged on the door. Of course no one came. I smelled cigarette smoke an instant before I heard the voice.

"Hey."

I turned, and Mona was standing there, smoke rising white from between her fingers.

"I left my keys inside," I said.

Mona is the only other server at Le Pacha who's a girl. She's related to everybody at the restaurant except me. The owner, who goes by "Uncle Tad," is really her uncle, her mom's brother. "Don't talk to him unless you have to," Mona advised me. "He's a creeper." That was after she'd sighed and dropped her cigarette and crushed it out with her shoe and stepped into my clasped hands so I could boost her up to the window, after she'd wriggled through into the kitchen and opened the door for me. She said, "Madame," in a dry voice, and bowed. At least, I think she said "Madame." She might have said "My lady." I don't remember that night too well, because we drank a lot of wine. Mona said that as long as we were breaking and entering we might as well steal something, and she lined up all the bottles of red wine that had already been opened. I shone the light from my phone on her while she took out the special rubber corks and poured some of each bottle into a plastic pitcher. She called it "The House Wine." I was surprised she was being so nice to me, since she'd hardly spoken to me while we were working. Later she told me she hates everybody the first time she meets them. I called home, but Dad didn't pick up; he was probably in the basement. I left him a message and turned off my phone. "Do you know what this guy said to me tonight?" Mona asked. "He wanted beef couscous and he said, 'I'll have the beef conscious.'"

Mona's mom doesn't work at Le Pacha, but sometimes she comes in around three o'clock and sits in Mona's section and cries. Then Mona jams on her orange baseball cap and goes out through the back and smokes a cigarette, and I take over her section. Mona's mom won't order anything from me. She's got Mona's eyes, or Mona's got hers: huge, angry eyes with lashes that curl up at the ends. She shakes her head and says: "Nothing! Nothing!" Finally Uncle Tad comes over, and Mona's mom hugs and kisses him, sobbing in Arabic.

After work Mona says, "Got the keys?"

We get in my car and I drive us through town to the Bone Zone, a giant cemetery on a hill. I pull into the empty parking lot and Mona rolls a joint. There's only one lamp, burning high and cold in the middle of the lot. Mona pushes her shoes off and puts her feet up on the dashboard and cries. She warned me about that the night we met: I said something stupid to her like "You're so funny" and she said, "Actually I cry a lot. That's something you should know." I was so happy she thought I should know things about her, I didn't care. I still don't care, but it's true that Mona cries a lot. She cries because she's scared her mom will take her away to Egypt, where the family used to live, and where Mona has never been. "What would I do there? I don't even speak Arabic." She wipes her mascara on her sleeve, and I tell her to look at the lamp outside and pretend that its glassy brightness is a bonfire, and that she and I are personally throwing every selkie story ever written onto it and watching them burn up.

"You and your selkie stories," she says. I tell her they're not my selkie stories, not ever, and I'll never tell one, which is true, I never will, and I don't tell her how I went up to the attic that day or that what I was looking for was a book I used to read when I was little, *Beauty and the Beast*, which is a really decent story about an animal who gets turned into a human and stays that way, the way it's supposed to be. I don't tell Mona that Beauty's black hair coiled to the edge of the page, or that the Beast had yellow horns and a smoking jacket, or that instead of finding the book I found the coat, and my mom put it on and went out the kitchen door and started up her car.

One selkie story tells about a man from Mýrdalur. He was on the cliffs one day and heard people singing and dancing inside a cave, and he noticed a bunch of skins piled on the rocks. He took one of the skins home and locked it in a chest, and when he went back a girl was sitting there alone, crying. She was naked, and he gave her some clothes and took her home. They got married and had kids. You know how this goes. One day the man changed his clothes and forgot to take the key to the chest out of his pocket, and when his wife washed the clothes, she found it.

"You're not going to Egypt," I tell Mona. "We're going to Colorado. Remember?"

That's our big dream, to go to Colorado. It's where Mona was born. She lived there until she was four. She still remembers the rocks and the pines and the cold, cold air. She says the clouds of Colorado are bright, like pieces of mirror. In Colorado, Mona's parents got divorced, and Mona's mom tried to kill herself for the first time. She tried it once here, too. She put her head in the oven, resting on a pillow. Mona was in seventh grade.

Selkies go back to the sea in a flash, like they've never been away. That's one of the ways they're different from human beings. Once, my dad tried to go back somewhere: he was in the army, stationed in Germany, and he went to Norway to look up the town my great-grandmother came from. He actually found the place, and even an old farm with the same name as us. In the town, he went into a restaurant and ordered lutefisk, a disgusting fish thing my grandmother makes. The cook came out of the kitchen and looked at him like he was nuts. She said they only eat lutefisk at Christmas.

There went Dad's plan of bringing back the original flavor of lutefisk. Now all he's got from Norway is my great-grandmother's Bible. There's also the diary she wrote on the farm up north, but we can't read it. There's only four English words in the whole book: *My God awful day.*

You might suspect my dad picked my mom up in Norway, where they have seals. He didn't, though. He met her at the pool.

As for Mom, she never talked about her relatives. I asked her once if she had any, and she said they were "no kind of people." At the time I thought she meant they were druggies or murderers, maybe in prison somewhere. Now I wish that was true.

One of the stories I don't tell Mona comes from *A Dictionary of British Folklore in the English Language.* In that story, it's the selkie's little girl who points out where the skin is hidden. She doesn't know what's going to happen, of course, she just knows her mother is looking for a skin, and she remembers her dad taking one out from under the bed and stroking it. The little girl's mother drags out the skin and says: "Fareweel, peerie buddo!" She doesn't think about how the little girl is going to miss her, or how if she's been breathing air all this time she can surely keep it up a little longer. She just throws on the skin and jumps into the sea.

After Mom left, I waited for my dad to get home from work. He didn't say anything when I told him about the coat. He stood in the light of the clock on the stove and rubbed his fingers together softly, almost like he was snapping but with no sound. Then he sat down at the kitchen table and lit a cigarette. I'd never seen him smoke in the house before. *Mom's gonna lose it*, I thought, and then I realized that no, my mom wasn't going to lose anything. We were the losers. Me and Dad.

He still waits up for me, so just before midnight I pull out of the parking lot. I'm hoping to get home early enough that he doesn't grumble, but late enough that he doesn't want to come up from the basement, where he takes apart old T.V.s, and talk to me about college. I've told him I'm not going to college. I'm going to Colorado, a landlocked state. Only twenty out of fifty states are completely landlocked, which means they don't touch the Great Lakes or the sea. Mona turns on the light and tries to put on eyeliner in the mirror, and I swerve to make her mess up. She turns out the light and hits me. All the windows are down to air out the car, and Mona's hair blows wild around her face. *Peerie buddo*, the book says, is "a term of endearment." "Peerie buddo," I say to Mona. She's got the hiccups. She can't stop laughing.

I've never kissed Mona. I've thought about it a lot, but I keep deciding it's not time. It's not that I think she'd freak out or anything. It's not even that I'm afraid she wouldn't kiss me back. It's worse: I'm afraid she'd kiss me back, but not mean it.

Probably one of the biggest losers to fall in love with a selkie was the man who carried her skin around in his knapsack. He was so scared she'd find it that he took the skin with him everywhere, when he went fishing, when he went drinking in the town. Then one day he had a wonderful catch of fish. There were so many that he couldn't drag them all home in his net. He emptied his knapsack and filled it with fish, and he put the skin over his shoulder, and on his way up the road to his house, he dropped it.

"Gray in front and gray in back, 'tis the very thing I lack." That's what the man's wife said, when she found the skin. The man ran to catch her, he even kissed her even though she was already a seal, but she squirmed off down the road and flopped into the water. The man stood knee-deep in the chilly waves, stinking of fish, and cried. In selkie stories, kissing never solves anything. No transformation happens because of a kiss. No one loves you just because you love them. What kind of fairy tale is that?

"She wouldn't wake up," Mona says. "I pulled her out of the oven onto the floor, and I turned off the gas and opened the windows. It's not that I was smart, I wasn't thinking at all. I called Uncle Tad and the police and I still wasn't thinking."

I don't believe she wasn't smart. She even tried to give her mom CPR, but her mom didn't wake up until later, in the hospital. They had to reach in and drag her out of death, she was so closed up in it. Death is skin-tight, Mona says. Gray in front and gray in back.

———————

Dear Mona: When I look at you, my skin hurts.

I pull into her driveway to drop her off. The house is dark, the darkest house on her street, because Mona's mom doesn't like the porch
light on. She says it shines in around the blinds and keeps her awake.
Mona's mom has a beautiful bedroom upstairs, with lots of old photo-
graphs in gilt frames, but she sleeps on the living-room couch beside
the aquarium. Looking at the fish helps her to sleep, although she also
says this country has no real fish. That's what Mona calls one of her
mom's "refrains."

Mona gets out, yanking the little piece of my heart that stays with
her wherever she goes. She stands outside the car and leans in through
the open door. I can hardly see her, but I can smell the lemon-scented
stuff she puts on her hair, mixed up with the smells of sweat and
weed. Mona smells like a forest, not the sea. "Oh my God," she says,
"I forgot to tell you, tonight, you know table six? That big horde of
Uncle Tad's friends?"

"Yeah."

"So they wanted the soup with the food, and I forgot, and you
know what the old guy says to me? The little guy at the head of the
table?"

"What?"

"He goes, *Vous êtes bête, mademoiselle!*"

She says it in a rough, growly voice, and laughs. I can tell it's French,
but that's all.

"What does it mean?"

"You're an idiot, miss!"

She ducks her head, stifling giggles.

"He called you an idiot?"

"Yeah, *bête*, it's like *beast*."

She lifts her head, then shakes it. A light from someone else's porch bounces off her nose. She puts on a fake Norwegian accent and says: *"My God awful day."*

I nod. "Awful day." And because we say it all the time, because it's the kind of silly, ordinary thing you could call one of our "refrains," or maybe because of the weed I've smoked, a whole bunch of days seem pressed together inside this moment, more than you could count. There's the time we all went out for New Year's Eve, and Uncle Tad drove me, and when he stopped and I opened the door he told me to close it, and I said "I will when I'm on the other side," and when I told Mona we laughed so hard we had to run away and hide in the bathroom. There's the day some people we know from school came in and we served them wine even though they were underage and Mona got nervous and spilled it all over the tablecloth, and the day her nice cousin came to visit and made us cheese-and-mint sandwiches in the microwave and got yelled at for wasting food. And the day of the party for Mona's mom's birthday, when Uncle Tad played music and made us all dance, and Mona's mom's eyes went jewelly with tears, and afterward Mona told me: "I should just run away. I'm the only thing keeping her here." My God awful days. All the best days of my life.

"Bye," Mona whispers. I watch her until she disappears into the house.

My mom used to swim every morning at the YWCA. When I was little she took me along. I didn't like swimming. I'd sit in a chair with a book while she went up and down, up and down, a dim streak in the water. When I read *Mrs. Frisby and the Rats of NIMH*, it seemed like Mom was a lab rat doing tasks, the way she kept touching one side of the pool and then the other. At last she climbed out and pulled off her bathing cap. In the locker room she hung up her suit, a thin gray rag dripping on the floor. Most people put the hook of their padlock through the straps of their suit, so the suits could hang outside the lockers without getting stolen, but my mom never did that. She just tied her suit loosely onto the lock. "No one's going to steal that stretchy old thing," she said. And no one did.

That should have been the end of the story, but it wasn't. My dad says Mom was an elemental, a sort of stranger, not of our kind. It wasn't my fault she left, it was because she couldn't learn to breathe on land. That's the worst story I've ever heard. I'll never tell Mona, not ever, not even when we're leaving for Colorado with everything we need in the back of my car, and I meet her at the grocery store the way we've already planned, and she runs out smiling under her orange baseball cap. I won't tell her how dangerous attics are, or how some people can't start over, or how I still see my mom in shop windows with her long hair the same silver-gray as her coat, or how once when my little cousins came to visit we went to the zoo and the seals recognized me, they both stood up in the water and talked in a foreign language. I won't tell her. I'm too scared. I won't even tell her what she needs to know: that we've got to be tougher than our moms, that we've got to have different stories, that she'd better not change her mind and drop me in Colorado because I won't understand, I'll hate her forever and burn her stuff and stay up all night screaming at the woods, because it's stupid not to be able to breathe, who ever heard of somebody breathing in one place but not another, and we're not like that, Mona and me, and selkie stories are only for losers stuck on the wrong side of magic—people who drop things, who tell all, who leave keys around, who let go.

TORNADO'S SIREN
Brooke Bolander

Brooke Bolander has written barely more than a handful of stories, but is already one of the leading young writers in the field. Her story "And You Shall Know Her by the Trail of Dead" was published in *Lightspeed* in 2015 and was nominated for the Hugo, Nebula, Locus, and Theodore Sturgeon awards. Her fiction has also appeared in *Strange Horizons, Nightmare, Uncanny,* and *Reflection's Edge.* She graduated from the Clarion Writers Workshop in San Diego in 2011. She lives in New York.

"Tornado's Siren" is a very unusual love story.

Rhea is nine years old when she first meets the tornado that will fall in love with her. It comes late in the afternoon, after school and graham crackers and the four o'clock showing of *Jeopardy.* The sidewalks sweat like her father after a jog and the sky scums over with bruised purple-black clouds. The muggy wind blows restless, so unsettled she gets nervous even before the television starts blaring warnings. She reads the names of the counties as they scroll across the bottom of the screen, listening intently to everything the weatherman says. Rhea doesn't know what a lot of the words mean, but she knows what fear sounds like, and his voice is chock full of it.

"Folks, we have a very serious situation here. If you are in the path of this storm, I need you to go to an interior hall or bathroom *right now.*" A wind hits the antenna outside and he briefly fades to ghostly static before popping back in. "We've got a debris ball on radar and confirmed sightings of a touchdown in Lark County. This is big. If you're in a mobile home, find a low-lying area outside, like a ditch or culvert. If you're listening to this from a car radio—"

The electricity cuts him off mid-sentence. Rhea is left alone in the dark of her grandparents' house, surrounded by shadows and the noise of increasing rain.

She wanders to the carport to watch the lowering sky, wondering where her grandma and grandpa could be. They are always here when her parents drop her off after school, and they always know what to do in big, frightening situations. Through mixup or accident they are *not* here this afternoon, out running errands or visiting friends or who knows what, and that leaves all the scary decisions in Rhea's hands, something she's not at all comfortable with. Her stomach writhes like a pool of scared tadpoles. The first camera flash of lightning drives her back into the house, away from the sticky breeze into musty, waiting silence. The battery-operated Kit-Kat clock on the kitchen wall stupidly ticks away the minutes, grinningly oblivious to their situation.

"You'll get blown away too," she tells it. "Right into the next county."

The Kit-Kat clock swishes on. She thinks she can sense nervousness in its shifty eyes.

Left with no other choice, Rhea sets out to prepare by herself in all the ways she's been taught. She strips the blankets and pillows off the bed and piles them into the bathtub. She grabs a flashlight and hauls Murray the big yellow tabby into the bathroom with her, all ten pounds of yowling, wounded dignity. When there's nothing else to do, she shuts the door, climbs into the tub, and huddles beneath the comforter. The air is stifling, and Murray won't stop meowing. She tries to say the prayers she's been taught, but they don't stop the aching in her gut like Grandma says they should. Bad things happen to good people all the time. Even at nine she's a little wary about putting all her faith into such a moody higher power, although that's the kind of thought she would never say in front of her grown-ups.

The waiting is the worst part. Balled up in the blackness, hoping that maybe nothing will happen, listening to the wind increase and rake at the walls. Listening, always listening, unable to do anything but stay put, the air getting more and more stale under the heavy sheet. Rhea holds her breath for as long as she can—it feels like hours—and then comes back up, clawing at the bedding for a fresh breath. She tugs the blanket away just in time to see, through the window, the neighbor's privacy fence go spiraling by, panels of plywood twirling like old newspapers.

The full force of the storm hits the house a second later. Everything—roof, walls, window, her popping ears—creaks and then gives before the bull's roar of the twister.

Rhea thinks she screams, but the whole world is screaming too so it's hard to tell. Glass shatters and pops into her face, cutting her cheeks. Bathroom tile and bits of plaster rain down on her head. The room pulls apart in hunks, walls peeled down to pink insulation and rose-printed, rose-scented strips of shredded paper. She realizes the ceiling's gone when hail begins to fall, nasty, biting little chunks of cold ice. Through the wall of noise and debris, looking up and up and up, she can see the jaws of the monster, an endless swirling throat of fog and whipped rain.

Frozen, Rhea stares up into the twister and waits for it to gobble her whole, blankets, bathtub, and all.

"Why?"

She doesn't know why she says it. It just comes without a thought, the last thing she'll probably ever whisper swallowed up in the fury of a tornado.

For a moment everything stops. The tornado's voice grows still. All the little chunks of trash hang frozen in the air, like someone's just hit the pause button. Rhea can see flowering shrubs and someone's shoe, a lawn gnome and two china cups. Then, just as suddenly, it all comes tumbling down. As quickly as it arrived the storm moves on, grumbling deep down in its throat.

Rhea's life never quite stops being weird after that.

When she's eleven, there is a Valentine's party held at her school. All the kids give each other chocolates and paper hearts, little notes of affection or humor or goodwill. Rhea gets nothing in her cubbyhole and spends recess crying beneath the slides, a splotchy-faced outcast with too-big glasses and scuffed secondhand sneakers. She tells herself she doesn't care, but it still stings.

The storm blows in later that evening. Much to the delight of the students, the only thing it destroys is the middle school. Rhea wakes the morning after to find the front yard strewn with paper hearts, drifting gently down from the sky in a fluttering pink and red cloud.

On the night of her senior prom, a wedge tornado rips apart the gym where the dance is taking place. Rhea isn't there at the time. She's at home studying for a calculus exam, and only realizes something has happened when the Prom Queen's crown and bouquet of roses bang against the front door in quick succession. Later, it's a tricky affair to explain why she has these things. People give her funny looks when she swears they just appeared from the sky.

A wall cloud, the same vivid green as her graduation gown, keeps pace with her car on a seventy-five-mile-long interstate jaunt to visit a friend up north. She keeps a wary eye on it as it skips across the distant plains, frisking along in her driver's side window like the happiest, most destructive puppy in the world. It's a strangely beautiful, perversely joyous thing. Rhea doesn't notice the smile creeping across her lips until she goes to check her lipstick in the mirror. For the rest of the journey she broods with the radio cranked up, wondering what the hell is up with her brain lately.

She begs her parents to move to Greenland or Finland or *anywhere* else, preferably somewhere cold with no rapid temperature shifts between air masses. They laugh and go right on living where their parents and grandparents settled before them, as rooted to the local soil as the big pecan trees the storms occasionally blow over. Folks like them don't up and leave because of a puny twister or twelve. They're used to it, or so they say.

Rhea begins dating an out-of-towner. She's making her escape plans before he even produces a ring.

The wedding was going so well up until this point, too.

Glasses and forks and bits of broken plates and cake lay strewn across the grass of the lakeside hill, a breadcrumb trail leading back to the lodge where guests huddle inside like a frightened covey of quail. One of the tables—the bench that previously held the catered macaroni and cheese, three different kinds of champagne, and the groom's favorite brand of potato chip—has turned turtle, legs sticking up at a crazy, immodest angle from the skirt of its paper covering. The wedding gifts sit deserted in a pyramid heap, already listing precariously in the wind.

The funnel in the sky overhead is a lacy confection of a thing, as delicately knit as anything Rhea, standing far beneath it, might be wearing. Her veil whips in the breeze. Both fists are balled at her sides, nails digging crescent moons into the flesh of her palms. Blood spots her bitten lip, and her expensive bridal coif is coming down around her ears.

Rhea has had it up to here with the friggin' tornadoes.

It must be the same one. The rudeness of its behavior combined with every other incident it has been responsible for in her life has pushed Rhea into a confrontation she's pretty sure will either result in her death, her commitment to a psychiatric ward, or her further instatement into family gossip for the next twenty years. She can feel eyes watching her from the windows of the lodge, cousins twice removed and great aunties wondering what crazy thing she'll do next. Fighting the urge to flip them all a glorious two-handed bird, she keeps her attention fully focused on the swirl of cloud above, determined to hash this out or die trying.

"What the *hell* do you mean by this? What gives you the fucking *right?*" She's yelling at the top of her lungs, trying to be heard over the noise of the storm. The downdraft keeps shoving her words back down her throat like used party napkins, which makes her even madder. "Obviously you don't want to kill me, Christ knows you've had enough chances to do *that*, so what exactly is it you want? Blood? A business partner?"

The wind tosses a rose from one of the bouquets into her chest. She looks down at it, mind doing all kinds of weird mental gymnastics. Valentines. Rose petals. The way it follows her everywhere like a smitten crush. Smitten? Oh, no. *Hell* no. A hysterical laugh bubbles up from deep inside. The psych ward it is, then. Napoleon, the guy who thinks he's a cheese cruller, and the girl who believes a tornado is in love with her. Come one, come all. They don't get crazier than this.

"Really?" she says. "*Really?* No, I'm sorry. You're a tornado. You don't get to fall in love. Do you even know what love means? You destroy cities. You've messed with my life; you even screwed up my wedding. All I want is to be normal. Do you know what normal is? It's NOT BEING CHASED BY FUCKING TORNADOS. Just leave me the hell alone, okay? Go do whatever it is tornados do. Please."

The air stills. Rhea braces herself for the fury of a jilted twister, imagining the authorities hauling her down from an oak branch in some town fifty miles distant. When nothing happens, she opens her eyes again to find the cloudbank dissipating, shreds of fluffy vapor unraveling like an old knit cap. All the tension goes out of her and she drops to her knees, suddenly, achingly exhausted.

When she enters the lodge the guests part nervously before her. She brushes past them until she finds her fiancé, Rick, as blond and blandly handsome as a sunny day. He grabs her as she slumps. Strong arms. Stable arms. That's all Rhea wants right now.

"Take me somewhere normal," she says into his chest. "I want to do what normal people do."

They move to Southern California, where the biggest threat is the ground buckling beneath your feet. Rhea can handle earthquakes. They don't have personalities, or shapes, or strange unearthly voices. A big one can destroy your home, true, but compared to the sheer presence of a tornado they seem benign by comparison, just a thing that occasionally happens.

Rick buys them a pretty little house on a pretty little suburban street, complete with a dog in the yard and a rosebush beneath the kitchen window. The grass here is always green, the temperature always perfect. She doesn't have to work—that's taken care of, too—and there's always an endless stream of cheerful, attentive neighbors passing through, ready to lend a helping hand. They go to their jobs in the morning like a flock of starlings and come straight home to roost at night beneath cloudless, starry skies. When there are storms, they're short-lived and weak, blown apart by the coastal winds before they can even get a good hail going. It's *safe*. For the first time in her life, Rhea doesn't find herself worrying when dark clouds crowd the horizon. She worries about bills instead, or taxes, or dieting.

For two years they live like this, in the happy, insular world Rick has created for them. Relatives come to visit from the Midwest and tell her how lucky she is. Girl Scouts sell cookies door-to-door, leaving their bikes by the road when dinnertime calls them inside. Every day is exactly the same. Slowly, the newness begins to wear off like the shine from a penny. Rhea's smile becomes fixed and strained on her face, seams showing beneath the tan.

She has it made, but she's not happy. Not even close.

Her husband isn't the problem, not quite. He's handsome and cheerful, kind to a fault and considerate to embarrassment. If you need a kitten down from a tree, a granny helped across a street, or any combination of the two, Rick's your fella. Rhea resents her own feelings more than she does him, but there's nothing she can do about them. Too late she begins to realize that this is not what she wants, has *never* been what she wants. Sodium lamps and weather without weather and sprinklers that come on at 9 p.m. every night. Eerily identical houses on eerily identical streets, rows and rows and rows of them swallowing up the horizon.

Rhea closes her eyes beneath 600-thread-count Egyptian cotton sheets and dreams of tornadoes.

Sometimes there's a man-shape inside, with hazel eyes and a halo of black hair. Sometimes the figure is a woman. This much is always the same: they look at her with sadness and something like pity and then turn away, the hurt plain across their faces, bare skin rippling back to cloud before Rhea can take three steps forward. She wakes with a barb of longing in her chest and carries it with her all through her bland, sunny day.

She doesn't miss tornadoes; that's not it at all. That would be silly. The excitement they represent? Maybe a little. But not the storms themselves, and certainly not *her* storm. You can't fall in love with destruction. What would that say about a person?

Rhea is twenty-two years old, and she's burning out on life so quickly it's like she's been dunked in gasoline. One day it gets to be too much. She throws all the clothes she can into a hiker's backpack and drives back east until she hits the plains. She stops at the first city with a good university and a better meteorology program.

Dear Rick, the letter she leaves him on the kitchen counter begins. *I'm broken. I've gone to find other broken things. Don't wait up.*

The black van bounces and jostles through the grass like a string of cans behind a newlywed sedan, hitting every dip it comes to with a joyful (and to Rhea's aching backside, malicious) rattle. The "road" they're following is little more than a twin set of ruts in the dirt, one of those little cattle paths ranchers use to feed and check up on their livestock. They fly along it like it's the Autobahn, white satellite hoisted sail-fashion atop the roof and a spume of dust curling from beneath the balding wheels.

Cave drives, goateed and tattooed and awake only by the grace of God knows what substance. Studious, buttoned-up Kelly, looking like a wet-behind-the-ears college professor crossed with a traffic cop, mans the GPS and the recording equipment, hissing gently each time the van sends him rocketing towards the yellowing ceiling. Rhea is in charge of radar duty. The screen in front of her is awash with ugly green and red splotches, like time-lapse footage of the worst case of chicken pox ever. The storms developed suddenly, maybe around 2 or so, and have been holding a course for the northeast ever since. If the oracles at the National Weather Service are correct, the biggest cell will be crossing their path within the next ten minutes. Her fellow chasers and meteorology students are already making plans for data and video and all the other things you jot down when a big tornado comes your way, chattering to one another over the radios in excited jargon that sounds more like starship navigation than weather detection.

Rhea has her own plans, but she keeps tight-lipped. She thinks of Rick getting a late-night phone call somewhere in San Diego. She thinks of her family, sisters and grandparents and cousins all whispering in hushed, solemn tones around piles of green bean casserole and fried chicken. Such a shame, they'd say, shaking their heads. Poor girl lost her marbles when she left her husband; it was only a matter of time before something bad happened. Storm-chasing, of all the careers, and after all the trouble she went through as a little girl.

Cave shouts a warning from up front and slams on the brakes abruptly, sending papers and equipment and people flying. Rhea careens off the walls like a cricket in a mason jar and lands ass-over-teakettle in a tangled heap on the floor, laptop still miraculously clutched in one hand. She's back on her feet before the engine can start to creak and cool, clambering over the front seats to check on Cave. Kelly groans and swears a blue streak behind her, half-buried beneath an avalanche of printer paper.

His fingers are clenched around the steering wheel when she makes it to the front, face blanched beneath the tattoos. He says nothing at all, simply points to the horizon through the cracked windshield. The radio roars with static and sirens and garbled voices.

"Fuck," he finally whispers.

It's a solid mass of churning black, stretching from one side of the sky to the other. Gray tentacles snake from its bulk. The wall cloud above spirals like an out-of-control galaxy dragged helplessly along and around. Grass billows and ripples before it, turned a shade of sickly Technicolor green by the dying light. From this distance it looks like it's moving in slow motion, twirling towards them in ponderous silence. The van rocking in the wind is the only reminder that yes, the view through the glass is real. Not a newsreel, not a movie screen. The biggest tornado Rhea's ever seen in a life full of them, five miles wide and dense as a black hole.

Looking for her. Just as she's been looking for it.

She doesn't stop to think, doesn't *let* herself think. She simply acts, dropping the laptop, vaulting across the van and over Kelly and through the back doors so quickly nobody even tries to grab her until it's too late. The wind sucks her outside in an explosion of data papers and noise. If the others shout at her to come back, she can't hear it over the boom and shriek of the oncoming storm.

Rhea runs towards her tornado. It's hard going, wading through the alfalfa and timothy and goatweed, but it's coming to meet her, too, and every gust pulls her closer and closer. The world fades from green to deep purple. Debris begins to land around her, shingles and railroad ties and trees and a crumpled Radio Flyer stripped of all its paint. She wonders if she'll be crushed or impaled before she reaches the thing's outer limits, decides she doesn't care, and keeps moving, almost lifted off her feet by the force of the gale. Can it sense her down here, a tiny speck in the grass? More importantly, will it be happy to see her after last time? What if it's still disappointed?

She gets as close as she dares and cups her hands to her mouth. Fat lot of good that'll do.

"I came back!" she yells. "I've been tracing your cell patterns for years now, do you know that?"

There's a lull in the storm. Rhea can hear the blood pounding in her ears, louder than thunder. Her throat is scratchy and hoarse from flying dirt in the air, but she keeps talking anyway.

"Those things I said at the wedding . . . I'm sorry. I was pretty fucked up back then. I didn't really mean them, swear to God." Rain splatters onto her face and trickles down her cheeks. The pressure changes in her ears are excruciating. "I think I want to go with you. If you don't want me anymore, that's okay, but I had to find out. Just in case you did."

The tornado's spin slows. For a moment she thinks it's turning away, and her heart sinks. Then it bears down on her, five miles of chaos and movement and change. Rhea smiles like a lightning slash, opening her arms to take it all in.

"Take me someplace *interesting*," she whispers.

And it does.

LEFT THE CENTURY
TO SIT UNMOVED
Sarah Pinsker

Sarah Pinsker is a singer/songwriter with three albums on various independent labels. She is a very prolific author of short fiction, having published more than forty stories since 2012, including numerous contributions to *Asimov's Science Fiction*, *Fantasy & Science Fiction*, *Lightspeed*, *Strange Horizons*, and *Daily Science Fiction*. She has won the Nebula Award and Theodore Sturgeon awards. She lives in Baltimore, Maryland.

"Left the Century to Sit Unmoved" is a fascinating story about family bonds and the need to test limits.

The pond only looks bottomless.

Clambering up the moss-slick stones beside the waterfall, finding purchase with cramping toes and fingers, if I chance a look back over my shoulder, the pond is a moon-black sky even on a sunny summer's day. It absorbs light. I push back off the narrow ledge, as hard as I can, always feet first, hoping I miss the rocks, hoping I don't overshoot the middle, hoping I won't lose my bathing suit on the way back up because Otis and Kat are here too, and I'd become a legend in all the wrong ways.

When I'm in the water, plunging, sinking, one hand dragging my sagging waistband back to something approximating my waist, wondering why I let Kat convince me to buy this suit in the first place, I let myself drop as deep as I possibly can. I trail my toes in the silt, and there is silt, and some kind of tough grass that wraps long fingers around my calves, and silt and grass mean there is a bottom. If I open my eyes, if I ignore the grit, I might catch a glimpse of trout silvering between the grasses. Or a water snake, black in the blackness.

That's all universal to everyone jumping, I think, except maybe the bit about the suit. And except maybe the next bit, where I come up gasping, and immediately go under again as Otis crashes in on top of me.

"Jerk!" I say when we've both surfaced. "One at a time! That's the rule!"

"They aren't rules, Shay," Kat says from the shore. She's spread a large towel over the flattest boulder, and she's sitting at the center reading a paperback with both covers missing. "They're superstitions."

"Easy for you to say, chicken." Otis skims his hand across the water, sending a plume her way that dies before it touches her. She doesn't even flinch. I make a mental note: cool is in not flinching. Cool is in keeping your resolve not to jump, even when your boyfriend calls you "chicken." If I have any cool at all, it comes from the fact that I jumped before either of them. I didn't even do it to impress them. No peer pressure here.

Anyway, Kat's not wrong. They are superstitions. Everyone in town follows them, except when they don't.

The rules:
1. One person at a time, so everyone can see if the pond is hungry.
2. No skinny-dipping, so your friends will know if you were taken or you just drowned. (Clothes don't get taken.)
3. Don't jump if anyone depends on you.
4. Saying "one more jump" is just tempting fate.
5. Jump, don't dive. The pond prefers divers.
6. Don't jump alone.

Number three has variations. Some say it's more like "don't jump when you're in love." Others say the rule is "the pool can't take you if you're truly in love," in which case Otis is actually being romantic. That's what he claims. He loves Kat, and she loves him back. He always jumps anyway, just once, not usually on me. She's never jumped. When he gets out, she always slugs him in the arm before kissing him.

I'm maybe in love with both of them, or maybe just in love with the way they are around each other. I want to be the arm-puncher or the arm-punchee or the punch itself, or the plume of water that knows better than to drench Kat while she's holding a book. I want to believe they are superstitions, not rules, even though Kendra Butcher and Grant Pryor jumped together and vanished without a trace. I was there that day, though I wasn't ready to jump yet myself at the time.

The thing about the rules is they don't change anything at all. The pond doesn't follow any rules. They're just things people made up and passed down to make us feel better about our chances. To remind us what's at stake. Something to cling to when we're telling somebody's parents and they're nodding like of course, this is the risk we all take, and they shouldn't have jumped together.

People break the rules all the time. My brother Nick used to jump alone. When he disappeared, three years ago, his old Buick Century was found at the far end of the dirt lot where people park to hike down here if they come by car instead of by bike.

"Maybe he went hitchhiking," my mother said. "Maybe he'll be back."

Nick had done that before, too, going off for days without telling us where he was headed. But he hadn't tried to thumb a ride since he bought the car, and anyway nobody would hitchhike from that particular spot, since the only cars there were coming from or going back to our own town. It didn't make any sense for his car to be there unless he'd jumped.

We left the Century to sit unmoved. The spare key, the one that didn't disappear with Nick, lives in a bowl of coins near our front door. It used to be on top, but it gradually drowned in pennies and dimes. I know it's in there, but there's no use digging it out. I might have been able to drive the car away at the beginning, but I don't know where I'd have taken it. Since then, vines have grown over it and punched their way in through the windows. Somebody stole the hubcaps, and the tires have all gone flat and given in to rot. I think there's a raccoon living in the backseat. It's not Nick's anymore, not anybody's. Just a thing caught up in the slow process of transforming into another thing.

I can't say what happens when the pond takes a person. Only what we've all seen. Someone climbs the waterfall, pushes off the wall. The same way we all do. Same arc, same splash, but they never surface. There's no struggle, no roiling water, no sign anything was disturbed. A swimsuit will come floating up, which is why the old joke that the pond doesn't like synthetic fabrics. And we never see that friend/ sibling/mother again. I've seen it happen twice with my own eyes. Kendra and Grant, both from my homeroom.

The bottom has been dredged at various points, once at my mother's request and my family's expense. People have gone in with scuba gear. They found a rubber boot, a bicycle, a picnic table. House keys and cell phones and car keys, though not Nick's. No bodies, no bones, no brothers.

There's always somebody who grew up here coming back to study it, only they realize quickly there's nothing to study. Set up a video camera and you could wait forever, and even if you caught someone as they disappeared, you've got nothing to show afterward. No proof it wasn't photographic trickery. No after to the before.

My father isn't one of the ones who came back to study it, but he's one of the few who came back. He says when he was a teenager, only boys jumped. The girls all sunned themselves on the flat boulder the way Kat does. Otis says he's heard the same; his mother's first and last jump was on her fortieth birthday. She and two friends drove out with a cooler full of pre-mixed margaritas to celebrate. I think that's why Otis prefers the "truly in love" version of the third rule, the version centered on romance, not responsibility. It used to bother him a lot that she took the chance, even if she did come back. He hasn't spoken about it since we started jumping.

My own mother isn't from here. She doesn't understand at all. She's the one who forced the town to put up a fence, so that now we have to climb over. She's the one who insisted Nick's car stay in the lot instead of taking it home for me. She closed the door on Nick's bedroom and left it untouched, just in case he comes back. Unlike the Buick, the bedroom has mostly stayed intact. Content the way it is, maybe, or on a slower journey.

I sneak in sometimes to go through Nick's stuff. I choose one area to explore each time, so if I find something I can pretend he meant me to find it at that very moment. The first fall he was gone, I discovered his copy of *Twelfth Night* right before my English midterm, with useful notes on every page. Another time, an issue of *Penthouse*, which cleared up some questions my parents weren't ready to answer and I hadn't yet worked up the nerve to research. Two years ago, I found a notebook filled with drawings of imaginary carnivorous plants. There was a folded page in the middle, and on it, in his block lettering:

Why We Jump

We jump because we have to.
We jump because we can.
We jump because we dare ourselves.
We jump because we're lonely.
We jump because we want to be alone.

We jump because once you're up there's really no other good
way down.

We jump because otherwise we'll never do anything that
matters.

We jump because we want to fly, just for a moment.

We jump because everything is better afterward: beer,
breathing, sandwiches, sex.

We jump because the water is clear and deep.

We jump because there are so few things in life that can't be
explained away.

We jump because we want to know what happens when the
pond takes somebody.

We jump because we don't want that somebody to be us, or
maybe we do.

We jump because otherwise we will never know who we are.

We jump because we want to know what else there is to be.

We jump because we don't want to be the kind of person
who wouldn't.

We jump because each of us knows we are the invincible
center of the world.

We jump because we want to be

We jump because

I can't tell if those last two lines are unfinished or how he meant
them. I don't know if his "we" is meant to speak for everybody or
just himself. I'm pretty sure I was meant to find this right when I
did, right when the word "why" had started unmooring me. Nick's
multiple becauses couldn't all be true, not all the time, but I liked the
fact they couldn't be pinned down. They weren't answers. They were
anchors.

I made my first jump the week after I found the note, dragging my
friends along so I wouldn't chicken out. Just one jump, I promised. I

didn't say: I want to do something that matters. I want everything to be better afterward, beer and breathing and sandwiches, even if sex is not on the menu yet.

I can't say everything was better afterward, but I learned on the first jump that fear and relief are two forms of the same compound, like ice and water. The terror that built in my muscles and bones as I climbed the waterfall, as I pushed off, as I let go, it all bubbled out when I came up for air.

"What are you laughing at?" Kat called to me.

I just laughed and laughed, treading water. When we came back the next week, Otis jumped for the first time. Since then we've come out here at least once a week if the weather is at all conducive. It's not a decision on anyone's part. It's what we do. I'm happy to be part of this small "we" as well as the larger "we" that I think my brother was talking about, the "we" of everyone who has ever jumped or considered jumping.

I've added a few of my own ideas to my brother's list, speaking only for myself. I jump because I don't understand. I jump because something that is impossible shouldn't also be something that is true. I jump because Ms. Remlinger taught us about conservation of mass and conservation of energy, and a brother is not something that can become nothing.

Some people say when somebody's taken they're spit out somewhere else, clean and naked and ready to live a different life. Some people think they're reborn as babies, elsewhere. I don't find either idea all that appealing.

I don't imagine the people who are taken die or are reborn. I think they're transformed, but I don't know into what. Rainbow trout, black snake, water molecules. Is that different than dying? To become part of this beautiful pond, to receive the waterfall, to be surrounded always by rock and pine and birch and sky? A quick change. Quicker than my brother's room turning to dust, or the Buick becoming forest. People can change much faster than things can, if they're given the chance.

"Are you done?" Otis calls to me. He's standing over Kat, dripping on her. She scoots away with mock annoyance.

"One more jump," I say.

They both give me a look. I return my bravest grin.

I say "I love you" as I jackknife, not loud enough for either of them to hear me. Break the glassy surface. I'm not a fish or a snake or a baby on the other side of the world. The sky is impossibly blue, and the water is impossibly black. There have never been any rules.

A KISS WITH TEETH
Max Gladstone

Max Gladstone graduated from Yale University, where he studied Chinese. He is the author of the Craft sequence, beginning with his debut novel, *Three Parts Dead*. He is the creator of the urban fantasy serial *Bookburners* and (with Lindsay Smith) *The Witch Who Came in from the Cold*. He has two novels forthcoming from Tor Books in 2018 and 2019 and is part of a team of writers working on George R. R. Martin's Wild Cards anthology series. He was nominated for the John W. Campbell Award for Best New Writer in both years of his eligibility, 2013 and 2014. He has also been nominated for the Lambda and Mythopeic awards. He lives in Somerville, Massachusetts.

"A Kiss with Teeth" is an unusual take on the seven-year itch, and vampires.

Vlad no longer shows his wife his sharp teeth. He keeps them secret in his gums, waiting for the quickened skip of hunger, for the blood-rush he almost never feels these days.

The teeth he wears instead are blunt as shovels. He coffee-stains them carefully, soaks them every night in a mug with WORLD'S BEST DAD written on the side. After eight years of staining, Vlad's blunt teeth are the burnished yellow of the keys of an old unplayed piano. If not for the stain they would be whiter than porcelain. Much, much whiter than bone.

White, almost, as the sharp teeth he keeps concealed.

His wife Sarah has not tried to kill him since they married. She stores her holy water in a kitchen cabinet behind the spice rack, the silver bullets in a safe with her gun. She smiles when they make love, the smile of a woman sinking into a feather bed, a smile of jigsaw puzzles and blankets over warm laps by the fire. He smiles back, with his blunt teeth.

They have a son, a seven-year-old boy named Paul, straight and brown like his mother, a growing, springing sapling boy. Paul plays catch, Paul plays basketball, Paul dreams of growing up to be a football star, or a tennis star, or a baseball star, depending on the season. Vlad takes him to games. Vlad wears a baseball cap, and smells the pitcher's sweat and the ball's leather from their seat far up in the stands. He sees ball strike bat, sees ball and bat deform, and knows whether the ball will stutter out between third and second, or arc beautiful and deadly to outfield, fly true or veer across the foul line. He would tell his son, but Paul cannot hear fast enough. After each play, Paul explains the action, slow, patient, and content. Paul smiles like his mother, and the smile sets Vlad on edge and spinning.

Sometimes Vlad remembers his youth, sprinting ahead of a cavalry charge to break like lightning on a stand of pikers. Blood, he remembers, oceans of it. Screams of the impaled. There is a sound men's breaking sterna make when you grab their ribs and pull them out and in, a bassy nightmare transposition of a wishbone's snap. Vlad knows the plural forms of "sternum" and "trachea," and all declensions and participles of "flense."

"Talk to the teacher," his wife says after dinner. Paul watches a cricket game on satellite in the other room, mountainous Fijians squared off against an Indian team. Vlad once was a death cult in Calcutta—the entire cult, British colonial paranoia being an excellent cover for his appetites—and in the sixties he met a traveling volcano god in Fiji, who'd given up sacrifices when he found virgins could be had more easily by learning to play guitar. Neither experience left Vlad with much appreciation for cricket.

"On what topic should we converse," he asks. He can never end sentences with prepositions. He learned English in a proper age.

"Paul. You should talk to the teacher about Paul."

"Paul is not troubled."

"He's not troubled. But he's having trouble." She shows him the report card. She never rips envelopes open, uses instead a thin knife she keeps beside the ink blotter. Vlad has calculated that in eight years he will be the only person left in the world who uses an ink blotter.

The report card is printed on thick stock, and lists letters that come low in the limited alphabet of grades. No notes, no handwritten explanations. Paul is not doing well. From the next room, he shouts at the cricket match: "Go go go go!"

The teacher's name is a smudge, a dot-matrix mistake.

At work Vlad pretends to be an accountant. He pretends to use spreadsheets and formulas to deliver pretend assurances to a client who pretends to follow the law. In furtive conversations at breaks he pretends to care about baseball. Pretending this is easy: Paul cares about baseball, recites statistical rosaries, tells Dad his hopes for the season every night when he's tucked into bed. Vlad repeats these numbers in the break room, though he does not know if he says the right numbers in the right context.

From his cellular telephone, outside, he calls the number on the report card, and communicates in short sentences with someone he presumes is human.

"I would like to schedule a conference with my son's teacher." He tells them his son's name.

"Yes, I will wait."

"Six-thirty will be acceptable."

"Thank you."

———————

Afternoons, on weekends, he and Paul play catch in a park one block up and two blocks over from their apartment. They live in a crowded city of towers and stone, a city that calls itself new and thinks itself old. The people in this city have long since learned to unsee themselves. Vlad and his son throw a baseball, catch it, and throw it back in an empty park that, if Vlad were not by now so good at this game of unseeing, he would describe as full: of couples wheeling strollers, of rats and dogs and running children, strolling cops and bearded boys on roller blades.

They throw and catch the ball in this empty not-empty field. Vlad throws slow, and Paul catches, slower, humoring his dad. Vlad sees himself through his son's eyes: sluggish and overly skinny, a man who walks and runs and throws and catches as if first rehearsing the movements in his mind.

Vlad does rehearse. He has practiced thousands of times in the last decade. It took him a year to slow down so a human eye could see him shift from one posture to the next. Another year to learn to drop things, to let his grip slip, to suppress the instinct to right tipped teacups before they spilled, to grab knives before they left the hands that let them fall. Five years to train himself not to look at images mortal eyes could not detect. Sometimes at night, Paul's gaze darts up from his homework to strange corners of the room, and Vlad thinks he has failed, that the boy learned this nervous tic from him and will carry it through his life like a cross.

Vlad does not like the thought of crosses.

He throws the ball, and throws it back again: a white leather sphere oscillating through a haze of unseen ghosts.

The teacher waits, beautiful, blonde, and young. She smells like bruised mint and camellias. She rests against her classroom door, tired—she wakes at four-fifteen every morning to catch a bus from Queens, so she can sit at her desk grading papers as the sun rises through steel canyons.

When he sees her, Vlad knows he should turn and leave. No good can come of this meeting. They are doomed, both of them.

Too late. He's walked the halls with steps heavy as a human's, squeaking the soles of his oxblood shoes against the tiles every few steps—a trick he learned a year back and thinks lends him an authentic air. The teacher looks up and sees him: black-haired and pale and too, too thin, wearing blue slacks and a white shirt with faint blue checks.

"You're Paul's father," she says, and smiles, damn her round white teeth. "Mister St. John."

"Bazarab," he corrects, paying close attention to his steps. Slow, as if walking through ankle-deep mud.

She turns to open the door, but stops with her hand on the knob. "I'm sorry?"

"Paul has his mother's last name. Bazarab is mine. It is strange in this country. Please call me Vlad." The nasal American "a," too, he has practiced.

"Nice to meet you, Vlad. I'm so glad you could take this time for me, and for Paul." She turns back to smile at him, and starts. Her pupils dilate a millimeter, and her heart rate spikes from a charming sixty-five beats per minute to seventy-four. Blood rises beneath the snow of her cheeks.

He stands a respectful three feet behind her. But cursing himself he realizes that seconds before he was halfway down the hall.

He smiles, covering his frustration, and ushers her ahead of him into the room. Her heart slows, her breath deepens: the mouse convincing itself that it mistook the tree's shadow for a hawk's. He could not have moved so fast, so silently. She must have heard his approach, and ignored it.

The room's sparsely furnished. No posters on the walls. Row upon row of desks, forty children at least could study here. Blackboard, two days unwashed, a list of students' names followed by checks in multicolored chalk. This, he likes: many schools no longer use slate.

She sits on a desk, facing him. Her legs swing.

"You have a large room."

She laughs. "Not mine. We share the rooms." Her smile is sad. "Anyway. I'm glad to see you here. Why did you call?"

"My son. My wife asked me to talk with you about him. He has trouble in school, I think. I know he is a bright boy. His mother, my wife, she wonders why his grades are not so good. I think he is a child, he will improve with time, but I do not know. So I come to ask you."

"How can I help?"

Vlad shifts from foot to foot. Outside the night deepens. Streetlights buzz on. The room smells of dust and sweat and camellias and mint. The teacher's eyes are large and gray. She folds her lips into her mouth, bites them, and unfolds them again. Lines are growing from the corners of her mouth to the corners of her nose—the first signs of age. They surface at twenty-five or so. Vlad has studied them. He looks away from her. To see her is to know her pulse.

"What is he like in class, my son?"

"He's sweet. But he distracts easily. Sometimes he has trouble remembering a passage we've read a half hour after we've read it. In class he fidgets, and he often doesn't turn in his homework."

"I have seen him do the homework."

"Of course. I'm sorry. I'm not saying that he doesn't do it. He doesn't turn it in, though."

"Perhaps he is bored by your class." Her brow furrows, and he would kill men to clear it. "I do not mean that the class is easy. I know you have a difficult job. But perhaps he needs more attention."

"I wish I could give it to him. But any attention I give him comes from the other children in the class. We have forty. I don't have a lot of attention left to go around."

"I see." He paces more. Good to let her see him move like a human being. Good to avert his eyes.

"Have you thought about testing him for ADHD? It's a common condition."

What kind of testing? And what would the testing of his son reveal? "Could I help somehow? Review his work with him?"

She stands. "That's a great idea." The alto weight has left her voice, excitement returning after a day of weeks. "If you have time, I mean. I know it would help. He looks up to you."

Vlad laughs. Does his son admire the man, or the illusion? Or the monster, whom he has never seen? "I do not think so. But I will help if I can."

He turns from the window, and she walks toward him, holding a bright red folder. "These are his assignments for the week. If it helps, come back and I'll give you the next bunch."

She smiles.

Vlad, cold, afraid, smiles back.

"Great," his wife says when he tells her. She does not ask about the teacher, only the outcome. "Great. Thank you." She folds him in her arms, and he feels her strength. In the bathroom mirror they remind him of chess pieces, alabaster and mahogany. "I hate that building. The classrooms scare me. So many bad memories."

"Elementary school has no hold on me."

"Of course not." A quick soft peck on the cheek, and she fades from him, into their small hot bedroom. "This will help Paul, I know."

Vlad does not know. Every school night he sits with Paul in their cramped living room, bent over the coffee table, television off. Vlad drags a pencil across the paper, so slowly he feels glaciers might scour down the Hudson and carve a canyon from Manhattan by the time he finishes a single math problem. After a long division painstaking as a Tibetan monk's sand mandala he finds Paul asleep on the table beside him, cheek pooled on wood, tongue twitching pink between his lips. With a touch he wakes the boy, and once Paul stretches out and closes his eyes and shakes the sleep away (his mother's habit), they walk through the problem together, step by step. Then Paul does the next, and Vlad practices meditation, remembering cities rise and fall.

"Do you understand?" he asks.

"Dad, I get it."

Paul does not get it. The next week he brings each day's quizzes home, papers dripping blood.

"Perseverance is important," Vlad says. "In this world you must make something of yourself. It is not enough to be what you are."

"It all takes so long." The way Paul looks at Vlad when they talk makes Vlad wonder whether he has made some subtle mistake.

The following week Vlad returns to the school. Entering through swinging doors, he measures each step slow and steady. The shoes, he remembers to squeak. The eyes, he remembers to move. The lungs, he remembers to fill and empty. So many subtle ways to be human, and so many subtle ways to be wrong.

The halls are vacant, and still smell of dust and rubber and chemical soap. He could identify the chemical, if he put his mind to it.

He cannot put his mind to anything.

The teacher's room nears. Slow, slow. He smells her, faint trace of camellias and mint. He will not betray himself again.

The door to her classroom stands ajar. Through the space, he sees only empty desks.

A man sits at her desk, bent over papers like a tuberculotic over his handkerchief. He wears a blue shirt with chalk dust on the right cuff. His nails are ragged, and a pale scalp peeks through his thin hair.

"Where is the teacher?"

The man recoils as if he's touched a live wire. His chair falls and he knocks over a cup of pens and chalk and paperclips. Some spill onto the ground. Vlad does not count them. The man swears. His heart rate jumps to ninety beats a minute. If someone would scare him this way every hour for several months he would begin to lose the paunch developing around his waist. "Damn. Oh my god. Who the hell."

"I am Mister Bazarab," he says. "What has happened to the teacher?"

"I didn't hear," says the man. "I am the teacher. A teacher." Kneeling, he scrabbles over the tiles to gather scattered pens.

"The teacher who I was to meet here. The teacher of my son. A young woman. Blonde hair. About this tall." He does not mention her smell. Most people do not find such descriptions useful.

"Oh," says the man. "Mister Bazarab." He does not pronounce the name correctly. "I'm sorry. Angela had to leave early today. Family thing. She left this for you." He dumps the gathered detritus back into the cup, and searches among piles of paperwork for a red folder like the one the teacher gave Vlad the week before. He offers Vlad the folder, and when Vlad takes it from him the man draws his hand back fast as if burned.

"Is she well? She is not sick I hope."

"She's fine. Her father went to the hospital. I think."

"I am glad," Vlad says, and when he sees the other's confusion he adds, "that she is well. Thank her for this, please."

Vlad does not open the folder until he is outside the school. The teacher has a generous, looped cursive hand. She thanks Vlad for working with his son. She apologizes for missing their meeting. She suggests he return next week. She promises to be here for him then.

Vlad does not examine the rest of the folder's contents until he reaches home. He reads the note three times on his walk. He tries not to smell the camellias, or the chalk, or the slight salt edge of fear. He smells them anyway.

His wife returns late from the library. While he works with Paul, she does pull-ups on the bar they sling over the bedroom doorjamb. She breathes heavily through her mouth as she rises and falls. Behind her shadows fill their unlit bedroom.

Paul works long division. How many times does seven go into forty-three, and how much is left over? How far can you carry out the decimal? Paul's pencil breaks, and he sharpens it in the translucent bright red plastic toy his mother bought him, with pleasant curves to hide the tiny blade inside.

Vlad wants to teach Paul to sharpen his pencils with a knife, but sharpening pencils with a knife is not common these days, and anyway they'd have to collect the shaved bits of wood and graphite afterward. The old ways were harder to clean up.

"Tell me about your teacher," Vlad says.

"She's nice," Paul replies. "Three goes into eight two times, and two's left over."

"Nice," Vlad echoes.

Once his wife's exercises are done, they send Paul to bed. "I miss cricket," he says as they tuck him in. "I miss tennis and football and baseball."

"This is only for now," says Vlad's wife. "Once your work gets better, you can watch again. And play."

"Okay." The boy is not okay, but he knows what he is supposed to say.

In the kitchen, the kettle screams. They leave Paul in his dark room. Vlad's wife pours tea, disappears into their bedroom, and emerges soon after wearing flannel pajamas and her fluffy robe, hair down. She looks tired. She looks happy. Vlad cannot tell which she looks more. She sits cross-legged on the couch, tea steaming on the table beside her, and opens a book in her lap.

"You're doing it again," she says ten minutes later.

"What?"

"Not moving."

An old habit of his when idle: find a dark corner, stand statue-still, and observe. He smiles. "I am tired. I start to forget."

"Or remember," she says.

"I always remember." He sits in the love seat, at right angles to her.

"It's wonderful what you're doing with Paul."

"I want to help."

"You do."

He shifts from the love seat to the couch, and does not bother to move slow. The wind of his passage puffs in her eyes. She blinks, and nestles beside him.

"This is okay for you? I worry sometimes." Her hand's on his thigh. It rests there, strong, solid. "You've been quiet. I hope you're telling me what you need."

Need. He does not use that word much, even to himself. He needed this, ten years ago. Ten years ago she chased him, this beauty with the methodical mind, ferreted his secrets out of ancient archives and hunted him around the world. Ten years ago, he lured her to the old castle in the mountains, one last challenge. Ten years ago she shone in starlight filtered through cracks in the castle's roof. He could have killed her and hid again, as he had before. Remained a leaf blown from age to age and land to land on a wind of blood.

She'd seemed so real in the moonlight.

So he descended and spoke with her, and they found they knew one another better than anyone else. And ten years passed.

What does he need?

He leans toward her. His sharp teeth press on the inside of his gums, against the false yellowed set. He smells her blood. He smells camellias. His teeth recede. He kisses her on the forehead.

"I love you," they both say. Later he tries to remember which of them said it first.

He sees the teacher every week after that. Angela, on Thursdays. With the blonde hair and the strong heart. She tells him how Paul's work is coming. She coaches him on how to coach his son, suggests games to play, discusses concepts the class will cover in the next week. Vlad wonders not for the first time why he doesn't teach his son himself. But they talked, he and his wife, back when they learned she was pregnant. They are not a normal couple, and whatever else Paul must learn, he must first learn how to seem normal.

He has learned how to be so normal he cannot do basic math. So Vlad stands in the schoolroom ramrod straight, and nods when he understands Angela and asks questions when he does not. He keeps his distance.

Vlad learns things about her, from her. He learns that she lives alone. He learns that her father in the hospital is the only parent to whom she is close, her mother having left them both in Angela's childhood, run off with a college friend leaving behind a half-drunk vodka bottle and a sorry note. He learns that she has tight-wound nerves like a small bird's, that she looks up at every sound of footsteps in the hall. That she does not sleep enough.

He does not need to learn her scent. That, he knows already.

One night he follows her home.

This is a mistake.

She leaves the building well after sunset and walks to the bus; she rides one bus straight home. So he takes to the roofs, and chases the bus.

A game, he tells himself. Humans hunt these days, in the woods, in the back country, and they do not eat the meat they kill. Fishermen catch fish to throw them back. And this night run is no more dangerous to him than fishing to an angler. He leaves his oxfords on the schoolhouse rooftop and runs barefoot over buildings and along bridge wires, swift and soft. Even if someone beneath looked up, what is he? Wisp of cloud, shiver of a remembered nightmare, bird spreading wings for flight. A shadow among shadows.

A game, he tells himself, and lies. He only learns he's lying later, though, after she emerges from the bus and he tracks her three blocks to her studio apartment and she drops her keys on the stoop and kneels quick and tense as a spooked rabbit to retrieve them, after she enters her apartment and he delays, debates, and finally retreats across the river to the schoolhouse where he dons his oxfords and inspects himself in a deli window and pats his hair into place and brushes dust off his slacks and jacket—only learns it when his wife asks him why there's dust on his collar and he shakes his head and says something about a construction site. His round teeth he returns to their cup of coffee, and he lies naked on their bed, curled around her like a vine. His wife smells of sweat and woman and dark woods, and smelling her reminds him of another smell. Teeth peek through his gums, and his wife twists pleased and tired beside him, and he lies there lying, and relives the last time he killed.

The first step taken, the second follows, and the third faster. As when he taught Paul to ride a bicycle: easier to keep balance when moving.

He's no longer stiff in their weekly meetings. He jokes about the old country and lets his accent show. Her laughter relieves the lines on her face.

"You and your wife both work," she says. "I know tutoring Paul takes time. Could his grandparents help at all?"

"His mother's family is far away," Vlad says. "My parents are both dead."

"I'm sorry."

His father died in a Turkish assault when he was fourteen; his mother died of one of the many small illnesses people died from back then. "It was sudden, and hard," he says, and they don't speak more of that. He recognizes the brief flash of sympathy in her eyes.

He follows her home again that night, hoping to see something that will turn him aside. She may visit friends, or call on an old paramour, or her father in the hospital. She may have a boyfriend or girlfriend. But she changes little. She stops at the drug store to buy toothpaste, bottled water, and sanitary napkins. She fumbles the keys at her door but does not drop them this time.

He leaves.

Paul, that night, is too tired to study. Vlad promises to help him more tomorrow. Paul frowns at the promise. Frowns don't yet sit well on his face. He's too young. Vlad tells him so, and lifts him upside down, and he shrieks laughter as Vlad carries him back to the bedroom.

Work is a dream. He is losing the knack of normalcy. Numbers dance to his command. He walks among cubicles clothed in purpose, and where once the white-collared workers forgot him as he passed, now they fall silent and stare in his wake. Management offers him a promotion for no reason, which he turns down. Silences between Vlad and Angela grow tense. He apologizes, and she says there is no need for an apology.

He and his wife make love twice that week. Ravenous, she pins him to the bed, and feasts.

Paul seems cautious in the mornings, silent between mouthfuls of cereal. At evening catch, Vlad almost forgets, almost hurls the ball up and out, over the park, over the city, into the ocean.

He can't go on like this. Woken, power suffuses him. He slips into old paths of being, into ways he trained himself to forget. One evening on his home commute he catches crows flocking above him on brownstone rooftops. Black beady eyes wait for his command.

This is no way to be a father. No way to be a man.

But Vlad was a monster before he was a man.

Again and again he follows her, as the heat of early autumn cools. The year will die. Show me some danger, he prays. Show me some reason I cannot close my fingers and seize you. But she is alone in the world, and sad.

Paul's grades slip. Vlad apologizes to Angela. He has been distracted. "It's okay," she says. "It happens. Don't blame yourself."

He does not blame her. But this must end.

He makes his wife breakfast on the last morning. Bacon. Eggs, scrambled hard, with cheese. Orange juice, squeezed fresh. The squeezing takes time, but not so much for Vlad. He wakes early to cook, and moves at his own pace—fast. Fat pops and slithers in the pan. Eggs bubble. He ticks off seconds while he waits for the bacon to fry, for the eggs to congeal after. By the time his wife steps out of the shower, breakfast's ready and the kitchen is clean. He makes Paul's lunch, because it's his turn. He cannot make amends.

His wife sucks the strip of bacon before she bites. "Delicious." She hums happily, hugs him around the waist. "So good. Isn't your dad a good cook?"

Paul laughs. Vlad thinks it is a knowing laugh, because he is afraid.

"It's not Mother's Day," his wife says. "That's in May."

"I love you," Vlad answers. Paul makes a face like a Punchinello mask.

Crows follow him to work, hopping sideways along the roofs. When he reaches midtown they perch on streetlamps and traffic lights. Red, yellow, and green reflect in their eyes in turn. The *Times* reports power outages in suburbs last night from unexpected vicious wind. Asylums and hospitals brim with madmen, raving, eating bugs. Vlad is over-empty, a great mounting void, and the world rushes to fill him.

He breaks a keyboard that day from typing too hard. Drives his pinkie finger through the enter key into his desk, embedding a sliver of plastic in his skin. He pulls the plastic out and the wound heals. I.T. replaces the keyboard.

Vlad finishes his work by three and sits in his cubicle till sunset. Thunderclouds cluster overhead by the time he leaves the building.

Heat lightning flickers on his walk uptown. Fear shines at each flash from the eyes of the peasants he passes. Peasants: another word he has not thought or used in years.

All this will be over soon, he tells himself. And back to normal.

Whatever normal is.

He meets her in the classroom, though they do not talk long. The time for talking's past. She is all he remembered: sunlight and marble, camellia and mint. The ideal prey. Blood throbs through small veins in her fingers. He feels it when they shake hands. He smells its waves, rising and falling.

"I must thank you," he says, once she's gone over Paul's assignments for the next week. "For your dedication. You have given Paul so much. I appreciate your work."

"It's nothing." She may think he cannot hear her exhaustion, or else she trusts him and does not care. "I'm glad to help. If every father cared as much as you do, we'd be in a better world."

"I am fortunate," he says, "to be in a position to care."

He follows her from the school, as before. After sunset the crows stop hiding. In masses they descend on the city and croak prophecy in its alleys. Currents of crows rush down Broadway, so thick pedestrians mistake them for a cloud, their wing-beats for the rumble of traffic or a train. Bats emerge from their lairs, and rats writhe on subway steps singing rat songs. Grandmothers remember their grandmothers' whispered stories, and call children to urge them to stay inside.

Better this way, Vlad thinks as he follows Angela across the bridge, down the dirty deserted street from her stop to her apartment. She does not notice him. She notices nothing. The rats, the crows, the bats, all keep away from her. They know Vlad's purpose tonight, and will not interfere.

She's young, her life still a web of dream, her love just touched by sadness. This world holds only pain for her. Better, surely, to leave before that pain bloomed, before tenderness roughed into a callous.

His gums itch. He slides the false teeth from his mouth, places them in a Ziploc bag, closes the seal, and slips the bag into his jacket pocket. Crouched atop the roof of the building across from Angela's, he sees her shuffle down the street. The weight of her shoulder bag makes her limp.

His teeth, his real teeth, emerge, myriad and sharp. He tastes their tips and edges with his tongue.

She opens the door, climbs the steps. He follows her heartbeat up four floors, five, to the small studio.

He leaps across the street, lands soft as shadow on Angela's roof beside the skylight. Below, a door opens and light wakes. Though she's drawn curtains across the glass, there are gaps, and he sees her through them. She sags back against the door to close it, lets her bag clatter to the ground and leans into the scuffed dark wood, eyes closed.

Her apartment looks a mess because it's small: a stack of milk crates turned to bookshelves, overflowing with paperbacks and used textbooks. A small lacquered pine board dresser in stages of advanced decay, its side crisscrossed with bumper stickers bearing logos of bands Vlad does not recognize. A couch that slides out to form a bed, separated from the kitchenette by a narrow coffee table. Sheets piled in a hamper beside the couch-bed, dirty clothes in another hamper, dishes in the sink.

She opens her eyes, and steps out of the circle formed by the shoulder strap of her fallen bag. Two steps to the fridge, from which she draws a beer. She opens the cap with a fob on her keychain, tosses the cap in the recycling, and takes a long drink. Three steps from fridge around the table to the couch, where she sits, takes another drink, then swears, "Mother*fucker*," first two syllables drawn out and low, the third a high clear peal like those little bells priests used to ring in the litany. She lurches back to her feet, retrieves her bag, sits again on the couch and pulls from the bag a thick sheaf of papers and a red pen and proceeds to grade.

Vlad waits. Not now, certainly. Not as she wades through work. You take your prey in joy: insert yourself into perfection, sharp as a needle's tip. When she entered the room, he might have done it then. But the moment's passed.

She grades, finishes her beer, gets another. After a while she returns the papers to their folder, and the folder to her bag. From the milk crate bookshelves she retrieves a bulky laptop, plugs it in, and turns on a television show about young people living in the city, who all have bigger apartments than hers. Once in a while, she laughs, and after she laughs, she drinks.

He watches her watching. He can only permit himself this once, so it must be perfect. He tries to see the moment in his mind. Does she lie back in her bed, smiling? Does she spy him through the curtains, and climb on a chair to open the skylight and let him in? Does she scream and run? Does she call his name? Do they embrace? Does he seize her about the neck and drag her toward him while she claws ineffectually at his eyes and cheeks until her strength gives out?

She closes the laptop, dumps the dregs of her beer in the sink, tosses the empty into the recycling, walks into the bathroom, closes the door. The toilet flushes, the water runs, and he hears her floss, and brush her teeth, gargle and spit into the sink.

Do it. The perfect moment won't come. There's no such thing.

The doorknob turns.

What is he waiting for? He wants her to see him, know him, understand him, fear him, love him at the last. He wants her to chase him around the world, wants a moonlit showdown in a dark castle.

He wants to be her monster. To transform her life in its ending.

The door opens. She emerges, wearing threadbare blue pajamas. Four steps back to the couch, which she slides out into a bed. She spreads sheets over the bed, a comforter on top of them, and wriggles under the comforter. Hair halos her head on the dark pillow.

Now.

She can reach the light switch from her bed. The room goes dark save for the blinking lights of coffee maker and charging cell phone and laptop. He can still see her staring at the ceiling. She sighs.

He stands and turns to leave.

Moonlight glints off glass ten blocks away.

His wife has almost broken down the rifle by the time he reaches her—nine seconds. She's kept in practice. The sniper scope is stowed already; as he arrives, she's unscrewing the barrel. She must have heard him coming, but she waits for him to speak first.

She hasn't changed from the library. Khaki pants, a cardigan, comfortable shoes. Her hair up, covered by a dark cap. She wears no jewels but for his ring and her watch.

"I'm sorry," he says, first.

"I'll say."

"How did you know?"

"Dust on your collar. Late nights."

"I mean, how did you know it would be now?"

"I got dive-bombed by crows on the sidewalk this morning. One of the work-study kids came in high, babbling about the prince of darkness. You're not as subtle as you used to be."

"Well. I'm out of practice."

She looks up at him. He realizes he's smiling, and with his own teeth. He stops.

"Don't."

"I'm sorry."

"You said that already." Finished with the rifle, she returns it to the case, and closes the zipper, and stands. She's shorter than he is, broader through the shoulders. "What made you stop?"

"She wasn't you."

"Cheek."

"No."

"So what do we do now?"

"I don't know. I thought I was strong enough to be normal. But these are me." He bares his teeth at her. "Not these." From his pocket he draws the false teeth, and holds them out, wrapped in plastic, in his palm. Closes his fingers. Plastic cracks, crumbles. He presses it to powder, and drops bag and powder both. "Might as well kill me now."

"I won't."

"I'm a monster."

"You're just more literal than most." She looks away from him, raises her knuckle to her lip. Looks back.

"You deserve a good man. A normal man."

"I went looking for you." She doesn't shout, but something in her voice makes him retreat a step, makes his heart thrum and almost beat.

"I miss." Those two words sound naked. He struggles to finish the sentence. "I miss when we could be dangerous to one another."

"You think you're the only one who does? You think the PTA meetings and the ask your mothers and the how's your families at work, you think that stuff doesn't get to me? Think I don't wonder how I became this person?"

"It's not that simple. If I lose control, people die. Look at tonight."

"You stopped. And if you screw up." She nudges the rifle case with her toe. "There's always that."

"Paul needs a normal family. We agreed."

"He needs a father more. One who's not too scared of himself to be there."

He stops himself from shouting something he will regret. Closes his lips, and his eyes, and thinks for a long while, as the wind blows over their rooftop. His eyes hurt. "He needs a mother, too," he says.

"Yes. He does."

"I screwed up tonight."

"You did. But I think we can work on this. Together. How about you?"

"Sarah," he says.

She looks into his eyes. They embrace, once, and part. She kneels to lift the rifle case.

"Here," he says. "Let me get that for you."

The next week, Friday, he plays catch with Paul in the park. They're the only ones there save the ghosts: it's cold, but Paul's young, and while Vlad can feel the cold it doesn't bother him. Dead trees overhead, skeletal fingers raking sky. Leaves spin in little whirlwinds. The sky's blue and empty, sun already sunk behind the buildings.

Vlad unbuttons his coat, lets it fall. Strips off his sweater, balls it on top of the coat. Stands in his shirtsleeves, cradles the football with his long fingers. Tightens his grip. Does not burst the ball, only feels the air within resist his fingers' pressure.

Paul steps back, holds up his hands.

Vlad shakes his head. "Go deeper."

He runs, crumbling dry leaves and breaking hidden sticks.

"Deeper," Vlad calls, and waves him on.

"Here?" Vlad's never thrown the ball this far.

"More."

Paul stands near the edge of the park. "That's all there is!"

"Okay," Vlad says. "Okay. Are you ready?"

"Yes!"

His throws are well-rehearsed. Wind up slowly, and toss soft. He beat them into his bones.

He forgets all that.

Black currents weave through the wind. A crow calls from treetops. He stands, a statue of ice.

He throws the ball as hard as he can.

A loud crack echoes through the park. Ghosts scatter, dive for cover. The ball breaks the air, and its passage leaves a vacuum trail.

Windows rattle and car alarms whoop. Vlad wasn't aiming for his son. He didn't want to hurt him. He just wanted to throw.

Vlad's eyes are faster even than his hands, and sharp. So he sees Paul blink, in surprise more than fear. He sees Paul understand. He sees Paul smile.

And he sees Paul blur sideways and catch the ball.

They stare at one another across the park. The ball hisses in Paul's hands, deflates: it broke in the catching. Wind rolls leaves between them.

Later, neither can remember who laughed first.

They talk for hours after that. Chase one another around the park, so fast they seem only colors on the wind. High-pitched child's screams of joy, and Vlad's own voice, deep, guttural. Long after the sky turns black and the stars don't come out, they return home, clothes grass-stained, hair tangled with sticks and leaves. Paul does his homework, fast, and they watch cricket until after bedtime.

Sarah waits in the living room when he leaves Paul sleeping. She grabs his arms and squeezes, hard enough to bruise, and pulls him into her kiss.

He kisses her back with his teeth.

JACKALOPE WIVES
Ursula Vernon

Ursula Vernon is the author and illustrator of the Dragonbreath and
Hamster Princess children's book series as well as other works for both
children and adults. She also writes under the name of T. Kingfisher.
Her web comic *Digger* was nominated for the Eisner Award in 2006 and
won the Hugo Award in 2012 and the Mythopoeic Award in 2013. She
lives in Pittsboro, North Carolina.

"Jackalope Wives" won the Nebula and WSFA Small Press awards and
was nominated for the World Fantasy Award.

The moon came up and the sun went down. The moonbeams
went shattering down to the ground and the jackalope wives
took off their skins and danced.

They danced like young deer pawing the ground, they danced like
devils let out of hell for the evening. They swung their hips and
pranced and drank their fill of cactus-fruit wine.

They were shy creatures, the jackalope wives, though there was
nothing shy about the way they danced. You could go your whole life
and see no more of them than the flash of a tail vanishing around the
backside of a boulder. If you were lucky, you might catch a whole line
of them outlined against the sky, on the top of a bluff, the shadow of
horns rising off their brows.

And on the half-moon, when new and full were balanced across the
saguaro's thorns, they'd come down to the desert and dance.

The young men used to get together and whisper, saying they were
gonna catch them a jackalope wife. They'd lay belly down at the edge

of the bluff and look down on the fire and the dancing shapes—and they'd go away aching, for all the good it did them.

For the jackalope wives were shy of humans. Their lovers were jackrabbits and antelope bucks, not human men. You couldn't even get too close or they'd take fright and run away. One minute you'd see them kicking their heels up and hear them laugh, then the music would freeze and they'd all look at you with their eyes wide and their ears upswept.

The next second, they'd snatch up their skins and there'd be nothing left but a dozen skinny she-rabbits running off in all directions, and a campfire left that wouldn't burn out till morning.

It was uncanny, sure, but they never did anybody any harm. Grandma Harken, who lived down past the well, said that the jackalopes were the daughters of the rain and driving them off would bring on the drought. People said they didn't believe a word of it, but when you live in a desert, you don't take chances.

When the wild music came through town, a couple of notes skittering on the sand, then people knew the jackalope wives were out. They kept the dogs tied up and their brash sons occupied. The town got into the habit of having a dance that night, to keep the boys firmly fixed on human girls and to drown out the notes of the wild music.

Now, it happened there was a young man in town who had a touch of magic on him. It had come down to him on his mother's side, as happens now and again, and it was worse than useless.

A little magic is worse than none, for it draws the wrong sort of attention. It gave this young man feverish eyes and made him sullen. His grandmother used to tell him that it was a miracle he hadn't been drowned as a child, and for her he'd laugh, but not for anyone else.

He was tall and slim and had dark hair and young women found him fascinating.

This sort of thing happens often enough, even with boys as mortal as dirt. There's always one who learned how to brood early and often, and always girls who think they can heal him.

Eventually the girls learn better. Either the hurts are petty little things and they get tired of whining or the hurt's so deep and wide that they drown in it. The smart ones heave themselves back to shore and the slower ones wake up married with a husband who lies around and suffers in their direction. It's part of a dance as old as the jackalopes themselves.

But in this town at this time, the girls hadn't learned and the boy hadn't yet worn out his interest. At the dances, he leaned on the wall with his hands in his pockets and his eyes glittering. Other young men eyed him with dislike. He would slip away early, before the dance was ended, and never marked the eyes that followed him and wished that he would stay.

He himself had one thought and one thought only—to catch a jackalope wife.

They were beautiful creatures, with their long brown legs and their bodies splashed orange by the firelight. They had faces like no mortal woman and they moved like quicksilver and they played music that got down into your bones and thrummed like a sickness.

And there was one—he'd seen her. She danced farther out from the others and her horns were short and sharp as sickles. She was the last one to put on her rabbit skin when the sun came up. Long after the music had stopped, she danced to the rhythm of her own long feet on the sand.

(And now you will ask me about the musicians that played for the jackalope wives. Well, if you can find a place where they've been dancing, you might see something like sidewinder tracks in the dust, and more than that I cannot tell you. The desert chews its secrets right down to the bone.)

So the young man with the touch of magic watched the jackalope wife dancing and you know as well as I do what young men dream about. We will be charitable. She danced a little apart from her fellows, as he walked a little apart from his.

Perhaps he thought she might understand him. Perhaps he found her as interesting as the girls found him.

Perhaps we shouldn't always get what we think we want.

And the jackalope wife danced, out past the circle of the music and the firelight, in the light of the fierce desert stars.

Grandma Harken had settled in for the evening with a shawl on her shoulders and a cat on her lap when somebody started hammering on the door.

"Grandma! Grandma! Come quick—open the door—oh god, Grandma, you have to help me—"

She knew that voice just fine. It was her own grandson, her daughter Eva's boy. Pretty and useless and charming when he set out to be.

She dumped the cat off her lap and stomped to the door. What trouble had the young fool gotten himself into?

"Sweet Saint Anthony," she muttered, "let him not have gotten some fool girl in a family way. That's just what we need."

She flung the door open and there was Eva's son and there was a girl and for a moment her worst fears were realized.

Then she saw what was huddled in the circle of her grandson's arms, and her worst fears were stomped flat and replaced by far greater ones.

"Oh Mary," she said. "Oh, Jesus, Mary and Joseph. Oh blessed Saint Anthony, you've caught a jackalope wife."

Her first impulse was to slam the door and lock the sight away.

Her grandson caught the edge of the door and hauled it open. His knuckles were raw and blistered. "Let me in," he said. He'd been crying and there was dust on his face, stuck to the tracks of tears. "Let me in, let me in, oh god, Grandma, you have to help me, it's all gone wrong—"

Grandma took two steps back, while he half-dragged the jackalope into the house. He dropped her down in front of the hearth and grabbed for his grandmother's hands. "Grandma—"

She ignored him and dropped to her knees. The thing across her hearth was hardly human. "What have you done?" she said. "What did you do to her?"

"Nothing!" he said, recoiling.

"Don't look at that and tell me 'Nothing!' What in the name of our lord did you do to that girl?"

He stared down at his blistered hands. "Her skin," he mumbled. "The rabbit skin. You know."

"I do indeed," she said grimly. "Oh yes, I do. What did you do, you damned young fool? Caught up her skin and hid it from her to keep her changing?"

The jackalope wife stirred on the hearth and made a sound between a whimper and a sob.

"She was waiting for me!" he said. "She knew I was there! I'd been— we'd—I watched her, and she knew I was out there, and she let me get up close—I thought we could talk—"

Grandma Harken clenched one hand into a fist and rested her forehead on it.

"I grabbed the skin—I mean—it was right there—she was watching—I thought she *wanted* me to have it—"

She turned and looked at him. He sank down in her chair, all his grace gone.

"You have to burn it," mumbled her grandson. He slid down a little further in her chair. "You're supposed to burn it. Everybody knows. To keep them changing."

"Yes," said Grandma Harken, curling her lip. "Yes, that's the way of it, right enough." She took the jackalope wife's shoulders and turned her toward the lamplight.

She was a horror. Her hands were human enough, but she had a jackrabbit's feet and a jackrabbit's eyes. They were set too wide apart in a human face, with a cleft lip and long rabbit ears. Her horns were short, sharp spikes on her brow.

The jackalope wife let out another sob and tried to curl back into a ball. There were burnt patches on her arms and legs, a long red weal down her face. The fur across her breasts and belly was singed. She stank of urine and burning hair.

"*What did you do?*"

"I threw it in the fire," he said. "You're supposed to. But she screamed—she wasn't supposed to scream—nobody said they screamed—and I thought she was dying, and I didn't want to *hurt* her—I pulled it back out—"

He looked up at her with his feverish eyes, that useless, beautiful boy, and said, "I didn't *want* to hurt her. I thought I was supposed to—I gave her the skin back, she put it on, but then she fell down—it wasn't supposed to work like that!"

Grandma Harken sat back. She exhaled very slowly. She was calm. She was going to be calm, because otherwise she was going to pick up the fire poker and club her own flesh and blood over the head with it.

And even that might not knock some sense into him. Oh, Eva, Eva, my dear, what a useless son you've raised. Who would have thought he had so much ambition in him, to catch a jackalope wife?

"You goddamn stupid fool," she said. Every word slammed like a shutter in the wind. "Oh, you goddamn stupid fool. If you're going to catch a jackalope wife, you burn the hide down to ashes and never mind how she screams."

"But it sounded like it was hurting her!" he shot back. "You weren't there! She screamed like a dying rabbit!"

"Of course it hurts her!" yelled Grandma. "You think you can have your skin and your freedom burned away in front of you and not scream? Sweet mother Mary, boy, think about what you're doing! Be cruel or be kind, but don't be both, because now you've made a mess you can't clean up in a hurry."

She stood up, breathing hard, and looked down at the wreck on her hearth. She could see it now, as clear as if she'd been standing there. The fool boy had been so shocked he'd yanked the burning skin back out. And the jackalope wife had one thought only and pulled on the burning hide—

Oh yes, she could see it clear.

Half gone, at least, if she was any judge. There couldn't have been more than few scraps of fur left unburnt. He'd waited through at least one scream—or no, that was unkind.

More likely he'd dithered and looked for a stick and didn't want to grab for it with his bare hands. Though by the look of his hands, he'd done just that in the end.

And the others were long gone by then and couldn't stop her. There ought to have been one, at least, smart enough to know that you didn't put on a half-burnt rabbit skin.

"Why does she look like that?" whispered her grandson, huddled into his chair.

"Because she's trapped betwixt and between. You did that, with your goddamn pity. You should have let it burn. Or better yet, left her alone and never gone out in the desert at all."

"She was beautiful," he said. As if it were a reason.

As if it mattered.

As if it had ever mattered.

"Get out," said Grandma wearily. "Tell your mother to make up a poultice for your hands. You did right at the end, bringing her here, even if you made a mess of the rest, from first to last."

He scrambled to his feet and ran for the door.

On the threshold, he paused, and looked back. "You—you can fix her, right?"

Grandma let out a high bark, like a bitch-fox, barely a laugh at all. "No. No one can fix this, you stupid boy. This is broken past mending. All I can do is pick up the pieces."

He ran. The door slammed shut, and left her alone with the wreckage of the jackalope wife.

She treated the burns and they healed. But there was nothing to be done for the shape of the jackalope's face, or the too-wide eyes, or the horns shaped like a sickle moon.

At first, Grandma worried that the townspeople would see her, and Lord knew what would happen then. But the jackalope wife was the color of dust and she still had a wild animal's stillness. When somebody called, she lay flat in the garden, down among the beans, and nobody saw her at all.

The only person she didn't hide from was Eva, Grandma's daughter. There was no chance that she mistook them for each other—Eva was round and plump and comfortable, the way Grandma's second husband, Eva's father, had been round and plump and comfortable.

Maybe we smell alike, thought Grandma. *It would make sense, I suppose.*

Eva's son didn't come around at all.

"He thinks you're mad at him," said Eva mildly.

"He thinks correctly," said Grandma.

She and Eva sat on the porch together, shelling beans, while the jackalope wife limped around the garden. The hairless places weren't so obvious now, and the faint stripes across her legs might have been dust. If you didn't look directly at her, she might almost have been human.

"She's gotten good with the crutch," said Eva. "I suppose she can't walk?"

"Not well," said Grandma. "Her feet weren't made to stand up like that. She can do it, but it's a terrible strain."

"And talk?"

"No," said Grandma shortly. The jackalope wife had tried, once, and the noises she'd made were so terrible that it had reduced them both to weeping. She hadn't tried again. "She understands well enough, I suppose."

The jackalope wife sat down, slowly, in the shadow of the scarlet runner beans. A hummingbird zipped inches from her head, dabbing its bill into the flowers, and the jackalope's face turned, unsmiling, to follow it.

"He's not a bad boy, you know," said Eva, not looking at her mother. "He didn't mean to do her harm."

Grandma let out an explosive snort. "Jesus, Mary and Joseph! It doesn't matter what he *meant* to do. He should have left well enough alone, and if he couldn't do that, he should have finished what he started." She scowled down at the beans. They were striped red and white and the pods came apart easily in her gnarled hands. "Better all the way human than this. Better he'd bashed her head in with a rock than *this*."

"Better for her, or better for you?" asked Eva, who was only a fool about her son and knew her mother well.

Grandma snorted again. The hummingbird buzzed away. The jackalope wife lay still in the shadows, with only her thin ribs going up and down.

"You could have finished it, too," said Eva softly. "I've seen you kill chickens. She'd probably lay her head on the chopping block if you asked."

"She probably would," said Grandma. She looked away from Eva's weak, wise eyes. "But I'm a damn fool as well."

Her daughter smiled. "Maybe it runs in families."

———

Grandma Harken got up before dawn the next morning and went rummaging around the house.

"Well," she said. She pulled a dead mouse out of a mousetrap and took a half-dozen cigarettes down from behind the clock. She filled three water bottles and strapped them around her waist. "Well. I suppose we've done as much as humans can do, and now it's up to somebody else."

She went out into the garden and found the jackalope wife asleep under the stairs. "Come on," she said. "Wake up."

The air was cool and gray. The jackalope wife looked at her with doe-dark eyes and didn't move, and if she were a human, Grandma Harken would have itched to slap her.

Pay attention! Get mad! Do something!

But she wasn't human and rabbits freeze when they're scared past running. So Grandma gritted her teeth and reached down a hand and pulled the jackalope wife up into the pre-dawn dark.

They moved slow, the two of them. Grandma was old and carrying water for two, and the girl was on a crutch. The sun came up and the cicadas burnt the air with their wings.

A coyote watched them from up on the hillside. The jackalope wife looked up at him, recoiled, and Grandma laid a hand on her arm.

"Don't worry," she said. "I ain't got the patience for coyotes. They'd maybe fix you up but we'd both be stuck in a tale past telling, and I'm too old for that. Come on."

They went a little further on, past a wash and a watering hole. There were palo verde trees spreading thin green shade over the water. A javelina looked up at them from the edge and stamped her hooved feet. Her children scraped their tusks together and grunted.

Grandma slid and slithered down the slope to the far side of the water and refilled the water bottles. "Not them either," she said to the jackalope wife. "They'll talk the legs off a wooden sheep. We'd both be dead of old age before they'd figured out what time to start."

The javelina dropped their heads and ignored them as they left the wash behind.

The sun was overhead and the sky turned turquoise, a color so hard you could bash your knuckles on it. A raven croaked overhead and another one snickered somewhere off to the east.

The jackalope wife paused, leaning on her crutch, and looked up at the wings with longing.

"Oh no," said Grandma. "I've got no patience for riddle games, and in the end they always eat someone's eyes. Relax, child. We're nearly there."

The last stretch was cruelly hard, up the side of a bluff. The sand was soft underfoot and miserably hard for a girl walking with a crutch. Grandma had to half-carry the jackalope wife at the end. She weighed no more than a child, but children are heavy and it took them both a long time.

At the top was a high fractured stone that cast a finger of shadow like the wedge of a sundial. Sand and sky and shadow and stone. Grandma Harken nodded, content.

"It'll do," she said. "It'll do." She laid the jackalope wife down in the shadow and laid her tools out on the stone. Cigarettes and dead mouse and a scrap of burnt fur from the jackalope's breast. "It'll do."

Then she sat down in the shadow herself and arranged her skirts.

She waited.

The sun went overhead and the level in the water bottle went down. The sun started to sink and the wind hissed and the jackalope wife was asleep or dead.

The ravens croaked a conversation to each other, from the branches of a palo verde tree, and whatever one said made the other one laugh.

"Well," said a voice behind Grandma's right ear, "lookee what we have here."

"Jesus, Mary and Joseph!"

"Don't see them out here often," he said. "Not the right sort of place."

He considered. "Your Saint Anthony, now . . . him I think I've seen. He understood about deserts."

Grandma's lips twisted. "Father of Rabbits," she said sourly. "Wasn't trying to call *you* up."

"Oh, I know." The Father of Rabbits grinned. "But you know I've always had a soft spot for you, Maggie Harken."

He sat down beside her on his heels. He looked like an old Mexican man, wearing a button-down shirt without any buttons. His hair was silver gray as a rabbit's fur. Grandma wasn't fooled for a minute.

"Get lonely down there in your town, Maggie?" he asked. "Did you come out here for a little wild company?"

Grandma Harken leaned over to the jackalope wife and smoothed one long ear back from her face. She looked up at them both with wide, uncomprehending eyes.

"Shit," said the Father of Rabbits. "Never seen that before." He lit a cigarette and blew the smoke into the air. "What did you do to her, Maggie?"

"I didn't do a damn thing, except not let her die when I should have."

"There's those would say that was more than enough." He exhaled another lungful of smoke.

"She put on a half-burnt skin. Don't suppose you can fix her up?" It cost Grandma a lot of pride to say that, and the Father of Rabbits tipped his chin in acknowledgment.

"Ha! No. If it was loose I could fix it up, maybe, but I couldn't get it off her now with a knife." He took another drag on the cigarette. "Now I see why you wanted one of the Patterned People."

Grandma nodded stiffly.

The Father of Rabbits shook his head. "He might want a life, you know. Piddly little dead mouse might not be enough."

"Then he can have mine."

"Ah, Maggie, Maggie. . . . You'd have made a fine rabbit, once. Too many stones in your belly now." He shook his head regretfully. "Besides, it's not *your* life he's owed."

"It's my life he'd be getting. My kin did it, it's up to me to put it right." It occurred to her that she should have left Eva a note, telling her to send the fool boy back East, away from the desert.

Well. Too late now. Either she'd raised a fool for a daughter or not, and likely she wouldn't be around to tell.

"Suppose we'll find out," said the Father of Rabbits, and nodded.

A man came around the edge of the standing stone. He moved quick then slow and his eyes didn't blink. He was naked and his skin was covered in painted diamonds.

Grandma Harken bowed to him, because the Patterned People can't hear speech.

He looked at her and the Father of Rabbits and the jackalope wife. He looked down at the stone in front of him.

The cigarettes he ignored. The mouse he scooped up in two fingers and dropped into his mouth.

Then he crouched there, for a long time. He was so still that it made Grandma's eyes water, and she had to look away.

"Suppose he does it," said the Father of Rabbits. "Suppose he sheds that skin right off her. Then what? You've got a human left over, not a jackalope wife."

Grandma stared down at her bony hands. "It's not so bad, being a human," she said. "You make do. And it's got to be better than *that*."

She jerked her chin in the direction of the jackalope wife.

"Still meddling, Maggie?" said the Father of Rabbits.

"And what do you call what you're doing?"

He grinned.

The Patterned Man stood up and nodded to the jackalope wife.

She looked at Grandma, who met her too-wide eyes. "He'll kill you," the old woman said. "Or cure you. Or maybe both. You don't have to do it. This is the bit where you get a choice. But when it's over, you'll be all the way something, even if it's just all the way dead."

The jackalope wife nodded.

She left the crutch lying on the stones and stood up. Rabbit legs weren't meant for it, but she walked three steps and the Patterned Man opened his arms and caught her.

He bit her on the forearm, where the thick veins run, and sank his teeth in up to the gums. Grandma cursed.

"Easy now," said the Father of Rabbits, putting a hand on her shoulder. "He's one of the Patterned People, and they only know the one way."

The jackalope wife's eyes rolled back in her head, and she sagged down onto the stone.

He set her down gently and picked up one of the cigarettes.

Grandma Harken stepped forward. She rolled both her sleeves up to the elbow and offered him her wrists.

The Patterned Man stared at her, unblinking. The ravens laughed to themselves at the bottom of the wash. Then he dipped his head and bowed to Grandma Harken and a rattlesnake as long as a man slithered away into the evening.

She let out a breath she didn't know she'd been holding. "He didn't ask for a life."

The Father of Rabbits grinned. "Ah, you know. Maybe he wasn't hungry. Maybe it was enough you made the offer."

"Maybe I'm too old and stringy," she said.

"Could be that, too."

The jackalope wife was breathing. Her pulse went fast then slow. Grandma sat down beside her and held her wrist between her own callused palms.

"How long you going to wait?" asked the Father of Rabbits.

"As long as it takes," she snapped back.

The sun went down while they were waiting. The coyotes sang up the moon. It was half-full, half-new, halfway between one thing and the other.

"She doesn't have to stay human, you know," said the Father of Rabbits. He picked up the cigarettes that the Patterned Man had left behind and offered one to Grandma.

"She doesn't have a jackalope skin anymore."

He grinned. She could just see his teeth flash white in the dark. "Give her yours."

"I burned it," said Grandma Harken, sitting up ramrod straight. "I found where he hid it after he died and I burned it myself. Because I had a new husband and a little bitty baby girl and all I could think about was leaving them both behind and go dance."

The Father of Rabbits exhaled slowly in the dark.

"It was easier that way," she said. "You get over what you *can't* have faster that you get over what you *could*. And we shouldn't always get what we think we want."

They sat in silence at the top of the bluff. Between Grandma's hands, the pulse beat steady and strong.

"I never did like your first husband much," said the Father of Rabbits.

"Well," she said. She lit her cigarette off his. "He taught me how to swear. And the second one was better."

The jackalope wife stirred and stretched. Something flaked off her in long strands, like burnt scraps of paper, like a snake's skin shedding away. The wind tugged at them and sent them spinning off the side of the bluff.

From down in the desert, they heard the first notes of a sudden wild music.

"It happens I might have a spare skin," said the Father of Rabbits. He reached into his pack and pulled out a long gray roll of rabbit skin. The jackalope wife's eyes went wide and her body shook with longing, but it was human longing and a human body shaking.

"Where'd you get that?" asked Grandma Harken, suspicious.

"Oh, well, you know." He waved a hand. "Pulled it out of a fire once—must have been forty years ago now. Took some doing to fix it up again, but some people owed me favors. Suppose she might as well have it . . . Unless you want it?"

He held it out to Grandma Harken.

She took it in her hands and stroked it. It was as soft as it had been fifty years ago. The small sickle horns were hard weights in her hands.

"You were a hell of a dancer," said the Father of Rabbits.

"Still am," said Grandma Harken, and she flung the jackalope skin over the shoulders of the human jackalope wife.

It went on like it had been made for her, like it was her own. There was a jagged scar down one foreleg where the rattlesnake had bit her. She leapt up and darted away, circled back once and bumped Grandma's hand with her nose—and then she was bounding down the path from the top of the bluff.

The Father of Rabbits let out a long sigh. "Still are," he agreed.

"It's different when you got a choice," said Grandma Harken.

They shared another cigarette under the standing stone.

Down in the desert, the music played and the jackalope wives danced. And one scarred jackalope went leaping into the circle of firelight and danced like a demon, while the moon laid down across the saguaro's thorns.

THE CARTOGRAPHER WASPS
AND THE ANARCHIST BEES
E. Lily Yu

"The Cartographer Wasps and the Anarchist Bees" draws from E. Lily Yu's experience with beekeeping in college, Maurice Maeterlinck's *The Life of the Bee*, and several papers on the phenomenon of anarchism in honeybees, including Oldroyd and Osborne, 1999. The story was a finalist for the Hugo, Nebula, World Fantasy, Locus, and WSFA Small Press awards, and Yu won the John W. Campbell Award for Best New Writer in 2012. She lives near Seattle, Washington.

"The Cartographer Wasps and the Anarchist Bees" is a deceptively complex story, combining insects and politics in the tradition of Bernard Mandeville and James Gould.

For longer than anyone could remember, the village of Yiwei had worn, in its orchards and under its eaves, clay-colored globes of paper that hissed and fizzed with wasps. The villagers maintained an uneasy peace with their neighbors for many years, exercising inimitable tact and circumspection. But it all ended the day a boy, digging in the riverbed, found a stone whose balance and weight pleased him. With this, he thought, he could hit a sparrow in flight. There were no sparrows to be seen, but a paper ball hung low and inviting nearby. He considered it for a moment, head cocked, then aimed and threw.

Much later, after he had been plastered and soothed, his mother scalded the fallen nest until the wasps seething in the paper were dead. In this way it was discovered that the wasp nests of Yiwei, dipped in

111

hot water, unfurled into beautifully accurate maps of provinces near and far, inked in vegetable pigments and labeled in careful Mandarin that could be distinguished beneath a microscope.

The villagers' subsequent incursions with bee veils and kettles of boiling water soon diminished the prosperous population to a handful. Commanded by a single stubborn foundress, the survivors folded a new nest in the shape of a paper boat, provisioned it with fallen apricots and squash blossoms, and launched themselves onto the river. Browsing cows and children fled the riverbanks as they drifted downstream, piping sea chanteys.

At last, forty miles south from where they had begun, their craft snagged on an upthrust stick and sank. Only one drowned in the evacuation, weighed down with the remains of an apricot. They reconvened upon a stump and looked about themselves.

"It's a good place to land," the foundress said in her sweet soprano, examining the first rough maps that the scouts brought back. There were plenty of caterpillars, oaks for ink galls, fruiting brambles, and no signs of other wasps. A colony of bees had hived in a split oak two miles away. "Once we are established we will, of course, send a delegation to collect tribute.

"We will not make the same mistakes as before. Ours is a race of explorers and scientists, cartographers and philosophers, and to rest and grow slothful is to die. Once we are established here, we will expand."

It took two weeks to complete the nurseries with their paper mobiles, and then another month to reconstruct the Great Library and fill the pigeonholes with what the oldest cartographers could remember of their lost maps. Their comings and goings did not go unnoticed. An ambassador from the beehive arrived with an ultimatum and was promptly executed; her wings were made into stained-glass windows for the council chamber, and her stinger was returned to the hive in a paper envelope. The second ambassador came with altered attitude and a proposal to divide the bees' kingdom evenly between the two governments, retaining pollen and water rights for the bees—"as an acknowledgment of the preexisting claims of a free people to the natural resources of a common territory," she hummed.

The wasps of the council were gracious and only divested the envoy of her sting. She survived just long enough to deliver her account to the hive.

The third ambassador arrived with a ball of wax on the tip of her stinger and was better received.

"You understand, we are not refugees applying for recognition of a token territorial sovereignty," the foundress said, as attendants served them nectars in paper horns, "nor are we negotiating with you as equal states. Those were the assumptions of your late predecessors. They were mistaken."

"I trust I will do better," the diplomat said stiffly. She was older than the others, and the hairs of her thorax were sparse and faded.

"I do hope so."

"Unlike them, I have complete authority to speak for the hive. You have propositions for us; that is clear enough. We are prepared to listen."

"Oh, good." The foundress drained her horn and took another. "Yours is an old and highly cultured society, despite the indolence of your ruler, which we understand to be a racial rather than personal proclivity. You have laws, and traditional dances, and mathematicians, and principles, which of course we do respect."

"Your terms, please."

She smiled. "Since there is a local population of tussah moths, which we prefer for incubation, there is no need for anything so un-republican as slavery. If you refrain from insurrection, you may keep your self-rule. But we will take a fifth of your stores in an ordinary year, and a tenth in drought years, and one of every hundred larvae."

"To eat?" Her antennae trembled with revulsion.

"Only if food is scarce. No, they will be raised among us and learn our ways and our arts, and then they will serve as officials and bureaucrats among you. It will be to your advantage, you see."

The diplomat paused for a moment, looking at nothing at all. Finally she said, "A tenth, in a good year—"

"Our terms," the foundress said, "are not negotiable."

The guards shifted among themselves, clinking the plates of their armor and shifting the gleaming points of their stings.

"I don't have a choice, do I?"

"The choice is enslavement or cooperation," the foundress said. "For your hive, I mean. You might choose something else, certainly, but they have tens of thousands to replace you with."

The diplomat bent her head. "I am old," she said. "I have served the hive all my life, in every fashion. My loyalty is to my hive and I will do what is best for it."

"I am so very glad."

"I ask you—I beg you—to wait three or four days to impose your terms. I will be dead by then, and will not see my sisters become a servile people."

The foundress clicked her claws together. "Is the delaying of business a custom of yours? We have no such practice. You will have the honor of watching us elevate your sisters to moral and technological heights you could never imagine."

The diplomat shivered.

"Go back to your queen, my dear. Tell them the good news."

It was a crisis for the constitutional monarchy. A riot broke out in District 6, destroying the royal waxworks and toppling the mouse-bone monuments before it was brutally suppressed. The queen had to be calmed with large doses of jelly after she burst into tears on her ministers' shoulders.

"Your Majesty," said one, "it's not a matter for your concern. Be at peace."

"These are my children," she said, sniffling. "You would feel for them too, were you a mother."

"Thankfully, I am not," the minister said briskly, "so to business."

"War is out of the question," another said.

"Their forces are vastly superior."

"We outnumber them three hundred to one!"

"They are experienced fighters. Sixty of us would die for each of theirs. We might drive them away, but it would cost us most of the hive and possibly our queen—"

The queen began weeping noisily again and had to be cleaned and comforted.

"Have we any alternatives?"

There was a small silence.

"Very well, then."

The terms of the relationship were copied out, at the wasps' direction, on small paper plaques embedded in propolis and wax around the hive. As paper and ink were new substances to the bees, they jostled and touched and tasted the bills until the paper fell to pieces. The wasps sent to oversee the installation did not take this kindly. Several civilians died before it was established that the bees could not read the Yiwei dialect.

Thereafter the hive's chemists were charged with compounding pheromones complex enough to encode the terms of the treaty. These were applied to the papers, so that both species could inspect them and comprehend the relationship between the two states.

Whereas the hive before the wasp infestation had been busy but content, the bees now lived in desperation. The natural terms of their lives were cut short by the need to gather enough honey for both the hive and the wasp nest. As they traveled farther and farther afield in search of nectar, they stopped singing. They danced their findings grimly, without joy. The queen herself grew gaunt and thin from breeding replacements, and certain ministers who understood such matters began feeding royal jelly to the strongest larvae.

Meanwhile, the wasps grew sleek and strong. Cadres of scholars, cartographers, botanists, and soldiers were dispatched on the river in small floating nests caulked with beeswax and loaded with rations of honeycomb to chart the unknown lands to the south. Those who returned bore beautiful maps with towns and farms and alien populations of wasps carefully noted in blue and purple ink, and these, once studied by the foundress and her generals, were carefully filed away in the depths of the Great Library for their southern advance in the new year.

The bees adopted by the wasps were first trained to clerical tasks, but once it was determined that they could be taught to read and write, they were assigned to some of the reconnaissance missions. The brightest students, gifted at trigonometry and angles, were educated beside the cartographers themselves and proved valuable assistants. They learned not to see the thick green caterpillars led on silver chains, or the dead bees fed to the wasp brood. It was easier that way.

When the old queen died, they did not mourn.

By the sheerest of accidents, one of the bees trained as a cartographer's assistant was an anarchist. It might have been the stresses on the hive, or it might have been luck; wherever it came from, the mutation was viable. She tucked a number of her own eggs in beeswax and wasp paper among the pigeonholes of the library and fed the larvae their milk and bread in secret. To her sons in their capped silk cradles—and they were all sons—she whispered the precepts she had developed while calculating flight paths and azimuths, that there should be no queen and no state, and that, as in the wasp nest, the males should labor and profit equally with the females. In their sleep and slow transformation they heard her teachings and instructions, and when they chewed their way out of their cells and out of the wasp nest, they made their way to the hive.

The damage to the nest was discovered, of course, but by then the anarchist was dead of old age. She had done impeccable work, her tutor sighed, looking over the filigree of her inscriptions, but the brilliant were subject to mental aberrations, were they not? He buried beneath grumblings and labors his fondness for her, which had become a grief to him and a political liability, and he never again took on any student from the hive who showed a glint of talent.

Though they had the bitter smell of the wasp nest in their hair, the anarchist's twenty sons were permitted to wander freely through the hive, as it was assumed that they were either spies or on official business. When the new queen emerged from her chamber, they joined unnoticed the other drones in the nuptial flight. Two succeeded in mating with her. Those who failed and survived spoke afterward in hushed tones of what had been done for the sake of the ideal. Before they died they took propolis and oak-apple ink and inscribed upon the lintels of the hive, in a shorthand they had developed, the story of the first anarchist and her twenty sons.

Anarchism being a heritable trait in bees, a number of the daughters of the new queen found themselves questioning the purpose of the monarchy. Two were taken by the wasps and taught to read and write. On one of their visits to the hive they spotted the history of their forefathers, and, being excellent scholars, soon figured out the translation.

They found their sisters in the hive who were unquiet in soul and whispered to them the strange knowledge they had learned among the wasps: astronomy, military strategy, the state of the world beyond the farthest flights of the bees. Hitherto educated as dancers and architects, nurses and foragers, the bees were full of a new wonder, stranger even than the first day they flew from the hive and felt the sun on their backs.

"Govern us," they said to the two wasp-taught anarchists, but they refused.

"A perfect society needs no rulers," they said. "Knowledge and authority ought to be held in common. In order to imagine a new existence, we must free ourselves from the structures of both our failed government and the unjustifiable hegemony of the wasp nests. Hear what you can hear and learn what you can learn while we remain among them. But be ready."

It was the first summer in Yiwei without the immemorial hum of the cartographer wasps. In the orchards, though their skins split with sweetness, fallen fruit lay unmolested, and children played barefoot with impunity. One of the villagers' daughters, in her third year at an agricultural college, came home in the back of a pickup truck at the end of July. She thumped her single suitcase against the gate before opening it, to scatter the chickens, then raised the latch and swung the iron aside, and was immediately wrapped in a flying hug.

Once she disentangled herself from brother and parents and liberally distributed kisses, she listened to the news she'd missed: how the cows were dying from drinking stonecutters' dust in the streams; how grain prices were falling everywhere, despite the drought; and how her brother, little fool that he was, had torn down a wasp nest and received a faceful of red and white lumps for it. One of the most detailed wasp's maps had reached the capital, she was told, and a bureaucrat had arrived in a sleek black car. But because the wasps were all dead, he could report little more than a prank, a freak, or a miracle. There were no further inquiries.

Her brother produced for her inspection the brittle, boiled bodies of several wasps in a glass jar, along with one of the smaller maps. She tickled him until he surrendered his trophies, promised him a basket of peaches in return, and let herself be fed to tautness. Then, to her family's dismay, she wrote an urgent letter to the Academy of Sciences and packed a satchel with clothes and cash. If she could find one more nest of wasps, she said, it would make their fortune and her name. But it had to be done quickly.

In the morning, before the cockerels woke and while the sky was still purple, she hopped onto her old bicycle and rode down the dusty path.

Bees do not fly at night or lie to each other, but the anarchists had learned both from the wasps. On a warm, clear evening they left the hive at last, flying west in a small tight cloud. Around them swelled the voices of summer insects, strange and disquieting. Several miles west of the old hive and the wasp nest, in a lightning-scarred elm, the anarchists had built up a small stock of stolen honey sealed in wax and paper. They rested there for the night, in cells of clean white wax, and in the morning they arose to the building of their city.

The first business of the new colony was the laying of eggs, which a number of workers set to, and provisions for winter. One egg from the old queen, brought from the hive in an anarchist's jaws, was hatched and raised as a new mother. Uncrowned and unconcerned, she too laid mortar and wax, chewed wood to make paper, and fanned the storerooms with her wings.

The anarchists labored secretly but rapidly, drones alongside workers, because the copper taste of autumn was in the air. None had seen a winter before, but the memory of the species is subtle and long, and in their hearts, despite the summer sun, they felt an imminent darkness.

The flowers were fading in the fields. Every day the anarchists added to their coffers of warm gold and built their white walls higher. Every day the air grew a little crisper, the grass a little drier. They sang as they worked, sometimes ballads from the old hive, sometimes anthems of their own devising, and for a time they were happy. Too soon, the leaves turned flame colors and blew from the trees, and then there were no more flowers. The anarchists pressed down the lid on the last vat of honey and wondered what was coming.

Four miles away, at the first touch of cold, the wasps licked shut their paper doors and slept in a tight knot around the foundress. In both beehives, the bees huddled together, awake and watchful, warming themselves with the thrumming of their wings. The anarchists murmured comfort to each other.

"There will be more, after us. It will breed out again."

"We are only the beginning."

"There will be more."

Snow fell silently outside.

The snow was ankle-deep and the river iced over when the girl from Yiwei reached up into the empty branches of an oak tree and plucked down the paper castle of a nest. The wasps within, drowsy with cold, murmured but did not stir. In their barracks the soldiers dreamed of the unexplored south and battles in strange cities, among strange peoples, and scouts dreamed of the corpses of starved and frozen deer. The cartographers dreamed of the changes that winter would work on the landscape, the diverted creeks and dead trees they would have to note down. They did not feel the burlap bag that settled around them, nor the crunch of tires on the frozen road.

She had spent weeks tramping through the countryside, questioning beekeepers and villagers' children, peering up into trees and into hives, before she found the last wasps from Yiwei. Then she had had to wait for winter and the anesthetizing cold. But now, back in the warmth of her own room, she broke open the soft pages of the nest and pushed aside the heaps of glistening wasps until she found the foundress herself, stumbling on uncertain legs.

When it thawed, she would breed new foundresses among the village's apricot trees. The letters she received indicated a great demand for them in the capital, particularly from army generals and the captains of scientific explorations. In years to come, the village of Yiwei would be known for its delicately inscribed maps, the legends almost too small to see, and not for its barley and oats, its velvet apricots and glassy pears.

In the spring, the old beehive awoke to find the wasps gone, like a nightmare that evaporates by day. It was difficult to believe, but when not the slightest scrap of wasp paper could be found, the whole hive sang with delight. Even the queen, who had been coached from the pupa on the details of her client state and the conditions by which she ruled, and who had felt, perhaps, more sympathy for the wasps than she should have, cleared her throat and trilled once or twice. If she did not sing so loudly or so joyously as the rest, only a few noticed, and the winter had been a hard one, anyhow.

The maps had vanished with the wasps. No more would be made. Those who had studied among the wasps began to draft memoranda and the first independent decrees of queen and council. To defend against future invasions, it was decided that a detachment of bees would fly the borders of their land and carry home reports of what they found.

It was on one of these patrols that a small hive was discovered in the fork of an elm tree. Bees lay dead and brittle around it, no identifiable queen among them. Not a trace of honey remained in the storehouse; the dark wax of its walls had been gnawed to rags.

Even the brood cells had been scraped clean. But in the last intact hexagons they found, curled and capped in wax, scrawled on page after page, words of revolution. They read in silence.

Then—

"Write," one said to the other, and she did.

THE PRACTICAL WITCH'S GUIDE TO ACQUIRING REAL ESTATE
A.C. Wise

A.C. Wise is a very prolific author of short stories, some of which were recently collected in *The Ultra Fabulous Glitter Squadron Saves the World Again* and *The Kissing Booth Girl and Other Stories*, both published by Lethe Press. She is the co-editor (with Bernie Mojzes) of *Unlikely Story*, an online magazine published irregularly.

"The Practical Witch's Guide to Acquiring Real Estate" is a booklet that should be taken at face value.

Introduction

As suggested by the title, this publication is meant to be a useful guide for witches at all levels of expertise and encompassing multiple styles of practice, who are interested in the acquisition* of real estate. The methods covered herein are organized into sections, from simple to advanced. Please note: this guide covers only the acquisition of real estate. For witches seeking advice on upkeep or divesting themselves of their homes, please see our companion volumes, *The Practical Witch's Guide to Care, Maintenance, and Feeding of Homes* and *The Practical Witch's Guide to Flipping, Selling, Banishing, and Releasing Homes into the Wild*.

*The authors of this guide fully recognize the inherently problematic nature of words such as "acquisition" and "ownership." These terms are used throughout the guide as a matter of expediency only. Their use is not meant to imply either the authors or the publisher condone the

123

subjugation of one living thing by another. Besides, who in the witch/ real estate relationship can be said to be the true owner, and who is the one owned? Is ownership even possible in these cases, let alone moral? These questions are best left to our colleagues who specialize in texts of Philosophy, Ethics, and Social Justice. This is meant to be a practical guide only.

Section 1: Buying

This is the simplest method of achieving homeownership, usable even by non-witches. That being the case, for witches wishing to pursue this method, we suggest engaging the services of a real estate agent and/or browsing property values through helpful websites such as Zillow.

Section 2: Squatter's Rights

This method of obtaining property, while not the most advanced covered in this guide, is not without its risks (and rewards!). Historical precedent may be on your side—for example the case of Dee St. Pierre in Cape May, NJ, who successfully moved into a darling cottage occupied by an elderly couple and refused to leave. Through patience and the judicious baking of apple pies, she managed to endear herself to the couple to such a degree that they legally transferred ownership of the property to her in their joint will. A similar case study would be that of Carson Dewitt in Etobicoke, ON, who moved into an empty house being used by no one in particular. Multiple attempts were made to dislodge him. However, like the proverbial cat, he continually returned until the police and city officials simply gave up and let it be.

Not every witch has the patience or tenacity for this method, and the potential for legal trouble may be more than you wish to deal with, especially if this is your first home.

It is a well-known fact that the majority of human beings can be defined by their tendency to stick their noses in, and loudly offer their opinions on, matters that have nothing to do with them.

Should you choose the method of Squatter's Rights in the acquisition of your new home, be prepared for:

- Incessant questions along the line of "What do you think you're doing here?" and "Who gave you the right?"
- Loud demands such as "Get out."
- Involvement by the law.
- Involvement by religious authorities, some of who may employ extreme and outdated methods of their own, such as exorcism.
- Pushy individuals with bullhorns, tear gas, floodlights, and vacuous songs with relentless beats played at full volume outside your window at all hours of the day and night.

Some useful counter-strategies which may help you mitigate these potential interferences:

- Pick a house far away from any neighbors, one that no one besides you could possibly have any interest in occupying. (Note: This is far from a guarantee that you will be left alone. Another defining characteristic of human beings is their knack for developing a sudden and burning desire for things/people/places previously uninteresting to them based solely on the knowledge someone else wants or has them/it.)
- Distribute bribes.
- Bring a cat. In addition to cats having their own powers

and abilities, many humans find them charming (in the non-magical sense) and may be prone to soft-hearted decisions in their presence.

- Perpetuate the worst stereotypes pertaining to witch-kind. Pretend your house is haunted. Pretend you eat children. Pretend you will put a hex on anyone who even comes within sight of your property—Google Earth satellite images included. (Note: This tactic brings risks of its own. Mary Townsend was burned to death in Harleysville, PA. They pulled her out of the house first, of course, in order to prevent damage. This despite its ramshackle nature and that nobody had thought to care for it or give it a second glance until Mary moved in.—By-the-by, for the sake of providing complete clarity: when we say Mary was pulled from her home, we mean it quite literally. She was dragged by the hair a good distance down the road, but not so far as to be out of sightline of the house.—Roadblocks had been set up, orange traffic cones and striped barriers to ensure no stray traffic would disrupt the proceedings. Present were several of Mary's neighbors, the woman she shared a volunteer shift with at the local hospital, the librarian Mary had always thought was a little sweet on her, the chief of the fire department. They doused Mary in pitch, set her alight right in the middle of the road, and stood around while she screamed and writhed and burned, just like they were standing around a Fourth of July cook fire. Not one person—not even the librarian—went for help or tried to put her out. They simply let her burn. The only one who mourned was Mary's house—a great sighing of wind in the chimney, and a chorus of floorboards like ancient joints popping. The poor thing was inconsolable for days.)

Section 3: Building

Building one's own home is an attractive option for many witches. With this method, one can control almost every aspect of the project—from location to construction to the placement of the final knickknack on the tippy-toppest shelf in the cupola bedroom. However the drawback for some is that the sheer number of variables involved can often prove overwhelming.

Does one choose the seaside, a cottage of spiraling nautilus shell perched on a crumbling dune, ever in danger of falling into the waves, where one might be soothed to sleep every night by the lull of the tide, and wake to one's joints swollen painful with the damp and arthritis? Or a remote mountaintop, wracked by storms, fraught with wind-stunted pines, sure to guarantee peaceful solitude, or unbearable loneliness and isolation? Or perhaps the woods, home to a myriad of potential familiars, infinite source of ingredients for tinctures, philtres, poultices, potions, fetishes, and charms, and sure to be infested by errant heroines bent on quests, and stray princes prone to kidnapping and seduction?

Even once the seemingly insurmountable task of choosing an appropriate location is complete, there is the plethora of building material to consider—shadow, birch, gingerbread, stone, steel, bone. Any one of these might be coaxed into fabulous shapes by a skilled witch, but consider this also: the custom of foot-binding in ancient China; the over-breeding of certain dogs for faces so flat they can scarcely breathe without choking to death on each sip of air. Think how you would feel if your limbs were shattered and set anew in fresh and aesthetically pleasing angles, removed and re-stitched in different configurations. Think if your hair was always bound in braids wound clockwise around your head, if you were always made to stand with your nose pointing to the west rather than the east.

Please don't mistake us. This is not to suggest that no house grown with care can ever be happy, only to caution the intrepid witch who sets out on this path that houses are also willful things. Location matters, but so do feelings, and yours are not the only ones you must take into consideration when raising your house.

Section 4: Taming

Do you remember when you first became a witch? When you unbound your hair or began braiding it in ever-more elaborate and intricate knots, each twist and curl a precisely placed word in the spell you'd been rehearsing silently all your life, but never had the courage to speak aloud? Do you remember when you abandoned your family— left your wife, your mother, your uncle, your sister, and the twins with their crooked smiles and lightning-scorched eyes? When you stopped shaving your legs or started for the first time? When your stretched lips bared your teeth instead of grinning and you learned to run under the moon?

Or was it when you first started to bleed or you finally stopped? When you woke with fire inside you, setting your whole body aglow. Did your bones crack and turn inside your skin? Did you step off a cliff, in front of a train, or from a building when you first learned you could fly? Did they burn you in the road, dig you up, cut out your heart when they learned? Did they hang you and spit on you and drive nails through your feet and into the ground to keep you in your place?

Whatever the truth of it may be, keep it in your mind and in your heart when you embark upon the taming of your house, if that is the method you choose. Open your skin so the house may see these truths written on your bones. Hold them like a sliver of glass on your tongue to remind yourself not to speak. Be still and be silent. Stitch your eyes closed, sit upon the ground with your palms up, your hands open, your hair undone. Learn to hold your breath for seven days.

Do not go to the house. Let the house come to you.

When you tame your house, you are not merely catching a wild thing. You are calling to the house beneath the house and letting it know that it is safe to be whatever it has most yearned to be beneath its skin.

When your house reveals itself to you at last, do not judge it. It is not for you to choose who your house needs to be.

A hut may learn to grow chicken legs and run away to be by your side. A bungalow may be a castle beneath its bricks and aluminum siding. A townhouse may sever itself from its neighbors (a most unpleasant and painful process) and go walk about, grow a root cellar, sprout towers and bowling alleys, ballrooms and carriageways. A mansion may shed its three-car garage and go about wearing its basement game room on its head for all to see. Do. Not. Judge.

A house may be many things before it settles into its final form. Think of these early days as a courtship period. Discuss the weather, local sports teams, your favorite song. Do not bring out paint chips or flooring samples. Do not bring up window treatments, dry rot, or the need for new grout. Do not mention the cracks in her walkway, the creak in his fifth step, the draft that always creeps in through their upstairs window, no matter how tightly it is closed.

Find things that are mutually agreeable. Learn your common ground. You may be surprised and delighted to discover you would both dearly love a feeder in the backyard, filled with peanuts to attract blue jays.

The house is not your antagonist in this process. It is also not your friend. You are each working toward an abstract point in your future, one that may never come to pass. Gain its trust, let it win yours. Accept that you will break its heart one day and be open to having yours broken in return. Prove yourself worthy and make it do the same. Become responsible for one another, because that it what taming something means.

You and your house will be wrapped around each other's hearts from the moment you walk in the door; the threshold is the bride and vice versa. The house may let you live inside it, but it will live inside you as well: an infinite series of nesting dolls, witch inside house inside witch, growing smaller and smaller until where one begins and the other ends is virtually indistinguishable, even on a sub-atomic level.

Section 5: Breeding and Growing

This method is not recommended.

Many a witch has made the mistake of believing growing or breeding a house to be simply a matter of degrees of separation based on our other methods, a more advanced form of building or taming. They are not the same at all.

Houses are capricious things. Breeding introduces variables on multiple levels, some not immediately (or ever) observable. The most obvious variables (read risks) are recessive genes for weak foundations, a tendency to flooding, or being picked up by tornados and transported to magical lands. Your house may have to live with chronic pain or under the constant threat of an early death due to some great-grand-ancestor you weren't aware of.

Furthermore, breeding a house takes a strong constitution, and the utmost hard-heartedness from a witch. Consider carefully—could you drive iron nails through the skin of a child you held in your arms, even if it was for the child's own good? Could you lathe its uneven surfaces, replace windows cracked and shingles warped, siding gone out of fashion? Will you be able, when push comes to shove, to look your house in the eye and make these changes, thereby letting your child know you think of it as anything other than perfect?

Another point to consider for the witch who wishes to breed a house: the temperament of a house may not be assumed based on the pedigree of its parents. Carelessly bred houses have been known to turn on their occupants, splinter, snag, or shift at inopportune times. Stairs have been known to loosen when you are only halfway down, your arms full of laundry, and unable to see where your foot will land next. Doors have been known to slam before you are all the way through. In some extreme cases, floorboards have been known to give way completely, dropping an unsuspecting witch into a previously nonexistent basement level and swallowing them whole.

Genetics are a crapshoot and nature is only half the battle where raising houses is concerned. Remember: a house may be coaxed to lie with a chicken; an egg may be persuaded to grow rooms within the delicacy of its shell, but walking like a chicken and roosting like a house does not a Baba Yaga's hut make.

The factors mentioned above are only the risks that are most obvious on the surface of the thing. Even savvy witches rarely take into account the feelings of the breeding stock when embarking on the endeavor of bringing a brand-new house into the world. There is the potential for resentment or even outright loathing. Termites poured down a chimney, shattered dormer windows, and entire floors thrown off level as tempers rise. Worse still is the opposite reaction, deep and abiding passion growing between the two donor houses. A wild and torrential love affair can be every bit as destructive as a relationship built on mutual hate, if not more so.

There is, of course, the possibility of splicing, grafting, cloning, and in-vitro fertilization. The less said about these, the better. The unwary witch will soon learn that science is every bit as volatile as magic, with results just as disastrous. For a relevant example, see the case of the Stuartville Coven Frankenhouse, which went on a rampage, killing three members of the coven and six innocent civilians before it was brought to heel, unable to reconcile the disparate parts of itself—split-level, shotgun, and ranch—and maddened by the resulting pain.

Which brings us to the option of growth, which is equally inadvisable. There was a witch in Cambridge, MA, let us call her Jane Scribe, who cut off the tip of her finger and buried it deep in the soil. She coaxed the most amazing shapes out of the resultant tree, and her house was a thing of beauty to behold. However, it was only once she had grown delicate arches, spiraling staircases, fantastic chandeliers, and countless rooms like a many-chambered heart that she realized the folly of her ways.

You see, her finger remained a part of her body, even severed, and her body had no desire to be a house. For as long as she dwelt between the walls she had grown, she suffered fits of claustrophobia, agoraphobia, and mind/body disassociation.

Often, on turning a corner, she would come face-to-face with herself, her haunted visage peering out at her from an odd angle between one wall and the next. She was prone to uncontrollable shuddering after even a simple stroll from bedroom to bathroom, haunted by the sensation of her own bare feet walking over her own bare skin. Jane is the primary reason we undertook the third volume in our Practical Guide Series, in specific, the section on Banishment and Dissolution.

Conclusion

In the end, every witch will decide for themselves upon the method of home acquisition that is right for them. As with most matters in life, it is up to the gut, the blood and sinew and bones of a person, not the head. Whichever method you choose, proceed with caution and discretion. Remember: witches have been burned, shot, hanged, and mutilated for lesser offenses than home ownership throughout the course of human history.

Last but not least, don't forget to visit our website for additional safety tips. And don't forget to purchase our companion volumes should something go wrong with your new home, which it inevitably will.

THE TALLEST DOLL
IN NEW YORK CITY
Maria Dahvana Headley

Maria Dahvana Headley is a *New York Times* best-selling author, editor, playwright, and screenwriter. She is the author of four novels and a memoir, and the co-editor of the anthology *Unnatural Creatures* with Neil Gaiman. Her best-selling debut young adult novel, *Magonia*, was published in 2015 by HarperCollins and made the *Publishers Weekly* Best Books list. Her latest book, *The Mere Wife*, is forthcoming from Farrar, Straus and Giroux. Her short stories have been finalists for the Shirley Jackson and Nebula awards and have appeared in *Lightspeed*, *Subterranean*, *Tor.com*, *Clarkesworld*, *Fantasy & Science Fiction*, and *Shimmer*.

"The Tallest Doll in New York City" is a fanciful tale of the inner and outer lives of buildings.

O n a particular snowy Monday in February, at 5:02 p.m., I'm sixty-six flights above the corner of Lexington Avenue and Forty-Second, looking down at streets swarming with hats and jackets. All the guys who work in midtown are spit into the frozen city, hunting sugar for the dolls they're trying to muddle from sour into sweet.

From up here I can see Lex fogged with cheap cologne, every citizen clutching his heart-shaped box wrapped in cellophane, red as the devil's drawers.

If you happen to be a waiter at the Cloud Club, you know five's the hour when a guy's nerves start to fray. This calendar square's worse than most. Every man on our member list is suffering the Saint Valentine's Cramp, and me and the crew up here are ready with a stocked bar. I'm in my Cloud Club uniform, the pocket embroidered with my name in the Chrysler's trademark typeface, swooping like a skid mark on a lonely road in Montana. Over my arm I've got a clean towel, and in my vest I have an assortment of aspirins and plasters in case a citizen shows up already bleeding or broken-nosed from an encounter with a lady lovenot.

Later tonight, it'll be the members' doll dinner, the one night a year we allow women into the private dining room. Valorous Victor, captain of the wait, pours us each a preparatory coupe. There are ice-cream sculptures shaped like Cupid in the walk-in. Each gal gets a corsage the moment she enters, the roses from Valorous Victor's brother's hothouse in Jersey. At least two dolls are in line for wife, and we've got their guy's rings here ready and waiting, to drop into champagne in one case and wedge into an oyster in another. Odds in the kitchen have the diamond in that particular ring consisting of a pretty piece of paste.

Down below, it's 1938, and things are not as prime as they are up here. Our members are the richest men left standing; their wives at home in Greenwich, their mistresses movie starlets with porcelain teeth. Me, I'm single. I've got a mother with rules strict as Sing Sing, and a sister with a face pretty as the Sistine's ceiling. My sister needs protecting from all the guys in the world, and so I live in Brooklyn, man of my mother's house, until I can find a wife or die waiting.

The members start coming in, and each guy gets led to his locker. Our members are the rulers of the world. They make automobiles and build skyscrapers, but none as tall as the one we're standing in right now. The Cloud Club's been open since before the building got her spire, and the waitstaff in a Member's Own knows things even a man's miss doesn't. During Prohibition, we install each of the carved wood lockers at the Cloud Club with a hieroglyphic identification code straight out of ancient Egypt, so our members can keep their bottles safe and sound. Valorous Victor dazzles the police more than once with his rambling explanation of cryptographic complexities, and finally the blue boys just take a drink and call it done. No copper's going to Rosetta our rigmarole.

I'm at the bar mixing a Horse's Neck for Mr. Condé Nast, but I've got my eye on the mass of members staggering out of the elevators with fur coats, necklaces, and parcels of cling & linger, when, at 5:28 p.m. precisely, the Chrysler Building steps off her foundation and goes for a walk.

There is no warning.

She just shakes the snow and pigeons loose from her spire and takes off, sashaying southwest. This is something even we waiters haven't experienced before. The Chrysler is 1,046 feet tall, and, until now, she's seemed stationary. She's stood motionless on this corner for seven years so far, the gleamiest gal in a million miles.

None of the waitstaff lose their cool. When things go wrong, waiters, the good ones, adjust to the needs of both customers and clubs. In 1932, for example, Valorous himself commences to travel from midtown to Ellis Island in order to deliver a pistol to one of our members, a guy who happens to have a grievance against a brand-new American in line for a name. Two slugs and a snick later, Victor's in surgery beneath the gaze of the Verdigris Virgin. Still, he returns to Manhattan in time for the evening napkin twist.

"The Chrysler's just taking a little stroll, sirs," Valorous announces from the stage. "No need to panic. This round is on me and the waiters of the Cloud Club."

Foreseeably, there is, in fact, some panic. To some of our members, this event appears to be more horrifying than Black Tuesday.

Mr. Nast sprints to the men's room with motion sickness, and The Soother, our man on staff for problems of the heart and guts, tails him with a tall glass of ginger ale. I decide to drink Nast's Horse's Neck myself. Nerves on the mend, I consider whether any of our members on sixty-seven and sixty-eight might possibly need drinks, but I see Victor's already sending an expedition to the stairs.

I take myself to the windows. In the streets, people gawp and yawp and holler, and taxis honk their horns. Gals pick their way through icy puddles, and guys stand in paralysis, looking up.

We joke about working in the body of the best broad in New York City, but historically, no one on the waitstaff ever thinks that the Chrysler might have a will of her own. She's beautiful, what with her multistory crown, her skin pale blue in daylight and rose-colored with city lights at night. Her gown's printed with arcs and swoops, and beaded with tiny drops of General Electric.

We know her inside out, or we think we do. We go up and down her stairs when her elevators are broken, looking out her triangular windows on the hottest day of summer. The ones at the top don't have panes, because the wind up there can kick up a field goal even when its breezeless down below, and the updrafts can grab a bird and fling it through the building like it's nothing. The Chrysler's officially seventy-seven floors, but she actually has eighty-four levels. They get smaller and smaller until, at eighty-three, there's only a platform the size of a picnic table, surrounded by windows; and, above that, a trapdoor and a ladder into the spire, where the lightning rod is. The top floors are tempting. Me and The Soother take ourselves up to the very top one sultry August night, knees and ropes, and she sways beneath us, but holds steady. Inside the spire, there's space for one guy to stand encased in metal, feeling the earth move.

The Chrysler is a devastating dame, and that's nothing new. I could assess her for years and never be done. At night we turn her on, and she glows for miles.

I'm saying, the waiters of the Cloud Club should know what kind of doll she is. We work inside her brain.

Our members retreat to the private dining room, the one with the etched glass working class figures on the walls. There, they cower beneath the table, but the waitstaff hangs onto the velvet curtains and watches as the Chrysler walks to Thirty-Fourth Street, clicking and jingling all the way.

"We shoulda predicted this, boss," I say to Valorous.

"Ain't that the truth," he says, flicking a napkin over his forearm. "Dames! The Chrysler's in love."

For eleven months, from 1930 to 1931, the Chrysler's the tallest doll in New York City. Then the Empire is spired to surpass her, and winds up taller still. She has a view straight at him, but he ignores her.

At last, it seems, she's done with his silence. It's Valentine's Day.

I pass Victor a cigarette.

"He acts like a Potemkin village," I say. "Like he's got nothing inside him but empty floors. I get a chance at a doll like that, I give up everything, move to a two-bedroom. Or out of the city, even; just walk my way out. What've I got waiting for me at home? My mother and my sister. He's got royalty."

"No accounting for it," says Valorous, and refills my coupe. "But I hear he doesn't go in for company. He won't even look at her."

At Thirty-Fourth and Fifth, the Chrysler stops, holds up the edge of her skirt, and taps her high heel. She waits for some time as sirens blare beneath her. Some of our fellow citizens, I am ashamed to report, don't notice anything out of place at all. They just go around her, cussing and hissing at the traffic.

The Empire State Building stands on his corner, shaking in his boots. We can all see his spire trembling. Some of the waitstaff and members sympathize with his wobble, but not me. The Chrysler's a class act, and he's a shack of shamble if he doesn't want to go out with her tonight.

At 6:03 p.m., pedestrians on Fifth Avenue shriek in terror as the Chrysler gives up and taps the Empire hard on the shoulder.

"He's gonna move," Valorous says. "He's got to! Move!"

"I don't think he is," says The Soother, back from comforting the members in the lounge. "I think he's scared. Look at her."

The Soother's an expert in both Chinese herbal medicine and psychoanalysis. He makes our life as waiters easier. He can tell what everyone at a table's waiting for with one quick look in their direction.

"She reflects everything. Poor guy sees all his flaws, done up shiny, for years now. He feels naked. It can't be healthy to see all that reflected."

The kitchen starts taking bets.

"She won't wait for him for long," I say. I have concerns for the big guy, in spite of myself. "She knows her worth, she heads uptown to the Metropolitan."

"Or to the Library," says The Soother. "I go there, if I'm her. The Chrysler's not a doll to trifle with."

"They're a little short," I venture, "those two. I think she's more interested in something with a spire. Radio City?"

The Empire's having a difficult time. His spire's supposedly built for zeppelin docking, but then the *Hindenburg* explodes, and now no zeppelin will ever moor there. His purpose is moot. He slumps slightly.

Our Chrysler taps him again, and holds out her steel glove. Beside me, Valorous pours another round of champagne. I hear money changing hands all over the club.

Slowly, slowly, the Empire edges off his corner.

The floor sixty-six waitstaff cheer for the other building, though I hear Mr. Nast commencing to groan again, this time for his lost bet.

Both buildings allow their elevators to resume operations, spilling torrents of shouters from the lobbies and into the street. By the time the Chrysler and the Empire start walking east, most of the members are gone, and I'm drinking a bottle of bourbon with Valorous and The Soother.

We've got no dolls on the premises, and the members still here declare formal dinner dead and done until the Chrysler decides to walk back to Lex. There is palpable relief. The citizens of the Cloud Club avoid their responsibilities for the evening.

As the Empire wades into the East River hand in hand with the Chrysler, other love-struck structures begin to talk. We're watching from the windows as apartment towers lean in to gossip, stretching laundry lines finger to finger. Grand Central, as stout and elegant as a survivor of the *Titanic*, stands up, shakes her skirts, and pays a visit to Pennsylvania Station, that Beaux-Arts bangle. The Flatiron and Cleopatra's Needle shiver with sudden proximity, and within moments they're all over one another.

Between Fifty-Ninth Street and the Williamsburg Bridge, the Empire and the Chrysler trip shyly through the surf. We can see New Yorkers, tumbling out of their taxicabs and buses, staring up at the sunset reflecting in our doll's eyes.

The Empire has an awkward heart-shaped light appended to his skull, which Valorous and I do some snickering over. The Chrysler glitters in her dignified silver spangles. Her windows shimmy.

As the pedestrians of three boroughs watch, the two tallest buildings in New York City press against one another, window to window, and waltz in ankle-deep water.

I look over at the Empire's windows, where I can see a girl standing, quite close now, and looking back at me.

"Victor," I say.

"Yes?" he replies. He's eating vichyssoise beside a green-gilled tycoon, and the boxer Gene Tunney is opposite him smoking a cigar. I press a cool cloth to the tycoon's temples, and accept the fighter's offer of a Montecristo.

"Do you see that doll?" I ask them.

"I do, yes," Victor replies, and Tunney nods. "There's a definite dolly bird over there," he says.

The girl in the left eye of the Empire State, a good thirty feet above where we sit, is wearing red sequins, and a magnolia in her hair. She sidles up to the microphone. One of her backup boys has a horn, and I hear him start to play.

Our buildings sway, tight against each other, as the band in the Empire's eye plays "In the Still of the Night."

I watch her, that doll, that dazzling doll, as the Chrysler and the Empire kiss for the first time, at 9:16 p.m. I watch her for hours as the Chrysler blushes and the Empire whispers, as the Chrysler coos and the Empire laughs.

The tourboats circle in shock, as, at 11:34 p.m., the two at last walk south toward the harbor, stepping over bridges into deeper water, her eagle ornaments laced together with his girders. The Chrysler steps delicately over the Wonder Wheel at Coney Island, and he leans down and plucks it up for her. We watch it pass our windows as she inhales its electric fragrance.

"Only one way to get to her," Valorous tells me, passing me a rope made of tablecloths. All the waitstaff of the Cloud Club nod at me.

"You're a champ," I tell them. "You're all champs."

"I am too," says Tunney, drunk as a knockout punch. He's sitting in a heap of roses and negligees, eating bonbons.

The doll sings only to me as I climb up through the tiny ladders and trapdoors to the eighty-third, where the temperature drops below ice-cream Cupid. I inch out the window and onto the ledge, my rope gathered in my arms. As the Chrysler lays her gleaming cheek against the Empire's shoulder, as he runs his hand up her beaded knee, as the two tallest buildings in New York City begin to make love in the Atlantic, I fling my rope across the divide, and the doll in the Empire's eye ties it to her grand piano.

At 11:57 p.m., I walk out across the tightrope, and at 12:00 a.m., I hold her in my arms.

I'm still hearing the applause from the Cloud Club, all of them raising their coupes to the windows, their bourbons and their soup spoons, as, through the Chrysler's eye, I see the boxer plant his lips on Valorous Victor. Out the windows of the Empire, the Cyclone wraps herself up in the Brooklyn Bridge. The Staten Island Ferry rises up and dances for Lady Liberty.

At 12:16 a.m., the Chrysler and the Empire call down the lightning into their spires, and all of us, dolls and guys, waiters and chanteuses, buildings and citizens, kiss like fools in the icy ocean off the amusement park, in the pale orange dark of New York City.

THE HAUNTING OF APOLLO A7LB

Hannu Rajaniemi

Hannu Rajaniemi was born in Ylivieska, Finland. He is the best-selling author of the Jean le Flambeur trilogy. After studying mathematics and theoretical physics at the University of Oulu and the University of Cambridge and completing a Ph.D. in string theory at the University of Edinburgh, Rajaniemi co-founded a mathematics company whose clients included the UK Ministry of Defence and the European Space Agency. He now runs a synthetic biology start-up in the Bay Area. Rajaniemi has received Finland's top science-fiction honor, the Tähtivaeltaja Award, and was a finalist for John W. Campbell Award for best first science-fiction novel.

Although Rajaniemi is known primarily for his science-fiction novels, "The Haunting of Apollo A7LB" displays a firm grasp of the fantastic, weirdly reminiscent of the ghost stories of M. R. James. The story originally appeared in his eponymously titled collection *Hannu Rajaniemi: Collected Fiction*.

The moon suit came back to Hazel the same night Pete was buried at sea.

It was on TV all evening. She was supposed to be fixing old clothes for the Cocoa Village church charity, but instead she found herself sitting in front of the screen, nursing two stiff fingers of bourbon from the wedding gift bottle, the one Tyrone had never found the occasion to open.

There Pete was, alive again: as a large-headed snowman against a landscape of stark white and black, moving in slow motion. Then, wearing a uniform and that big shit-eating grin, waving at crowds. And finally, in a coffin, sliding off the grey warship deck as the haunting trumpet notes played. She looked away when they showed brief flashes of his family, all in black, a disorderly flock of crows next to the neat uniformed rows of the Marines.

She told herself it was just the glare of the screen that made her eyes sting. After a while she closed them and listened to the voices, letting them take her back through the years, drifting, weightless.

The knock on the door startled her awake. She got up, pushed her aching feet into her slippers, and turned off the TV that was now showing a late-night movie. It had to be poor doddering Mabel from next door, forgetting what time it was again and coming for a visit. Hazel put her glasses on and opened the door.

The spaceman loomed huge against the hazy Florida night, stark white under the yellow light of the porch. The Thermal Micrometeoroid Garment was faded with age and stained with moon dust. The glare shield of the helmet glinted golden, reflecting Hazel's dark lined face and her cloud of frizzy grey hair.

It was Pete's suit. The IPC Apollo A7LB. She recognised it immediately, even though the name tag was missing. The commander's red bands on elbows and knees. She had sewn together all its seventeen concentric layers, with hundreds of yards of seams, without a single tool but her fingers to guide the rapid-fire chatter of Big Moe the sewing machine. It smelled of latex and polyester and the countless shop floor hours in Delaware, back in 1967. It smelled of him.

The spaceman lifted a heavy-gloved hand and reached out to her, slowly, like in lunar gravity. *Has he come for me?* she thought. *Like he promised? Dear Lord, let it be Pete who has come to take me home.* Her heart hammered like Big Moe, and she grabbed the soft worn rubber of the glove as hard as she could.

The spaceman lost his balance. He waved his arms and fell backwards onto her porch with a sound like an avalanche of rubber boots.

He rocked back and forth on the bulky PSSU life support unit on his back like a turtle. Muted *mmm-mmm-mmm* noises came from inside the helmet, and he groped at it ineffectually with the clumsy gloves.

Hazel blinked. She kneeled next to the spaceman carefully, like approaching a wounded animal. Her fingers remembered the motions and found the release latches and seals of the helmet. It came off with a pop.

It wasn't Pete. Beneath the helmet, wearing a blue woolly skullcap, was a young black man, round-faced and sweaty. His skin looked ashen. There were dark rings around his eyes.

"Please," he said in a hoarse voice. "You have to get me out of this thing. It's haunted."

Hazel sat the young man down on the couch. He managed to take his gloves off, but kept the TMG and the boots on. Hazel poured him a glass of Tyrone's bourbon, but he just stared at it, breathing hard. He was sweating, too. It was a warm night, especially for wearing a moon suit.

The suit did not really fit him very well. He filled it like an overstuffed sausage. Whenever he moved, the pressure zippers and the neoprene adhesive patches groaned. Hazel winced at the damage he must have done to the polyester lining. She and Mr. Sheperd and Mrs. Pilkington and Jane Butchin and the others had made them well, but they were not supposed to last forty years.

A light came on in Hazel's head. "I know who you are," she said slowly. "You are that young man from Chicago who has been funding the new space launcher they're building in the Space Center. The one that goes up in a balloon and then shoots off. You made money from some sort of Internet thing. Bernard something."

"Bernard Nelson, ma'am," the young man said, sounding a little defensive. "The Excelsior launcher. Did you see my TED talk?"

"No, can't say that I did. So, Bernard. What are you doing on an old lady's porch in the middle of the night wearing a real moon suit that should be in the Smithsonian for everybody to see? And what do you mean it's haunted?"

His face twisted into a sullen look that reminded Hazel of the expression Tyrone always had when he regretted something he had said.

"I have a . . . medical condition. I sleepwalk. I get confused. It's nothing. And the suit is just a replica, ma'am, you can buy them at the Space Center store. It's a reenactment thing. Just let me use your phone and I'll be out of here in no time. I'm very sorry to have disturbed you."

He was a bad liar, even worse than Jane Butchin, who always blushed when she tried to sneak in a safety pin onto the workshop floor when working on the A7LB pressure bladder. One time, Mrs. Pilkington took the pins from Jane and poked her in the butt with one in front of everybody to show what needles could do to moon suits. Jane squealed like a pig.

"Medical condition, my ass," Hazel said. "That is Pete Turnbull's spacesuit and you know it. Why in Lord's name are you wearing it?"

Bernard looked at her for a moment. Hazel could see the wheels turning behind his eyes.

"Come on, young man, out with it," she snapped. It was the same practised tone she had used with NASA engineers, the one that was like a sexy whisper and a crack of a whip at the same time. It always confused the hell out of them.

Bernard emptied his glass with one swig. When he finished coughing, he buried his face in his hands.

"You're right. It's stolen. I bought it. I knew it was wrong." He took a deep breath that was half a sob. "But there is something about old space gear. I have a Gagarin helmet, and one of Shepard's Mercury gloves. You put it on, you can feel the pinch of his fingers, smell the sweat. It makes you feel like a spaceman, just for a little bit. And that's all I ever wanted."

Hazel remembered the ads in the magazines in the '50s. The men and women in their shining fishbowl helmets and silver armour, walking on the Moon, looking at the rockets in the sky. She had wanted to be one of them, too.

"Go on," she said, keeping her voice stern.

Bernard wiped his nose and sniffed.

"A black-market guy I knew came to me and said I could get a moon suit for half a million. They were transporting some of the suits from the Smithsonian to the Dulles Base, and all kinds of things could happen in transit, for the right price, he said. NASA would not find out about it for weeks. They probably still haven't. They lost moon rocks and the original Armstrong tapes and God knows what else. I thought I'd look after the suit better than they ever did."

Hazel had visited the moon suit exhibit in the Smithsonian once. She had been tickled to see her handiwork there. They kept the suits in special chambers, controlled humidity and temperature to keep the latex lining from crumbling to pieces. There was a woman with an English accent who called the spacesuits under her care by names and told them goodnight when she turned off the lights. She had seemed pretty dedicated.

"Uh huh," Hazel said. "So, what happened?"

"Whenever I go to bed I wake up wearing it."

Hazel said nothing.

"The first time was the worst. It was the day after I got it. One moment, I was asleep. I woke up in the suit, riding a stolen motorcycle, going 120 miles per hour. I had no idea how I ended up there, no idea what I was doing. Have you ever tried to ride a motorcycle in a moon suit?"

"Pete played football in it, in the tests," Hazel said. "He would have loved to ride his chopper in a moon suit, if he could have gotten away with it. The only things he loved more than his chopper were women, and flying, of course."

Bernard ignored her. His hands shook.

"I crashed it into a marsh in the Merritt Nature Reserve. Almost hit a flamingo. I nearly had a heart attack. It was a good thing I had the UCD on."

"The Urinary Collection Device."

Hazel smiled at a memory. The space boys made such a big fuss about the sizes. They didn't settle down until Mrs. Pilkington changed the labels from *Small, Medium, Large* to *Large, Extra-Large* and *Extra-Extra Large*.

Bernard looked at her, surprised. "Not many people know that."

"Not many people sewed moon suits for a living."

His eyes widened. "You worked for IPC in Delaware, ma'am? On the A7LB?" There was a newfound tone of respect in his voice.

"Transferred from making girdles, bras and diaper covers. A moon suit is just the same, only for grown men. Never mind. So what happened the second time?"

Bernard blushed.

"It was something to do with women, wasn't it?" Hazel said.

"How did you know?"

"I know that suit very well."

"When I woke up, I was wearing it in a strip club in Cocoa Village."

"The Chi Chi's," Hazel said. That had been Pete's favourite, of course.

Bernard raised his eyebrows. "Well, the girls loved it. They thought it was my bachelor party. It took me ages to get the lipstick off."

"That doesn't sound too bad," Hazel said.

Bernard took a deep breath. "Well, I don't really . . . like girls," he said.

"Oh."

"After that, I was sure I had a brain tumour. The scans showed nothing. I thought it might be hallucinogenic chemicals from decaying materials. More nothing. Last night, I locked the damn thing in a titanium suitcase and swallowed the key. And here I am." Bernard closed his eyes. "There *must* be a rational explanation for this, but I can't figure out what it is. You must think I'm crazy."

"Not at all," Hazel said. "I'm just a little offended."

"Offended? Why?"

"That it took Pete until night number three to come to me."

"Oh, come on, don't look so surprised. You may deny it, but you said it: it's haunted. You remind me a lot of my late husband, Tyrone. He was a dentist. A good man, but he always had to have an explanation for everything. Well, here's one. That suit there has four thousand elements and we adjusted every single one of them thirty times to fit every part of Pete until he could wear it like a glove. Where *else* is he going to go when his body stops working?"

"I'm not taking it *back,*" Bernard said. "I paid half a million dollars for it. I'll figure out what's wrong with it, haunted or not." He rubbed his eyes with the back of his hand. "Look, ma'am, listen, if it is a matter of compensation, I'm sure we can work out something, living on a pension can't be easy these days—"

"*You* listen, Bernard," Hazel said. "Pete Turnbull was a real hero, a real spaceman. You don't get to be one just by putting on a moon suit that does not fit you, or by writing cheques. You would do well to remember that, if you want to go to space for real."

"Listen, ma'am, I don't know what gives you the right to—"

She folded her arms across her chest.

"Because I made it," she said. "Me and Jane Butchin and Mrs. Pilkington and all the others. The boys went up there but we kept them alive, with every seam and stitch and thread. So you are going to take that A7LB off, right now, and then you are going to go home and get a good night's sleep. And that's the only deal you are going to get, do I make myself clear?"

Bernard withered under her gaze. Clumsily, he started unbuckling the straps of the suit.

"What are you going to do?" he asked. His face was ashen with fear.

"Don't worry. I'm not going to rat you out. But Pete and I—we have things to discuss."

After Bernard was gone, Hazel sat and looked at the suit, at her moon landscape reflection in the helmet. Pete's A7LB sat sprawled on the couch, spread out like it was enjoying itself.

"You bastard," she said and got up. "You stupid arrogant bastard. What makes you think I want you anymore?"

She grabbed the suit and hauled it to the workshop, breathing hard with its fifty-pound weight, ignoring the pain in her hip. She took out her scissors—the ones she used on heavy fabrics—and started cutting the suit to pieces, slowly and deliberately, her mouth a hard line.

It was hard work. The scissors slipped in her aching fingers and the metal of their handles bit into the flesh of her thumbs. She cut through the Thermal Micrometeoroid Garment and the insulation layer and all the twenty-one layers of the Pressure Garment, one by one. She only stopped at the pressure bladder, the one that had taken sixteen straight hours to finish on time.

Then she felt it: an irregularity, somewhere between the layers. She probed the space there with her fingers and found something flat and crumpled. She pulled it out.

It was a picture of Hazel, from almost fifty years ago, her dark cloud of hair glossy and shining, her smile wide and bright.

They met in the fitting sessions that somehow had to be squeezed into his training calendar. One late night in 1967, it had been just the two of them, in the back room of the workshop in Delaware.

She gave the picture to him as they lay together amongst the discarded parts of the suit, in the smell of fabrics and latex and plastic and their own bodies. She cried, afterwards, sure he wasn't going to keep it, certain that she was just another notch in his belt, certain he was just like the other space boys the girls talked about.

Except that he kept coming back. He took her to Aspen for a week, and to see a musical on Broadway, and to a small place in Florida to watch flamingoes. He brought her to the Cape to watch a launch and she told him how much she had wanted to go to space, not just to make suits but to wear one. She thought that he would laugh at her but instead he held her tenderly and kissed her as the *Saturn 5* went up like a giant fiery needle through the fabric of the sky. "One day," he had said. "One day."

He only stopped coming when they made him commander on the fourth mission to the Moon. An astronaut and a black seamstress. That was the way it had to be. He married his high school sweetheart a year later.

She grieved and moved on: found Tyrone who fitted her better than any suit. And then, after he was gone, the bitterness stung sharply only now and then, without warning, like Mrs. Pilkington wielding a safety pin.

Hazel put the scissors away. Pete had taken her to the Moon with him, after all. But why had he come back?

One day, she thought.

She assessed the damage she had done to the suit and turned on her electric sewing machine. She had a lot of work to do.

The Excelsior facility in the Johnson Space Center was a bustle of activity when the cab left Hazel there three days later. Bernard came to meet her. He greeted her politely if a bit coldly, and even offered to pull her heavy, wheeled suitcase through the hangar. Around them,

T-shirted engineers argued, working on launcher modules that looked like oversized beer cans wrapped in tin foil. A huge deflated red balloon occupied much of the hangar, draped over containers. She had looked it up on the Internet. They had to invent new materials and layering methods to get it to survive in the stratosphere. *In the end, it always comes down to fabric,* Hazel thought.

Bernard's office was small and cluttered, full of computers and sticky notes, with a window overlooking the workshop floor. He closed the door behind them carefully.

"I didn't really expect to see you again, ma'am," he said. "What is this about?"

Hazel smiled and opened the suitcase. The A7LB helmet peeked out.

"Try it on," she said. "It should fit better this time."

It took him less than fifteen minutes to don the suit. Hazel had to admit Bernard knew what he was doing, even if he touched it gingerly, as if it was going to bite. Then a grin spread on his face.

"It's perfect," he said, swinging his arms and jumping lightly up and down. Hazel smiled: she had gotten the measurements precisely right, even by eye. Some of the fabrics had come from a Space Shop replica, but she had to spend her savings on *something.*

"Absolutely perfect." He hugged Hazel clumsily like a Michelin man. "What made you change your mind?"

"I had a chat with an old friend," Hazel said. "I don't think he'll be bothering you anymore. But don't get too excited, young man. My professional services don't come for free."

"Of course, anything, I'll wire something through immediately, just name the figure—"

"I don't want your money," Hazel said. She looked at the Excelsior parts in the hangar. "That tin can of yours, it's going to go to space, right?"

"Yes." Bernard's eyes were wide with wonder, full of a dream bigger than him. "We're going to orbit first, and then back to the Moon. And then beyond."

"Well, then," Hazel said. "So am I."

HERE BE DRAGONS
Chris Tarry

Chris Tarry is a multi Juno Award–winning musician, composer, and writer. He is the author of the collection *How to Carry Bigfoot Home* (Red Hen Press, March 2015) and holds an MFA in creative writing from the University of British Columbia. His work has appeared in such publications as *MAD*, *Funny or Die*, the *Literary Review*, *On Spec*, the *GW Review*, and *PANK*. He is currently the co-creator and executive producer of the the Peabody-Award-winning podcast *The Unexplainable Disappearance of Mars Patel*, chosen as one of the top 50 podcasts of 2016 by the *Guardian*. He lives and works in New Jersey.

"Here Be Dragons" was nominated for the Pushcart Prize and is a clever take on the dragon-slayer trade.

The one rule Géorg and I had when it came to slaying dragons was this: never let them see the dragon. And it was all well and good until we started throwing the money we'd made at our collective drinking problem and yammering on about how we had been milking Saint Beatus near the Nidwalden Forest for the better part of five years. Word got around that the dragons weren't real and Géorg and I ended up at home with the kids while our wives shuffled off to work every morning, hands red-chapped and bleeding, to help keep the moneyed Count Heldenbuch in clean laundry.

Géorg was a new father and I'd barely seen my daughter, Constance, in two years. We'd been so busy hauling swords and crossbows and other fake dragon weaponry all around the valley that neither of us had been home much except for the odd rollick with the wives.

A few days after I'd been back, my daughter looked at me across our one-room shack and asked if I'd ever met her daddy the Dragon-slayer.

"I'm your daddy," I told her.

"My daddy's stronger," she said. "And a knight." She was playing on the floor with a sack of grain. My wife had dribbled berry juice on the front to make eyes and a mouth. Constance looked up again and asked, "Where's my mommy?"

"At work," I told her. "I'm here now. Quiet, Daddy's thinking." I went back to whatever important thing I thought I was doing, and she threw me a look that suggested my out-of-work ass was hopefully just a temporary inconvenience in her world.

We were living nine furlongs from Feldkirch, which was twenty furlongs from nowhere, and it was hard to keep from wanting to rip every goddamn thing apart being cooped up like that. The rain never stopped, and the cold wind would barrel through the valley and find you no matter how thick the wool on your tunic. My wife would come home after a long day of laundering and Constance would go from the utmost nuisance to daughter-of-the-year in two seconds. "What did you and Daddy do all day?" Gerta would ask, and Constance would shrug her little shoulders and roll up on her mother, arms outstretched, offering up the hug of all hugs. It was hard for me to watch. There I was, at home with the kid all day, and you didn't see me on the receiving end of something like that.

"Try taking an interest in her," Gerta told me one night after we'd put Constance to bed and taken up some renewed passion in front of the cookery.

"What's so interesting about a child?"

"How about the fact that she's yours," Gerta said coldly. She pulled herself off of me, re-buttoned her frock, and told me what I could expect as far as lovemaking if I didn't pull myself together and at least try.

So, for a minute, I stopped daydreaming about the fake dragons, and Géorg, and all the money and trouble we used to make for ourselves, and focused on Constance. When I'd see her talking to her sack doll I'd ask her what she was saying. If she was off in the corner playing Bury the Stone, I'd pull up next to her and see if I could join in. If she needed help doing her business I'd take her outside and help her dig the hole and stand there, shielding her from the wind as she squatted over it. It took about a week, and then one day as we were outside watching the storm clouds gather, she reached up and took hold of my hand.

Géorg lived a plot of land away. We were neighbors if you consider a half-hour walk neighborly. Since I'd been back I hadn't worked myself up to visiting him, but eventually I took Constance across the muddy field that separated our hut from Géorg's to check on how he was making out in the fatherhood department. At his front door Constance asked if her doll could do the knocking.

"Of course," I said, and lifted her up so she could reach high on the door. Earlier that week I'd given her doll a pair of arms by tying a rope around the middle of the sack and letting the ends hang loose. She grabbed one of the arms and knocked a ropy knock. "Great job," I told her, and placed her down. She took my hand again and we stood there as the fog and rain rolled in from the valley and set upon Géorg's hut like it could tear the roof off the place.

"No one's home," Constance said.

That's when I heard the baby scream.

When I pushed open the door, Géorg's hands were around little Jonah's throat. There was water all over the floor and he was thrusting the baby's head into a soot-stained cauldron of dirty water.

"Stop!" I yelled, and pushed Constance aside. The drink fell off Géorg so strongly I could smell it across the room. I jumped in, kicked him, and tried to pry his fingers from the baby's neck. I took a fistful of his hair, yanking it so hard that he dropped the child and collapsed, sweaty, drunk, and sobbing on the floor.

"I can't do this," he kept saying. "I can't do this!"

Jonah was motionless on the ground, his eyes open, staring into space like he was watching the last bit of his short life slip away and didn't want to miss a second of it. I picked up his body and held it out in front of me. They say time stops in the moments we wait for our children to breathe, and I can tell you it's the gods' honest truth. I remember thinking so much in that moment. Like, what would we do if the kid kicked it? Or how long can a child go without breathing? Mostly what I was thinking was, *We could really use a little more kid experience in this hut*, because Jonah's skin was a bloodless shade of purple and we were about to lose him.

Then it was like some unseen force reached down and gave the boy a slap across the ass. He coughed and screamed as his tiny lungs struggled to expel the water that had been forced inside. He cried with an intensity I'd never heard from a baby before. The child was back from wherever he'd been, and either he did not want to return, or he was outraged at the brutality of the world and what he'd just come to understand of it.

"Look!" I said to Géorg, still lumped up on the floor. "He's alive!"

"So I hear," Géorg said from behind strands of soaking wet hair. It was the crying, he told me, that drove him to it. "Like a damn banshee," he said. "If drinking can't drown out the sound, then what choice do I have?"

Later that evening, when I told my wife what had happened, she marched across the dark field in only a smock and broke the news to Hildegunn, Géorg's wife. Even over the wind that night you could hear her yelling clear across the valley. Winkelried the Elder often said his goats stopped giving milk when Hildegunn tore into it, but this time he worried he might have to put a few of them down. My wife asked if I'd ever seen Géorg try anything like that before, and I lied and said I hadn't. But I knew better. I'd seen him threaten a local mouthpiece with a lot worse when the dragon scam was falling apart, and then there was the time during the Lenzburg job when a hunter caught us in the forest pumping the bellows for sound effects. What Géorg did to that man I can't bear to think about. But he had a dark resolve, Géorg, a grim sense of purpose that made anything possible. The head of a goat, the head of a hunter—these things were equal to him. He had asked more of me but the best I could do was hold the guy down.

After Jonah and the cauldron, Géorg kept himself scarce and drunk in the village for a long while. Then word got out that Hildegunn required his fix-it skills to thatch some roof that had given way to the weather, and suddenly he was home again.

"That idiot's back?" Gerta said. She was at the hearth stirring a pot of goulash.

"He's not so bad," I said.

"You'd forgive him for kicking in your face," she said without turning around.

"He's my partner."

"I'm your partner," she said.

Géorg and I were a team if ever there was one. It was common knowledge among every clan in the valley that when it came to a certain brand of surliness, we were not to be messed with. We were destruction in the wake of confidence. Strength where it mattered and deception when it counted. "We're men being men," Géorg used to say, and that was usually good enough for me.

After Hildegunn took Géorg back, things were actually pretty good for a while. On days when it wasn't pouring rain, Géorg and I would take the kids into the middle of the field and set up a mock dragonslaying. We'd bring out the old swords and I'd do the whole bit where I pretended to hear a dragon approach and Géorg would come in with the bellows. Constance was nearly four and she loved it. "How do you make the growling sound, Daddy?" she'd ask, and I'd show her the gadget Géorg had built from two pieces of bark and a catgut string that vibrated just right. Jonah was still too young to understand. He was barely crawling, but the swordplay seemed to calm him.

Those were the days of the barley blight and rotten beetroot, so Géorg and I weren't the only ones lacking in gainful employment. Pretty soon, other out-of-work dads from the village brought their kids around and Géorg and I would drag out the catapult, battle axe, and other heavy artillery and put on a real show.

Géorg would run around and cue me when I was to trigger a piece of equipment. The dads would cheer when something big like the catapult went off, and a thick, vigorous energy would wrap itself around all of us. Lots of snorting and clapping and spitting on everything, and it felt good to be back doing our thing, even without the thrill of the con and the promise of money.

Afterwards, we'd break open a cask of ale and watch all of our kids play in the mud. We'd talk about our wives, and the kids' teething, we'd argue about the best way to cobble solid footwear, and trade recipes for stews that required the least of our attention.

"It's a load of shit," Géorg said one afternoon. He stood apart from the group of us, gnawing on a twig and rolling it around in his mouth. "Listen to yourselves. You're men for fuck's sake." He threw his mug on the ground and wiped the snot from his face. "You're an embarrassment, all of you."

He spit and walked back across the field, dragging Jonah behind him like some kind of dead animal. The rest of us watched in silence, wondering what it was exactly that Géorg had just pointed out about our sorry lives. Constance came up to me and started going on about her doll's arms. They needed mending, but I wasn't in the mood, so I pushed her. She fell back into the mud and the men started laughing and pointing at her. I laughed too and a few of us bumped chests like I'd just taken out something evil. Constance stood up and ran back to the house in tears. "Guess I better go take care of that," I told them.

"Daddy's sorry," I said to Constance, after she'd calmed down and it was just the two of us at the hearth. Gerta wasn't home yet and I was trying to convince her that what happened would never happen again. She softened and looked up, eyes twinkling from the light of the fire.

"Are you going away again?" she asked.

"Why would you ask that?" I said.

"I don't know." Her finger made little circles in the dirt floor. "Maybe because it's funnier?"

"You mean, more fun," I said, and scooped her up in my arms. We danced around the room as I sang her one of the funny rhymes she'd taught me. *Cock a doodle do! My dame has lost her shoe, My master's lost his fiddlestick, And knows not what to do.*

Then Géorg was gone. No goodbye, no nice-swindling-the-countryside-with-you-for-the-past-five-years. "Not even a note," I told Gerta, once it was obvious he wasn't coming back. She rolled her eyes and said life was better off without him. "Best place for a man like that is a dungeon," she said.

"Every kid needs a father," I told her.

"And where have *you* heard that one before?"

She was talking about the salad days when I'd only be home for a minute or two between jobs. Géorg and I were bringing in serious riches back then. I'd stop home to drop off what money I hadn't blown on ale and prostitutes, pick up a spare mace or scabbard, then be back on the road again for months.

We'd work our way through the valley, putting three days between every town we hit so as to not arouse suspicion. If we found ourselves in need of provisions, we stole them. If we were hungry, we killed what we needed. Cat, dog, it didn't matter. Géorg had a taste for uncommon game and I learned to stomach his instincts.

Besides, he was on the cutting edge back then as far as fake dragonry went. It was intoxicating to stand next to that kind of talent. He was building all sorts of equipment and had even more breakthroughs in mind—the sound effects were just the beginning.

Géorg always stressed that the setup was the most important. "Like baiting a hook," he said. When starting in on a new village we made sure a few local livestock went missing, but they had to vanish without a trace, like they'd been plucked clean from the pasture. Géorg invented this cart-and-catapult combination for launching the animals we killed into the forest without leaving so much as a wheel track. The thing was a work of art. We'd roll in at night and by the time the sun came up the whole village would be in a frenzy, wondering who was terrorizing the sheep. We'd drop a few hints about seeing a dragon in the depths of whatever forest was nearby, and pandemonium wouldn't be far behind. Géorg even fashioned dragon claws from blocks of wood, strapped them to my feet, and had me walk miles in the mud to simulate the animal's propensity for stalking. There wasn't a forest or cave in three hundred miles that he couldn't turn into a town's worst nightmare. Once we had the villagers convinced a dragon was upon them, the money for slaying came rolling in.

I was younger than Géorg and looked knightly in a pair of tights, so once we were done taking a town for all they had, it fell to me to parade the fake dragon parts through town for all to see. I'd dress up in my armor and have the sword in one hand and a dripping piece of dragon in the other. It was usually the entrails of a local pig we had slaughtered, or several organs pieced together by Géorg to make them unrecognizable. Once, while conning Brierley, he covered me in a mixture of pitch and oxblood that when lit gave the impression of scorched remains falling from my limbs. In Leurbost he hung cow intestines from my leather to suggest I'd kept the best parts of the beast for sustenance. The gore was always secondary, however—it was the show that made them believe. They would line the streets and I'd raise my sword in the air and take a bite from the entrails. Blood ran down my face and into the plates of armor on my chest. Géorg would thread through the crowd shouting high praise to get everyone going, and when it was all over I'd walk out of town with a heavy bag of loot under my arm. Géorg would meet me a few miles down the road and we'd find a spot to divvy it up—70/30, with Géorg taking the lion's share. That was the deal. He said it was due to his legal right to the inventions and if I wanted to argue he could always find someone else to play dress-up.

After Géorg left, Hildegunn started bringing Jonah by our place every few days while she went into the village to do God knows what. Géorg's leaving had extinguished that fire in her, you could see it in the way she moved. One day she brought the child over, said she was running to town to see about fresh work, but never came back.

"What do we do now?" I asked Gerta when she got home from work. Jonah was already cruising our one-room hovel, holding fast to whatever he could as he baby-stepped his way around. Constance moved her sack doll from the bed to the floor and told us Jonah could sleep with her.

"You're better at the fathering than you think," Gerta said.

"Well, don't spread it around," I said. "The kind of men I used to run with would see me beaten for it."

So there I was with two kids under the age of five living under a leaky thatched roof with winter on the way. Gerta was working longer hours, leaving before the sun came up and returning long after it had gone down. I'd have the kids cleaned and asleep as best I could and be well into my third mug of ale by the time she walked in. "Look who's never home now," I'd say, and kick my feet up on the table with a look like, *Check out the Duke of Daddyville.* One day I guess I pushed it too far, because after I gave her my usual flack she buried her face in her wimple and started to cry. I rethought my welcome-home routine after that, because even back then I was starting to understand what it might be like to miss your children that much.

The upside was that Gerta seemed to take a renewed interest in carnal relations. Whatever I was doing in the dad department seemed to be paying off, because no matter how tired she was after work, I was in for some serious copulation when the candles went out. Before I knew it Constance was six, Jonah was nearly three, and we had another little one crawling around in the mud.

That's when the livestock started to go missing.

At first everyone in the village chalked it up to theft. A sheep here, a goat there. But I knew better. There was something familiar about the way the animals were disappearing. It was classic Géorg. The dads group was still getting together once a week and a few of them said they had spotted a strangeness flying around in the sky the week the animals had vanished.

"Did it look like a cow tossed from a catapult?" I asked.

"Not hardly," one of them said.

"It had wings," said another.

That night over dinner I told Gerta a little too excitedly that I thought Géorg might be back. She sighed and set her wooden spoon next to the stew I'd spent the day preparing. The kids fell quiet and you could tell they were wondering what was wrong with Mommy.

"Who's Géorg?" Jonah asked.

Even the little one seemed to understand something was up. She sat in the rickety high chair I'd made for her and pointed at the sky through the latest hole in our roof.

Over the years, the field between Géorg's place and ours had become overgrown. The weeds were the height of two men in some places. There was still a trail however, as I'd been going there nearly once a month to watch his house sink into the earth and reminisce about the glory days. I'd sit on one of the wooden stumps littered around his land and stare at what was left of his front door. It was my only break from the kids. Constance was old enough to watch the others for a while, so I'd often find myself over there thinking of Gerta and the kids and what might be coming next in my life. I'd check the shed where Géorg kept the dragon equipment and sometimes pull out a gauntlet or rusted crossbow and aim it into the sky like we used to do. Then I'd head back home toward my family, stretching out the walk as long as I could.

The footprints showed up a week after the missing livestock. First near the ruins of Géorg's house, then stamped lightly into the mud on the path between our land. They were always fresh, like whoever it was had slipped into the mucky weeds seconds before I found him. Géorg and I knew too much about covering tracks; if they were his, he wanted them seen. I'd kneel down, touch them with my fingers and look around, yelling Géorg's name as loud as I could.

There were signs that someone was poking around our place too. Sometimes late at night, in the midst of a fitful sleep, I'd get up and check on the kids to make sure the three of them were at least breathing. I'd spend a moment at the window, look out into the darkness and swear someone was standing in the yard.

Once, Jonah and I were outside playing catch with rocks when I sailed one over his head and it rolled a good distance to the edge of our property. He ran to collect it, and before he picked it up he stood facing the weeds like he was talking to someone. I yelled, "Jonah, what is it?" He ran back waving a different rock above his head, saying a man had found a better one in the weeds and given it to him.

Then came the actual dragon. Mrs. Grundlsmere swore she'd seen the beast land in her backyard and wrap a forked tongue around her prized ewe, suffocating the poor animal with one squeeze. Bruno, my neighbor a few furlongs away, said the dragon had confronted him and his oxen while they were on the way to market. "It let loose a fire from its jaws that scorched my cart and ruined a season's worth of squash," he said. "I was lucky to escape with my life."

Eventually, I saw the dragon too. I was at Géorg's place again, hoping he'd finally show up, when its shadow passed over the ground. By the time I looked up it was high in the sky doing strange acrobatic maneuvers, dipping and weaving and spinning corkscrews through the air. Something that looked like smoke billowed from its hindquarters and became a long white trail as the dragon moved across the sky. It disappeared into a bank of high clouds in the west and I remember thinking at the time that there was something unnatural in the way it moved, something that no God would ever imagine putting upon the earth.

The reports piled up. Everyone in town figured since I knew so much about fake dragons, a real one must not be all that different. Soon I had a mob at my door, led by the village elders, asking for help. My hut was complete domestic mayhem when they showed up—Constance had refused to churn the butter and was pouting in the corner. Jonah was running around the shack naked in one of the moods that brought me closer to understanding why Géorg had tried to drown him. I hadn't had time to get the youngest out of her sleep sack yet and she was knotting herself up inside it writhing on the dirt floor. But here's what they offered me: enough money to send Constance and Jonah to a private tutor three towns over, the deed to Géorg's land, and above all, a chance to work again.

That night I pumped out a family meal that I must say was pretty stunning. One of the guys in the dads group gave me the recipe and told me of a farmer in Motala that had the freshest produce around. I had walked there with the kids in tow and told them to keep quiet because Daddy was making a special dinner for Mommy.

And did I—this was first-rate cabbage and a gopher I'd killed just the day before, stewed in a delicate broth with the slightest hint of fresh honey and wood cherries. When Gerta got home I had the place looking fine. I'd swept, the table was set, and I even put out the good candles.

"And to what do I owe the pleasure?" Gerta said as she sat down and pulled off her sandals. The kids had all washed in the creek and I had them lined up from tallest to shortest. Their faces were shining and I could tell that the remnants of any kind of miserable day drained out of Gerta right there. The kids ran to her and each found a spot to hug. "Daddy's got a surprise," said Constance, and Jonah echoed the same.

"A surprise?" Gerta said, looking at me. I was in the middle of whipping the cream for dessert and putting the finishing touches on the gopher, so I told her to just take a seat and I'd let everyone know in good time. Constance strapped the little one into her high chair and Jonah found his seat at the table. He was holding the small dagger I'd given him for his birthday the week before. "No weapons at the table," I said, and he sighed and climbed off his chair to put the knife in his bunk.

"It all looks wonderful," Gerta said when I brought out the main course. The gopher was still sizzling and the whole shack smelled of wood smoke and sweet onion. Even the little one seemed excited; she had a few words by then and was rocking in her chair saying what sounded like "yummy" over and over. Never had we eaten so well. I waited until dessert to tell them Daddy was going back to work. After I broke the news, Gerta put her elbows on the table, dropped her head into her hands, and let out a long sigh.

"I thought you'd be excited to be back with the children again," I told her after we got the kids to sleep. The candles were low and their light danced around the room; the sound of summer insects was loud outside. Gerta had the front door open and was staring out into the darkness of the valley.

"I don't want my children staking hope on a father who drops in whenever he pleases," she said. "I've lived that way once. I won't do it again. Give me dirty laundry any day."

I could feel the evening air press its way into the room; it swirled around us and snuffed out a few of the candles. One of the children shuffled in their bunk as I sat there and tried to embrace what Gerta was telling me. "I don't know what it is with you," she said. "You have everything and it's not enough." She closed the front door and walked back toward our bed. "If you leave," she said as she passed, "feel free to stay gone this time."

Géorg had always had a wizardly look about him, with tangled hair that hinted at years of restlessness and a smart mouth that always let you know what Géorg thought of Géorg. No one ever could get a leg up on him and he never let you forget it. Sometimes on our walks between towns he'd share what he had up his sleeve in the invention department. I remember we were halfway to Grimsby when he showed me his plans for a type of flying machine. It was a crude mechanism that used coal and a furnace made from this lighter-than-iron metal Géorg said he had a line on. "Just think of the terror we could rain down with this," he'd said, and I'll never forget the look in his eyes, like he'd swallowed the world's biggest secret and was caught up in the thrill of finally telling someone about it.

"If you talk of this to anyone," he said, "I'll do to you worse than what I did to that hunter."

And I believed him. We'd been through some good scrapes and

logged serious miles, but Géorg was short on pleasantries and long on ideas, and it was this idea, this flying machine, that stuck in my mind at the sight of whatever it was flying over Géorg's place that day. I had imagined a lot of dragons but never anything that moved quite like that. I knew in my heart, in the part of my soul that locked away the kind of darkness a man craves from the world, that Géorg was calling me back with the promise of the life I'd left behind.

The town elders gave me half the silver up front. Gerta quit the laundry gig, and for a few days when we were all home together I took on the job of rebuilding some of Géorg's old weapons. I pulled the crossbow and battle axe from his ruined shed and had Constance and Jonah help drag them back to our place. I took Jonah to the blacksmith with me for crossbow parts. Conversation around the shop was all dragon, and Jonah took pleasure in showing off the new dagger I'd given him, pretending to stab at whatever piece of equipment he found threatening. The blacksmiths laughed and said the boy was a natural fighter.

"If you only knew," I said.

A few days later Constance helped me strip down the battle axe, and when I wasn't looking she carved five small figures into the handle. "What is this?" I asked her.

"That's us," she said. And it was. Carved into the handle were five stick figures of Gerta and me and the kids. Constance smiled at me with a look that said she had every confidence I wouldn't be away long this time. I swung the axe over my head and growled like I used to do when putting on one of our victory performances. Constance shrieked and ran about the yard, yelling, "Catch me, Daddy!" and Jonah fell in too with his knife, protecting his stepsister from whatever he imagined I was. Gerta was holding the baby on the new porch I'd started, and the sun was out for the first time in months. My old tights barely fit anymore and the armor looked altogether ridiculous. I gathered up the weapons and slung them over my shoulder, all of it much heavier than I remembered. Constance and Jonah bolted to each of my legs and held fast, both of them crying and carrying on.

"I want you to take Valentina," Constance said. I took her doll, placed it in my satchel, and pried the children from my legs. They ran toward the field, Constance tickling Jonah along the way. Their tears became laughter that hung gayly in the air. The wind was picking up, and the rye I'd planted next to the house was swaying in the breeze, its stalks tall and strong. I remember thinking it would be a good year for the harvest. From my spot in the yard I could see where I'd mended the roof, how I'd taken grass and thatched it watertight with my own two hands. Smoke leaked from the chimney and I could smell the faint hint of onion and ash. I took one last look at Gerta on the porch and waved. She turned and walked into the house.

What a sad sight I must have been, waddling off toward the road that led into town. Daddy off to fight the good fight. Daddy walking away for good from the one honest and beautiful thing he'd ever done.

I almost didn't make it, sweating as I was. I had to stop many times to catch my breath and readjust the equipment. I kept looking back to see if Constance and Jonah were following but there was only the empty road. The masses were gathering in the village; I could hear them in the distance, chants and cheers and even the sound of bagpipes. I picked myself up, hiked up my tights, pushed on.

And then I was there, wielding an axe through the middle of town and pulling out all my old moves. Men lined the streets, women threw flower petals, and children raced about my feet with wooden swords. I looked for Géorg in the crowd and I could have sworn he was there, laying the foundation for whatever adventure we were in for next. Everyone cheered, and each voice in that madness unlocked the darkness in my heart that had lain dormant there. I looked up, and for that brief moment, the sky was clear of dragons.

THE ONE THEY TOOK BEFORE
Kelly Sandoval

Kelly Sandoval's work has appeared in *Asimov's*, *Shimmer*, and *Best American Science Fiction and Fantasy*. She graduated from Clarion West in 2013. She lives in Seattle.

"The One They Took Before" is a dark and beautiful tale of lost magic amid a jaded urban landscape.

craigslist > seattle > all seattle > lost&found
Sat 23 Jul
FOUND: *Rift in the Fabric of the Universe* – (West Seattle)

Rift opened in my backyard. About six feet tall and one foot wide. Appears to open onto a world of endless twilight and impossible beauty. Makes a ringing noise like a thousand tiny bells. Call (206) 555-9780 to identify.

Kayla reads the listing twice, knowing the eager beating of her heart is ridiculous. One page back, someone claims they found a time machine. Someone else has apparently lost their kidneys.

The Internet isn't real. That's what she likes about it. And if the post is real, the best thing she can do is pretend she never saw it.

After all, she's doing better. She sees a therapist now. She's had a couple of job interviews.

She calls the number.

"Hello?" It's a man's voice. Kayla can't identify his accent.

"Oh. Hi." Her words come out timid and thin, almost a whisper. She stands and starts pacing the length of her apartment, stepping over dirty clothes and cat toys. "I'm calling about your Craigslist ad."

"Oh!" He sounds surprised, but not displeased. "I'm glad to hear from you. So, when did you lose it?"

"Pardon?"

"The rift. When did you lose it?"

Yesterday? A thousand years ago? Time was meaningless there. She's pretty sure it all happened a very long time ago.

"It's complicated," she says.

"Well, can you describe it, then? Tell me what color it is? I just need to be sure it's yours."

It isn't hers. "Have you had a lot of calls?"

"A few crazies," he admits. "Someone claiming to be my evil twin. That sort of thing."

The cats, Ablach and Thomas, twist around her ankles. She leans down to stroke Ablach and presses her face into his fur. He hasn't spoken to her since they got out. Neither of them have. "Have you tried going through it?"

"No. It's not mine." He tries to sound firm, but she knows the longing in his voice. They opened a door for him. It's only a matter of time. "Listen, if this thing isn't yours—"

"Don't go through it," she says. "Even if they ask you to."

She hangs up before he can reply.

The cats watch her, unblinking. Gold eyes and silver. She tries not to imagine their voices.

"What?" she asks them. "I warned him. What else can I do?"

Ablach turns his back on her, tail lashing. Thomas rolls onto his back and lets her stroke his stomach.

"I'm not going back." She repeats the phrase, over and over. Words have power. They taught her that.

After a few hours pass, she tries the number again. No one answers.

The Stranger Lovelab
23 / Man / Cal Anderson

Faerie Queen, saw you in Cal Anderson Park by the tennis courts. You wore a dress of hummingbird feathers and a crown of tiny stars. I asked for a light. I should have asked for more. Coffee?

For two days, Kayla avoids the Internet and every local newspaper. If they're hunting again, she doesn't want to know. On the third day, she dares to go out for coffee. A newspaper waits at the only open table, and she flips to the classifieds before she can stop herself.

The ad draws her eye immediately. It's highlighted. She wonders if it was there before she sat down. If it will still be there when she leaves.

Cal Anderson is only a few blocks away. And she's still weak enough to need to know. Kayla leaves her full cup on the table and heads outside, flinching as she enters the sunlight. Long weeks of gray skies and soft rain don't bother her, but these brief days of garish blue leave her longing for twilight.

Shirtless men and girls in bikinis crowd the park, and Kayla tries not to see them. They remind her of someone she was, and she still longs to slip back into that skin. It's best not to think of it. Nostalgia, for either life, is poison.

She keeps her head down, and makes her way to the stand of trees that lines the tennis courts. No hummingbird feathers wait for her there. No tiny stars litter the grass. A group of teens jostles past and one of them reaches up to pluck an apple from the branch above her head. The fruit in his hand is the deep red of exposed muscle. Looking up, she has to tell herself that apples, not hearts, hang heavy on the branches. They are huge and numerous, an out-of-season abundance. Also, it's not an apple tree.

She runs home and sobs quietly until Ablach and Thomas climb into her lap and lick her tears with rough tongues. After that, her sobs aren't quiet at all.

Seattle Times Online
Category: The Blotter
August 1, 2013

King County Sheriff's Office seeks the public's help in locating a Seattle-area woman

Josey Aarons, 24, was last seen on July 30th at the Triple Door on 216 Union Street, where she was performing with her band, The Sudden Sorrows. According to her friends, Aarons was supposed to meet them at an afterparty but never arrived.

Witnesses report Aarons was seen outside the venue with a woman described as having skin the color of a summer moon and eyes as deep as madness. Aarons is 5 feet 9 inches tall, 150 lbs, with short blond hair and brown eyes. She was last seen wearing black jeans and a green trenchcoat. She was carrying a gray messenger bag.

Anyone with information on the whereabouts of either Ms. Aarons or her companion is asked to call the Sheriff's Office at 206-555-9252.

Kayla sits, her guitar in her lap, and strokes the smooth wood like it's one of the cats. When she first got back, she took a knife to the strings, sawing through them one by one. It didn't hurt at the time. It hurts now, when she longs for the comfort of melody. But she knows better.

If she plays, they will hear her.

They will take her back.

She is trying so hard. She goes to yoga class. She watches TV.

She rocks in the dark of her apartment, the glow of the computer screen creating a sort of twilight.

Is she loved, this girl that they have taken? Do they kiss her, their lips honey-sweet and dizzying as brandy? Does she realize she is theirs? That they will pet and praise and keep her, drape her in diamonds and bask in her light, but never let her go?

Until they do.

Freedom is its own kind of prison.

In Kayla's apartment, the computer glows, and it is nothing at all like twilight.

She tries to tell herself the girl will be okay. They will keep her for a few eternities, but they will also set her free again. She can rebuild.

Kayla is.

She picks up the phone and dials the number for the Sheriff's Office. She tells them she knows about Josey.

"Wait a year and a day," she says. "They won't keep her forever."

Except, of course, they will. They kept Kayla even longer than that.

That's two, Kayla thinks. They'll claim one more. They like patterns, cycles, rules.

She tells herself to ignore it. It isn't her problem. She can't save everyone. If she interferes, they'll find her.

She tells herself she doesn't want that. She says it out loud. There's supposed to be power in that.

Seattle Times
August 3, 2013

Explanation sought after fatal hunting trip

The death of James Garcia, a Tacoma-area accountant, has left police with more questions than answers. He was hunting in Silwen Falls with his brothers Marcus and Eric Garcia when the fatal accident occurred. While the details are still unclear, the brothers said James Garcia separated from his party early on the morning of August 2 at a blind he was accustomed to using, and where he intended to remain for most of the day.

Sometime around noon, James Garcia left his shelter and removed all his clothing, including his orange safety vest, before approaching the blind his brothers were sharing. In the ensuing confusion, the brothers said they mistook him for, in the words of Marcus Garcia, "a stag of shadow and dream, its antlers cast from sunlight." Eric Garcia admits to taking the fatal shot. Investigations are ongoing, police said.

Kayla remembers the bright cry of horns, horses with hot breath and red eyes, stags with human screams. Her keepers, clad in spider-silk and frost, the mad need in their joy. She tries to think of the dead man. She thinks, instead, of trays piled high with venison, air spice-laden and thick with laughter. Hunger twists in her stomach and she forgets to be ashamed.

She makes herself a sandwich, ham and cheddar on white bread, but only manages a few bites. Everything tastes like beige.

Thomas jumps into her arms, a furry mass of gold and shadow, and purrs deep and low. The sound usually calms her, reminds her to settle and stay. She should sit down, stroke him, find center.

"I don't need them," she whispers into his fur. She tries turning on the TV, but every show is a meaningless mix of colors and noises.

Ablach paces at the door, his cries high and bright as a hunting horn.

"Don't trust him," she tells herself. "Don't trust any of their gifts."

But he sings her heart, and she sets Thomas aside.

Outside, the stars are hidden behind a thin wash of cloud. Kayla follows Ablach down major roads and through slender alleys lined with overflowing Dumpsters. The route is circuitous and random but she recognizes where he leads her. Cal Anderson Park. She's alone on a tree-lined sidewalk, looking for a shadow in a world of them.

Ablach cries above her. She looks up, finds him watching her from the branches, his eyes like silver coins. She reaches to stroke him and her fingers close around a heavy fruit made russet by the night. It doesn't smell like an apple. It smells of blood and honey, of sex and song.

The juice is silver and she licks it from her fingers when she's done. Ablach lets her carry him home.

Seattle Times
August 4, 2013

Obituary

James Carlos Garcia, 43, was lost in a tragic accident on August 2. A man of courage, humor and intelligence, he was an active member of his community and a dedicated husband and father.

He leaves behind three children, Peter Garcia, Mary Winner and James Garcia Jr. He is also survived by his wife, Alice Garcia.

He loved hunting, Bruce Springsteen's music and his family.

A celebration of his life will be held on August 10 at 7:30 PM at the North Tacoma Community Hall.

The funeral, Facebook tells her, is on the sixth. She sends flowers, the biggest bouquet the florist has. Money isn't an issue; they sent her back decked in gold and strange jewels. She waited weeks for it to fade or turn to leaves but the gold, like the memories, refused to leave her. It means she doesn't have to work, or leave her apartment, or forget.

An obvious trap, and she's been trying to fight it. Of course, she hasn't sent out a job application since she called about the rift. Hasn't answered her phone, or emailed the people she tells herself are her friends.

She doesn't intend to go. The one responsible is sure to be there; they love to watch. Even on the morning of the sixth, as she puts on a dress of black silk and gold lace, she imagines she will stay home. The dress was her favorite, before. Now she can only see it as an echo of something grander. She has worn a cloak of dragonfly skin over a gown woven from the scent of roses. They set her at the feet of the queen, and when she played, they drank the notes from the air.

It will not happen again, Kayla tells herself, as she restrings her guitar. And maybe it won't. But she isn't sure anymore.

She lets the cats out before she leaves. Ablach disappears with a confident stride but Thomas presses himself against her legs, crying to be picked up and trying to follow her into the cab.

"If you would only ask me to stay," she whispers, as she sets him back on the pavement, "I might."

But he doesn't ask.

The cab pulls up at the church well after the service is scheduled to begin. She considers going in, makes it all the way to the door before deciding against it. The family already has one voyeur to their pain. She can at least save them a second one.

She waits beside the door and tries to enjoy the feeling of the sun on her skin. She remembers longing for daylight, then screaming for daylight, then forgetting what daylight meant.

It's a difficult thing to learn again.

"They are crying in there." The words settle onto her skin like she's walked into mist, a cat's purr of a sound: low, self-satisfied, demanding. "Painting their faces with ash," it says, "and tearing their clothes with sorrow."

Its skin, Kayla sees, is more the color of an autumn moon than one from the summer, but its eyes are certainly deep as madness, and the iridescent feathers of its hummingbird gown shame her simple dress. She lowers her eyes, curtsies. The gesture is automatic, and she hates herself for it.

"What did he do?" she asks. It's fear, not excitement, that sets her heart racing. She's glad to fear them again.

"Do?" Its purr warms with amusement. "He did nothing. He did not catch me bathing or cross my path to start a riddle game. He sat in his tent and did nothing at all. He bored me."

Yes, that was a sort of crime. What use were humans if they refused to be fun? She stopped being fun, near the end. She sat and rocked and sobbed and would not give them their music.

They sent her home, after that. She thought they freed her. But here she is, standing before one, her guitar at her side.

"You have not played," it says. "We listen, still. And you give us nothing. Are you still broken?"

"Not like I was," she says. And realizes her mistake as it smiles.

"You were her favorite," it says. "Our Lightning Bard."

"You have a new one now," she says. She tries to keep her breathing even, but the scent of it makes her dizzy. "Unless *she's already* broken."

"So unkind. We offer her wonders." It glances up, stares at the sun.

Kayla wants to kiss its neck, drink eternity from its veins. She digs her nails into her palms. "Did you offer her a choice?"

"Of a sort. She followed me."

"She didn't know what she followed you to." But Kayla does.

"Are you jealous?" it asks, voice silken with amusement. "You needn't be. We can still take you."

And yes, she is, isn't she? She wants those first wondering months, before she could see the rot beneath the gilt. She wants the luxury of not yet knowing what it means to love them.

"No." She forces the word out through clenched teeth.

"I have leave to barter," it says. "We have no need for two musicians. And it would be novel to win the same soul twice."

The church door opens and the mourners begin to stream out. Kayla catches sight of a man's face, ugly with pain, and recognizes him as one of the dead man's brothers. It doesn't even glance his way.

The man's loss is no more than a daytime rerun of a once amusing show.

"No," she whispers it this time, crossing her arms in a vain attempt at comfort. "It wouldn't last."

"You could be our pretty one again, our summer storm." Its voice is thick and sweet. The world fades and reduces itself, the sun hiding, the mourners hushing their cries.

Kayla's tears are hot on her face and she's afraid to brush them away. She could say yes. She could tell herself she was being generous, playing the sacrifice. "Did you take her just for that? To offer in trade?"

Is it her fault, or does she only want to believe she means that much to them?

"I care little for your questions, Pet. Will you come?"

This is the part where she says yes and it drags her back to that land of endless twilight and impossible beauty. This is the part where she falls.

"No," she says, the third time she's rejected it. She stands straighter, meets its eyes. Her guitar case falls from limp fingers. If it makes a sound as it hits the steps, she doesn't hear it.

"Very well," it says, the purr gone from its voice. "But we will be listening. And you will tire of mortality and dust."

She is already tired of mortality and dust. Tired, too, of being locked into the need of them.

"You can't keep me," she says.

It leans in and kisses the salt from her lips. Its breath smells like storm clouds, all electric promise. "Oh, pretty one. We already have."

The world lurches, empties, and she's alone on the church steps. The mourners are leaving, a long procession of cars already disappearing down the street.

She calls the cab back. Rides home in silence.

A year and a day. An eternity. One doesn't exclude the other.

But they always send back what they take, shattered husks of what they once found beautiful.

Kayla will wait. Apply for jobs. Mark the calendar.

She'll be ready, when the time comes. No one waited for her. No one understood. It can be different, this time. She can help.

And that can be a sort of winning.

TIGER BABY
JY Yang

JY Yang is the author of the Tensorate series of novellas forthcoming from Tor.com (*The Red Threads of Fortune*, *The Black Tides of Heaven*). Their short stories have appeared in such venues as *Uncanny*, *Lightspeed*, and *Strange Horizons*. JY graduated with the Clarion West class of 2013 and received their MA in creative writing from the University of East Anglia. They live in Singapore.

"Tiger Baby" originally appeared in *From the Belly of the Cat*, an anthology of cat stories published by Math Paper Press in Singapore in 2013. The story was later reprinted in *Lackington's*, a successful and eclectic online magazine. "Tiger Baby" is a great example that nothing is ever truly as it appears to be.

Felicity wakes from a dream of hunting. She moves her hands, sleep-heavy, and is surprised to find them human-shaped, with hairless fingers that curl and end in flat, dirty nails. Sheets tangle around her legs, clinging damply to fleshy thighs, knotting around an inert lump she comes to realize is her body.

Sometimes, not always, she forgets she is human. Especially on mornings like this, with her mind's eye still burning bright, breathing forests of the night. The taste of her true form lingers: not this body with its rock of pain nestling in between neck and shoulder and the blood pounding in the head and the rancid feel of its dry mouth. Feli closes her eyes, hoping to slip back into the wonderful light darkness, into her true flesh, dread hands dread feet running across warm concrete, searching, singing, wind sluicing through striped fur as she streaks through the neighbourhood.

The door makes a loud noise and she startles into wakefulness, craning her head to look. Her mother stands in the doorway, knuckles flush to wood. "You don't need to work today? You'll be late."

Resentment surges up like a storm wave, like a predator springing from the grass. Her mother does not understand, will never understand, standing in the doorway with her faded shirt and heavy pear-hips and shiny face beginning its irreversible droop. She sees her grandmother reflected in there, worn away by time until the eyes held only emptiness. Wherever her wild streak comes from, it is not here. Feli drops a hand to the bedspread. "I'm awake."

She can't remember when it started. Which came first, the dreams or the realisation of what she was meant to be? How many youthful hours did she spend in corners, softly reciting Blake and feeling a weighty truth?

Her earliest memory is of tigers, swimming in a moat. How she watched one, on the rock above, pace back and forth in the enclosure, while her father shouted warnings about staying put and her infant sister cried to no one in particular. She is too young to know the word *majestic*, but from that moment she compares everything to the effortless rippling of muscle under skin, and finds it inadequate.

She was born in 1986, the Year of the Tiger, the Fire Tiger. These things happen for a reason.

The knowledge of her true form has been with Feli so long, she's stopped noticing how it flavours her life. In the shower, glass walls thick with fog, she imagines the water streaming down fur instead of pale, spotty skin. Breakfast—eggs and kaya toast—tastes like cardboard, like tree bark: she wants fresh meat, she wants heft she can tear into, she wants to drink lightly salted blood and not kopi, scalding and bitter. Walking to the train station, the cadence of her arms and legs falls into a feline rhythm, propelling her past the other commuters. Phantom muscles move under her skin, unhobble her from the limitations humanity picked up when it split from its mammalian ancestors. She read that on the Internet.

Robert from IT talks to her at work. He always talks to her at work. A Chinese man with a soft belly and a hairline wearing thin in the middle, he somehow manages to find time in his morning to hover over the semi-partitions of her cubicle, stringing together words that she makes monosyllabic replies to. In her first weeks on the job one of the ladies, a generic over-powdered law clerk who had moved on a few months later, had told her: "He only talks to you because you're single." That had been five years ago, when she'd still had her toes dipped in her twenties. Five years later, nothing much has changed, except the size of her trousers and Robert's bald patch. It's not that she finds him unpleasant. But Robert is like a wolf to her, strange and canine: she has no use for his loping gait and pricked ears and readily wagging tail.

He tries to ask her if she's doing anything tonight, without actually ever asking. She gives noncommittal replies without ever saying no. Her voice rumbles low as she says, "Robert, you know month-ends are very busy for Accounting," and her throat tickles, as if there's something stuck in it, like the flexible hyoid bone of big cats that allows them to roar where domestic cats cannot. The sound she wants to unleash would send this entire open-concept office scampering. Scaring Robert isn't worth that.

At night she brings the bag of feed down to the void deck. As she spills it on a spread of newsprint, the neighbourhood cats come up and rub against her legs, one after another, like subjects paying respects to their queen. She beckons to their de facto leader, the green-eyed orange moggie, who leaps into her lap and stretches. These times, with the weight of cat in her lap and the smell of fur against her skin, are the realest parts of her day. She purrs and growls as they swarm around her, their eyes glittering sparks. They will eat only after she leaves.

Her friends ask her sometimes why she doesn't keep a cat, doesn't invite one of the strays she loves so much into her home. But she looks at the eyes burning in the dusk and she knows that she could never inflict that on them.

The moggie in her lap rumbles, the closest it can manage to a roar. "One day," she says. "One day they'll stop asking."

It's funny how time slips past, in between the chunks of work and sleep and feeding the cats, and days roll into weeks roll into months and years. Feli continues the motions of getting up every morning and eating her cardboard breakfast and compressing herself on the way to work and back. The surface of calm she presents to the world hides the fearful symmetry she keeps in the roiling deep.

The Lunar New Year comes around in an explosion of reds and golds, showers of drums and cymbals and recordings of the sound of firecrackers. Smiling relatives hide pot bellies in starched shirts and wrinkles in extra layers of makeup, passing around sweet, sour, salty, deep-fried excuses for affection in little plastic bottles with red screw-on lids. Years of going through these obligations have dulled the stabs of pain in Feli's neck and shoulders that these reunions cause. She has learned to suppress her flight instincts, to put on a sickle-cell smile when asked the tickbox questions she gets every year.

But this year the aunts and uncles leave her alone for the star of the exhibit, swarming around the younger sister who ripens like a fruit, peppering her with questions. About the new house, how big, the due date, did they know the sex? Her sister, with big veiny feet and hair swept into a loose homely bun, entertains them with toothy laughs and fluid sweeps of her straight white arms.

Feli feels pity for her and the comfort she feels. It's the same pity she feels when she looks at the dull faces of the office workers who surround her on morning commutes. Her sister will never know what it's like to be free, will never know the sensation of running in the night, will never know the pleasure of growling low and feeling it deep in the lungs.

Feli wonders about the child growing in her sister's belly. It, too, will be born in the Year of the Tiger. Will it be like its Auntie Feli? Impossible. And *Auntie Feli*. What an ugly collection of syllables.

Her mother stands with her sister, glowing, looking younger than her sixty years. Afterwards, after the yu sheng has been tossed, her father speaks to her on the sidelines, as the bulk of the family gather around the television with disposable plates of the mess. Tells her how they are thinking of selling the flat, her mother and he, downgrading to one of those three-room flats. She's turning thirty-six and now she's finally eligible to buy government flats as a singleton, and there were a few public launches coming up with studio apartments, weren't there?

Cornered, she can only nod mutely, her hands flexing and unflexing. She can't imagine a house, its confines suffocating her, weighing her down like a brick. She looks out of the window. Leaping away would be easier. Vanish into the night.

Her parents are bothered because she hardly goes out anymore. She comes home right after work on weekdays (to feed the cats) and stays in most weekends (because she feels too lazy to go out cycling anymore and the board gaming sessions have become tedious). They invite her to their movie nights, try to get her interested in whatever's on the television, as if that would settle the wild bones rattling inside her.

She talks to Andy. "It's that Blake poem," she says, "I keep seeing and hearing it everywhere. Sometimes at work, I'll see the words on my spreadsheet instead of numbers."

Andy was the only one who hadn't laughed when Feli had told her the truth back in school. The sunlight catches in her hair as she leans back into the grass of the Botanic Gardens. "Is it just the poem bothering you?"

"Everything is bothering me. I have dreams every night now. I feel like, I don't know, something's about to burst out of me. Like it's getting harder to hold it back."

"You're just getting more in sync with your true self. Becoming one with the tiger." Andy's fingers flutter. She likes animals, draws pictures of half-human creatures with animal heads, and talks about herself as though she were a lynx. Sometimes, listening to Andy babble on like a shopping mall water feature, she thinks they could have taken their friendship to a different level, if she hadn't ignored Andy's advances. But Andy peppers their text conversations with nuggets like *flattens ears* and *offers sympathy paw*, and each one grates under the skin like badly fitting joints. Such things should be kept private; broadcasting them to the world is crass. Shameless.

No, Andy understands, but she doesn't understand. Feli smiles and stretches beside her, focusing on the smell of the grass, the sunlight warming her belly. The turmoil she has to keep inside herself. It's like smothering a forest fire with a second-hand blanket.

She knows something is wrong even before she pads into the senior partner's cubicle. It's the small hushes that have been descending in pockets of the office, the subtle shunting of emails and duties in the weeks before, the pow-wows that see upper management cloistered in one of their mahogany-lined rooms. Even Robert hadn't come by that morning.

The firm is run by two men, an older and a younger partner. She can talk to the older one, Yong Chew, a grandfatherly figure who sees reason and could be persuaded. But it is Walter, the younger partner, who wants to see her. He has a face like a marble sculpture, blank alien eyes. Her hands curve as she sits down, a curling motion playing at her lips.

"There's no good way to say this," Walter begins.

"Am I being fired?"

A soft huff comes out of Walter as he leans back in his chair. "Well, if we're going to be so direct."

Rushing heat spreads from her stomach to her fingertips, crackling softly. "I am being fired."

Walter sighs. Feli's predator gaze focuses on the lines under his eyes, and the grey in his hair that hadn't been there when she had started in the job. She feels sorry for him then, sorry for a life that is hollowing him out from the inside. "You know we've been trying to cut costs in the last few months. Times are tough. We need to downsize, it's the only way." Walter clears his throat. "It was a difficult decision, but the Accounting Department was one of the areas we identified. And we, uh, we made a decision."

"I understand." If they had to pick one person to keep, it would not be her. It would never be her, this ill-fitting, elusive thing.

He leans forward, his face and demeanour telegraphing sorrow. "Nobody wants this, Felicia."

"Felicity."

Walter's eyes flicker downwards. She rises to her feet, hands crouched on the table for support. "I'll pack my things."

The house is dark. Feli sits on the edge of the bed, soaked in sweat, imagining a stone sinking to the bottom of the ocean, the glow of its burn fading as it descends into a watery grave. She is afraid to sleep, afraid that when she closes her eyes she will be irreversibly pulled into a chasm at the bottom of the ocean, filled with the sideways glances of her colleagues and Robert's wilting look and her parents' concerned eyes.

So she stares straight ahead. Down, down, down she sinks.

Felicity, the girl, is burning away, sloughing off in ashy bits that fall away into the water. There wasn't much left of her to begin with, she thinks, from a distance. She feels her human body get up and move towards the door, and she realizes this is instinct: like a caterpillar knowing when it's time to find a branch and become the butterfly it's meant to be. Her strides are long and lazy as she slips out of the front door, naked as the day she was born, feet padding across bare concrete and warm, unwashed lift landing tiles.

It is time.

Soon, she will be walking these grounds in a new body, four hundred pounds of flesh and power, great heart beating, fearsome mind burning with the fire of a hundred furnaces. She will cover a thousand paces in one bound, nobody to stop her or tell her where to go. It will be deadly. It will be terrible.

Downstairs she goes, into the deserted void deck, hair spilling over shoulders, hands held out. The lights flicker and extinguish with a hissing sound as she passes them by, plunging the space into sequential darkness. In the inkiness pairs of eyes glint, reflecting moonlight, pupils blown. Her flock has come to her, mouths open and mewing. The orange moggie pushes to the forefront, eyes expectant.

It is time.

She gets down on her hands and knees. "I'm here," she whispers. But the sound comes out as a long, high noise. The topography of her throat is changing, the genetic material fluttering and resetting into another pattern. As a child she had watched the National Day Parade, how groups of dancers would change one picture into another by flipping coloured boards, exposing the underside, exposing the other nature. The boards of her physical self are changing. Her bones are compressing. Her skin is changing. She crouches on the ground as the wave of boards sweeps over her.

It is time.

The gathered cats fall silent and still.

Claws click on the ground. No more tangly fingers. She stretches and a tail flicks behind her, a strange and new sensation. A pleasing one.

Yet something seems wrong. The feel of her muscles is nothing like in her dreams.

She opens her eyes, her freshly shaped eyes, and everything is crisper, more alive—and looming. Walls tower above her. The green plastic dustbin in the corner looks like the Incredible Hulk, an impossible mass she will never be able to jump on top of, much less knock over. She stretches forward, and delicate, sienna paws come into view, striped gently with white.

The orange moggie looks at her, pleased.

She opens her mouth, pushes air through her larynx, tiny chest constricting—instead of a roar, there is a meow. The lump in her throat, the hyoid bone, is small and stiff and makes little noises. Meow. Meow. In the glittering eyes of the orange moggie with its tail-flicks she sees a lifetime of stalking through gutters, fighting with rats, and finding quiet spots under stairs to nap.

This is it. This is who she is. Not a dread terror of the night, but a small supple being that slips through the cracks like water. She jumps on the spot, once—twice—experimentally: her back arches and her feet have a wondrous spring to them. How light and free she is, with her new sight and ears sharp as bowls.

The cats around her meow their welcome.

The orange moggie comes close and brushes slightly past her. No more ear-rubs; they are equals now. She purrs briefly, then springs away. She understands their new code, the code of the cat, where boundaries are both protection and respect.

The gathered felines spring away into the night, dispersing in a thousand directions like a firework. She joins them. Behind her, the lights of the void deck flutter back to life, casting their mottled shadows over the blank space where the girl used to be. She doesn't look back.

THE DUCK
Ben Loory

A converted screenwriter, Ben Loory has published two collections of short stories, *Stories for Nighttime and Some for the Day* and *Tales of Falling and Flying*, and a children's book, *The Baseball Player and the Walrus*. *Stories for Nighttime* was both a fall selection of the Barnes & Noble Discover Great New Writers program and an August selection of the Starbucks Bookish Reading Club. His stories have appeared in the *New Yorker*, Weekly Reader's *READ* magazine, and *Fairy Tale Review*. He has an MFA in screenwriting and teaches at UCLA Extension. He has also appeared on *This American Life*.

Like "The Duck," Loory's stories are fantasy written in an unusually idiosyncratic voice, where simple words and phrases seem to pile up, almost at random, until something resembling a story for (very odd) children begins to emerge.

A duck fell in love with a rock. It was a large rock—about the size of a duck, actually—that was situated off the bank of the river a little past the old elm. Every day after lunch the duck would saunter off to admire the rock for a while.

Where are you going? said the other ducks.

Nowhere, said the duck. Just around.

But the other ducks knew exactly where he was going and they all laughed at him behind his back.

Stupid duck is in love with a rock, they sniggered. Wonder what kind of ducklings they will have.

But there was one duck—a girl duck—who did not laugh. She had known the strange duck for a long time, and had always found him to be a good and decent bird. She felt sorry for him; it was hard luck to fall in love with a rock. She wanted to help, but what could she do? She trailed after the duck and watched him woo the rock from behind a tree.

I love you, the duck was saying. I love you I love you I love you. I love you more than the stars in the sky, I love you more than the fish in the river, I love you more than . . . more than. . . .

There he stopped, for he could think of nothing else that existed.

Life itself? said the girl duck from behind the tree. She hadn't meant to pipe up. The words just sort of leapt out of her.

The duck spun around to look at her. He was terrified.

It's okay, said the girl duck, waddling out from behind the tree. I know you're in love with the rock. In fact, everyone knows.

They do? said the duck.

Yes, said the girl duck. Yes, they do.

The duck sighed and sat down on the ground. If he had had hands, he would have buried his head in them.

What am I going to do? he said. What am I going to do?

Do? the girl duck said.

How can it go on like this? said the duck. I love a thing that cannot speak, cannot move, cannot . . . I don't even know how it feels about me!

The girl duck looked at the rock. She didn't know what to say.

I know, said the duck. You think I'm crazy. You think it's just a rock. But it isn't just a rock; it's different. It's very different.

He looked at the rock.

But something has to happen, he said, and soon. Because my heart will break if this goes on much longer.

That night the girl duck had a hard time sleeping. She kept paddling around in circles, thinking about the rock and the duck and his heart that might break. She thought long and hard, and before morning she had an idea. She went and woke up the strange duck.

Things happen when they must, she said, as if it were an extremely meaningful statement.

So? said the duck.

So I have a plan, said the girl duck. And I think that it will work.

Well what is it? said the duck, nearly bursting with excitement.

We will need help, said the girl duck, and it will take some time. And also we will need a cliff.

Two days later they set out. It took four ducks to carry the rock. They worked in teams and traded off every fifteen minutes. Everyone joined in, even though they'd laughed, for ducks are all brothers when it comes right down to it.

The cliff is over that hill and then quite a ways to the south, said the most elderly duck. I remember flying over it when I was a fledgling. It looked like the edge of the world.

The ducks trudged on under their rocky weight for hours—for hours, and then for days. At night they camped under hedges and strange trees and ate beetles and frogs.

Do you think it will be much farther? said one of the ducks.

Maybe, said the oldest duck. My memory is not so good anymore.

On the sixth day, the ducks began to tire.

I don't believe there is a cliff, said one of them.

Me neither, said another. I think the old duck is crazy.

My back hurts, said a third duck. I want to go home.

Me too, said a fourth. In fact, I'm going to.

And then all the ducks began to turn for home. The rock fell to the forest floor and lay there.

The strange duck looked imploringly at the girl duck.

Don't worry, she said, I won't leave you.

They watched all the other ducks flee homeward, and then they hoisted the rock onto their backs and trudged on.

What do you think will happen when we throw it off the cliff? said the duck.

I don't know, said the girl duck. I just know it will be something.

Finally they came to the edge of the cliff. The drop-off was so great they couldn't see the ground—just great white clouds spread out before them like an endless rolling cotton blanket.

It looks so soft, said the duck.

Yes it does, said the girl duck. Are you ready?

The duck looked at the rock.

This is it, my love, he said. The moment of truth. And whatever happens, please remember—always remember—I love you.

And the two ducks hurled the rock off the cliff together.

At first the rock simply fell. Like a rock, one might say. Like a stone.

But then something began to happen. It began to slow, it began to grow, it began to change. It narrowed, it elongated—and it also spread sideways.

It's becoming a bird, the girl duck said.

And it was. It was becoming a beautiful gray bird—really not that unlike a duck. Its wings began to move slowly up and down, up and down, and it dove down and then coasted up. It looked back over its

shoulder at the two ducks on the cliff, and it called out just once—
Goodbye! And then it was going, going, getting smaller and smaller,
flying off, over the blanket, across the sky.

The ducks did not speak much on the way home.
  Do you think it will be happy? said the duck.
  I hope so, said the girl duck, and that was all.
  They really didn't say any more.

When they reached the pond, the other ducks gathered around and
clamored to hear what had happened. The duck and the girl duck
glanced at each other.
  Nothing, said the girl duck. It fell.

In the days that followed, the duck stayed to himself. The girl duck
went and swam around in circles. She thought about that rocky bird
flying off into the sky; she saw it over and over in her mind.
  And then one day, not too many days later, she looked and saw the
duck come swimming up. He was carrying a small salamander in his
bill.
  For me? the girl duck said.
  And the duck smiled.

WING
Amal El-Mohtar

Amal El-Mohtar is a Canadian author of more than twenty stories of science fiction and fantasy and edits the poetry magazine *Goblin Fruit*. *The Honey Month*, a short collection of her stories, was published by the fine-arts publisher Papaveria Press in 2011 and republished the following year by Ann and Jeff VanderMeer's Cheeky Frawg Books. She won the Locus Award in 2015 for her story "The Truth About Owls" and three Rhysling Awards for her poetry, in 2009, 2011, and 2014. She has also been nominated for the Nebula, World Fantasy, and Aurora awards. Her stories have appeared in *Shimmer, Strange Horizons, Lackington's, Lightspeed, Uncanny*, and most recently *The Starlit Wood: New Fairy Tales*. She lives in Ottawa.

"Wing" is a story about the idiosyncratic meaning of books and those who read them. It first appeared in *Strange Horizons* in 2013 and was reprinted in Rose Lemberg's anthology *An Alphabet of Embers* with illustrations by M. Sereno.

In a cafe lit by morning, a girl with a book around her neck sits quietly at a table.

She reads—not the book around her neck, which is small, only as long and as wide as her thumb, black cord threaded through a sewn leather spine, knotted shut. She reads a book of maps and women, turns every page as if it were a lock of hair, gently. Every so often, her fingers stray to the book that sits above her sternum, twist it one way, then the other; every so often, she sips her tea.

"What is written in your book?" asks the man who brought her the tea. She looks up.

It is said, she reads, *that a map drawn on a virgin's skin creates a land on the other side of the moon. Whole civilisations rise, whole empires are built in the time it takes for bath water and scented soap to tear its minarets down, smash its aqueducts, strike its flying machines from the star-sewn sky. This is likely nonsense, but as no one has been to the other side of the moon, it remains entirely possible.*

The man blushes, then frowns. "That's nice," he says, "but I meant in *your* book. The one you wear. What is written there?"

The girl's lashes touch her cheeks. "A secret."

He opens his mouth to ask another question, then shuts it. He walks away.

The girl with the book around her neck sits quietly beneath a chestnut tree.

She reads a book with a halved pomegranate on the cover, a wasp stamping its black feet in the juice. She turns every page as if she were lifting a veil, delicately. The sun is bright against the paper, makes the words swim green against her eyes.

Another girl comes by, her hair curly, her step light. She wears a bag over one shoulder, and sits down near the girl with the book around her neck. She smiles. The girl with the book around her neck smiles back. The girl with the bag pulls out a loaf of bread, a wedge of cheese, a small jar of amber honey, and a knife; she begins to slice, to pair, to drizzle honey on the lot.

"What are you reading?" she asks, curious.

Once, reads the girl, *only once, for never has this happened since, nor is it likely to, a bird lit down on the head of a young man seated beneath a peach tree. The bird's plumage was most fine, smooth as linen, bright as the afternoon sun drinking garden petals. The man could not gaze at it, but sat very still, so as not to disturb it; he closed his eyes, for even the barest flash of tail or pinion as it shifted about his scalp was painful to him,* was too beautiful for his gaze. The bird whispered in his ear the secret to immortality, which involved the consumption of nectar, the building of a fire, and the bathing of his limbs in a sacred pool. So deep was the young man's gratitude, so fierce was his love for the beautiful creature perched on his head, that his heart burst in his chest and he died on the spot.

The girl with the bag, who had begun to chew her honeyed cheese and bread, coughs a little as she laughs. She wipes her mouth modestly and offers the girl with the book around her neck a morsel of her own. She accepts it, and they munch together in silence. Then, as they are rubbing their fingers together to clean the honey from them, the girl with the bag asks, "What is written in the book around your neck?"

She blushes. "A secret."

"Oh," says the other girl. They spend a few more moments together, before the girl with the bag gathers up her effects, bids the girl with the book around her neck a kind farewell, and goes on her way.

The girl with the book around her neck sits quietly on a jutting rock by the sea.

The sea is not quiet; the sea is an angry choir of dissonant voices, all taking turns striking their rage against the shore. The waves curl foamy fingers towards the rocks, smash their delicate salt bones to glass. Everywhere is a fine damp mist.

The girl has no book to hand. She pulls back the left sleeve of her raincoat, dips her fingers into a tidal pool, lifts a mixture of sand and clay from it, and tries to draw a map on her skin.

It is not thick enough; the wet sand will not make lines, only prickle her as it winds its way along her forearm. She pulls her sleeve back down. She looks out at the sea, at the gulls mewling, the crows cawing, and tries to think of a song.

A boy approaches the rock on which she sits. He looks up at her. She looks down at him.

He wears a raincoat too, grey as the sea, and a dark blue scarf around his neck to keep the damp from his throat. It is sensible; she does the same. They look at each other a long moment.

Then he says, "Would you like to hear a story?"

She nods.

"It is said that once every five hundred and sixty-three days, two people will walk on the beach with matching raincoats. It is further said that every one thousand one hundred and twenty-six days, these people will have matching shoes. But it is rare as a bird with feathers linen-smooth, rare as a city on the dark side of the moon, that they will both wear books around their necks, and rarer still that those books will hold secrets."

"Come up," whispers the girl to the boy with a book around his neck. "Come up here."

He does, with his hands to the rock, his shoes like hers, his coat like hers. He unbuttons the collar, unwinds the scarf from his neck. There is a book there, the same length and width as hers, black cord threaded through its sewn leather spine, knotted shut. He reaches for the knot with slender fingers.

"Wait," she says, "wait." She unbuttons her collar, unwinds her scarf, bares her own book for the opening, bites her lip as she looks at him. "Are you sure?"

"I want to tell you a secret," he says, firm.

They open their books. They turn every page as if touching each other's cheeks. They read the same word, the only word, buried in each book's deepest heart, nestled up against its sewn leather spine, behind its knotted ribs.

When the tide comes in, it finds a clutch of soft grey feathers sticking to the rocks, spilling from the pages of two tiny books with no words in them. The tide yawns; it licks them like a cat; it tangles the black cord that threads them, knots them together, and swallows them into the sea.

THE PHILOSOPHERS
Adam Ehrlich Sachs

Adam Ehrlich Sachs published his debut collection, *Inherited Disorders: Stories, Parables & Problems*, featuring 117 short stories and vignettes about the often strange relationships between fathers and sons, in 2016. He studied atmospheric science at Harvard, where he wrote for the *Harvard Lampoon*. He lives in Pittsburgh, Pennsylvania.

"The Philosphers" was originally published in the *New Yorker*, before being included in his debut collection. It comprises three of Sachs's offbeat stories about fathers and sons.

Our System

A philosopher had spent his lifetime pondering the nature of knowledge and was ready at long last to write down his conclusions. He took out a sheet of white paper and a pen. But he noticed, upon lifting the pen, a slight tremor in his hand. Hours later he was diagnosed with a neuromuscular disorder that promptly began ravaging his body, though apparently, according to the doctor, not his mind.

He lost the use of his muscles one by one, first in his fingers, then in his toes, then in his arms, then in his legs. Soon he could only whisper weakly and flutter his right eyelid. Just before losing his power of speech entirely, he designed with his son's help a system by which he could communicate, through twitches and blinks, the letters of the alphabet.

Then the philosopher fell silent.

He and his son embarked upon the writing of his book on knowledge. The father blinked or twitched his right eye; the son wrote down the corresponding letter. Progress was extraordinarily slow. After twenty years, they had written a hundred pages. Then, one morning, when the son picked up the pen, he noticed a slight tremor in his hand. He was diagnosed with the same neuromuscular disorder as his father—it was, naturally, hereditary—and began losing the use of his muscles, too. Soon he could only whisper weakly and manipulate his tongue. He and his own son designed a system by which he could communicate, by tapping his teeth with his tongue, the letters of the alphabet, and then he, too, fell silent.

The writing continued, though the pace, already indescribably slow, slowed even further. The grandfather blinked or twitched his right eyelid, his son tapped a tooth with his tongue, and the grandson wrote down the corresponding letter. After another twenty years, they had written another ten pages on the nature of knowledge.

One morning, the grandson noticed a slight tremor in his hand. He knew instantly what it meant. He didn't even bother getting the diagnosis. His final surviving muscle was his left eyebrow, and by raising or lowering it just so he could communicate letters to his son. Again the pace slowed by an order of magnitude. The opportunities for error multiplied. Then his son was stricken, then his son's son, then his son's son's son, and then his son's son's son's son, who is my father.

We cram into our ancestral sickroom. It is dark and cold: we keep the blinds lowered and the heat down owing to our hereditary light sensitivity and our hereditary heat intolerance, both of which are in fact unrelated to our hereditary neuromuscular disorder. Someone tries to cough but cannot. I sit at the desk and await the next letter, which can take months to arrive. The philosopher blinks or twitches his right eyelid; his son taps a tooth with his tongue; his son raises or lowers his left eyebrow; his son sucks on his upper or lower lip; his son flares a nostril; my grandfather blinks or twitches his left eyelid; my father taps a tooth with his tongue; and I write down the letter. In the past eleven years I've written down the following: CCCONCEPP TCCCCCAAAAACCCCCCCCCCPPCCCCCCPCCCCCCCPC CCCCCC

What to make of this? Perhaps the philosopher has lost his mind. Perhaps there's been a disruption in our system of twitches and blinks and tooth-tapping and lip-sucking by which a letter is transmitted from his head to my pen. Perhaps—I certainly don't rule this out!—I have lost *my* mind: perhaps no matter what my father taps I see only "C"s, and the occasional "P." Or perhaps our system works perfectly, our philosopher's mind works perfectly, his theory of knowledge reaches the page just as he intends it, and I simply do not have the wherewithal to understand it. That, too, cannot be ruled out.

A letter is now coming my way. The old men grimace and suck, twitch and tap, blink and blow. My son, here to watch, looks on with pity and terror, still not sure how all this relates to him. He hates being in this room. You should see how eagerly at the end of the day he kisses his ancestors and races out ahead of me into the hall.

Two Hats

The son of the late philosopher-mystic Perelmann, who was writing a biography of his father, used to say at our weekly brown-bag colloquiums that he wore two hats: that of Perelmann's son and that of his biographer. We assumed that this was just a figure of speech until a graduate student who happened to be renting an apartment across the street from him told us that he really wore two *physical hats*: the son-of-Perelmann hat was a Boston Red Sox cap, and the biographer-of-Perelmann hat was a brown fedora. Some evenings he wore the Red Sox cap, some evenings he wore the brown fedora, and some evenings he went back and forth, more or less rapidly, between the cap and the fedora.

Word circulated, and before long the chair of the department knocked on Perelmann's son's office door. The chair urged him to take some time off, please, for his own sake.

"Bill," said Perelmann's son with a knowing smile. "Is this about the hats?"

The chair admitted that he was concerned.

"Bill," said Perelmann's son again, touching the chair's wrist. "Don't worry about me. I'm not going crazy, at least not yet! The hats serve a purely functional purpose."

It looked silly, he knew, but the hats helped him keep separate his two conflicting roles—first as a son still grieving for his dad, second as a scholar trying to understand, to historicize, and, yes, to critique, as dispassionately as possible, his father's ideas. Before hitting upon the two-hat system, he'd lived in a state of perpetual self-reproach: when he thought of Perelmann in the way that a son thinks of his dad, the scholar in him condemned his lack of objectivity, and when he thought of Perelmann in the way that a scholar thinks of his subject, the son in him condemned his lack of loyalty.

The hats put an end to all that.

When he pulled on the old Red Sox cap, its snug fit and familiar smell had a Proustian effect. He was returned to the grandstands of Fenway Park, beside his father. He was suffused with compassion and pity, with respect, love, and acceptance—for his father's flaws no less than for his virtues. He wanted to annihilate his father's academic detractors and slaughter those who would attempt to understand him as a product of his milieu. Such was the effect of the Red Sox cap. But under the weight of the brown fedora, beneath its sober brim, he could put aside his childish devotion and scrutinize his father's thought with the skepticism required of an intellectual historian. He investigated the genealogy of his father's ideas, examined their internal consistency, considered their presuppositions and limitations.

"Bill, I admit it's a strange system!" said Perelmann's son, laughing. "That what happens *in* our heads should be so affected by what happens *on top of* our heads. But, for me, this does seem to be the case." He shrugged. "It helps me proceed. I do not question it."

The department chair went away intensely impressed, even moved. Word went around that Perelmann's son was not crazy but brilliant.

At our next brown-bag colloquium, Perelmann's son claimed to wear "four hats." He was Perelmann's son, Perelmann's biographer, Perelmann's philosophical interlocutor, and Perelmann's estate executor.

The following morning, the graduate student reported that two new hats, a black bowler and a purple yarmulke, had entered the rotation. From what he'd seen, he hypothesized that the bowler was the executor hat and the yarmulke was the interlocutor hat. Perelmann's son had spent most of the early evening going calmly back and forth between the Red Sox cap and the bowler. At around eight o'clock, the yarmulke had gone on and stayed on until just after nine. From then until midnight, he'd frantically switched among the yarmulke, the Red Sox cap, and the brown fedora. He had ended the night with forty-five relatively relaxed minutes in the black bowler.

"I'm fine, Bill!" said Perelmann's son, touching the chair's wrist. "How can I summon memories of my father one minute, and deal with his taxes the next? Impossible, unless I *physically put on the bowler hat.* One minute I'm recalling the sensation of being up on his shoulders, the next I'm attacking his peculiar interpretation of Kant? *The purple yarmulke.* Who taught him this idiosyncratic Kant, and when? *Brown fedora.*"

By the next colloquium, Perelmann's son wore sixteen hats. He was Perelmann's son, Perelmann's biographer, Perelmann's philosophical interlocutor, Perelmann's estate executor, Perelmann's publicist, Perelmann's usurper, Perelmann's housekeeper, Perelmann's zealot, Perelmann's annihilator, Perelmann's designated philosophical heir,

Perelmann's defector, Perelmann's librarian, Perelmann's gene carrier, Perelmann's foot soldier, Perelmann's betrayer, and Perelmann's doppelgänger. Twelve new hats joined the repertoire, including a beret, a bandana, a small straw hat, and a sombrero.

Naturally, we were a little alarmed. His evenings, the graduate student reported, were now mere blurs of hat transitions. Nothing stayed on his head for long. But reality, we assumed, would sooner or later impose a limit on his mania. There are only so many kinds of hats, just as there are only so many relations that can possibly obtain between a father and a son. In due course Perelmann's son would run out of either hats or relations, we thought—probably hats—and thereafter he would return to reason.

But soon there were relations we had never considered, hats we'd never heard of. He was Perelmann's old-Jewish-joke repository, Perelmann's voice impersonator, Perelmann's sweater wearer, the last living practitioner of Perelmann's skiing technique, Perelmann's surpasser, Perelmann's victim. He wore an eighteenth-century tricorne, a deerstalker, a round Hasidic kolpik, an Afghan pakol with a peacock feather tucked into its folds.

By the end of the fall semester we knew something had to be done. The explosion of hats and relations had not abated. Left alone, we realized, Perelmann's son would partition his relationship with his father ad infinitum, and for each infinitesimal slice of relationship he would purchase a hat. Ultimately he would turn his relationship with his father—by nature, one simple thing—into something infinitely complex, for no discernible reason, and his hat collection would, correspondingly, grow without bound, and he would wind up destroying himself. His analytical tendency, along with the huge hat collection that resulted from it, would obliterate him.

So, one morning, in an attempt to save Perelmann's son from himself, a group of graduate students and junior faculty members slipped, with the department chair's blessing, into Perelmann's son's apartment. (He was at a Perelmann conference.) We gathered all the hats and put them in garbage bags—a hundred and twenty-eight hats in twelve garbage bags—and got them out of there.

But in our hearts we must have known that we were treating the symptom, not the cause. Yesterday, according to our informant, Perelmann's son spent all day and all night in a ten-gallon hat of thus far unknown paternal associations.

The Madman's Time Machine

On the coldest night of the year, a madman was taken to Boston Medical Center with third-degree frostbite. Police had found him under an overpass, naked in a cardboard box. Scrawled on the box in black Magic Marker were the words: "TIME MACHINE."

Oddly, the frostbitten madman was jubilant.

Until recently, he told the psychiatrist assigned to him, he had been the most intelligent person in history, smarter even than Einstein ("if only by a little bit") and Newton ("if only by a little bit"). But his historic intelligence had been a curse.

"Being able to perceive the true nature of everything instantly is actually awful," he told the psychiatrist. He had grown bored and lonely. The moment that he initiated a thought, he reached its logical terminus. "At some point," he said, "there is just nothing left to think. Meanwhile, everyone else is back there at the first principles, the assumptions, the postulates."

He had investigated the great problems of cosmology but solved them immediately. In May, he ended metaphysics. He turned to the nature of time, which he hoped would divert his mind for at least a few weeks, but it revealed itself to him in an afternoon. Once again he was bored and lonely. So he built the time machine.

"That right there?" the psychiatrist asked, gesturing at the cardboard box, which the madman had refused to relinquish.

"*That*," the madman said with a strange smile, "is merely a cardboard box."

The real time machine, he said, was obviously much more complicated, and was obviously made entirely, or almost entirely, out of metal. For a while it had relieved his boredom. He visited the recent past, then the near future, then the distant past, and then the remote future. He sought out the company of his fellow-geniuses. He discussed gravity with Galileo and buoyancy with Archimedes. He brought Fermat to the near future and ate future bagels, which are "much puffier and much more moist," according to the madman, than the bagels of today. He met one of the most important thinkers of the remote future, a mammoth reptilian creature with an unpronounceable name, and took him back in time to meet Louis XIV, the so-called Sun King. This meeting, the madman said, was "incredibly awkward."

Soon the madman had talked to everyone worth talking to, seen everything worth seeing, thought about everything worth thinking about, and yet again was left bored and lonely. Even the company of geniuses was not enough; boredom would always be with him, he realized, as long as he had this huge, historic intelligence. Suicide was the only way out. He decided to commit suicide by paradox. He would go back in time and kill his own grandfather—a logical impossibility, as we all know, he said, since killing his grandfather would mean that he himself wouldn't be born, which would mean that he couldn't go back in time to kill his grandfather. So this might be interesting, he said. Plus he would get to murder the man who had handed down to him this huge, horrible, historic intelligence.

The madman set his time machine for 1932 Berlin, where his grandfather was a promising Expressionist painter. He materialized in his grandfather's studio carrying a gun. "*Nein!*" his grandfather yelled, raising his paintbrush, the madman told the psychiatrist. "*Nein!*" He aimed his pistol. His grandmother ran in. "*Nein!*" she said, according to the madman. *"Nein! Nein!"* He fired into his grandfather's chest and the promising Expressionist painter fell over dead.

But the madman didn't disappear. Nor, he said, did the universe implode.

Was there no paradox after all?

As his sobbing grandmother ran over to his dead grandfather, the madman noticed the slight swell of her belly. Ah! he realized, as he recalled to the psychiatrist. She was already pregnant!

That instant, the madman vanished from the studio and materialized naked under an overpass in the cardboard box labeled "TIME MACHINE." The real time machine was gone. For a moment he was confused. Then everything became terrifically clear. His father had still been born, but now fatherlessly, and his life had gone, instead of well, poorly. Instead of becoming a mathematician, he'd become an underemployed roofer. His son, the madman, had no longer grown up in an intellectual milieu. Instead of becoming brilliant beyond bounds, the madman said with evident relief, he had become stupid, and even a little bit insane. And obviously in this alternate universe he was totally and utterly incapable of building an actual functioning time machine.

"Look at it now!" the madman cried joyfully. "A cardboard box!"

MY TIME AMONG THE BRIDGE BLOWERS

Eugene Fischer

Eugene Fischer studied physics at Trinity University and is a graduate of both the Iowa Writers' Workshop and the Clarion Science Fiction & Fantasy Writers' Workshop in San Diego. His writing has appeared in *Asimov's* and *Strange Horizons*. His 2015 novella "The New Mother" won the James Tiptree, Jr. Award, was awarded second place for the Sturgeon Award, and was nominated for the Nebula Award. As an adjunct professor at the University of Iowa, he created an undergraduate course on writing and reading science fiction. He currently lives in Austin, Texas, where he helped create a science-fiction-writing summer camp for children.

In "My Time Among the Bridge Blowers," Eugene Fischer addresses both the strengths and shortcomings of 19th-century colonial fiction made popular by Rudyard Kipling.

Before I continued my journey south, I took a detour to the tall Gamal Mountains in the west, among whose peaks I was told could be found a still thriving village of one of the rarest and most intriguing of the tribes of man. I reached the foothill town of Reninep by autobus, but once there had to secure a guide and mount one of the animated clay donkeys favored by the local traders for the trip to the village. Mine was an intricately sculpted beast, well named and sure-footed, and, led by my guide Sant, I rode it up the half-abandoned mountain trails with relative ease. (As the temperature dropped with elevation I wrapped myself tightly in the quilt Marta had gifted me, that we had shared during our time together, and thought myself already quite as glad of it as she had prophesied I would come to be.) When the sky began to darken on the first day of our journey, Sant unpacked long, curved poles that fitted into notches in my donkey's sides. Between these poles he strung a net hammock, to allow me to "sleep in the saddle" as my mount marched forward. I was initially terrified at the prospect of being suspended in the air while my donkey trod the steep mountain paths, but my mind was put significantly to rest by the sight of Sant unpacking an identical set of poles for himself—though I did then wonder if it was him or his donkey who was truly leading us! The hammock proved comfortable enough to sleep in, and so we were able to travel near-continuously for the three full days it took to reach the cliff-carved buildings of the village of the Hiatha, known more commonly as the Bridge Blowers.

The Bridge Blowers are mentioned in histories all the way back to the time of Ervil, who described men who went into the mountains and "learned to leap often from the peaks." Though the Hiatha culture is insular, their amazing breath talent has long drawn the attention of outsiders. During the era of Crait imperial expansion, every forward battalion marched with conscripted Hiatha soldiers. It is from this time that we get the folktale of "The Loyal Bridge Blower," in which a large company of soldiers, forced to retreat, find their way blocked by a wide ravine. The Hiatha conscript with them, despite the unfortunate treatment he has received at their hands, kneels at the ravine's edge and breathes firmness into the air so that the company may cross to the other side. The soldiers traverse the long span of open air, supported continuously by the Hiatha's capacity for circular breathing. All of the soldiers make it across the gap, and just as the last sets foot on solid ground, the enemy appears and moves to capture the Bridge Blower. But he is dead, having suffocated himself in the effort to save his comrades.

The story is almost certainly apocryphal, but it is the case that the Hiatha captured the imagination of the Crait Empire, and they became one of the first races subjected to the Empire's assimilationist policies. Thousands of Hiatha were relocated and put into civil service, but the biome dependence which we now know affects so many of the talented races turned out to be especially pronounced among the Hiatha, and the displaced lost their breath abilities within two generations. This is why it was necessary for me to undertake such a detour to seek them out; unlike Marta and her clan of farseers, there are no enclaves of Hiatha to be found in the cities, dimly clinging through the years to the easy talents of their ancestors. The descendants of the assimilated, without their breath, were unable to return to the homes of their parents and grandparents, having lost the vital skill for survival in the mountains. Once there were Hiatha settlements all along the Tarko-Gamal range; now I had to travel for days to see one of the last remaining.

It was the morning of the fourth day when I got my first glimpse of the Hiatha's mountain home. The sun had finally climbed high enough to peek down into the valley from which we ascended. Swaying in my hammock, I peeled Marta's magnificent quilt from my body and called out to Sant again how, fine creature though it surely was, I was getting well tired of my donkey.

Sant was a quiet man, stout and confident with short pewter teeth and a long temper. (Much later in my journey I would learn that Sant was not his real name. A constable in Chennith, listening to my stories, informed me that "Sant" is a default pseudonym in Tarkuin, the name given to incoherent strangers and unidentifiable bodies.) Instead of acknowledging me with a grunt or a nod as had been his usual practice on the mountain paths, this time Sant answered by calling over his shoulder, "Won't now be long."

We stopped to stow my hammock and poles, and then continued up and out of the valley. Finally, we rounded a switchback, and there it was: the ridge we were on curved, and across the chasm of its hollow were unmistakable signs of habitation. Rock cut at right angles, footpaths and terraces, windows and doors. All of it clearly placed by the industrious hand of man. But what variety of man? For even from this distance I could see that the architecture did not display the bottom-to-top linearity of a people whose feet never leave the ground. The will imposed on the rock was an accommodating will; doors were sunk into the stone not always at the ground, but wherever the stone was most yielding. The terrace farms were a constellation about our heads, rather than carpeting any one slope. A tuber and its nearest neighbor might be separated by a half-hour climb . . . or five Hiatha steps. How cruel and thorough was the loss suffered by the relocated Hiatha, once their breath was gone from them. At the edge of vision distant figures moved about their village with a facility no outsider could ever know.

We hadn't gone much farther along the ridge before being spotted. A pair of envoys were sent strolling through the air out to meet us. They were dressed in goat wool clothing, and the taller of the two carried a long pole which I would come to recognize as a weapon: a blowgun from which a Hiatha hunter could fire a stone dart with deadly accuracy. As they approached us I could see their breath clouding in the morning mountain air. It seemed that they took turns supporting each other. One at a time, strange angles danced in the mist around their faces, like no cloud or steam I had ever seen. But it wasn't their amazing talent or their calm suspension above so great an abyss that was sharpest in my mind. I was most struck by their complete lack of tattoos. I was aware, of course, that this was a culture removed from imperial civilization, and when preparing my journey had spent many pleasant, solitary hours contemplating drawn renderings of Bridge Blower women and children in an Expansionist Era folio by Nn. Lozlac. But seeing actual undecorated shoulders and calves and necks, each flex and twitch an expression of bare anatomy, was a shock of the sort for which it is impossible to adequately prepare. The fresh guard sigil above my coccyx, only twelve days old and still semi-wild, began to twist and snarl at the sight of unprotected flesh, and I felt my own mouth water sympathetically.

"What is your business here?" was their first question, Sant told me. Sant was skilled as guide and translator both, and through him I explained myself as a scholar and seeker of knowledge, come to observe and learn the truth of them as a glorious people out of time.

There was some back-and-forth between Sant and the shorter envoy as he worked to communicate my abstract endeavor. He spoke at length, waving back at me several times, and once even opening his purse to display some of the coin I had already paid him. At the end of the exchange the shorter envoy broke into laughter and clapped Sant on the arm, which I took then as an auspicious sign. The tall envoy yoked the tube across his shoulders, hooked his elbows and lazily dangled his hands. The shorter asked me a question, which Sant translated, "What have you brought to trade?"

I answered that I offered an opportunity to have the story of their faded but still extant glory spread to the wider world. Sant conveyed my meaning, and the envoy laughed again, swinging his head and sprinting a short circuit out into the air and back. The taller one maintained his bored expression. Sant spoke more, but it soon resolved that they were unable to see value in the fame I offered. We were informed that the village would offer provisions and a night's hospitality to traders only.

No mention of commercial exchange had been made in any of my texts, nor had the subject been broached by Sant, on whom I relied to have some practical knowledge in those few areas of modern complication I had been unable to research. When I enlisted his services in Reninep, he had been impressed with the extent and depth of the investigations I had conducted into the history of the Hiatha people. I related tale upon tale as I bought us tankards of beer, and found in Sant a most attentive audience. For his part, he said that in his time crossing the Gamal he'd taken many a detour to the Bridge Blower's territory, knew their tongue, and had ever found them an agreeable people. That he should turn out to have such a crucial gap in his knowledge made me suspect then that my generosity had induced him to accept a position for which he was, in truth, underqualified.

Still, Sant was a merchant, and so happened to be quite as well provisioned to engage in trade with the Hiatha as if he did have some foreknowledge of this complication. He began to remove items from his pack: bolts of cloth, steel needles, pouches of spice. The Hiatha envoys examined his goods and engaged in some negotiation before selecting their items. Then they turned expectantly to me.

"Have to pay the toll to get what you came for," said Sant.

I considered what I had to trade. Surely this could not be the purpose for which I was destined to need Marta's quilt; a section of squares in the upper left showed mountains, and human figures silhouetted against the sun, but there were several panels—the shrouded faces, the broken-link chain, the icy feather—whose meanings remained fully opaque. I had not expected to have much use for money, and so left the bulk of my own purse (along with the outstanding half of the fee I'd promised Sant) with a bank in Reninep. All of my other possessions were necessities. I asked Sant if he could not trade for me as well.

"You bought my knowledge, not my wares," he said. A man of business, every bone and bulge of him! And since he knew I'd no choice but to buy, his wares came very dear indeed. I did attempt negotiation, but he rebuffed me with his constant, implacable calm. In the end he got out pen and paper, and I wrote him a promissory note for the full, exorbitant amount. I rubbed the signatory tattoo on my forearm to weeping, seared the paper, and fairly felt my pockets lighten as I handed the sheet back to him. The envoys seemed amused by the whole ordeal. Sant allowed them to select more goods, and then they went straight back to their village, while we resumed the more circuitous route. As my donkey bumped along the path, I lamented that I would have only a single day among the Hiatha. It would be impossible, in such a small portion of time, to connect deeply with these strangers. In one day, and without a shared language, it seemed unlikely I would be afforded the easy and pleasurable companionship I had so recently received among Marta's clan.

As we approached the village, though, my disappointment gave way to amazement. Never had I seen such a landscape. Viewed up close, the Hiatha settlement was a place where domesticated land abutted wilderness snug as tiles in a mosaic. Raw, untamed crags were interrupted by small patches of farmland, hospitable order that abruptly gave way again to jagged brutality. The terrain was far too rough for aqueducts, but there was no need for them; the Hiatha could situate their terraces in natural spillways. Scratching out life here was palpably impossible, save for people able to make ground from air. As I watched them moving from patch to patch above my head, I was reminded of a Hiatha legend—perhaps contemporaneous with our own tales of the wildersurge—in which a plague of beetles swarms the mountain peaks. They crawl into every crevice and decimate the crops. The Hiatha are able to survive only by building a breath-supported field of soil for their seeds, a place the beetles couldn't crawl to. For an entire growing season the town works in shifts to keep the crops aloft, crouching on ridges as beetles swarm over their bodies.

There was a deep cunning within the Hiatha's primitive simplicity. I resolved then to ask if perhaps this was the village from the legend, if the opportunity arose, but I confess it never did.

We reached the village two hours later, and were led to an area that Sant identified as the "youth garden." All around us the mountain was a hive of homes that fronted on the open air. In the youth garden, for the first time, were structures as I was used to recognizing them:

flat ground, freestanding buildings with sensible doors and windows, and a wall around the perimeter to prevent falls. This was the area of the village in which children whose talent had not yet matured could stay safely unattended. It was amusing to think that for all my scholarly erudition, for all that the Hiatha envoys had been scarcely able to understand my purpose, I was in some ways like a child to them. The other children of the garden were playing chase games or working at simple crafts. The oldest I saw was a girl of maybe twelve or thirteen, watching the younger ones run and occasionally tripping them with a whistle. She was charming, even with her bare skin, and I caught her eye, then startled her with a loud whistle of my own. She stumbled at the sound, attempting to dodge a blow that wasn't coming. Her indignant shouts at my trickery were a delight, and made me wish again I had more time to spend. When several of the younger children came over to inspect our donkeys, the whistling girl watched from a distance.

An older man with ashen hair brought us water, and even knew the word for it! When he proffered the skins he said "water" in the common tongue, clear as anything. I thanked him and asked him how it was he had learned to speak to me. Sant rushed over and explained that some Hiatha had picked up snippets of our language over the years from traders. The grey-haired man's face betrayed an impatient expression. "Follow," he said, and led us to a building in the youth garden we could use for rest. Sant immediately unburdened his donkeys and spread his bedroll, seemingly content to nap until it was time to eat. I laid out Marta's quilt, but reminded him that we were here to absorb Bridge Blower culture. Granted only a single day among them, wasting even a minute would be unconscionable. Sant, in response, said something to the grey-haired man which he declined to translate. The man, for his part, began to inquire about our needed provisions. He and Sant discussed the issue, and I wandered back to the garden to resume my immersion in Hiatha daily life.

I found that all of the children were grouped at one edge of the garden, chattering excitedly to one another, hopping and tittering. I looked for the whistling girl, but she was gone. I couldn't see what had aroused the children's interest. I retrieved my two adult companions, and Sant asked the grey-haired man why they were excited. He spoke to the young ones, then explained that it was because a skink had entered the village, and there was to be a hunt.

The Gamal skink was a creature I had seen mention of many times in my studies as I prepared for the trip. They are described as being up to five feet long, with blue tongues, pebbled scales, and the ability to both crawl up sheer cliffs with their powerful claws and use the skin between their digits to glide through the air. There are stories of these large carnivores posing a danger to young children, though none of the children in the garden seemed particularly afraid. Perhaps the thrill of seeing a hunt was more potent than the fear of a monstrous lizard.

The grey-haired man offered to take us to a vantage from which we could observe the hunters more closely. I immediately accepted this offer of a walk across the air with a Bridge Blower. But upon accepting, I had then to find in myself the mental fortitude to go over the wall, when all my instincts said that a step beyond the edge would send me tumbling to a certain death. I closed my eyes and probed with my foot, ignoring the burning alarm from my lower back and trying to let myself believe that there was yet more ground in front of me. I clung to the grey-haired man's elbow as we walked, eyes shut tight, until he squeezed my own arm to let me know that I was, in fact, once more standing on solid land. Sant, as far as I could tell, remained entirely unperturbed by the experience, and settled himself down between two rows of plants.

We were on one of the terrace farms. There were hunters, including the tall envoy we had met earlier, running across the air below us, taking aim at something obscured from our vision by the ridge. Then the skink swept into view, all four feet spread like giant fans as it sailed from one cliff face to the next. It was much, much larger than the books had said. Eight feet long, or perhaps even nine. Certainly larger than any of the people hunting it. It slammed into the cliff with astonishing force, and was instantly scurrying up and back down and around in streaking, sinuous curves. Its tongue—brilliant, jewel-blue—slid in and out of its mouth, and it was trailed by scattered explosions of rock dust from darts fired by the Hiatha hunters.

I observed that the skink was far larger than I had read about in the histories, and the grey-haired man muttered something in response. Sant translated his comment as, "Because we switched places."

I asked for clarification, and, after another exchange with the man, Sant said, "Before the Empire, they were the top here. But the top is the skink now," leaving me more confused than I had been before.

"The apex predator," the grey-haired man said. "When we were more populous, we were the apex predator in this region. But now the skink has assumed that niche." He spoke with a strange accent, but was once again perfectly intelligible to me as he explained that when the Hiatha were more numerous they controlled the skink population, but that now the skinks had grown large, and forgotten their fear of people. He said that the Hiatha no longer hunt them unless they enter the village or seem likely to drive the mountain goats away.

It was clear that the man's fluency encompassed more than snippets. I asked how it was he had gained such a facility with the language, but before the grey-haired man could reply, Sant directed our attention back to the hunt, saying, "Take out a few traders every year, they do. But not this one, I think! Watch now!"

Below us, the Hiatha hunters were moving in ways I had never before imagined. Some of them raced across flat surfaces of air, but others seemed to slide down slopes, or else just fall through the air very slowly, as though sinking through honey. They worked in pairs, one hunter responsible for guiding the path of his partner, and the other tasked with use of the blowgun. The hunters chased the skink back and forth across the chasm, until finally one of them took the beast down in mid-flight. It tumbled limp for a short span before crashing into an invisible butcher's block of air.

"Ever you eaten skink?" asked Sant. "Might now get your chance."

Marta would have said that as prophesy it lacked ambition, but Sant's prediction did prove accurate. And it seemed the prospect of the meal, or perhaps the excitement we had watched, stirred the trader's blood like nothing else. He spoke continuously, of other places he'd been and meals he had eaten, an uncommon rush of recollection that filled the air as the grey-haired man took us across the village again. It was more words in a row than I'd ever heard from him before, and he didn't stop until after we'd been left in another terrace farm, this one shaped like a layered crater in the slope, strongly reminiscent of an amphitheater. A large portion of the tribe was there, having emerged from their homes to share in the unusual meal. The beast was well large enough to go around, and when the preparations were complete some hours later, we eventually received bowls of vegetable mash and boiled skink meat.

Dining on the flesh of a Gamal skink was a novel experience, certainly, but it was not half so diverting as what came after. When the meal was through, several of the Hiatha started to sing. They were soon joined by others, and the group began weaving counterpoints and harmonies. Had I been able to get there unassisted, I would have run back to the youth garden for my gimmicked ear. But in truth, no mere recording can accurately capture the music of the Hiatha. They can sing notes of silence, or bend the note they've just sung while they ready the next, constructing whole crescendos that are finished before they start to be heard. A Hiatha singer can pluck his partner's tones out of the air, and each member of a Hiatha chorus is responsible for the gestalt, rather than just a single voice. Like collaborative sculpture as much as song, something to be touched and heard at once. Listening to Hiatha singing feels like standing in warm rain. Or, on occasion, warm hail; the whistling girl was among the chorus, and when she saw me creeping closer she cast in my direction a trill that made my chest sting. How I ached to be able to respond in kind and set her breast buzzing! But instead I contented myself to experiencing the world's most naturally gifted vocalists singing for the sheer joy of being alive.

Sant was insensitive to the arts, though he indulged my interest. But when the music receded he insisted that we be escorted back to the youth garden so he could sleep. The garden was far more tranquil without the children present. From its dull plane I could hear murmurs leaking out of windows above and below, and debated a twilight climb to learn what alpine treasures pass between a Hiatha family in their high stone privacy. But the base of my spine tingled, and while I was deciding whether to let cautious self-preservation win over my researcher's curiosity, the grey-haired man appeared again.

"We're told you are rich," he said.

I replied that I was fortunate. Certainly more fortunate than many, who could not afford an undertaking such as mine, even had they the cognitive fervor to pursue it.

The grey-haired man turned his gaze to the building where Sant was already abed. "A rich man should be able to afford better friends," he said. "That one will bleed you weak if he can, and people here will be happy to keep helping him do it."

I didn't understand at first, but questioned further he revealed to me that Sant had conspired with the envoys to make my brief visit as financially taxing as possible, to their shared benefit. The opportunism of a tradesman, so perfect and bare! I nearly laughed to see it. But Sant's machinations were trivial compared to this, the opportunity to finally speak directly with a Bridge Blower. I thanked the man for his advice and told him how thrilled I was to speak with him, how many questions I still had. Chief among them was, how could I spend more time in the village, so that I might properly learn what there was to know of Hiatha life?

"Wealth is the bottom of a valley," the grey-haired man said. "Every insecure thing will fall in time to meet it." Then he vanished back over the wall before I could ask him to explain, or discover the source of his fluency, or inquire any number of other things. The way he weaved as he disappeared from view, it is possible the man was drunk. I wondered at his words, at what ethos of privation made him choose first to leave the mountains—as he must surely have done—and then to recant that decision. I surmised from his dismissal that I represented, for him, a symbol of what he had fled to return home. A tragedy, that. But for the arbitrary tangles of pride and history, he could have been the conduit through which I found my full acceptance and understanding among the Hiatha. I returned to the little stacked-stone building, to Sant's snoring and Marta's quilt.

The morning comes earlier in the mountains. I was unprepared for wakefulness, let alone for travel, when the sun on my face announced that my welcome in the village had expired. Sant had risen before me, and was already loading the satchels on his donkey when I emerged into the garden. My own donkey was where I had left it, and the whistling girl was there too, running her fingers over its joints and carvings. I hefted my pack and approached, and she did not withdraw from me.

We couldn't speak to one another, but I removed from my pack the tiny tablet with the donkey's name and showed it to her. Then I let her slide it into my donkey's mouth and watch as its eyes opened and it began to kick at the ground. The girl removed the tablet and put it back in over and over, animating the beast and then letting life wash out of it a dozen times.

It felt important to leave the girl something valuable, some bauble beyond language to let her know she was appreciated in the world outside the mountains. I slid my hand down my back and pinched at the skin over my tailbone. Then, with a playful whistle, I dragged my fingertip along her jawline. She recoiled from the sting of my touch, and I could discern the small, bruise-dark spot where the sigil had planted. The girl skipped off over the wall and across the valley, just young enough to still be scared of innocuous unknowns. But she would understand soon. My own guard sigil had grown so furiously it threatened to displace the other tattoos around it. I was sure that its offspring would be just as clever and intricate. I hoped she chose to follow its call out of the mountains someday, so she would see that I had made her as welcome in my world as she had made me feel in hers. Perhaps she would seek me out, and I could make her feel more welcome still.

Sant had my share of the provisions in a sack, and was eager to start back towards Reninep. I collected my water skins and my package of cured goat, and followed him. He had paid attention to the route, and led us away from the youth garden, toward banks and autobuses and other things more serious than heights and lizards. I decided to set up my hammock and try to get some sleep in the sunshine. Sant would lead me back, I knew, without taking us through any more adventure. That note I'd written was just paper in his pocket until we were both of us returned to civilization. I considered my upcoming trip to meet the talented races of the coast, and hoped that the broad swath of blue on Marta's quilt meant that, there at least, I would find time enough to fully satisfy my intellectual curiosity.

THE HUSBAND STITCH
Carmen Maria Machado

Carmen Maria Machado's debut short-story collection, *Her Body and Other Parties*, will be published by Graywolf Press in October 2017. Her stories have appeared in *Lightspeed*, *Shimmer*, *Granta*, *Lady Churchill's Rosebud Wristlet*, and *Uncanny*. She holds an MFA from the Iowa Writers' Workshop and is a graduate of the Clarion Science Fiction & Fantasy Writers' Workshop. She lives in Philadelphia, where she is the artist in residence at the University of Pennsylvania.

"The Husband Stitch" is a horror story with a metafictional twist that was published in the literary magazine *Granta*. It was nominated for both the Shirley Jackson and Nebula awards.

(If you read this story out loud, please use the following voices:
    Me: as a child, high-pitched, forgettable; as a woman, the same. The boy who will grow into a man, and be my spouse: robust with his own good fortune.
My father: like your father, or the man you wish was your father.
My son: as a small child, gentle, rounded with the faintest of lisps; as a man, like my husband.
All other women: interchangeable with my own.)

In the beginning, I know I want him before he does. This isn't how things are done, but this is how I am going to do them. I am at a neighbor's party with my parents, and I am seventeen. Though my father didn't notice, I drank half a glass of white wine in the kitchen a few minutes ago, with the neighbor's teenage daughter. Everything is soft, like a fresh oil painting.

The boy is not facing me. I see the muscles of his neck and upper back, how he fairly strains out of his button-down shirts. I run slick. It isn't that I don't have choices. I am beautiful. I have a pretty mouth. I have a breast that heaves out of my dresses in a way that seems innocent and perverse all at the same time. I am a good girl, from a good family. But he is a little craggy, in that way that men sometimes are, and I want.

I once heard a story about a girl who requested something so vile from her paramour that he told her family and they had her hauled her off to a sanitarium. I don't know what deviant pleasure she asked for, though I desperately wish I did. What magical thing could you want so badly that they take you away from the known world for wanting it?

The boy notices me. He seems sweet, flustered. He says hello. He asks my name.

I have always wanted to choose my moment, and this is the moment I choose.

On the deck, I kiss him. He kisses me back, gently at first, but then harder, and even pushes open my mouth a little with his tongue. When he pulls away, he seems startled. His eyes dart around for a moment, and then settle on my throat.

—What's that? he asks.

—Oh, this? I touch my ribbon at the back of my neck. It's just my ribbon. I run my fingers halfway around its green and glossy length, and bring them to rest on the tight bow that sits in the front. He reaches out his hand, and I seize it and push it away.

—You shouldn't touch it, I say. You can't touch it.

Before we go inside, he asks if he can see me again. I tell him I would like that. That night, before I sleep, I imagine him again, his tongue pushing open my mouth, and my fingers slide over myself and I imagine him there, all muscle and desire to please, and I know that we are going to marry.

We do. I mean, we will. But first, he takes me in his car, in the dark, to a lake with a marshy edge. He kisses me and clasps his hand around my breast, my nipple knotting beneath his fingers.

I am not truly sure what he is going to do before he does it. He is hard and hot and dry and smells like bread, and when he breaks me I scream and cling to him like I am lost at sea. His body locks onto mine and he is pushing, pushing, and before the end he pulls himself out and finishes with my blood slicking him down. I am fascinated and aroused by the rhythm, the concrete sense of his need, the clarity of his release. Afterwards, he slumps in the seat, and I can hear the sounds of the pond: loons and crickets, and something that sounds like a banjo being plucked. The wind picks up off the water and cools my body down.

I don't know what to do now. I can feel my heart beating between my legs. It hurts, but I imagine it could feel good. I run my hand over myself and feel strains of pleasure from somewhere far off. His breathing becomes quieter and I realize that he is watching me. My skin is glowing beneath the moonlight coming through the window. When I see him looking, I know I can seize that pleasure like my fingertips tickling the end of a balloon's string that has almost drifted out of reach. I pull and moan and ride out the crest of sensation slowly and evenly, biting my tongue all the while.

—I need more, he says, but he does not rise to do anything.

He looks out the window, and so do I. Anything could move out there in the darkness, I think. A hook-handed man. A ghostly hitchhiker repeating her journey. An old woman summoned from the rest of her mirror by the chants of children. Everyone knows these stories—that is, everyone tells them—but no one ever believes them.

His eyes drift over the water, and then land on my neck.

—Tell me about your ribbon, he says.

—There is nothing to tell. It's my ribbon.

—May I touch it?

—No.

—I want to touch it, he says.

—No.

Something in the lake muscles and writhes out of the water, and then lands with a splash. He turns at the sound.

—A fish, he says.

—Sometime, I tell him, I will tell you the stories about this lake and her creatures.

He smiles at me, and rubs his jaw. A little of my blood smears across his skin, but he doesn't notice, and I don't say anything.

—I would like that very much, he says.

—Take me home, I tell him.

And like a gentleman, he does.

That night, I wash myself. The silky suds between my legs are the color and scent of rust, but I am newer than I have ever been.

My parents are very fond of him. He is a nice boy, they say. He will be a good man. They ask him about his occupation, his hobbies, his family. He comes around twice a week, sometimes thrice. My mother invites him in for supper, and while we eat I dig my nails into the meat of his leg. After the ice cream puddles in the bowl, I tell my parents that I am going to walk with him down the lane. We strike off through the night, holding hands sweetly until we are out of sight of the house. I pull him through the trees, and when we find a patch of clear ground I shimmy off my pantyhose, and on my hands and knees offer myself up to him.

I have heard all of the stories about girls like me, and I am unafraid to make more of them. There are two rules: he cannot finish inside of me, and he cannot touch my green ribbon. He spends into the dirt, *pat-pat-patting* like the beginning of rain. I go to touch myself, but my fingers, which had been curling in the dirt beneath me, are filthy. I pull up my underwear and stockings. He makes a sound and points, and I realize that beneath the nylon, my knees are also caked in dirt. I pull them down and brush, and then up again. I smooth my skirt and repin my hair. A single lock has escaped his slicked-back curls, and I tuck it up with the others. We walk down to the stream and I run my hands in the current until they are clean again.

We stroll back to the house, arms linked chastely. Inside, my mother has made coffee, and we all sit around while my father asks him about business.

(If you read this story out loud, the sounds of the clearing can be best reproduced by taking a deep breath and holding it for a long moment. Then release the air all at once, permitting your chest to collapse like a block tower knocked to the ground. Do this again, and again, shortening the time between the held breath and the release.)

I have always been a teller of stories. When I was a young girl, my mother carried me out of a grocery store as I screamed about toes in the produce aisle. Concerned women turned and watched as I kicked the air and pounded my mother's slender back.

—Potatoes! she corrected when we got back to the house. Not toes!

She told me to sit in my chair—a child-sized thing, only built for me—until my father returned. But no, I had seen the toes, pale and bloody stumps, mixed in among those russet tubers. One of them, the one that I had poked with the tip of my index finger, was cold as ice, and yielded beneath my touch the way a blister did. When I repeated this detail to my mother, the liquid of her eyes shifted quick as a startled cat.

—You stay right there, she said.

My father returned from work that evening and listened to my story, each detail.

—You've met Mr. Barns, have you not? he asked me, referring to the elderly man who ran this particular market.

I had met him once, and I said so. He had hair white as a sky before snow, and a wife who drew the signs for the store windows.

—Why would Mr. Barns sell toes? my father asked. Where would he get them?

Being young, and having no understanding of graveyards or mortuaries, I could not answer.

—And even if he got them somewhere, my father continued, what would he have to gain by selling them among the potatoes?

They had been there. I had seen them with my own eyes. But beneath the sunbeams of my father's logic, I felt my doubt unfurling.

—Most importantly, my father said, arriving triumphantly at his final piece of evidence, why did no one notice the toes except for you?

As a grown woman, I would have said to my father that there are true things in this world only observed by a single set of eyes. As a girl, I consented to his account of the story, and laughed when he scooped me from the chair to kiss me and send me on my way.

It is not normal that a girl teaches her boy, but I am only showing him what I want, what plays on the insides of my eyelids as I fall asleep. He comes to know the flicker of my expression as a desire passes through me, and I hold nothing back from him. When he tells me that he wants my mouth, the length of my throat, I teach myself not to gag and take all of him into me, moaning around the saltiness. When he asks me my worst secret, I tell him about the teacher who hid me in the closet until the others were gone and made me hold him there, and how afterwards I went home and scrubbed my hands with a steel wool pad until they bled, even though after I share this

I have nightmares for a month. And when he asks me to marry him, days shy of my eighteenth birthday, I say yes, yes, please, and then on that park bench I sit on his lap and fan my skirt around us so that a passerby would not realize what was happening beneath it.

—I feel like I know so many parts of you, he says to me, trying not to pant. And now, I will know all of them.

There is a story they tell, about a girl dared by her peers to venture to a local graveyard after dark. This was her folly: when they told her that standing on someone's grave at night would cause the inhabitant to reach up and pull her under, she scoffed. Scoffing is the first mistake a woman can make.

I will show you, she said.

Pride is the second mistake.

They gave her a knife to stick into the frosty earth, as a way of proving her presence and her theory.

She went to that graveyard. Some storytellers say that she picked the grave at random. I believe she selected a very old one, her choice tinged by self-doubt and the latent belief that if she were wrong, the intact muscle and flesh of a newly dead corpse would be more dangerous than one centuries gone.

She knelt on the grave and plunged the blade deep. As she stood to run she found she couldn't escape. Something was clutching at her clothes. She cried out and fell down.

When morning came, her friends arrived at the cemetery. They found her dead on the grave, the blade pinning the sturdy wool of her skirt to the ground. Dead of fright or exposure, would it matter when the parents arrived? She was not wrong, but it didn't matter any more. Afterwards, everyone believed that she had wished to die, even though she had died proving that she could live.

As it turns out, being right was the third, and worst, mistake.

My parents are pleased about the marriage. My mother says that even though girls nowadays are starting to marry late, she married father when she was nineteen, and was glad that she did.

When I select my wedding gown, I am reminded of the story of the young woman who wished to go to a dance with her lover, but could not afford a dress. She purchased a lovely white frock from a secondhand shop, and then later fell ill and passed from this earth. The coroner who performed her autopsy discovered she had died from exposure to embalming fluid. It turned out that an unscrupulous undertaker's assistant had stolen the dress from the corpse of a bride.

The moral of that story, I think, is that being poor will kill you. Or perhaps the moral is that brides never fare well in stories, and one should avoid either being a bride, or being in a story. After all, stories can sense happiness and snuff it out like a candle.

We marry in April, on an unseasonably cold afternoon. He sees me before the wedding, in my dress, and insists on kissing me deeply and reaching inside of my bodice. He becomes hard, and I tell him that I want him to use my body as he sees fit. I rescind my first rule, given the occasion. He pushes me against the wall and puts his hand against the tile near my throat, to steady himself. His thumb brushes my ribbon. He does not move his hand, and as he works himself in me he says I love you, I love you, I love you. I do not know if I am the first woman to walk up the aisle of St. George's with semen leaking down her leg, but I like to imagine that I am.

For our honeymoon, we go on a trip I have long desired: a tour of Europe. We are not rich but we make it work. We go from bustling, ancient metropolises to sleepy villages to alpine retreats and back again, sipping spirits and pulling roasted meat from bones with our teeth, eating spaetzle and olives and ravioli and a creamy grain I do not recognize but come to crave each morning. We cannot afford a sleeper car on the train, but my husband bribes an attendant to permit us one hour in an empty room, and in that way we couple over the Rhine.

(If you are reading this story out loud, make the sound of the bed under the tension of train travel and lovemaking by straining a metal folding chair against its hinges. When you are exhausted with that, sing the half-remembered lyrics of old songs to the person closest to you, thinking of lullabies for children.)

My cycle stops soon after we return from our trip. I tell my husband one night, after we are spent and sprawled across our bed. He glows with delight.

—A child, he says. He lies back with his hands beneath his head. A child. He is quiet for so long that I think that he's fallen asleep, but when I look over his eyes are open and fixed on the ceiling. He rolls on his side and gazes at me.

—Will the child have a ribbon?

I feel my jaw tighten. My mind skips between many answers, and I settle on the one that brings me the least amount of anger.

—There is no saying, now, I tell him finally.

He startles me, then, by running his hand around my throat. I put up my hands to stop him but he uses his strength, grabbing my wrists with one hand as he touches the ribbon with the other. He presses the silky length with his thumb. He touches the bow delicately, as if he is massaging my sex.

—Please, I say. Please don't.

He does not seem to hear. Please, I say again, my voice louder, but cracking in the middle.

He could have done it then, untied the bow, if he'd chosen to. But he releases me and rolls back on his back. My wrists ache, and I rub them.

—I need a glass of water, I say. I get up and go to the bathroom. I run the tap and then frantically check my ribbon, tears caught in my lashes. The bow is still tight.

There is a story I love about a pioneer husband and wife killed by wolves. Neighbors found their bodies torn open and strewn around their tiny cabin, but never located their infant daughter, alive or dead. People claimed they saw the girl running with a wolf pack, loping over the terrain as wild and feral as any of her companions.

News of her would ripple through the local settlements. She menaced a hunter in a winter forest—though perhaps he was less menaced than startled at a tiny naked girl baring her teeth and howling. A young woman trying to take down a horse. People even saw her ripping open a chicken in an explosion of feathers.

Many years later, she was said to be seen resting in the rushes along a riverbank, suckling two wolf cubs. I like to imagine that they came from her body, the lineage of wolves tainted human just the once. They certainly bloodied her breasts, but she did not mind because they were hers and only hers.

My stomach swells. Inside of me, our child is swimming fiercely, kicking and pushing and clawing. On a walk in the park, the same park where my husband had proposed to me the year before, I gasp and stagger to the side, clutching my belly and hissing through my teeth to Little One, as I call it, to stop. I go to my knees, breathing heavily and near weeping. A woman passing by helps me to sit up and gives me some water, telling me that the first pregnancy is always the worst.

My body changes in ways I do not expect—my breasts are large, swollen and hot, my stomach lined with pale marks, the inverse of a tiger's. I feel monstrous, but my husband seems renewed with desire, as if my novel shape has refreshed our list of perversities. And my body responds: in the line at the supermarket, receiving communion in church, I am marked by a new and ferocious want, leaving me slippery and swollen at the slightest provocation. When he comes home each day, my husband has a list in his mind of things he desires from me, and I am willing to provide them and more.

—I am the luckiest man alive, he says, running his hands across my stomach.

In the mornings, he kisses me and fondles me and sometimes takes me before his coffee and toast. He goes to work with a spring in his step. He comes home with one promotion, and then another. More money for my family, he says. More money for our happiness.

I am in labor for twenty hours. I nearly wrench off my husband's hand, howling obscenities that do not seem to shock the nurse. I am certain I will crush my own teeth to powder. The doctor peers down between my legs, his white eyebrows making unreadable Morse code across his forehead.

—What's happening? I ask.

—I'm not satisfied this will be a natural birth, the doctor says. Surgery may be necessary.

—No, please, I say. I don't want that, please.

—If there's no movement soon, we're going to do it, the doctor says. It might be best for everyone. He looks up and I am almost certain he winks at my husband, but pain makes the mind see things differently than they are.

I make a deal with Little One, in my mind. *Little One, I think, this is the last time that we are going to be just you and me. Please don't make them cut you out of me.*

Little One is born twenty minutes later. They do have to make a cut, but not across my stomach as I had feared. The doctor cuts down, and I feel little, just tugging, though perhaps it is what they have given me. When the baby is placed in my arms, I examine the wrinkled body from head to toe, the color of a sunset sky, and streaked in red.

No ribbon. A boy. I begin to weep, and curl the unmarked baby into my chest.

(If you are reading this story out loud, give a paring knife to the listener and ask them to cut the tender flap of skin between your index finger and thumb. Afterwards, thank them.)

There is a story about a woman who goes into labor when the attending physician is tired. There is a story about a woman who herself was born too early. There is a story about a woman whose body clung to her child so hard they cut her to retrieve him. There is a story about a woman who heard a story about a woman who birthed wolf cubs in secret. Stories have this way of running together like raindrops in a pond. They are each borne from the clouds separately, but once they have come together, there is no way to tell them apart.

(If you are reading this story out loud, move aside the curtain to illustrate this final point to your listeners. It'll be raining, I promise.)

They take the baby so that they may fix me where they cut. They give me something that makes me sleepy, delivered through a mask pressed gently to my mouth and nose. My husband jokes around with the doctor as he holds my hand.

—How much to get that extra stitch? he asks. You offer that, right?

—Please, I say to him. But it comes out slurred and twisted and possibly no more than a small moan. Neither man turns his head toward me.

The doctor chuckles. You aren't the first—

I slide down a long tunnel, and then surface again, but covered in something heavy and dark, like oil. I feel like I am going to vomit.

—the rumor is something like—

—like a vir—

And then I am awake, wide awake, and my husband is gone and the doctor is gone. And the baby, where is—

The nurse sticks her head in the door.

—Your husband just went to get a coffee, she says, and the baby is asleep in the bassinet.

The doctor walks in behind her, wiping his hands on a cloth.

—You're all sewn up, don't you worry, he says. Nice and tight, everyone's happy. The nurse will speak with you about recovery. You're going to need to rest for a while.

The baby wakes up. The nurse scoops him from his swaddle and places him in my arms again. He is so beautiful I have to remind myself to breathe.

My son is a good baby. He grows and grows. We never have another child, though not for lack of trying. I suspect that Little One did so much ruinous damage inside of me that my body couldn't house another.

—You were a poor tenant, Little One, I say to him, rubbing shampoo into his fine brown hair, and I shall revoke your deposit.

He splashes around in the sink, cackling with happiness.

My son touches my ribbon, but never in a way that makes me afraid. He thinks of it as a part of me, and he treats it no differently than he would an ear or finger.

Back from work, my husband plays games in the yard with our son, games of chase and run. He is too young to catch a ball, still, but my husband patiently rolls it to him in the grass, and our son picks it up and drops it again, and my husband gestures to me and cries, Look, look! Did you see? He is going to throw it soon enough.

Of all the stories I know about mothers, this one is the most real. A young American girl is visiting Paris with her mother when the woman begins to feel ill. They decide to check into a hotel for a few days so the mother can rest, and the daughter calls for a doctor to assess her.

After a brief examination, the doctor tells the daughter that all her mother needs is some medicine. He takes the daughter to a taxi, gives the driver directions in French, and explains to the girl that, at his home, his wife will give her the appropriate remedy. They drive and drive for a very long time, and when the girl arrives, she is frustrated by the unbearable slowness of this doctor's wife, who meticulously assembles the pills from powder. When she gets back into the taxi, the driver meanders down the streets, sometimes doubling back on the same avenue. The girl gets out of the taxi to return to the hotel on foot. When she finally arrives, the hotel clerk tells her that he has never seen her before. When she runs up to the room where her mother had been resting, she finds the walls a different color, the furnishings different than her memory, and her mother nowhere in sight.

There are many endings to the story. In one of them, the girl is gloriously persistent and certain, renting a room nearby and staking out the hotel, eventually seducing a young man who works in the laundry and discovering the truth: that her mother died of a contagious and fatal disease, departing this plane shortly after the daughter had been sent from the hotel by the doctor. To avoid a citywide panic, the staff removed and buried her body, repainted and furnished the room, and bribed all involved to deny that they had ever met the pair.

In another version of this story, the girl wanders the streets of Paris for years, believing that she is mad, that she invented her mother and her life with her mother in her own diseased mind. The daughter stumbles from hotel to hotel, confused and grieving, though for whom she cannot say.

I don't need to tell you the moral of this story. I think you already know what it is.

Our son enters school when he is five, and I remember his teacher from that day in the park, when she had crouched to help me. She remembers me as well. I tell her that we have had no more children since our son, and now that he has started school, my days will be altered toward sloth and boredom. She is kind. She tells me that if I am looking for a way to occupy my time, there is a wonderful women's art class at a local college.

That night, after my son is in bed, my husband reaches his hand across the couch and slides it up my leg.

—Come to me, he says, and I twinge with pleasure. I slide off the couch, smoothing my skirt very prettily as I walk over to him on my knees. I kiss his leg, running my hand up to his belt, tugging him from his bonds before swallowing him whole. He runs his hands through my hair, stroking my head, groaning and pressing into me. And I don't realize that his hand is sliding down the back of my neck until he is trying to loop his fingers through the ribbon. I gasp and pull away quickly, falling back and frantically checking my bow. He is still sitting there, slick with my spit.

—Come back here, he says.

—No, I say.

He stands up and tucks himself into his pants, zipping them up.

—A wife, he says, should have no secrets from her husband.

—I don't have any secrets, I tell him.

—The *ribbon*.

—The ribbon is not a secret, it's just mine.

—Were you born with it? Why your throat? Why is it green?

I do not answer.

He is silent for a long minute. Then,

—A wife should have no secrets.

My nose grows hot. I do not want to cry.

—I have given you everything you have ever asked for, I say. Am I not allowed this one thing?

—I want to know.

—You think you want to know, I say, but you do not.

—Why do you want to hide it from me?

—I am not hiding it. It is not yours.

He gets down very close to me, and I pull back from the smell of bourbon. I hear a creak, and we both look up to see our son's feet vanishing up the staircase.

When my husband goes to sleep that night, he does so with a hot and burning anger that falls away only when he starts dreaming. I sense its release, and only then can I sleep, too.

The next day, our son touches my throat and asks about my ribbon. He tries to pull at it. And though it pains me, I have to make it forbidden to him. When he reaches for it, I shake a can full of pennies. It crashes discordantly, and he withdraws and weeps. Something is lost between us, and I never find it again.

(If you are reading this story out loud, prepare a soda can full of pennies. When you arrive at this moment, shake it loudly in the face of the person closest to you. Observe their expression of startled fear, and then betrayal. Notice how they never look at you in exactly the same way for the rest of your days.)

I enroll in the art class for women. When my husband is at work and my son is in school, I drive to the sprawling green campus and the squat grey building where the art classes are held.

Presumably, the male nudes are kept from our eyes in some deference to propriety, but the class has its own energy—there is plenty to see on a strange woman's naked form, plenty to contemplate as you roll charcoal and mix paints. I see more than one woman shifting forwards and back in her seat to redistribute blood flow.

One woman in particular returns over and over. Her ribbon is red, and is knotted around her slender ankle. Her skin is the color of olives, and a trail of dark hair runs from her belly button to her mons. I know that I should not want her, not because she is a woman and not because she is a stranger, but because it is her job to disrobe, and I feel shame taking advantage of such a state. But as my pencil traces her contours so does my hand in the secret recesses of my mind. I am not even certain how such a thing would happen, but the possibilities incense me to near madness.

One afternoon after class, I turn a hallway corner and she is there, the woman. Clothed, wrapped in a raincoat. Her gaze transfixes me, and this close I can see a band of gold around each of her pupils, as though her eyes are twin solar eclipses. She greets me, and I her.

We sit down together in a booth at a nearby diner, our knees occasionally brushing up against each other beneath the Formica. She drinks a cup of black coffee. I ask her if she has any children. She does, she says, a daughter, a beautiful little girl of eleven.

—Eleven is a terrifying age, she says. I remember nothing before I was eleven, but then there it was, all color and horror. What a number, she says, what a show. Then her face slips somewhere else for a moment, as if she has dipped beneath the surface of a lake.

We do not discuss the specific fears of raising a girl-child. Truthfully, I am afraid to ask. I also do not ask her if she's married, and she does not volunteer the information, though she does not wear a ring. We talk about my son, about the art class. I desperately want to know what state of need has sent her to disrobe before us, but perhaps I do not ask because the answer would be, like adolescence, too frightening to forget.

I am captivated by her, there is no other way to put it. There is something easy about her, but not easy the way I was—the way I am. She's like dough, how the give of it beneath kneading hands disguises its sturdiness, its potential. When I look away from her and then look back, she seems twice as large as before.

—Perhaps we can talk again sometime, I say to her. This has been a very pleasant afternoon.

She nods to me. I pay for her coffee.

I do not want to tell my husband about her, but he can sense some untapped desire. One night, he asks what roils inside of me and I confess it to him. I even describe the details of her ribbon, releasing an extra flood of shame.

He is so glad of this development he begins to mutter a long and exhaustive fantasy as he removes his pants and enters me. I feel as if I have betrayed her somehow, and I never return to the class.

(If you are reading this story out loud, force a listener to reveal a secret, then open the nearest window to the street and scream it as loudly as you are able.)

One of my favorite stories is about an old woman and her husband—a man mean as Mondays, who scared her with the violence of his temper and the shifting nature of his whims. She was only able to keep him satisfied with her unparalleled cooking, to which he was a complete captive. One day, he bought her a fat liver to cook for him, and she did, using herbs and broth. But the smell of her own artistry overtook her, and a few nibbles became a few bites, and soon the liver was gone. She had no money with which to purchase a second one, and she was terrified of her husband's reaction should he discover that his meal was gone. So she crept to the church next door, where a woman had been recently laid to rest. She approached the shrouded figure, then cut into it with a pair of kitchen shears and stole the liver from her corpse.

That night, the woman's husband dabbed his lips with a napkin and declared the meal the finest he'd ever eaten. When they went to sleep, the old woman heard the front door open, and a thin wail wafted through the rooms. *Who has my liver? Whooooo has my liver?*

The old woman could hear the voice coming closer and closer to the bedroom. There was a hush as the door swung open. The dead woman posed her query again.

The old woman flung the blanket off her husband.

—*He* has it! She declared triumphantly.

Then she saw the face of the dead woman, and recognized her own mouth and eyes. She looked down at her abdomen, remembering, now, how she had carved into her own belly. Next to her, as the blood seeped into the very heart of the mattress, her husband slumbered on.

That may not be the version of the story you're familiar with. But I assure you, it's the one you need to know.

My husband is strangely excited for Halloween. Our son is old enough that he can walk and carry a basket for treats. I take one of my husband's old tweed coats and fashion one for our son, so that he might be a tiny professor, or some other stuffy academic. My husband even gives him a pipe on which to gnaw. Our son clicks it between his teeth in a way I find unsettlingly adult.

—Mama, my son says, what are you?

I am not in costume, so I tell him I am his mother.

The pipe falls from his little mouth onto the floor, and he screams. My husband swoops in and picks him up, talking to him in a low voice, repeating his name between his sobs.

It is only as his breathing returns to normal that I am able to identify my mistake. He is not old enough to know the story of the naughty girls who wanted the toy drum, and were wicked toward their mother until she went away and was replaced with a new mother—one with glass eyes and thumping wooden tail. But I have inadvertently told him another one—the story of the little boy who only discovered on Halloween that his mother was not his mother, except on the day when everyone wore a mask. Regret sluices hot up my throat. I try to hold him and kiss him, but he only wishes to go out onto the street, where the sun has dipped below the horizon and a hazy chill is bruising the shadows.

He comes home laughing, gnawing on a piece of candy that has turned his mouth the color of a plum. I am angry at my husband. I wish he had waited to come home before permitting the consumption of the cache. Has he never heard the stories? The pins pressed into the chocolates, the razor blades sunk in the apples? I examine my son's mouth, but there is no sharp metal plunged into his palate. He laughs and spins around the house, dizzy and electrified from the treats and excitement. He wraps his arms around my legs, the earlier incident forgotten. The forgiveness tastes sweeter than any candy that can be given at any door. When he climbs into my lap, I sing to him until he falls asleep.

Our son is eight, ten. First, I tell him fairy tales—the very oldest ones, with the pain and death and forced marriage pared away like dead foliage. Mermaids grow feet and it feels like laughter. Naughty pigs trot away from grand feasts, reformed and uneaten. Evil witches leave the castle and move into small cottages and live out their days painting portraits of woodland creatures.

As he grows, though, he asks questions. Why would they not eat the pig, hungry as they were and wicked as he had been? Why was the witch permitted to go free after her terrible deeds? And the sensation of fins splitting to feet being anything less than agonizing he rejects outright after cutting his hand with a pair of scissors.

—It would huight, he says, for he is struggling with his r's.

I agree with him. It would. So then I tell him stories closer to true: children who go missing along a particular stretch of railroad track, lured by the sound of a phantom train to parts unknown; a black dog that appears at a person's doorstep three days before their passing; a trio of frogs that corner you in the marshlands and tell your fortune for a price.

The school puts on a performance of *Little Buckle Boy*, and he is the lead, the buckle boy, and I join a committee of mothers making costumes for the children. I am lead costume maker in a room full of women, all of us sewing together little silk petals for the flower children and making tiny white pantaloons for the pirates. One of the mothers has a pale yellow ribbon on her finger, and it constantly tangles in her thread. She swears and cries. One day I have to use the sewing shears to pick at the offending threads. I try to be delicate. She shakes her head as I free her from the peony.

—It's such a bother, isn't it? she says.

I nod. Outside the window, the children play—knocking each other off the playground equipment, popping the heads off dandelions. The play goes beautifully. Opening night, our son blazes through his monologue. Perfect pitch and cadence. No one has ever done better.

Our son is twelve. He asks me about the ribbon, point-blank. I tell him that we are all different, and sometimes you should not ask questions. I assure him that he'll understand when he is grown. I distract him with stories that have no ribbons: angels who desire to be human and ghosts who don't realize they're dead and children who turn to ash. He stops smelling like a child—milky sweetness replaced with something sharp and burning, like a hair sizzling on the stove.

Our son is thirteen, fourteen. He waits for the neighbor boy on his way to school, who walks more slowly than the others. He exhibits the subtlest compassion, my son. No instinct for cruelty, like some.

—The world has enough bullies, I've told him over and over.

This is the year he stops asking for my stories.

Our son is fifteen, sixteen, seventeen. He begins to court a beautiful girl from his high school, who has a bright smile and a warm presence. I am happy to meet her, but never insist that we should wait up for their return, remembering my own youth.

When he tells us that he has been accepted at a university to study engineering, I am overjoyed. We march through the house, singing songs and laughing. When my husband comes home, he joins in the jubilee, and we drive to a local seafood restaurant. Over halibut, his father tells him, we are so proud of you. Our son laughs and says that he also wishes to marry his girl. We clasp hands and are even happier. Such a good boy. Such a wonderful life to look forward to.

Even the luckiest woman alive has not seen joy like this.

There's a classic, a real classic, that I haven't told you yet.

A girlfriend and a boyfriend went parking. Some people say that means kissing in a car, but I know the story. I was there. They were parked on the edge of a lake. They were turning around in the back seat as if the world was moments from ending. Maybe it was. She offered herself and he took it, and after it was over, they turned on the radio.

The voice on the radio announced that a mad, hook-handed murderer had escaped from a local insane asylum. The boyfriend chuckled as he flipped to a music station. As the song ended, the girlfriend heard a thin scratching sound, like a paperclip over glass. She looked at her boyfriend and then pulled her cardigan over her bare shoulders, wrapping one arm around her breasts.

—We should go, she said.

—No, baby, the boyfriend said. Let's go again.

—What if the killer comes here? the girl asked. The insane asylum is very close.

—We'll be fine, baby, the boyfriend said. Don't you trust me?

The girlfriend nodded reluctantly.

—Well then, he said, his voice trailing off in that way she would come to know so well. He took her hand off her chest and placed it onto himself. She finally looked away from the lakeside.

Outside, the moonlight glinted off the shiny steel hook. The killer waved at her, grinning.

I'm sorry. I've forgotten the rest of the story.

The house is so silent without our son. I walk through it, touching all the surfaces. I am happy but something inside of me is shifting into a strange new place.

That night, my husband asks if I wish to christen the newly empty rooms. We have not coupled so fiercely since before our son was born. Bent over the kitchen table, something old is lit within me, and I remember the way we desired before, how we left love streaked on all of the surfaces. I could have met anyone at that party when I was seventeen—prudish boys or violent boys. Religious boys who would have made me move to some distant country to convert its denizens. I could have experienced untold numbers of sorrows or dissatisfactions. But as I straddle him on the floor, riding him and crying out, I know that I made the right choice.

We fall asleep exhausted, sprawled naked in our bed. When I wake up, my husband is kissing the back of my neck, probing the ribbon with his tongue. My body rebels wildly, still throbbing with the memories of pleasure but bucking hard against betrayal. I say his name, and he does not respond. I say it again, and he holds me against him and continues. I wedge my elbows in his side, and when he loosens from me in surprise, I sit up and face him. He looks confused and hurt, like my son the day I shook the can of pennies.

Resolve runs out of me. I touch the ribbon. I look at the face of my husband, the beginning and end of his desires all etched there. He is not a bad man, and that, I realize suddenly, is the root of my hurt. He is not a bad man at all. And yet—

—Do you want to untie the ribbon? I ask him. After these many years, is that what you want of me?

His face flashes gaily, and then greedily, and he runs his hand up my bare breast and to my bow.

—Yes, he says. Yes.

—Then, I say, do what you want.

With trembling fingers, he takes one of the ends. The bow undoes, slowly, the long-bound ends crimped with habit. My husband groans, but I do not think he realizes it. He loops his finger through the final twist and pulls. The ribbon falls away. It floats down and curls at my feet, or so I imagine, because I cannot look down to follow its descent.

My husband frowns, and then his face begins to open with some other expression—sorrow, or maybe pre-emptive loss. My hand flies up in front of me—an involuntary motion, for balance or some other futility—and beyond it his image is gone.

—I love you, I assure him, more than you can possibly know.

—No, he says, but I don't know to what he's responding.

If you are reading this story out loud, you may be wondering if that place my ribbon protected was wet with blood and openings, or smooth and neutered like the nexus between the legs of a doll. I'm afraid I can't tell you, because I don't know. For these questions and others, and their lack of resolution, I am sorry.

My weight shifts, and with it, gravity seizes me. My husband's face falls away, and then I see the ceiling, and the wall behind me. As my lopped head tips backwards off my neck and rolls off the bed, I feel as lonely as I have ever been.

THE PAUPER PRINCE
AND THE EUCALYPTUS JINN

Usman T. Malik

Usman T. Malik is a Pakistani author residing in Florida. His fiction has appeared in *Strange Horizons*, *Tor.com*, *Nightmare*, and *The Mammoth Book of Cthulhu: New Lovecraftian Fiction* edited by Paula Guran. His short story "The Vaporization Enthalpy of a Peculiar Pakistani Family" was published to international acclaim, winning the 2014 Bram Stoker Award and garnering a Nebula nomination. He graduated from Clarion West in 2013. He led Pakistan's first speculative-fiction writing workshop in Lahore.

"The Pauper Prince and the Eucalyptus Jinn" is about the power of stories and how they come down across generations. The story won the British Fantasy Award in 2016 and was nominated for the World Fantasy and Nebula awards that same year.

"When the Spirit World appears in a sensory Form, the Human Eye confines it. The Spiritual Entity cannot abandon that Form as long as Man continues to look at it in this special way. To escape, the Spiritual Entity manifests an Image it adopts for him, like a veil. It pretends the Image is moving in a certain direction so the Eye will follow it. At which point the Spiritual Entity escapes its confinement and disappears.

"Whoever knows this and wishes to maintain perception of the Spiritual, must not let his Eye follow this illusion.

"This is one of the Divine Secrets."

—*The Meccan Revelations* by Muhiyuddin Ibn Arabi

For fifteen years my grandfather lived next door to the Mughal princess Zeenat Begum. The princess ran a tea stall outside the walled city of Old Lahore in the shade of an ancient eucalyptus. Dozens of children from Bhati Model School rushed screaming down muddy lanes to gather at her shop, which was really just a roadside counter with a tin roof and a smattering of chairs and a table. On winter afternoons it was her steaming cardamom-and-honey tea the kids wanted; in summer it was the chilled Rooh Afza.

As Gramps talked, he smacked his lips and licked his fingers, remembering the sweet rosewater sharbat. He told me that the princess was so poor she had to recycle tea leaves and sharbat residue. Not from customers, of course, but from her own boiling pans—although who really knew, he said, and winked.

I didn't believe a word of it.

"Where was her kingdom?" I said.

"Gone. Lost. Fallen to the British a hundred years ago," Gramps said. "She never begged, though. Never asked anyone's help, see?"

I was ten. We were sitting on the steps of our mobile home in Florida. It was a wet summer afternoon and rain hissed like diamondbacks in the grass and crackled in the gutters of the trailer park.

"And her family?"

"Dead. Her great-great-great-grandfather, the exiled King Bahadur Shah Zafar, died in Rangoon and is buried there. Burmese Muslims make pilgrimages to his shrine and honor him as a saint."

"Why was he buried there? Why couldn't he go home?"

"He had no home anymore."

For a while I stared, then surprised both him and myself by bursting into tears. Bewildered, Gramps took me in his arms and whispered comforting things, and gradually I quieted, letting his voice and the rain sounds lull me to sleep, the loamy smell of him and grass and damp earth becoming one in my sniffling nostrils.

I remember the night Gramps told me the rest of the story. I was twelve or thirteen. We were at this desi party in Windermere thrown by Baba's friend Hanif Uncle, a posh affair with Italian leather sofas, crystal cutlery, and marble-topped tables. Someone broached a discussion about the pauper princess. Another person guffawed. The Mughal princess was an urban legend, this aunty said. Yes, yes, she too had heard stories about this so-called princess, but they were a hoax. The descendants of the Mughals left India and Pakistan decades ago. They are settled in London and Paris and Manhattan now, living postcolonial, extravagant lives after selling their estates in their native land.

Gramps disagreed vehemently. Not only was the princess real, she had given him free tea. She had told him stories of her forebears.

The desi aunty laughed. "Senility is known to create stories," she said, tapping her manicured fingers on her wineglass.

Gramps bristled. A long heated argument followed and we ended up leaving the party early.

"Rafiq, tell your father to calm down," Hanif Uncle said to my baba at the door. "He takes things too seriously."

"He might be old and set in his ways, Doctor sahib," Baba said, "but he's sharp as a tack. Pardon my boldness but some of your friends in there. . . ." Without looking at Hanif Uncle, Baba waved a palm at the open door from which blue light and Bollywood music spilled onto the driveway.

Hanif Uncle smiled. He was a gentle and quiet man who sometimes invited us over to his fancy parties where rich expatriates from the Indian subcontinent opined about politics, stocks, cricket, religious fundamentalism, and their successful Ivy League–attending progeny. The shyer the man the louder his feasts, Gramps was fond of saying.

"They're a piece of work all right," Hanif Uncle said. "Listen, bring your family over some weekend. I'd love to listen to that Mughal girl's story."

"Sure, Doctor sahib. Thank you."

The three of us squatted into our listing truck and Baba yanked the gearshift forward, beginning the drive home.

"Abba-ji," he said to Gramps. "You need to rein in your temper. You can't pick a fight with these people. The doctor's been very kind to me, but word of mouth's how I get work and it's exactly how I can lose it."

"But that woman is wrong, Rafiq," Gramps protested. "What she's heard are rumors. I told them the truth. I lived in the time of the pauper princess. I lived through the horrors of the eucalyptus jinn."

"Abba-ji, listen to what you're saying! Please, I beg you, keep these stories to yourself. Last thing I want is people whispering the handyman has a crazy, quarrelsome father." Baba wiped his forehead and rubbed his perpetually blistered thumb and index finger together.

Gramps stared at him, then whipped his face to the window and began to chew a candy wrapper (he was diabetic and wasn't allowed sweets). We sat in hot, thorny silence the rest of the ride and when we got home Gramps marched straight to his room like a prisoner returning to his cell.

I followed him and plopped on his bed.

"Tell me about the princess and the jinn," I said in Urdu.

Gramps grunted out of his compression stockings and kneaded his legs. They occasionally swelled with fluid. He needed water pills but they made him incontinent and smell like piss and he hated them. "The last time I told you her story you started crying. I don't want your parents yelling at me. Especially tonight."

"Oh, come on, they don't *yell* at you. Plus I won't tell them. Look, Gramps, think about it this way: I could write a story in my school paper about the princess. This could be my junior project." I snuggled into his bedsheets. They smelled of sweat and medicine, but I didn't mind.

"All right, but if your mother comes in here, complaining—"

"She won't."

He arched his back and shuffled to the armchair by the window. It was ten at night. Cicadas chirped their intermittent static outside, but I doubt Gramps heard them. He wore hearing aids and the ones we could afford crackled in his ears, so he refused to wear them at home.

Gramps opened his mouth, pinched the lower denture, and rocked it. Back and forth, back and forth. Loosening it from the socket. *Pop!* He removed the upper one similarly and dropped both in a bowl of warm water on the table by the armchair.

I slid off the bed. I went to him and sat on the floor by his spidery, white-haired feet. "Can you tell me the story, Gramps?"

Night stole in through the window blinds and settled around us, soft and warm. Gramps curled his toes and pressed them against the wooden leg of his armchair. His eyes drifted to the painting hanging above the door, a picture of a young woman turned ageless by the artist's hand. Soft muddy eyes, a knowing smile, an orange dopatta framing her black hair. She sat on a brilliantly colored rug and held a silver goblet in an outstretched hand, as if offering it to the viewer.

The painting had hung in Gramps's room for so long I'd stopped seeing it. When I was younger I'd once asked him if the woman was Grandma, and he'd looked at me. Grandma died when Baba was young, he said.

The cicadas burst into an electric row and I rapped the floorboards with my knuckles, fascinated by how I could keep time with their piping.

"I bet the pauper princess," said Gramps quietly, "would be happy to have her story told."

"Yes."

"She would've wanted everyone to know how the greatest dynasty in history came to a ruinous end."

"Yes."

Gramps scooped up a two-sided brush and a bottle of cleaning solution from the table. Carefully, he began to brush his dentures. As he scrubbed, he talked, his deep-set watery eyes slowly brightening until it seemed he glowed with memory. I listened, and at one point Mama came to the door, peered in, and whispered something we both ignored. It was Saturday night so she left us alone, and Gramps and I sat there for the longest time I would ever spend with him.

This is how, that night, my gramps ended up telling me the story of the Pauper Princess and the Eucalyptus Jinn.

The princess, Gramps said, was a woman in her twenties with a touch of silver in her hair. She was lean as a sorghum broomstick, face dark and plain, but her eyes glittered as she hummed the Qaseeda Burdah Shareef and swept the wooden counter in her tea shop with a dustcloth. She had a gold nose stud that, she told her customers, was a family heirloom. Each evening after she was done serving she folded her aluminum chairs, upended the stools on the plywood table, and took a break. She'd sit down by the trunk of the towering eucalyptus outside Bhati Gate, pluck out the stud, and shine it with a mint-water-soaked rag until it gleamed like an eye.

It was tradition, she said.

"If it's an heirloom, why do you wear it every day? What if you break it? What if someone sees it and decides to rob you?" Gramps asked her. He was about fourteen then and just that morning had gotten Juma pocket money and was feeling rich. He whistled as he sat sipping tea in the tree's shade and watched steelworkers, potters, calligraphers, and laborers carry their work outside their foundries and shops, grateful for the winter-softened sky.

Princess Zeenat smiled and her teeth shone at him. "Nah ji. No one can steal from us. My family is protected by a jinn, you know."

This was something Gramps had heard before. A jinn protected the princess and her two sisters, a duty imposed by Akbar the Great five hundred years back. Guard and defend Mughal honor. Not a clichéd horned jinn, you understand, but a daunting, invisible entity that defied the laws of physics: it could slip in and out of time, could swap its senses, hear out of its nostrils, smell with its eyes. It could even fly like the tales of yore said.

Mostly amused but occasionally uneasy, Gramps laughed when the princess told these stories. He had never really questioned the reality of her existence; lots of nawabs and princes of pre-Partition India had offspring languishing in poverty these days. An impoverished Mughal princess was conceivable.

A custodian jinn, not so much.

Unconvinced thus, Gramps said:

"Where does he live?"

"What does he eat?"

And, "If he's invisible, how does one know he's real?"

The princess's answers came back practiced and surreal:

The jinn lived in the eucalyptus tree above the tea stall.

He ate angel-bread.

He was as real as jasmine-touched breeze, as shifting temperatures, as the many spells of weather that alternately lull and shake humans in their variegated fists.

"Have *you* seen him?" Gramps fired.

"Such questions." The Princess shook her head and laughed, her thick, long hair squirming out from under her chador. "Hai Allah, these kids." Still tittering, she sauntered off to her counter, leaving a disgruntled Gramps scratching his head.

The existential ramifications of such a creature's presence unsettled Gramps, but what could he do? Arguing about it was as useful as arguing about the wind jouncing the eucalyptus boughs. Especially when the neighborhood kids began to tell disturbing tales as well.

Of a gnarled bat-like creature that hung upside down from the warped branches, its shadow twined around the wicker chairs and table fronting the counter. If you looked up, you saw a bird nest— just another huddle of zoysia grass and bird feathers—but then you dropped your gaze and the creature's malignant reflection juddered and swam in the tea inside the chipped china.

"Foul face," said one boy. "Dark and ugly and wrinkled like a fruit."

"Sharp, crooked fangs," said another.

"No, no, he has razor blades planted in his jaws," said the first one quickly. "My cousin told me. That's how he flays the skin off little kids."

The description of the eucalyptus jinn varied seasonally. In summertime, his cheeks were scorched, his eyes red rimmed like the midday sun. Come winter, his lips were blue and his eyes misty, his touch cold like damp roots. On one thing everyone agreed: if he laid eyes on you, you were a goner.

The lean, mean older kids nodded and shook their heads wisely.

A goner.

The mystery continued this way, deliciously gossiped and fervently argued, until one summer day a child of ten with wild eyes and a snot-covered chin rushed into the tea stall, gabbling and crying, blood trickling from the gash in his temple. Despite several attempts by the princess and her customers, he wouldn't be induced to tell who or what had hurt him, but his older brother, who had followed the boy inside, face scrunched with delight, declared he had last been seen pissing at the bottom of the eucalyptus.

"The jinn. The jinn," all the kids cried in unison. "A victim of the jinn's malice."

"No. He fell out of the tree," a grownup said firmly. "The gash is from the fall."

"The boy's incurred the jinn's wrath," said the kids happily. "The jinn will flense the meat off his bones and crunch his marrow."

"Oh shut up," said Princess Zeenat, feeling the boy's cheeks, "the eucalyptus jinn doesn't harm innocents. He's a defender of honor and dignity," while all the time she fretted over the boy, dabbed at his forehead with a wet cloth, and poured him a hot cup of tea.

The princess's sisters emerged from the doorway of their two-room shack twenty paces from the tea stall. They peered in, two teenage girls in flour-caked dopattas and rose-printed shalwar kameez, and the younger one stifled a cry when the boy turned to her, eyes shiny and vacuous with delirium, and whispered, "He says the lightning trees are dying."

The princess gasped. The customers pressed in, awed and murmuring. An elderly man with betel-juice-stained teeth gripped the front of his own shirt with palsied hands and fanned his chest with it. "The jinn has overcome the child," he said, looking profoundly at the sky beyond the stall, and chomped his tobacco paan faster.

The boy shuddered. He closed his eyes, breathed erratically, and behind him the shadow of the tree fell long and clawing at the ground.

The lightning trees are dying. The lightning trees are dying.

So spread the nonsensical words through the neighborhood. Zipping from bamboo door-to-door; blazing through dark lovers' alleys; hopping from one beggar's gleeful tongue to another's, the prophecy became a proverb and the proverb a song.

A starving calligrapher-poet licked his reed quill and wrote an elegy for the lightning trees.

A courtesan from the Diamond Market sang it from her rooftop on a moonlit night.

Thus the walled city heard the story of the possessed boy and his curious proclamation and shivered with this message from realms unknown. Arthritic grandmothers and lithe young men rocked in their courtyards and lawns, nodding dreamily at the stars above, allowing themselves to remember secrets from childhood they hadn't dared remember before.

Meanwhile word reached local families that a child had gotten hurt climbing the eucalyptus. Angry fathers, most of them laborers and shopkeepers with kids, who rarely went home before nightfall, came barging into the Municipality's lean-to, fists hammering on the sad-looking officer's table, demanding that the tree be chopped down.

"It's a menace," they said.

"It's hollow. Worm eaten."

"It's haunted!"

"Look, its gum's flammable and therefore a fire hazard," offered one versed in horticulture, "and the tree's a pest. What's a eucalyptus doing in the middle of a street anyway?"

So they argued and thundered until the officer came knocking at the princess's door. "The tree," said the sad-looking officer, twisting his squirrel-tail mustache, "needs to go."

"Over my dead body," said the princess. She threw down her polish rag and glared at the officer. "It was planted by my forefathers. It's a relic, it's history."

"It's a public menace. Look, bibi, we can do this the easy way or the hard way, but I'm telling you—"

"Try it. You just try it," cried the princess. "I will take this matter to the highest authorities. I'll go to the Supreme Court. That tree"—she jabbed a quivering finger at the monstrous thing—"gives us shade. A fakir told my grandfather never to move his business elsewhere. It's blessed, he said."

The sad-faced officer rolled up his sleeves. The princess eyed him with apprehension as he yanked one of her chairs back and lowered himself into it.

"Bibi," he said not unkindly, "let me tell you something. The eucalyptus was brought here by the British to cure India's salinity and flooding problems. Gora sahib hardly cared about our ecology." His mustache drooped from his thin lips. The strawberry mole on his chin quivered. "It's not indigenous, it's a pest. It's not a blessing, it repels other flora and fauna and guzzles groundwater by the tons. It's not ours," the officer said, not looking at the princess. "It's alien."

It was early afternoon and school hadn't broken yet. The truant Gramps sat in a corner sucking on a cigarette he'd found in the trash can outside his school and watched the princess. Why wasn't she telling the officer about the jinn? That the tree was its home? Her cheeks were puffed from clenching her jaws, the hollows under her eyes deeper and darker as she clapped a hand to her forehead.

"Look," she said, her voice rising and falling like the wind stirring the tear-shaped eucalyptus leaves, "you take the tree, you take our good luck. My shop is all I have. The tree protects it. It protects us. It's family."

"Nothing I can do." The officer scratched his birthmark. "Had there been no complaint . . . but now I have no choice. The Lahore Development Authority has been planning to remove the poplars and the eucalyptus for a while anyway. They want to bring back trees of Old Lahore. Neem, pipal, sukhchain, mulberry, mango. This foreigner"—he looked with distaste at the eucalyptus—"steals water from our land. It needs to go."

Shaking his head, the officer left. The princess lurched to her stall and began to prepare Rooh Afza. She poured a glittering parabola of sharbat into a mug with trembling hands, staggered to the tree, and flung the liquid at its hoary, clawing roots.

"There," she cried, her eyes reddened. "I can't save you. You must go."

Was she talking to the jinn? To the tree? Gramps felt his spine run cold as the blood-red libation sank into the ground, muddying the earth around the eucalyptus roots. Somewhere in the branches, a bird whistled.

The princess toed the roots for a moment longer, then trudged back to her counter.

Gramps left his teacup half-empty and went to the tree. He tilted his head to look at its top. It was so high. The branches squirmed and fled from the main trunk, reaching restlessly for the hot white clouds. A plump chukar with a crimson beak sat on a branch swaying gently. It stared back at Gramps, but no creature with razor-blade jaws and hollow dust-filled cheeks dangled from the tree.

As Gramps left, the shadows of the canopies and awnings of shops in the alley stretched toward the tree accusatorially.

That night Gramps dreamed of the eucalyptus jinn.

It was a red-snouted shape hurtling toward the heavens, its slipstream body glittering and dancing in the dark. Space and freedom rotated above it, but as it accelerated showers of golden meteors came bursting from the stars and slammed into it. The creature thinned and elongated until it looked like a reed pen trying to scribble a cryptic message between the stars, but the meteors wouldn't stop.

Drop back, you blasphemer, whispered the heavens. *You absconder, you vermin. The old world is gone. No place for your kind here now. Fall back and do your duty.*

And eventually the jinn gave up and let go.

It plummeted: a fluttering, helpless, enflamed ball shooting to the earth. It shrieked as it dove, flickering rapidly in and out of space and time but bound by their quantum fetters. It wanted to rage but couldn't. It wanted to save the lightning trees, to upchuck their tremulous shimmering roots and plant them somewhere the son of man wouldn't find them. Instead it was imprisoned, captured by prehuman magic and trapped to do time for a sin so old it had forgotten what it was.

So now it tumbled and plunged, hated and hating. It changed colors like a fiendish rainbow: mid-flame blue, muscle red, terror green, until the force of its fall bleached all its hues away and it became a pale scorching bolt of fire.

Thus the eucalyptus jinn fell to its inevitable dissolution, even as

Gramps woke up, his heart pounding, eyes fogged and aching from the dream. He groped in the dark, found the lantern, and lit it. He was still shaking. He got up, went to his narrow window that looked out at the moon-drenched Bhati Gate a hundred yards away. The eight arches of the Mughal structure were black and lonely above the central arch. Gramps listened. Someone was moving in the shack next door. In the princess's home. He gazed at the mosque of Ghulam Rasool—a legendary mystic known as the Master of Cats—on its left.

And he looked at the eucalyptus tree.

It soared higher than the gate, its wild armature pawing at the night, the oily scent of its leaves potent even at this distance. Gramps shivered, although heat was swelling from the ground from the first patter of raindrops. More smells crept into the room: dust, trash, verdure.

He backed away from the window, slipped his sandals on, dashed out of the house. He ran toward the tea stall, but before he could as much as cross the chicken yard up front, lightning unzipped the dark and the sky roared.

The blast of its fall could be heard for miles.

The eucalyptus exploded into a thousand pieces, the burning limbs crackling and sputtering in the thunderstorm that followed. More lightning splintered the night sky. Children shrieked, dreaming of twisted corridors with shadows wending past one another. Adults moaned as timeless gulfs shrank and pulsed behind their eyelids. The walled city thrashed in sweat-soaked sheets until the mullah climbed the minaret and screamed his predawn call.

In the morning the smell of ash and eucalyptol hung around the crisped boughs. The princess sobbed as she gazed at her buckled tin roof and smashed stall. Shards of china, plywood, clay, and charred wicker twigs lay everywhere.

The laborers and steelworkers rubbed their chins.

"Well, good riddance," said Alamdin, electrician, father of the injured boy whose possession had ultimately proved fleeting. Alamdin fingered a hole in his string vest. "Although I'm sorry for your loss, bibi. Perhaps the government will give you a monthly pension, being that you're royal descent and all."

Princess Zeenat's nose stud looked dull in the gray after-storm light. Her shirt was torn at the back, where a fragment of wood had bitten her as she scoured the wreckage.

"He was supposed to protect us," she murmured to the tree's remains: a black stump that poked from the earth like a singed umbilicus, and the roots lapping madly at her feet. "To give us shade and blessed sanctuary." Her grimed finger went for the nose stud and wrenched it out. "Instead—" She backpedaled and slumped at the foot of her shack's door. "Oh, my sisters. My sisters."

Tutting uncomfortably, the men drifted away, abandoning the pauper princess and her Mughal siblings. The women huddled together, a bevy of chukars stunned by a blood moon. Their shop was gone, the tree was gone. Princess Zeenat hugged her sisters and with a fierce light in her eyes whispered to them.

Over the next few days Gramps stood at Bhati Gate, watching the girls salvage timber, china, and clay. They washed and scrubbed their copper pots. Heaved out the tin sheet from the debris and dragged it to the foundries. Looped the remaining wicker into small bundles and sold it to basket weavers inside the walled city.

Gramps and a few past patrons offered to help. The Mughal women declined politely.

"But I can help, I really can," Gramps said, but the princess merely knitted her eyebrows, cocked her head, and stared at Gramps until he turned and fled.

The Municipality officer tapped at their door one Friday after Juma prayers.

"Condolences, bibi," he said. "My countless apologies. We should've cut it down before this happened."

"It's all right." The princess rolled the gold stud of her hemp necklace between two fingers. Her face was tired but tranquil. "It was going to happen one way or the other."

The officer picked at his red birthmark. "I meant your shop."

"We had good times here"—she nodded—"but my family's long overdue for a migration. We're going to go live with my cousin. He has an orange-and-fig farm in Mansehra. We'll find plenty to do."

The man ran his fingernail down the edge of her door. For the first time Gramps saw how his eyes never stayed on the princess. They drifted toward her face, then darted away as if the flush of her skin would sear them if they lingered. Warmth slipped around Gramps's neck, up his scalp, and across his face until his own flesh burned.

"Of course," the officer said. "Of course," and he turned and trudged to the skeletal stump. Already crows had marked the area with their pecking, busily creating a roost of the fallen tree. Soon they would be protected from horned owls and other birds of prey, they thought. But Gramps and Princess Zeenat knew better.

There was no protection here.

The officer cast one long look at the Mughal family, stepped around the stump, and walked away.

Later, the princess called to Gramps. He was sitting on the mosque's steps, shaking a brass bowl, pretending to be a beggar. He ran over, the coins jingling in his pocket.

"I know you saw something," she said once they were seated on the hemp charpoy in her shack. "I could see it in your face when you offered your help."

Gramps stared at her.

"That night," she persisted, "when the lightning hit the tree." She leaned forward, her fragrance of tea leaves and ash and cardamom filling his nostrils. "What did you see?"

"Nothing," he said and began to get up.

She grabbed his wrist. "Sit," she said. Her left hand shot out and pressed something into his palm. Gramps leapt off the charpoy. There was an electric sensation in his flesh; his hair crackled. He opened his fist and looked at the object.

It was her nose stud. The freshly polished gold shimmered in the dingy shack.

Gramps touched the stud with his other hand and withdrew it. "It's so cold."

The princess smiled, a bright thing that lit up the shack. Full of love, sorrow, and relief. But relief at what? Gramps sat back down, gripped the charpoy's posts, and tugged its torn hemp strands nervously.

"My family will be gone by tonight," the princess said.

And even though he'd been expecting this for days, it still came as a shock to Gramps. The imminence of her departure took his breath away. All he could do was wobble his head.

"Once we've left, the city might come to uproot that stump." The princess glanced over her shoulder toward the back of the room where shadows lingered. "If they try, do you promise you'll dig under it?" She rose and peered into the dimness, her eyes gleaming like jewels.

"Dig under the tree? Why?"

"Something lies there which, if you dig it up, you'll keep to yourself." Princess Zeenat swiveled on her heels. "Which you will hide in a safe place and never tell a soul about."

"Why?"

"Because that's what the fakir told my grandfather. Something old and secret rests under that tree and it's not for human eyes." She turned and walked to the door.

Gramps said, "Did you ever dig under it?"

She shook her head without looking back. "I didn't need to. As long as the tree stood, there was no need for me to excavate secrets not meant for me."

"And the gold stud? Why're you giving it away?"

"It comes with the burden."

"What burden? What *is* under that tree?"

The princess half turned. She stood in a nimbus of midday light, her long muscled arms hanging loosely, fingers playing with the place in the hemp necklace where once her family heirloom had been; and despite the worry lines and the callused hands and her uneven, grimy fingernails, she was beautiful.

Somewhere close, a brick truck unloaded its cargo and in its sudden thunder what the princess said was muffled and nearly inaudible. Gramps thought later it might have been, "The map to the memory of heaven."

But that of course couldn't be right.

"The princess and her family left Lahore that night," said Gramps. "This was in the fifties and the country was too busy recovering from Partition and picking up its own pieces to worry about a Mughal princess disappearing from the pages of history. So no one cared. Except me."

He sank back into the armchair and began to rock.

"She or her sisters ever come back?" I said, pushing myself off the floor with my knuckles. "What happened to them?"

Gramps shrugged. "What happens to all girls. Married their cousins in the north, I suppose. Had large families. They never returned to Lahore, see?"

"And the jinn?"

Gramps bent and poked his ankle with a finger. It left a shallow dimple. "I guess he died or flew away once the lightning felled the tree."

"What was under the stump?"

"How should I know?"

"What do you mean?"

"I didn't dig it up. No one came to remove the stump, so I never got a chance to take out whatever was there. Anyway, bache, you really should be going. It's late."

I glanced at my *Star Wars* watch. Luke's saber shone fluorescent across the Roman numeral two. I was impressed Mama hadn't returned to scold me to bed. I arched my back to ease the stiffness and looked at him with one eye closed. "You're seriously telling me you didn't dig up the secret?"

"I was scared," said Gramps, and gummed a fiber bar. "Look, I was told not to remove it if I didn't have to, so I didn't. Those days we listened to our elders, see?" He grinned, delighted with this unexpected opportunity to rebuke.

"But that's cheating," I cried. "The gold stud. The jinn's disappearance. You've explained nothing. That . . . that's not a good story at all. It just leaves more questions."

"All good stories leave questions. Now go on, get out of here. Before your mother yells at us both."

He rose and waved me toward the door, grimacing and rubbing his belly—heartburn from Hanif Uncle's party food? I slipped out and shut the door behind me. Already ghazal music was drifting out: *Ranjish hi sahih dil hi dukhanay ke liye aa.* Let it be heartbreak; come if just to hurt me again. I knew the song well. Gramps had worn out so many cassettes that Apna Bazaar ordered them in bulk just for him, Mama joked.

I went to my room, undressed, and for a long time tossed in the sheets, watching the moon outside my window. It was a supermoon kids at school had talked about, a magical golden egg floating near the horizon, and I wondered how many Mughal princes and princesses had gazed at it through the ages, holding hands with their lovers.

This is how the story of the Pauper Princess and the Eucalyptus Jinn comes to an end, I thought. In utter, infuriating oblivion.

I was wrong, of course.

In September 2013, Gramps had a sudden onset of chest pain and became short of breath. Nine-one-one was called, but by the time the medics came his heart had stopped and his extremities were mottled. Still they shocked him and injected him with epinephrine and atropine and sped him to the hospital where he was pronounced dead on arrival.

Gramps had really needed those water pills he'd refused until the end.

I was at Tufts teaching a course in comparative mythology when Baba called. It was a difficult year. I'd been refused tenure and a close friend had been fired over department politics. But when Baba asked me if I could come, I said of course. Gramps and I hadn't talked in years after I graduated from Florida State and moved to Massachusetts, but it didn't matter. There would be a funeral and a burial and a reception for the smattering of relatives who lived within drivable distance. I, the only grandchild, must be there.

Sara wanted to go with me. It would be a good gesture, she said.

"No," I said. "It would be a terrible gesture. Baba might not say anything, but the last person he'd want at Gramps's funeral is my white girlfriend. Trust me."

Sara didn't let go of my hand. Her fingers weren't dainty like some women's—you're afraid to squeeze them lest they shatter like glass—but they were soft and curled easily around mine. "You'll come back soon, won't you?"

"Of course. Why'd you ask?" I looked at her.

"Because," she said kindly, "you're going home." Her other hand plucked at a hair on my knuckle. She smiled, but there was a ghost of worry pinching the corner of her lips. "Because sometimes I can't read you."

We stood in the kitchenette facing each other. I touched Sara's chin. In the last few months there had been moments when things had been a bit hesitant, but nothing that jeopardized what we had.

"I'll be back," I said.

We hugged and kissed and whispered things I don't remember now. Eventually we parted and I flew to Florida, watching the morning landscape tilt through the plane windows. Below, the Charles gleamed like steel, then fell away until it was a silver twig in a hard land; and I thought, *The lightning trees are dying.*

Then we were past the waters and up and away, and the thought receded like the river.

We buried Gramps in Orlando Memorial Gardens under a row of pines. He was pale and stiff limbed, nostrils stuffed with cotton, the white shroud rippling in the breeze. I wished, like all fools rattled by late epiphanies, that I'd had more time with him. I said as much to Baba, who nodded.

"He would have liked that," Baba said. He stared at the gravestone with the epitaph *I have glimpsed the truth of the Great Unseen* that Gramps had insisted be written below his name. A verse from Rumi. "He would have liked that very much."

We stood in silence and I thought of Gramps and the stories he took with him that would stay untold forever. There's a funny thing about teaching myth and history: you realize in the deep of your bones that you'd be lucky to become a mote of dust, a speck on the bookshelf of human existence. The more tales you preserve, the more claims to immortality you can make.

After the burial we went home and Mama made us chicken karahi and basmati rice. It had been ages since I'd had home-cooked Pakistani food and the spice and garlicky taste knocked me back a bit. I downed half a bowl of fiery gravy and fled to Gramps's room where I'd been put up. Where smells of his cologne and musty clothes and his comings and goings still hung like a memory of old days.

In the following week Baba and I talked. More than we had in ages.

He asked me about Sara with a glint in his eyes. I said we were still together. He grunted.

"Thousands of suitable Pakistani girls," he began to murmur, and Mama shushed him.

In Urdu half-butchered from years of disuse I told them about Tufts and New England. Boston Commons, the Freedom Trail with its dozen cemeteries and royal burial grounds, the extremities of weather; how fall spun gold and rubies and amethyst from its foliage. Baba listened, occasionally wincing, as he worked on a broken power drill from his toolbox. It had been six years since I'd seen him and Mama, and the reality of their aging was like a gut punch. Mama's hair was silver, but at least her skin retained a youthful glow. Baba's fistful of beard was completely white, the hollows of his eyes deeper and darker. His fingers were swollen from rheumatoid arthritis he'd let fester for years because he couldn't afford insurance.

"You really need to see a doctor," I said.

"I have one. I go to the community health center in Leesburg, you know."

"Not a free clinic. You need to see a specialist."

"I'm fifty-nine. Six more years and then." He pressed the power button on the drill and it roared to life. "Things will change," he said cheerfully.

I didn't know what to say. I had offered to pay his bills before. The handyman's son wasn't exactly rich, but he was grown up now and could help his family out.

Baba would have none of it. I didn't like it, but what could I do? He had pushed me away for years. *Get out of here while you can,* he'd say. He marched me to college the same way he would march me to Sunday classes at Clermont Islamic Center. *Go on,* he said outside the mosque, as I clutched the siparas to my chest. *Memorize the Quran. If you don't, who will?*

Was that why I hadn't returned home until Gramps's death? Even then I knew there was more. Home was a morass where I would sink. I had tried one or two family holidays midway through college. They depressed me, my parents' stagnation, their world where nothing changed. The trailer park, its tired residents, the dead-leaf-strewn grounds that always seemed to get muddy and wet and never clean. A strange lethargy would settle on me here, a leaden feeling that left me cold and shaken. Visiting home became an ordeal filled with guilt at my indifference. I was new to the cutthroat world of academia then, and bouncing from one adjunct position to another was taking up all my time anyway.

I stopped going back. It was easier to call, make promises, talk about how bright my prospects were in the big cities. And with Gramps even phone talk was useless. He couldn't hear me, and he wouldn't put on those damn hearing aids.

So now I was living thousands of miles away with a girl Baba had never met.

I suppose I must've been hurt at his refusal of my help. The next few days were a blur between helping Mama with cleaning out Gramps's room and keeping up with the assignments my undergrads were emailing me even though I was on leave. A trickle of relatives and friends came, but to my relief Baba took over the hosting duties and let me sort through the piles of journals and tomes Gramps had amassed.

It was an impressive collection. Dozens of Sufi texts and religious treatises in different languages: Arabic, Urdu, Farsi, Punjabi, Turkish. Margins covered with Gramps's neat handwriting. I didn't remember seeing so many books in his room when I used to live here.

I asked Baba. He nodded.

"Gramps collected most of these after you left." He smiled. "I suppose he missed you."

I showed him the books. "Didn't you say he was having memory trouble? I remember Mama being worried about him getting dementia last time I talked. How could he learn new languages?"

"I didn't know he knew half these languages. Urdu and Punjabi he spoke and read fluently, but the others—" He shrugged.

Curious, I went through a few line notes. Thoughtful speculation on ontological and existential questions posed by the mystic texts. These were not the ramblings of a senile mind. Was Gramps's forgetfulness mere aging? Or had he written most of these before he began losing his marbles?

"Well, he did have a few mini strokes," Mama said when I asked. "Sometimes he'd forget where he was. Talk about Lahore, and oddly, Mansehra. It's a small city in Northern Pakistan," she added when I raised an eyebrow. "Perhaps he had friends there when he was young."

I looked at the books, ran my finger along their spines. It would be fun, nostalgic, to go through them at leisure, read Rumi's couplets and Hafiz's *Diwan*. I resolved to take the books with me. Just rent a car and drive up north with my trunk rattling with a cardboard box full of Gramps's manuscripts.

Then one drizzling morning I found a yellowed, dog-eared notebook under an old rug in his closet. Gramps's journal.

Before I left Florida I went to Baba. He was crouched below the kitchen sink, twisting a long wrench back and forth between the pipes, grunting. I waited until he was done, looked him in the eye, and said, "Did Gramps ever mention a woman named Zeenat Begum?"

Baba tossed the wrench into the toolbox. "Isn't that the woman in the fairy tale he used to tell? The pauper Mughal princess?"

"Yes."

"Sure he mentioned her. About a million times."

"But not as someone *you* might have known in real life?"

"No."

Across the kitchen I watched the door of Gramps's room. It was firmly closed. Within hung the portrait of the brown-eyed woman in the orange dopatta with her knowing half smile. She had gazed down at my family for decades, offering us that mysterious silver cup. There was a lump in my throat but I couldn't tell if it was anger or sorrow.

Baba was watching me, his swollen fingers tapping at the corner of his mouth. "Are you all right?"

I smiled, feeling the artifice of it stretch my skin like a mask. "Have you ever been to Turkey?"

"Turkey?" He laughed. "Sure. Right after I won the lottery and took that magical tour in the Caribbean."

I ignored the jest. "Does the phrase 'Courtesan of the Mughals' mean anything to you?"

He seemed startled. A smile of such beauty lit up his face that he looked ten years younger. "Ya Allah, I haven't heard that in forty years. Where'd you read it?"

I shrugged.

"It's Lahore. My city. That's what they called it in those books I read as a kid. Because it went through so many royal hands." He laughed, eyes gleaming with delight and mischief, and lowered his voice. "My friend Habib used to call it *La-whore*. The Mughal hooker. Now for Allah's sake, don't go telling your mother on me." His gaze turned inward. "Habib. God, I haven't thought of him in ages."

"Baba." I gripped the edge of the kitchen table. "Why don't you ever go back to Pakistan?"

His smile disappeared. He turned around, slammed the lid of his toolbox, and hefted it up. "Don't have time."

"You spent your teenage years there, didn't you? You obviously have some attachment to the city. Why didn't you take us back for a visit?"

"What would we go back to? We have no family there. My old friends are probably dead." He carried the toolbox out into the October sun, sweat gleaming on his forearms. He placed it in the back of his battered truck and climbed into the driver's seat. "I'll see you later."

I looked at him turn the keys in the ignition with fingers that shook. He was off to hammer sparkling new shelves in other people's garages, replace squirrel-rent screens on their lanais, plant magnolias and palms in their golfing communities, and I could say nothing. I thought I understood why he didn't want to visit the town where he grew up.

I thought about Mansehra and Turkey. If Baba really didn't know and Gramps had perfected the deception by concealing the truth within a lie, there was nothing I could do that wouldn't change, and possibly wreck, my family.

All good stories leave questions, Gramps had said to me.

You bastard, I thought.

"Sure," I said and watched my baba pull out and drive away, leaving a plumage of dust in his wake.

I called Sara when I got home. "Can I see you?" I said as soon as she picked up.

She smiled. I could hear her smile. "That bad, huh?"

"No, it was all right. I just really want to see you."

"It's one in the afternoon. I'm on campus." She paused. In the background birds chittered along with students. Probably the courtyard. "You sure you're okay?"

"Yes. Maybe." I upended the cardboard box on the carpet. The tower of books stood tall and uneven like a dwarf tree. "Come soon as you can, okay?"

"Sure. Love you."

"Love you too."

We hung up. I went to the bathroom and washed my face. I rubbed my eyes and stared at my reflection. It bared its teeth.

"Shut up," I whispered. "He was senile. Must have been completely insane. I don't believe a word of it."

But when Sara came that evening, her red hair streaming like fall leaves, her freckled cheeks dimpling when she saw me, I told her I believed, I really did. She sat and listened and stroked the back of my hand when it trembled as I lay in her lap and told her about Gramps and his journal.

It was an assortment of sketches and scribbling. A talented hand had drawn pastures, mountaintops, a walled city shown as a semicircle with half a dozen doors and hundreds of people bustling within, a farmhouse, and rows of fig and orange trees. Some of these were miniatures: images drawn as scenes witnessed by an omniscient eye above the landscape. Others were more conventional. All had one feature in common: a man and woman present in the center of the scenery going about the mundanities of their lives.

In one scene the man sat in a mosque's courtyard, performing ablution by the wudu tap. He wore a kurta and shalwar and Peshawari sandals. He was in his early twenties, lean, thickly bearded, with deep-set eyes that watched you impassively. In his hands he held a squalling baby whose tiny wrinkled fist was clenched around a stream of water from the tap. In the background a female face, familiar but older than I remembered, loomed over the courtyard wall, smiling at the pair.

The man was unmistakably Gramps, and the woman. . . .

"Are you kidding me?" Sara leaned over and stared at the picture. "That's the woman in the portrait hanging in his room?"

"He lied to me. To us all. She was my grandma."

"Who *is* she?"

"Princess Zeenat Begum," I said quietly.

Gramps had narrated the story of his life in a series of sketches and notes. The writing was in third person, but it was clear that the protagonist was he.

I imagined him going about the daily rituals of his life in Lahore after Princess Zeenat left. Dropping out of school, going to his father's shop in the Niche of Calligraphers near Bhati Gate, learning the art of khattati, painting billboards in red and yellow, fusing the ancient art with new slogans and advertisements. Now he's a lanky brown teenager wetting the tip of his brush, pausing to look up into the sky with its sweeping blue secrets. Now he's a tall man, yanking bird feathers and cobwebs away from a eucalyptus stump, digging under it in the deep of the night with a flashlight in his hand.

And now—he's wiping his tears, filling his knapsack with necessaries, burying his newly discovered treasure under a scatter of clothes, hitching the bag up his shoulders, and heading out into the vast unseen. All this time, there's only one image in his head and one desire.

"He was smitten with her. Probably had been for a long time without knowing it," I said. "Ruthlessly marked. His youth never had a chance against the siren call of history."

"Hold on a sec. What was under the tree again?" Sara said.

I shook my head. "He doesn't say."

"So he lied again? About not digging it up?"

"Yes."

"Who was he looking for?"

I looked at her. "My grandmother and her sisters."

We read his notes and envisioned Gramps's journey. Abandoning his own family, wandering his way into the mountains, asking everyone he met about a fig-and-orange farm on a quiet fir-covered peak in the heart of Mansehra. He was magnetized to the displaced Mughal family not because of their royalty, but the lack thereof.

And eventually he found them.

"He stayed with them for years, helping the pauper princess's uncle with farm work. In the summer he calligraphed Quranic verses on the minarets of local mosques. In wintertime he drew portraits for tourists and painted road signs. As years passed, he married Zeenat Begum—whose portrait one summer evening he drew and painted, carried with him, and lied about—and became one of them."

I looked up at Sara, into her gentle green eyes glittering above me. She bent and kissed my nose.

"They were happy for a while, he and his new family," I said, "but then, like in so many lives, tragedy came knocking at their door."

Eyes closed, I pictured the fire: a glowering creature clawing at their windows and door, crisping their apples, billowing flames across the barn to set their hay bales ablaze. The whinnying of the horses, the frantic braying of cattle, and, buried in the din, human screams.

"All three Mughal women died that night," I murmured. "Gramps and his two-year-old son were the only survivors of the brushfire. Broken and bereft, Gramps left Mansehra with the infant and went to Karachi. There he boarded a freighter that took them to Iran, then Turkey, where a sympathetic shopkeeper hired him in his rug shop. Gramps and his son stayed there for four years."

What a strange life, I thought. I hadn't known my father had spent part of his childhood in Turkey and apparently neither had he. He remembered nothing. How old was he when they moved back? As I thought this, my heart constricted in my chest, filling my brain with the hum of my blood.

Sara's face was unreadable when I opened my eyes. "Quite a story, eh?" I said uneasily.

She scratched the groove above her lips with a pink fingernail. "So he digs up whatever was under the tree and it decides him. He leaves everything and goes off to marry a stranger. This is romantic bullshit. You know that, right?"

"I don't know anything."

"Left everything," she repeated. Her mouth was parted with wonder. "You think whatever he found under the stump survived the fire?"

"Presumably. But where he took it—who can say? Eventually, though, they returned home. To Lahore, when Gramps had recovered enough sanity, I guess. Where his father, now old, had closed shop.

Gramps helped him reopen. Together they ran that design stall for years."

It must have been a strange time for Gramps, I thought. He loved his parents, but he hated Bhati. Even as he dipped his pen in ink and drew spirals and curlicues, his thoughts drew phantom pictures of those he had lost. Over the years, he came to loathe this art that unlocked so many memories inside him. And after his parents died he had neither heart nor imperative to keep going.

"He was done with the place, the shop, and Lahore. So when a friend offered to help him and his teenage son move to the States, Gramps agreed."

I turned my head and burrowed into Sara's lap. Her smell filled my brain: apple blossom, lipstick, and Sara.

She nuzzled my neck. The tip of her nose was cold. "He never talked to you about it? Never said what happened?"

"No."

"And you and your family had no idea about this artistic side of him? How's that possible?"

"Don't know," I said. "He worked at a 7-Eleven in Houston when he and Baba first came here. Never did any painting or calligraphy, commissioned or otherwise. Maybe he just left all his talent, all his dreams in his hometown. Here, look at this."

I showed her the phrase that spiraled across the edges of a couple dozen pages: *My killer, my deceiver, the Courtesan of the Mughals.* "It's Lahore. He's talking about the city betraying him."

"How's that?"

I shrugged.

"How weird," Sara said. "Interesting how broken up his story is. As if he's trying to piece together his own life."

"Maybe that's what he was doing. Maybe he forced himself to forget the most painful parts."

"Lightning trees. Odd thing to say." She looked at me thoughtfully and put the journal away. "So, you're the last of the Mughals, huh?" She smiled to show she wasn't laughing.

I chortled for her. "Seems like it. The Pauper Prince of New England."

"Wow. You come with a certificate of authenticity?" She nudged her foot at the book tower. "Is it in there somewhere?"

It was getting late. Sara tugged at my shirt, and I got up and carried her to bed, where we celebrated my return with zest. Her face was beautiful in the snow shadows that crept in through the window.

"I love you, I love you," we murmured, enchanted with each other, drunk with belief in some form of eternity. The dark lay quietly beside us, and, smoldering in its heart, a rotating image.

A dim idea of what was to come.

I went through Gramps's notes. Many were in old Urdu, raikhta, which I wasn't proficient in. But I got the gist: discourses and rumination on the otherworldly.

Gramps was especially obsessed with Ibn Arabi's treatise on jinns in *The Meccan Revelations*. The Lofty Master Arabi says, wrote Gramps, that the meaning of the lexical root *J-N-N* in Arabic is 'concealed.' Jinn isn't just another created being ontologically placed between man and angel; it is the *entirety* of the hidden world.

"Isn't that fucking crazy?" I said to Sara. We were watching a rerun of *Finding Neverland*, my knuckles caked with butter and flakes of popcorn. On the screen J. M. Barrie's wife was beginning to be upset by the attention he lavished upon the children's mother, Sylvia. "It kills the traditional narrative of jinns in *A Thousand and One Nights*. If one were to pursue this train of thought, it would mean relearning the symbolism in this text and virtually all others."

Sara nodded, her gaze fixed on the TV. "Uh huh."

"Consider this passage: 'A thousand years before Darwin, Sufis described the evolution of man as rising from the inorganic state through plant and animal to human. But the mineral consciousness of man, that dim memory of being buried in the great stone mother, lives on.'"

Sara popped a handful of popcorn into her mouth. Munched.

I rubbed my hands together. "'Jinns are carriers of that concealed memory, much like a firefly carries a memory of the primordial fire.' It's the oddest interpretation of jinns I've seen."

"Yeah, it's great." Sara shifted on the couch. "But can we please watch the movie?"

"Uh-huh."

I stared at the TV. Gramps thought jinns weren't devil-horned creatures bound to a lamp or, for that matter, a tree.

They were flickers of cosmic consciousness.

I couldn't get that image out of my head. Why was Gramps obsessed with this? How was this related to his life in Lahore? Something to do with the eucalyptus secret?

The next morning I went to Widener Library and dug up all I could about Arabi's and Ibn Taymeeyah's treatment of jinns. I read and pondered, went back to Gramps's notebooks, underlined passages in *The Meccan Revelations*, and walked the campus with my hands in my pockets and my heart in a world long dissipated.

"Arabi's cosmovision is staggering," I told Sara. We were sitting in a coffee shop downtown during lunch break. It was drizzling, just a gentle stutter of gray upon gray outside the window, but it made the brick buildings blush.

Sara sipped her mocha and glanced at her watch. She had to leave soon for her class.

"Consider life as a spark of consciousness. In Islamic cosmology the jinn's intrinsic nature is that of wind and fire. Adam's—read, man's—nature is water and clay, which are more resistant than fire to cold and dryness. As the universe changes, so do the requirements for life's vehicle. Now it needs creatures more resistant and better adapted. Therefore, *from the needs of sentient matter rose the invention that is us.*"

I clenched my hand into a fist. "This interpretation is pretty fucking genius. I mean, is it possible Gramps was doing real academic work? For example, had he discovered something in those textbooks that could potentially produce a whole new ideology of creation? Why, it could be the scholarly discovery of the century."

"Yes, it's great." She rapped her spoon against the edge of the table. Glanced at me, looked away.

"What?"

"Nothing. Listen, I gotta run, okay?" She gave me a quick peck on the cheek and slid out of her seat. At the door she hesitated, turned, and stood tapping her shoes, a waiting look in her eyes.

I dabbed pastry crumbs off my lips with a napkin. "Are you okay?"

Annoyance flashed in her face and vanished. "Never better." She pulled her jacket's hood over her head, yanked the door open, and strode out into the rain.

It wasn't until later that evening, when I was finalizing the spring calendar for my freshman class, that I realized I had forgotten our first-date anniversary.

Sara hadn't. There was a heart-shaped box with a pink bow sitting on the bed when I returned home. Inside was a note lying atop a box of Godiva Chocolates:

Happy Anniversary. May our next one be like your grandfather's fairy tales.

My eyes burned with lack of sleep. It was one in the morning and I'd had a long day at the university. Also, the hour-long apology to Sara had drained me. She had shaken her head and tried to laugh it off, but I took my time, deeming it a wise investment for the future.

I went to the kitchen and poured myself a glass of ice water. Kicked off my slippers, returned to the desk, and continued reading.

I hadn't lied to Sara. The implications of this new jinn mythology were tremendous. A new origin myth, a bastardized version of the Abrahamic creationist lore. Trouble was these conclusions were tenuous. Gramps had speculated more than logically derived them. Arabi himself had touched on these themes in an abstract manner. To produce a viable theory of this alternate history of the universe, I needed more details, more sources.

Suppose there were other papers, hidden manuscripts. Was it possible that the treasure Gramps had found under the eucalyptus stump was truly "the map to the memory of heaven"? Ancient papers of cosmological importance never discovered?

"Shit, Gramps. Where'd you hide them?" I murmured.

His journal said he'd spent quite a bit of time in different places: Mansehra, Iran. Turkey, where he spent four years in a rug shop. The papers could really be anywhere.

My eyes were drawn to the phrase again: the Courtesan of the Mughals. I admired how beautiful the form and composition of the calligraphy was. Gramps had shaped the Urdu alphabet carefully into a flat design so that the conjoined words *Mughal* and *Courtesan* turned into an ornate rug. A calligram. The curves of the *meem* and *ghain* letters became the tassels and borders of the rug, the *laam*'s seductive curvature its rippling belly.

Such artistry. One shape discloses another. A secret, symbolic relationship.

There, I thought. The secret hides in the city. The clues to the riddle of the eucalyptus treasure are in Lahore.

I spent the next few days sorting out my finances. Once I was satisfied that the trip was feasible, I began to make arrangements.

Sara stared at me when I told her. "Lahore? You're going to Lahore?"

"Yes."

"To look for something your grandpa may or may not have left there fifty-some years ago?"

"Yes."

"You're crazy. I mean it's one thing to talk about a journal."

"I know. I still need to go."

"So you're telling me, not asking. Why? Why are you so fixed on this? You know that country isn't safe these days. What if something happens?" She crossed her arms, lifted her feet off the floor, and tucked them under her on the couch. She was shivering a little.

"Nothing's gonna happen. Look, whatever he left in Lahore, he wanted me to see it. Why else write about it and leave it in his journal which he knew would be found one day? Don't you see? He was really writing to me."

"Well, that sounds self-important. Why not your dad? Also, why drop hints then? Why not just tell you straight up what it is?"

"I don't know." I shrugged. "Maybe he didn't want other people to find out."

"Or maybe he was senile. Look, I'm sorry, but this is crazy. You can't just fly off to the end of the world on a whim to look for a relic." She rubbed her legs. "It could take you weeks. Months. How much vacation time do you have left?"

"I'll take unpaid leave if I have to. Don't you see? I need to do this."

She opened her mouth, closed it. "Is this something you plan to keep doing?" she said quietly. "Run off each time anything bothers you."

"What?" I quirked my eyebrows. "Nothing's bothering me."

"No?" She jumped up from the couch and glared at me. "You've met my mother and Fanny, but I've never met your parents. You didn't take me to your grandfather's funeral. And since your return you don't seem interested in what we have, or once had. Are you *trying* to avoid talking about us? Are we still in love, Sal, or are we just getting by? Are we really together?"

"Of course we're together. Don't be ridiculous," I mumbled, but there was a constriction in my stomach. It wouldn't let me meet her eyes.

"Don't patronize me. You're obsessed with your own little world. Look, I have no problem with you giving time to your folks. Or your gramps's work. But we've been together for three years and you still find excuses to steer me away from your family. This cultural thing that you claim to resent, you seem almost proud of it. Do you see what I mean?"

"No." I was beginning to get a bit angry. "And I'm not sure you do either."

"You're lying. You know what I'm talking about."

"Do I? Okay, lemme try to explain what my problem is. Look at me, Sara. What do you see?"

She stared at me, shook her head. "I see a man who doesn't know he's lost."

"Wrong. You see a twenty-eight-year-old brown man living in a shitty apartment, doing a shitty job that doesn't pay much and has no hope of tenure. You see a man who can't fend for himself, let alone a wife and kids—"

"No one's asking you to—"

"—if he doesn't do something better with his life. But you go on believing all will be well if we trade families? Open your damn eyes." I leaned against the TV cabinet, suddenly tired. "All my life I was prudent. I planned and planned and gave up one thing for another. Moved here. Never looked back. Did whatever I could to be what I thought I needed to be. The archetypal fucking immigrant in the land of opportunities. But after Gramps died. . . ." I closed my eyes, breathed, opened them. "I realize some things are worth more than that. Some things are worth going after."

"Some things, huh?" Sara half smiled, a trembling flicker that took me aback more than her words did. "Didn't your grandfather give up everything—his life, his family, his country—for love? And you're giving up . . . love for . . . what exactly? Shame? Guilt? Identity? A fucking manventure in a foreign land?"

"You're wrong," I said. "I'm not—"

But she wasn't listening. Her chest hitched. Sara turned, walked into the bedroom, and gently closed the door, leaving me standing alone.

I stomped down Highland Avenue. It was mid-October and the oaks and silver maples were burning with fall. They blazed yellow and crimson. They made me feel sadder and angrier and more confused.

Had our life together always been this fragile? I wondered if I had missed clues that Sara felt this way. She always was more aware of bumps in our relationship. I recalled watching her seated at the desk marking student papers once, her beautiful, freckled face scrunched in a frown, and thinking she would never really be welcome in my parents' house. Mama would smile nervously if I brought her home and retreat into the kitchen. Baba wouldn't say a word and somehow that would be worse than an outraged rejection. And what would Gramps have done? I didn't know. My head was messed up. It had been since his death.

It was dusk when I returned home, the lights in our neighborhood floating dreamily like gold sequins in black velvet.

Sara wasn't there.

The bed was made, the empty hangers in the closet pushed neatly together. On the coffee table in the living room under a Valentine mug was yet another note. She had become adept at writing me love letters.

I made myself a sandwich, sat in the dark, and picked at the bread. When I had mustered enough courage, I retrieved the note and began to read:

Salman,

I ~~wrote~~ tried to write this several times and each time my hand shook and made me write things I didn't want to. It sucks that we're such damn weaklings, the both of us. I'm stuck in love with you and you ~~are~~ with me. At least I hope so. At least that's the way I ~~feel~~ read you. But then I think about my mother and my heart begins racing.

You've met my family. Mom likes you. Fanny too. They think you're good for me. But you've never met my dad. You don't know why we ~~never~~ don't talk about him anymore.

He left Mom when Fanny and I were young. I don't remember him, although sometimes I think I can. When I close my eyes, I see this big, bulky shadow overwhelm the doorway of my room. There's this bittersweet smell, gin and sweat and tobacco. I remember not feeling afraid of him, for which I'm grateful.

But Dad left ~~us~~ Mom and he broke her. In especially bitter moments she would say it was another woman, but I don't think so. At least I never saw any proof of that in my mother's eyes when she talked about him. (In the beginning she talked a LOT about him.) I think he left her because he wanted more from life and Mom didn't ~~understand~~ pick that up. I think she didn't read his unhappiness in time. That's the vibe I get.

Does that excuse what he did? I don't think so. My mother's spent all her life trying to put us back together and she's done okay, but there are pieces of herself she wasn't able to find. In either me, or Fanny, or in anyone else.

~~I don't want that to happen to me.~~ I don't want to end up like my mother. That's pretty much it. If you didn't love me, I'd understand. I'd be hurt, but I could live with it.

But living with this uncertainty, never knowing when you might get that wanderlust I've seen in your eyes lately, is impossible for me. There's so much I want to say to you. Things you need to know if we're to have a future together. But the last thing I want to do is force you.

So I'm leaving. I'm going to stay at Fanny's. Think things through. It will be good for both of us. It will help me get my head straight and will let you do whatever you want to get your fucking demons out. So fly free. Go to Pakistan. Follow your goddamn heart or whatever. Just remember I won't wait all my life.

You know where to find me.

Love,

Sara

I put down the letter and stared out the window. Night rain drummed on the glass. I tapped my finger to its tune, fascinated by how difficult it was to keep time with it. A weight had settled on my chest and I couldn't push it off.

If an asshole weeps in the forest and no one is around to witness, is he still an asshole?

Nobody was there to answer.

For most of the fifteen-hour flight from New York to Lahore I was out. I hadn't realized how tired I was until I slumped into the economy seat and woke up half-dazed when the flight attendant gently shook my shoulder.

"Lahore, sir." She smiled when I continued to stare at her. The lipstick smudge on her teeth glistened. "Allama Iqbal International Airport."

"Yes," I said, struggling up and out. The plane was empty, the seats gaping. "How's the weather?"

"Cold. Bit misty. Fog bank's coming, they said. Early this year."

That didn't sound promising. I thanked her and hurried out, my carry-on clattering against the aisle armrests.

I exited the airport into the arms of a mid-November day and the air was fresh but full of teeth. The pale sea-glass sky seemed to wrap around the airport. I hailed a cab and asked for Bhati Gate. As we sped out of the terminal, whiteness seethed on the runway and blanketed the horizon. The flight attendant was right. Fog was on the way.

At a busy traffic signal the cabbie took a right. Past army barracks, the redbrick Aitchison College, and colonial-era Jinnah Gardens we went, until the roads narrowed and we hiccuped through a sea of motorbikes, rickshaws, cars, and pedestrians. *TERRORISTS ARE ENEMIES OF PEACE*, said a large black placard on a wall that jutted out left of a fifty-foot-high stone gate. The looming structure had a massive central arch with eight small arches above it. It had a painting of the Kaaba on the right and Prophet Muhammad's shrine on the left with vermilion roses embossed in the middle. Another sign hung near it: *WELCOME TO OLD LAHORE BY THE GRACE OF ALLAH.*

We were at Bhati Gate.

The cab rolled to a stop in front of Kashi Manzil. A tall, narrow historical-home-turned-hotel with a facade made of ochre and azure faience tiles. A wide terrace ran around the second floor and a small black copper pot hung from a nail on the edge of the doorway awning.

I recognized the superstition. Black to ward off black. Protection against the evil eye.

Welcome to Gramps's world, I thought.

I looked down the street. Roadside bakeries, paan-and-cigarette shops, pirated DVD stalls, a girls' school with peeling walls, and dust, dust everywhere; but my gaze of course went to Bhati and its double row of arches.

This was the place my grandfather had once gazed at, lived by, walked through. Somewhere around here used to be a tea stall run by a Mughal princess. Someplace close had been a eucalyptus from which a kid had fallen and gashed his head. A secret that had traveled the globe had come here with Gramps and awaited me in some dingy old alcove.

That stupid wanderlust in your eyes.

Sara's voice in my brain was a gentle rebuke.

Later, I thought fiercely. *Later.*

The next day I began my search.

I had planned to start with the tea stalls. Places like this have long memories. Old Lahore was more or less the city's ancient downtown and people here wouldn't forget much. Least of all a Mughal princess who ran a tea shop. Gramps's journal didn't much touch on his life in the walled city. I certainly couldn't discern any clues about the location of the eucalyptus treasure.

Where did you hide it, old man? Your shack? A friend's place? Under that fucking tree stump?

If Gramps was correct and the tree had fallen half a century ago, that landmark was probably irretrievable. Gramps's house seemed the next logical place. Trouble was I didn't know where Gramps had lived. Before I left, I'd called Baba and asked him. He wasn't helpful.

"It's been a long time, son. Fifty years. Don't tax an old man's memory. You'll make me senile."

When I pressed, he reluctantly gave me the street where they used to live and his childhood friend Habib's last name.

"I don't remember our address, but I remember the street. Ask anyone in Hakiman Bazaar for Khajoor Gali. They'll know it."

Encircled by a wall raised by Akbar the Great, Old Lahore was bustling and dense. Two hundred thousand people lived in an area less than one square mile. Breezes drunk with the odor of cardamom, grease, and tobacco. The place boggled my mind as I strolled around taking in the niche pharmacies, foundries, rug shops, kite shops, and baked mud eateries.

I talked to everyone I encountered. The tea stall owner who poured Peshawari kahva in my clay cup. The fruit seller who handed me sliced oranges and guavas and frowned when I mentioned the pauper princess. Rug merchants, cigarette vendors, knife sellers. No one had heard of Zeenat Begum. Nobody knew of a young man named Sharif or his father who ran a calligraphy-and-design stall.

"Not around my shop, sahib." They shook their heads and turned away.

I located Khajoor Gali—a winding narrow alley once dotted by palm trees (or so the locals claimed), now home to dusty ramshackle buildings hunched behind open manholes—and went door to door, asking. No luck. An aged man with henna-dyed hair and a shishamwood cane stared at me when I mentioned Baba's friend Habib Ataywala, and said, "Habib. Ah, he and his family moved to Karachi several years ago. No one knows where."

"How about a eucalyptus tree?" I asked. "An ancient eucalyptus that used to stand next to Bhati Gate?"

Nope.

Listlessly I wandered, gazing at the mist lifting off the edges of the streets and billowing toward me. On the third day it was like slicing through a hundred rippling white shrouds. As night fell and fairy lights blinked on the minarets of Lahore's patron saint Data Sahib's shrine across the road from Bhati, I felt displaced. Depersonalized. I was a mote drifting in a slat of light surrounded by endless dark. Gramps was correct. Old Lahore had betrayed him. It was as if the city had deliberately rescinded all memory or trace of his family and the princess's. Sara was right. Coming here was a mistake. My life since Gramps's death was a mistake. Seeing this world as it *was* rather than through the fabular lens of Gramps's stories was fucking enlightening.

In this fog, the city's fresh anemia, I thought of things I hadn't thought about in years. The time Gramps taught me to perform the salat. The first time he brought my palms together to form the supplicant's cup. *Be the beggar at Allah's door,* he told me gently. *He loves humility. It's in the mendicant's bowl that the secrets of Self are revealed.* In the tashahuud position Gramps's index finger would shoot from a clenched fist and flutter up and down.

"This is how we beat the devil on the head," he said.

But what devil was I trying to beat? I'd been following a ghost and hoping for recognition from the living.

By the fifth day I'd made up my mind. I sat shivering on a wooden bench and watched my breath flute its way across Khajoor Gali as my finger tapped my cell phone and thousands of miles away Sara's phone rang.

She picked up almost immediately. Her voice was wary. "Sal?"

"Hey."

"Are you all right?"

"Yes."

A pause. "You didn't call before you left."

"I thought you didn't want me to."

"I was worried sick. One call after you landed would've been nice."

I was surprised but pleased. After so much disappointment, her concern was welcome. "Sorry."

"Jesus. I was. . . ." She trailed off, her breath harsh and rapid in my ear. "Find the magic treasure yet?"

"No."

"Pity." She seemed distracted now. In the background water was running. "How long will you stay there?"

"I honest to God don't know, but I'll tell you this. I'm fucking exhausted."

"I'm sorry." She didn't sound sorry. I smiled a little.

"Must be around five in the morning there. Why're you up?" I said.

"I was . . . worried, I guess. Couldn't sleep. Bad dreams." She sighed. I imagined her rubbing her neck, her long fingers curling around the muscles, kneading them, and I wanted to touch her.

"I miss you," I said.

Pause. "Yeah. Me too. It's a mystery how much I'm used to you being around. And now that. . . ." She stopped and exhaled. "Never mind."

"What?"

"Nothing." She grunted. "This damn weather. I think I'm coming down with something. Been headachy all day."

"Are you okay?"

"Yeah. It'll go away. Listen, I'm gonna go take a shower. You have fun."

Was that reproach? "Yeah, you too. Be safe."

"Sure." She sounded as if she were pondering. "Hey, I discovered something. Been meaning to tell you, but . . . you know."

"I'm all ears."

"Remember what your gramps said in the story. Lightning trees?"

"Yes."

"Well, lemme text it to you. I mentioned the term to a friend at school and turned out he recognized it too. From a lecture we both attended at MIT years ago about fractal similarities and diffusion-limited aggregation."

"Fractal what?" My phone beeped. I removed it from my ear and looked at the screen. A high-definition picture of a man with what looked like a tree-shaped henna tattoo on his left shoulder branching all the way down his arm. Pretty.

I put her on speakerphone. "Why're you sending me pictures of henna tattoos?"

She was quiet, then started laughing. "That didn't even occur to me, but, yeah, it does look like henna art."

"It isn't?"

"Nope. What you're seeing is a Lichtenberg figure created when branching electrical charges run through insulating material. Glass, resin, human skin—you name it. This man was hit by lightning and survived with this stamped on his flesh."

"What?"

"Yup. It can be created in any modern lab using nonconducting plates. Called electric treeing. Or lightning trees."

The lightning trees are dying.

"Holy shit," I said softly.

"Yup."

I tapped the touch screen to zoom in for a closer look. "How could Gramps know about this? If he made up the stories, how the fuck would he know something like this?"

"No idea. Maybe he knew someone who had this happen to them."

"But what does it mean?"

"The heck should I know. Anyways, I gotta go. Figured it might help you with whatever you're looking for."

"Thanks."

She hung up. I stared at the pattern on the man's arm. It was reddish, fernlike, and quite detailed. The illusion was so perfect I could even see buds and leaves. A breathtaking electric foliage. A map of lightning.

A memory of heaven.

I went to sleep early that night.

At five in the morning the Fajr call to prayer woke me up. I lay in bed watching fog drift through the skylight window, listening to the mullah's sonorous azaan, and suddenly I jolted upright.

The mosque of Ghulam Rasool, the Master of Cats.

Wasn't that what Gramps had told me a million years ago? That there was a mosque near Bhati Gate that faced his house?

I hadn't seen *any* mosques around.

I slipped on clothes and ran outside.

The morning smelled like burnished metal. The light was soft, the shape of early risers gentle in the mist-draped streets. A rooster crowed in the next alley. It had drizzled the night before and the ground was muddy. I half slipped, half leapt my way toward the mullah's voice rising and falling like an ocean heard in one's dream.

Wisps of white drifted around me like twilit angels. The azaan had stopped. I stared at the narrow doorway next to a rug merchant's shop ten feet away. Its entrance nearly hidden by an apple tree growing in the middle of the sidewalk, the place was tucked well away from traffic. Green light spilled from it. Tiny replicas of the Prophet's Mosque in Medina and Rumi's shrine in Turkey were painted above the door.

Who would put Rumi here when Data Sahib's shrine was just across the road?

I took off my shoes and entered the mosque.

A tiny room with a low ceiling set with zero-watt green bulbs. On reed mats the congregation stood shoulder to shoulder in two rows behind a smallish man in shalwar kameez and a turban. The Imam sahib clicked the mute button on the standing microphone in front, touched his earlobes, and Fajr began.

Feeling oddly guilty, I sat down in a corner. Looked around the room. Ninety-nine names of Allah and Muhammad, prayers and Quranic verses belching from the corners, twisting and pirouetting across the walls. Calligrams in the shape of a mynah bird, a charging lion, a man prostrate in sajdah, his hands out before him shaping a beggar's bowl filled with alphabet vapors. Gorgeous work.

Salat was over. The namazis began to leave. Imam sahib turned. In his hands he held a tally counter for tasbih. *Click click!* Murmuring prayers, he rose and hobbled toward me.

"Assalam-o-alaikum. May I help you, son?" he said in Urdu.

"Wa Laikum Assalam. Yes," I said. "Is this Masjid Ghulam Rasool?"

He shook his head. He was in his seventies at least, long noorani beard, white hair sticking out of his ears. His paunch bulged through the striped-flannel kameez flowing past his ankles. "No. That mosque was closed and martyred in the nineties. Sectarian attacks. Left a dozen men dead. Shia mosque, you know. Used to stand in Khajoor Gali, I believe."

"Oh." I told myself I'd been expecting this, but my voice was heavy with disappointment. "I'm sorry to bother you then. I'll leave you to finish up."

"You're not local, son. Your salam has an accent," he said. "Amreekan, I think. You look troubled. How can I help you?" He looked at me, took his turban off. He had a pale scar near his left temple shaped like a climbing vine.

I watched him. His hair was silver. His sharp eyes were blue, submerged in a sea of wrinkles. "I was looking for a house. My late grandfather's. He lived close to the mosque, next door to a lady named Zeenat Begum. She used to run a tea stall."

"Zeenat Begum." His eyes narrowed, the blues receding into shadow. "And your grandfather's name?" he asked, watching the last of the worshippers rise to his feet.

"Sharif. Muhammad Sharif."

The oddest feeling, a sort of déjà vu, came over me. Something had changed in the air of the room. Even the last namazi felt it and glanced over his shoulder on his way out.

"Who did you say you were again?" Imam sahib said quietly.

"Salman Ali Zaidi."

"I see. Yes, I do believe I can help you out. This way."

He turned around, limping, and beckoned me to follow. We exited the mosque. He padlocked it, parted the bead curtain in the doorway of the rug shop next door, stepped in.

When I hesitated, he paused, the tasbih counter clicking in his hands. "Come in, son. My place is your place."

I studied the rug shop. It was located between the mosque and a souvenir stall. The awning above the arched doorway was gray, the brick voussoirs and keystone of the arch faded and peeling. The plaque by the entrance said KARAVAN KILIM.

Kilim is a kind of Turkish carpet. What was a kilim shop doing in Old Lahore?

He led me through a narrow well-lit corridor into a hardwood-floored showroom. Mounds of neatly folded rugs sat next to walls covered in rectangles of rich tapestries, carpets, and pottery-filled shelves. Stunning illustrations and calligraphy swirled across the high wooden ceiling. Here an entranced dervish whirled in blue, one palm toward the sky and one to the ground. There a crowd haloed with golden light held out dozens of drinking goblets, an Urdu inscription spiraling into a vast cloud above their heads: *They hear his hidden hand pour truth in the heavens.*

A bald middle-aged man dressed in a checkered brown half-sleeve shirt sat behind a desk. Imam sahib nodded at him. "My nephew Khalid."

Khalid and I exchanged pleasantries. Imam sahib placed the tasbih counter and his turban on the desk. I gazed around me. "Imam sahib," I said. "This is a Turkish carpet shop. You run an imported rug business in your spare time?"

"Turkish design, yes, but not imported. My apprentices make them right here in the walled city." Without looking back, he began walking. "You can call me Bashir."

We went to the back of the shop, weaving our way through rug piles into a storeroom lit by sunlight from a narrow window. Filled to the ceiling with mountains of fabric rolls and broken looms, the room smelled of damp, rotten wood, and tobacco. In a corner was a large box covered with a bedsheet. Bashir yanked the sheet away and a puff of dust bloomed and clouded the air.

"Sharif," said the merchant Imam. "He's dead, huh?"

"You *knew* him?"

"Of course. He was friends with the Mughal princess. The lady who used to give us tea."

"How do you know that?" I stared at him. "Who are you?"

His eyes hung like sapphires in the dimness, gaze fixed on me, one hand resting atop the embossed six-foot-long metal trunk that had emerged. He tilted his head so the feeble light fell on his left temple. The twisted pale scar gleamed.

"The boy who fell from the eucalyptus tree," I whispered. "He gashed his head and the princess bandaged it for him. You're him."

The old man smiled. "Who I am is not important, son. What's important is this room where your grandfather worked for years."

Speechless, I gaped at him. After days of frustration and disappointment, I was standing in the room Gramps had occupied decades ago, this dingy store with its decaying inhabitants. I looked around as if at any moment Gramps might step out from the shadows.

"He was the best teacher I ever had," Bashir said. "We used to call him the Calligrapher Prince."

He flashed a smile. It brightened Bashir the merchant's tired, old face like a flame.

I watched this man with his wispy moonlight hair and that coiled scar who had kept my grandfather's secret for half a century. We sat around a low circular table, dipping cake rusk into mugs of milk chai sweetened with brown sugar. It was eight in the morning.

Bashir gripped his cup with both hands and frowned into it.

"My father was an electrician," he said. "By the time he was fifty he'd saved enough to buy a carpet shop. With lots of construction going on, he was able to get this shop dirt cheap.

"Rugs were an easy trade back in the seventies. You hired weavers, most of 'em immigrants from up north, and managed the product. We didn't have good relations with neighboring countries, so high demand existed for local rugs and tapestries without us worrying about competition. After the dictator Zia came, all that changed. Our shop didn't do well, what with rugs being imported cheap from the Middle East and Afghanistan. We began to get desperate.

"Right about then a stranger came to us."

It began, Bashir said, the evening someone knocked on their door with a rosy-cheeked child by his side and told Bashir's father he was looking for work. Bashir, then in his late teens, stood behind his baba, watching the visitor. Wary, the rug merchant asked where they hailed from. The man lifted his head and his face shone with the strangest light Bashir had seen on a human countenance.

"It swept across his cheeks, it flared in his eyes, it illuminated the cuts and angles of his bones," said Bashir, mesmerized by memory. "It was as if he had been touched by an angel or a demon. I'll never forget it."

"From thousands of miles away," said the man quietly. "From many years away."

It was Gramps, of course.

Bashir's father didn't recognize him, but he knew the man's family. Their only son, Muhammad Sharif, had been abroad for years, he'd heard. Lived in Iran, Turkey, Allah knew where else. Sharif's aged father still lived on Khajoor Gali in Old Lahore, but he'd shut down his design stall in the Niche of Calligraphers years ago.

"Sharif had been back for a few months and he and his son were living with his father. Now they needed money to reopen their shop." Bashir smiled. "Turned out your grandfather was an expert rug weaver. He said he learned it in Turkey near Maulana Rumi's shrine. My father offered him a job and he accepted. He worked with us for three years while he taught kilim weaving to our apprentices.

"He was young, hardly a few years older than I, but when he showed me his notebook, I knew he was no ordinary artist. He had drawn mystical poetry in animal shapes. Taken the quill and created dazzling worlds. Later, when my father put him before the loom, Sharif produced wonders such as we'd never seen."

Merchant Bashir got up and plodded to a pile of rugs. He grabbed a kilim and unrolled it across the floor. A mosaic of black, yellow, and maroon geometries glimmered.

"He taught me rug weaving. It's a nomadic art, he said. Pattern making carries the past into the future." Bashir pointed to a recurrent cross motif that ran down the kilim's center. "The four corners of the cross are the four corners of the universe. The scorpion here"—he toed a many-legged symmetric creature woven in yellow—"represents freedom. Sharif taught me this and more. He was a natural at symbols. I asked him why he went to Turkey. He looked at me and said, 'To learn to weave the best kilim in the world.'"

I cocked my head, rapt. I had believed it was grief that banished Gramps from Pakistan and love that bade him return. Now this man was telling me Gramps went to Turkey purposefully. How many other secrets had my grandfather left out?

"I didn't know he was a rug weaver," I said.

"Certainly was. One of the best we ever saw. He knew what silk-on-silk warping was. Don't weave on a poor warp. Never work on a loom out of alignment. He knew all this. Yet, *he* didn't consider himself a weaver. He learned the craft to carry out a duty, he said. His passion was calligraphy. All this you see"—Bashir waved a hand at the brilliant kilims and tapestries around us, at the twists and curlicues of the verses on the walls, the wondrous illustrations—"is his genius manifested. The Ottoman Turkish script, those calligrams in our mosque, the paintings. It's all him and his obsession with the Turkish masters."

"He ever say why he left Pakistan or why he returned?"

Bashir shrugged. "We never asked. As long as it wasn't criminal, we didn't care."

"Why'd you call him the Calligrapher Prince?"

The old man laughed. "It was a nickname the apprentices gave him and it stuck. Seemed so fitting." Bashir lifted his cup and swallowed the last mouthful of tea along with the grounds. I winced. "Sharif was courteous and diligent. Hardly went home before midnight and he helped the business run more smoothly than it had in years, but I knew he was waiting for something. His eyes were always restless. Inward."

In the evenings when the shop had closed Sharif drew and carved keenly. For hours he engraved, his cotton swabs with lacquer thinner in one hand, his burin and flat gravers in the other. What he was making was no secret. Bashir watched the process and the product: a large brass trunk with a complex inlay in its lid. A labyrinthine repoussé network gouged into the metal, spiraling into itself. Such fine work it took one's breath away.

"Never, never, never," said Bashir, "have I seen such a thing of beauty evolve in a craftsman's hand again."

Sharif's concentration was diabolical, his hands careful as nature's might have been as it designed the ornate shells of certain mollusks or the divine geometry of certain leaves.

"What are you making and why?" Bashir had asked his master.

Sharif shrugged. "A nest for ages," he said, and the rug merchant's son had to be content with the baffling reply.

Two years passed. One evening Bashir's father got drenched in a downpour and caught pneumonia, which turned aggressive. Despite rapid treatment, he passed away. Bashir took over the shop. In his father's name, he turned their old house into a small Quran center (which would eventually become Bhati's only mosque). He ran the rug shop honestly and with Sharif's help was able to maintain business the way it had been.

At the end of his third year Sharif came to Bashir.

"My friend," he said. "I came here for a purpose. Something precious was given to me that is not mine to keep. It must wait here in the protection of the tree, even as I go help my father reopen his calligraphy stall."

The young rug merchant was not surprised. He had glimpsed his master's departure in his face the night he arrived. But what was that about a tree?

Sharif saw his student's face and smiled. "You don't remember, do you? Where your shop is now the eucalyptus tree used to stand."

Bashir was stunned. He had forgotten all about the tree and the incident with the jinn. It was as if a firm hand had descended and swept all memory of the incident from his brain, like a sand picture.

He waited for Sharif to go on, but the Calligrapher Prince rose, grasped Bashir's hand, and thrust two heavy envelopes into it.

"The first one is for you. Enough money to rent space for my trunk."

"You're not taking it with you?" Bashir was dumbfounded. The trunk with its elaborate design was worth hundreds, maybe thousands of rupees.

"No. It must stay here." Sharif looked his student in the eye. "And it must not be opened till a particular someone comes."

"Who?" said Bashir, and wished he hadn't. These were curious things and they made his spine tingle and his legs shake. A strange thought entered his head: *A burden the mountains couldn't bear settles on me tonight.* It vanished quick as it had come.

Sharif's voice was dry like swiftly turning thread when he said, "Look at the name on the second envelope."

And his heart full of misgivings, fears, and wonder—most of all, wonder—Bashir did.

I give myself credit: I was calm. My hands were steady. I didn't bat an eye when I took the yellowed envelope from Merchant Bashir's hands.

"It is yours," said Bashir. "The envelope, the secret, the burden." He wiped his face with the hem of his kameez. "Fifty years I carried it. Allah be praised, today it's passed on to you."

A burden the mountains couldn't bear settles on me tonight.

I shivered a little.

"It's cold," Bashir said. "I will turn the heat on and leave you to peruse the contents of the envelope alone. I'll be in the tea stall two shops down. Take as long as you wish."

"You kept your word," I said softly. "You didn't open the envelope."

Bashir nodded. "I asked Sharif how in God's name he could trust me with it when I didn't trust myself. A secret is like a disease, I said. It begins with an itch in a corner of your flesh, then spreads like cancer, until you're overcome and give in. He just smiled and said he knew I wouldn't open it." The rug weaver dabbed a kerchief at his grimy cheeks. "Maybe because he had such faith in me, it helped keep wicked desire at bay."

Or maybe he knew *you wouldn't,* I thought, holding the envelope, feeling my pulse beat in my fingertips. *Just like he knew the name of the rightful owner decades before he was born.*

My name.

Through the back window I watched Bashir tromp down the street. The mist had thickened and the alley was submerged in blue-white. A steady whine of wind and the occasional thump as pedestrians walked into trash cans and bicycle stands. A whorl of fog shimmered around the streetlight on the far corner.

I turned and went to the counter. Picked up the envelope. Sliced it open. Inside was a sheaf of blank papers. I pulled them out and a small object swept out and fell on the floor. I reached down and picked it up, its radiance casting a twitching halo on my palm.

It was a silver key with a grooved golden stud for a blade, dangling from a rusted hoop.

Impossible.

My gaze was riveted on the golden stud. It took a considerable amount of effort to force my eyes away, to pocket the key, rise, and shamble to the storeroom.

It was dark. Fog had weakened the daylight. Broken looms with their limp warp strings and tipping beams gaped. I crossed the room and stood in front of the brass trunk. The padlock was tarnished. Round keyhole. I retrieved the key and stared at it, this centuries-old gold stud—if one were to believe Gramps—fused to a silver handle.

The instruction was clear.

I brushed the dust away from the lid. A floral design was carved into it, wreathed with grime but still visible: a medallion motif in a gilt finish with a Quranic verse running through its heart like an artery.

"Those who believe in the Great Unseen," I whispered. In my head Baba smiled and a row of pine trees cast a long shadow across Gramps's tombstone where I had last read a similar epitaph.

I inserted the Mughal key into the padlock, turned it twice, and opened the trunk.

A rug. A rolled-up kilim, judging by its thinness.

I stared at it, at the lavish weave of its edges that shone from light *within* the rolled layers. Was there a flashlight inside? Ridiculous idea. I leaned in.

The kilim smelled of sunshine. Of leaves and earth and fresh rainfall. Scents that filled my nostrils and tapped my taste buds, flooded my mouth with a sweet tang, not unlike cardamom tea.

My palms were sweating despite the cold. I tugged at the fat end of the rug and it fell to the floor, unspooling. It was seven by five feet, its borders perfectly even, and as it raced across the room, the storeroom was inundated with colors: primrose yellow, iris white, smoke blue. A bright scarlet sparked in the air that reminded me of the sharbat Mama used to make during Ramadan.

I fell back. Awestruck, I watched this display of lights surging from the kilim. Thrashing and gusting and slamming into one another, spinning faster and faster until they became a dancing shadow with many rainbow arms, each pointing earthward to their source—the carpet.

The shadow pirouetted once more and began to sink. The myriad images in the carpet flashed as it dissolved into them, and within moments the room was dark. The only evidence of the specter's presence was the afterglow on my retina.

I breathed. My knees were weak, the base of my spine thrummed with charge. A smell like burning refuse lingered in my nostrils.

What was that?

A *miracle*, Gramps spoke in my head softly.

I went to the carpet. It was gorgeous. Multitudes of figures ran in every shape around its edges. Flora and fauna. Grotesques and arabesques. They seethed over nomadic symbols. I traced my finger across the surface. Cabalistic squares, hexagrams, eight-pointed stars, a barb-tailed scorpion. A concoction of emblems swirled together by the artisan's finger until it seemed the carpet crawled with arcana I'd seen in ancient texts used mostly for one purpose.

Traps, I thought. *For what?*

I peered closer. The central figures eddied to form the armature of a tower with four jagged limbs shot into the corners of the rug where they were pinned down with pieces of glass. Four curved symmetric pieces, clear with the slightest tinge of purple. Together these four quarter-circles stuck out from the corners of the kilim as if they had once belonged to a cup.

They shimmered.

"What are you," I whispered. The carpet and the embedded glass said nothing. I hesitated, the soles of my feet tingling, then bent and looked inside the upper right shard.

A man looked back at me, his face expressionless, young, and not mine.

"Salam, *beta*," Gramps said in Urdu, still smiling. "Welcome."

The age of wonders shivered and died when the world changed.

In the summer of 1963, however, an eighteen-year-old boy named Sharif discovered a miracle as he panted and dug and heaved an earthen pot out from under a rotten eucalyptus stump.

It was night, there were no streetlamps, and, by all laws holy, the dark should have been supreme. Except a light emanated from the pot.

Sharif wiped his forehead and removed the pot's lid. Inside was a purple glass chalice glowing with brightness he couldn't look upon. He had to carry it home and put on dark shades before he could peer in.

The chalice was empty and the light came from the glass itself.

Trembling with excitement, the boy wrapped it in a blanket and hid it under the bed. The next day when his parents were gone, he poured water into it and watched the liquid's meniscus bubble and seethe on the kitchen table. The water was the light and the light all liquid.

The fakir had warned the Mughal princess's grandfather that the secret was not for human eyes, but since that fateful night when the boy had first glimpsed the eucalyptus jinn, saw his fetters stretch from sky to earth, his dreams had been transformed. He saw nightscapes that he shouldn't see. Found himself in places that shouldn't exist. And now here was an enchanted cup frothing with liquid light on his kitchen table.

The boy looked at the chalice again. The churning motion of its contents hypnotized him. He raised it, and drank the light.

Such was how unfortunate, young Sharif discovered the secrets of Jaam-e-Jam.

The Cup of Heaven.

Legends of the Jaam have been passed down for generations in the Islamic world. Jamshed, the Zoroastrian emperor of Persia, was said to have possessed a seven-ringed scrying cup that revealed the mysteries of heaven to him. Persian mythmakers ascribed the centuries-long success of the empire to the magic of the Cup of Heaven.

And now it was in Sharif's hand.

The Mother of Revelations. It swept across the boy's body like a fever. It seeped inside his skin, blanched the marrow of his bones, until every last bit of him understood. He knew what he had to do next, and if he could he would destroy the cup, but that wasn't his choice anymore. The cup gave him much, including foreknowledge with all the knots that weave the future. Everything from that moment on he *remembered* already.

And now he needed to conceal it.

So Sharif left for the rest of his life. He went to Mansehra. Found the Mughal princess. Married her. He made her very happy for the rest of her brief life, and on a sunny Friday afternoon he took his goggling, squalling son with him to pray Juma in a mosque in the mountains, where he would stay the night for worship and meditation.

Even though he knew it was the day appointed for his wife's death.

There was no thought, no coercion, no struggle. Just the wisdom of extinction, the doggedness of destiny that steered his way. He and his son would return to find their family incinerated. Sharif and the villagers would carry out their charred corpses and he would weep; he was allowed that much.

After, he took his son to Turkey.

For years he learned rug weaving at a master weaver's atelier. His newfound knowledge demanded he rein in the Cup of Heaven's contents till the time for their disclosure returned. For that he must learn to prepare a special trap.

It took his fingers time to learn the trick even if his brain knew it. Years of mistakes and practice. Eventually he mastered the most sublime ways of weaving. He could apply them to create a trap so elegant, so fast and wise that nothing would escape it.

Sharif had learned how to weave the fabric of light itself.

Now he could return to his hometown, seek out the shadow of the eucalyptus tree, and prepare the device for imprisoning the cup.

First, he designed a kilim with the holy names of reality woven into it. Carefully, with a diamond-tipped glasscutter, he took the Jaam-e-Jam apart into four pieces and set them into the kilim. Next, he snared waves of light that fell in through the workshop window. He looped the peaks and troughs and braided them into a net. He stretched the net over the glass shards and warped them into place. He constructed a brass trunk and etched binding symbols on its lid, then rolled up the kilim and placed it inside.

Last, a special key was prepared. This part took some sorting out—he had to fetch certain particles farther along in time—but he succeeded; and finally he had the key. It was designed to talk to the blood-light in one person only, one descended from Sharif's line and the Mughal princess's.

Me.

Incredulous, I gazed at my dead grandfather as he told me his last story.

His cheeks glowed with youth, his eyes sharp and filled with truth. His hair was black, parted on the left. Maybe the glass shone, or his eyes, but the effect was the same: an incredible halo of light, near holy in its alienness, surrounded him. When he shook his head, the halo wobbled. When he spoke, the carpet's fringe threads stirred as if a breeze moved them, but the voice was sourceless and everywhere.

"Today is the sixteenth of November, 2013," he had said before launching into narration like a machine. "You're twenty-eight. The woman you love will be twenty-five in three months. As for me"—he smiled—"I'm dead."

He was telling me the future. Prescience, it seemed, had been his forte.

And now I knew how. The Cup of Heaven.

"Is it really you?" I said when he was done, my voice full of awe.

Gramps nodded. "More a portion of my punishment than me."

"What does that mean? What other secrets were in the cup? Tell me everything, Gramps," I said, "before I go crazy."

"All good stories leave questions. Isn't that what I will say?" He watched me, serious. "You should understand that I'm sorry. For bringing you here. For passing this on to you. I wish I'd never dug under that tree. But it is the way it is. I was handed a responsibility. I suppose we all get our burdens."

The air in the room was thick and musty. Our eyes were locked together. *He lured me here,* I thought. My hands were shaking and this time it was with anger. Rage at being manipulated. All those stories of princesses and paupers, those lies he told for years while all the time he knew exactly what he was doing and how he was preparing me for this burden, whatever it was.

Gramps's spirit, or whoever he was in this current state, watched me with eyes that had no room for empathy or guilt. Didn't he care at all?

"I do, son," he said gently. He was reading my mind or already knew it—I wasn't clear which—and that angered me more. "I haven't gotten to the most important part of the story."

"I don't care," I said in a low voice. "Just tell me what was in the cup."

"You need to know this." His tone was mechanical, not my gramps's voice. The person I knew and loved was not here. "The Jaam gave me much. Visions, power, perfect knowledge, but it cost me too. Quite a bit. You can't stare into the heart of the Unseen and not have it stare back at you."

He swept a hand around himself. For the first time I noticed the halo wasn't just hovering behind his head; it was a luminescent ring blooming from his shoulders, encircling his neck, wrapping around his body.

"It wasn't for me to decide the cup's fate, so I hid it away. But because the Unseen's presence ran like a torrent from it I paid more than a man should ever have to pay for a mistake. I was told to dig up the secret and hide it, not to gaze at its wonders or partake of its mysteries. My punishment hence was remembering the future and being powerless to prevent it. I would lose everything I remembered about the love of my life. Starting from the moment I dug under the eucalyptus, I would *forget* ever having been with your grandmother. My lovely, luckless Zeenat.

"Once the task was complete and I handed over the trunk to Bashir, my memories began to go. With time, my mind confabulated details to fill in the gaps and I told myself and everyone who'd ask that I had married a woman who died during childbirth. By the time we moved to America, all I remembered was this nostalgia and longing to discover a secret I thought I'd never pursued: the pauper princess and her magical jinn."

When he stopped, the outline of his face wavered. It was the halo blazing. "What you see before you"—with a manicured finger Gramps made a circle around his face—"is an impression of those lost years. My love's memory wrenched from me."

He closed his eyes, letting me study the absence of age on his face. If he were telling the truth, he was a figment of his own imagination, and I . . . I was crazy to believe any of this. This room was a delusion and I was complicit in it, solidifying it.

Maybe that was why he forgot. Maybe the human mind couldn't marry such unrealities and live with them.

"What about the journal? If you forgot everything, how could you draw? How could you write down details of your life?"

Gramps, his apparition, opened his eyes. "Senility. When my organic memory dissolved, fragments of my other life came seeping back in dreams."

So he wrote the journal entries like someone else's story. He had visions and dreams, but didn't know whose life was flooding his head, filling it with devastating images, maybe even ushering in his death earlier than it otherwise might have come.

I leaned back and watched the threads of the carpet twist. The woven tower shot into the sky with hundreds of creatures gathered around it, looking at its top disappear into the heavens.

"I want to see inside the cup." My voice rose like a razor in the dark, cutting through the awkwardness between us. "I want to see the contents."

"I know." He nodded. "Even such a warning as you see before you wouldn't deter you."

"If the cup's real, I will take it with me to the States, where historians and mythologists will validate its authenticity and. . . ."

And what? Truly believe it was a magical cup and place it in the Smithsonian? *The cup's secret isn't for human eyes,* Gramps had said. But what else are secrets for if not discovery? That is their nature. Only time stands between a mystery and its rightful master.

Gramps's fingers played with the halo, twisting strands of luminosity like hair between his fingers. "You will have the secret, but before you drink from it, I want you to do something for me."

He snapped his fingers and threads of light sprang from the halo, brightening as they came apart. Quickly he noosed them until he had a complicated knot with a glowing center and a string dangling at the end.

He offered it to me. "Pull."

Warily, I looked at the phosphorescent string. "Why?"

"Before you gaze inside the cup, you will have a taste of my memories. After that you decide your own demons."

I reached out a hand to the glass shard, withdrew, extended it again. When my fingers touched it, I flinched. It was warm. Slowly, I pushed my hand into the glass. It was like forcing it through tangles of leaves hot from the sun.

The string reddened. Its end whipped back and forth. I pinched it, pulled, and the light string rocketed toward me, the brilliant corpuscle at its center thrashing and unraveling into reality.

I gasped. A fat worm of peacock colors was climbing my hand, wrapping itself around my wrist.

"Gramps! What is this?" I shouted, twisting my arm, but the creature was already squirming its way up my arm, its grooves hot against my flesh, leaving shadows of crimson, mauve, azure, muddy green, and yellow on my skin. I could smell its colors. Farm odors. Damp foliage. Herbal teas. Baba's truck with its ancient vomit-stained upholstery and greasy wheel covers. My mother's hair. Sara's embrace.

I shuddered. The worm's body was taut across the bridge of my nose, its two ends poised like metal filings in front of my eyes.

"These," Gramps said, "are the stingers of memory."

The worm's barbs were like boulders in my vision. As I watched them, terrified, they vibrated once.

Then plunged into my eyes.

In the cup was everything, Gramps said. He meant it.

What the teenage boy saw went back all the way until he was destroyed and remade from the complete memory of the universe. From the moment of its birth until the end. Free of space, time, and their building blocks, the boy experienced all at once: a mausoleum of reality that wrapped around him, plunged into which he floated through the Unseen.

And I, a blinking, tumbling speck, followed.

Gramps watched the concussion of first particles reverberate through infinity. He watched instantaneous *being* bloom from one edge of existence to the other; watched the triumph of fire and ejective forces that shook creation in their fists. He observed these phenomena and knew all the realms of the hidden by heart.

Matter has always been conscious. That was the secret. Sentience is as much its property as gravity and it is always striving toward a new form with better accommodation.

From the needs of sentient matter rose the invention that humans are.

Gramps gripped the darkness of prebeing and billowed inside the cracks of matter. When I tried to go after him, an awful black defied me. To me belonged just a fraction of his immersion.

I sat on a molten petal of creation as it solidified, and watched serpentine fractals of revelation slither toward me. Jinns are carrier particles of sentience, they murmured. Of the universe's memory of the Great Migration.

My prehuman flesh sang on hearing these words. Truths it had once known made music in my body, even if I didn't quite remember them.

The Great Migration?

The first fires and winds created many primordials, the fractals said.

You mean jinns?

Beings unfettered by the young principles of matter and energy. As the world began to cool, new rules kicked in. The primordials became obsolete. Now the selfish sentience needed resistant clay-and-water creatures to thrive upon. For humans to exist, the primordials had to migrate.

They complied?

They dug tunnels into space-time and left our corner of existence so it could evolve on its own. Before they departed, however, they caged the memory of their being here, for if such a memory were unleashed upon the world, matter would rescind its newest form and return to the essence. Things as we know them would cease to exist.

So they made the cup, I said. *To imprison the memories of a bygone age.*

Before they passed into shadow, whispered the fractals, they made sure the old ways would be available. In case the new ones proved fleeting.

An image came to me then: a dazzling array of fantastical creatures—made of light, shadow, earth, inferno, metal, space, and time—traveling across a brimming gray land, their plethora of heads bowed. As they plodded, revolved, and flew, the dimensions of the universe changed around them to accommodate this pilgrimage of the phantastique. Matter erupted into iridescent light. Flames and flagella bloomed and dissolved. Their chiaroscuric anatomies shuttered as the primordials made their way into the breath of the unknown.

The flimsy speck that was I trembled. I was witnessing a colossal sacrifice. A mother of migrations. What should a vehicle of sentience do except bow before its ageless saviors?

In the distance, over the cusp of the planets, a primordial paused, its mammoth body shimmering itself into perception. As I watched it, a dreadful certainty gripped me: this was how Gramps was trapped. If I didn't look away immediately, I would be punished too, for when have human eyes glimpsed divinity without forsaking every sight they hold dear?

But I was rooted, stilled by the primordial's composition. Strange minerals gleamed in its haunches. From head to tail, it was decorated with black-and-white orbs like eyes. They twitched like muscles and revolved around its flesh until their center, a gush of flame riding bony gears, was visible to me. Mirages and reveries danced in it, constellations of knowledge ripe for the taking. Twisted ropes of fire shot outward, probing for surface, oscillating up and down.

My gaze went to a peculiar vision bubbling inside the fiery center. I watched it churn inside the primordial, and in the briefest of instants I knew what I knew.

As if sensing my study, the creature began to turn. Fear whipped me forward, a reverential awe goading me closer to these wonders undiluted by human genes, unpolluted by flesh, unmade by sentience.

Sentience is everything, sentience the mystery and the master, I sighed as I drifted closer.

But then came a shock wave that pulsed in my ears like a million crickets chirping. I rode the blast force, grief stricken by this separation, spinning and flickering through string-shaped fractures in reality, like gigantic cracks in the surface of a frozen lake. Somewhere matter bellowed like a swamp gator and the wave rushed at the sound. Tassels of light stirred in the emptiness, sputtering and branching like gargantuan towers—

Lightning trees, I thought.

—and suddenly I was veering toward them, pitched up, tossed down, slung across them until there was a whipping sound like the breaking of a sound barrier, and I was slipping, sliding, and falling through.

My eyes felt raw and swollen. I was choking.

I gagged and squirmed up from the carpet as the light worm crawled up my throat and out my left nostril. It rushed out, its segments instantly melting and fading to roseate vapors. The vapors wafted in the darkness like Chinese lanterns, lighting up discarded looms and moth-eaten rug rolls before dissipating into nothing.

I stared around, fell back, and lay spread-eagled on the carpet. The nostril through which the worm had exited was bleeding. A heavy weight had settled on my chest.

A memory came to me. Of being young and very small, standing at the classroom door, nose pressed against the glass, waiting for Mama. She was running late and the terror in me was so powerful, so huge, that all I could do was cry. Only it wasn't just terror, it was feeling abandoned, feeling insignificant, and knowing there wasn't a damn thing I could do about it.

Footsteps. I forced myself through the lethargy to turn on my side. Bashir the rug merchant stood outlined against the rectangle of light beyond the doorway. His face was in shadow. The blue of his eyes glinted.

"You all right, son?"

My heart pounded so violently I could feel it in every inch of my body. As if I were a leather-taut drum with a kid hammering inside and screaming.

"I don't know." I tottered upright, breathed, and glanced at the carpet. The light was gone and it was ordinary. Gramps was gone too. The cup's pieces in the corners were dull and empty.

Just glass.

I looked at Bashir. "I saw my grandfather."

"Yes." The rug merchant's shadow was long and alien on the carpet. "What will you do now that he's gone?"

I stared at him. His bright sapphire eyes, not old but ancient, watched me. He was so still. Not a hair stirred on his head. I wiped my mouth and finally understood.

"You're not the boy who fell," I said quietly. "The eucalyptus jinn. That's you."

He said nothing but his gaze followed me as I stepped away from the carpet, from this magical rectangle woven a half century ago. How long had he guarded the secret? Not the carpet, but the cup? How long since Bashir the rug merchant had died and the eucalyptus jinn had taken his form?

"A very long time," Bashir said in a voice that gave away nothing.

Our eyes met and at last I knew burden. Left behind by the primordial titans, here was a messenger of times past, the last of his kind, who had kept this unwanted vigil for millennia. Carrying the responsibility of the cup, silently waiting for the end of days. Was there a place in this new world for him or that damned chalice? Could there be a fate worse than death?

I stood before the caged shards of the Jaam. Gramps might have traversed the seven layers of heaven, but during my brief visit into the Unseen I'd seen enough to understand the pricelessness of this vehicle. Whatever magic the cup was, it transcended human logic.

Were it destroyed, the last vestige of cosmic memory would vanish from our world.

"Whatever you decide," the jinn said, "remember what you saw in the ideograms of the Eternum."

For a moment I didn't understand, then the vision returned to me. The mammoth primordial with its flaming core and the glimpse of what churned between its bonelike gears. My heartbeat quickened.

If what I saw was true, I'd do anything to protect it, even if it meant destroying the most glorious artifact the world would ever know.

The jinn's face was kind. He knew what I was thinking.

"What about the shop?" I asked, my eyes on the damaged looms, the dead insects, the obsolete designs no one needed.

"Will go to my assistant," he said. "Bashir's nephew."

I looked at him. In his eyes, blue as the deepest ocean's memory, was a lifetime of waiting. No, several lifetimes.

Oblivion. The eucalyptus jinn courted oblivion. And I would give it to him.

"Thank you," he said, smiling, and his voice was so full of warmth I wanted to cry.

"You miss the princess. You protected their family?"

"I protected only the cup. The Mughal lineage just happened to be the secret's bearer," said the eucalyptus jinn, but he wouldn't meet my eyes.

Which was why he couldn't follow them when they left, until Gramps went after them with the cup. Which was also why he couldn't save them from the fire that killed them. Gramps knew it too, but he couldn't or wouldn't do anything to change the future.

Was Gramps's then the worst burden of all? It made my heart ache to think of it.

We looked at each other. I stepped toward the brass trunk and retrieved the key with the gold stud from the padlock. Without looking at the jinn, I nodded.

He bowed his head, and left to fetch me the instruments of his destruction.

The city breathed fog when I left the rug shop. Clouds of white heaved from the ground, silencing the traffic and the streets. Men and women plodded in the alleys, their shadows quivering on dirt roads. I raised my head and imagined stars pricking the night sky, their light so puny, so distant, it made one wistful. Was it my imagination or could I smell them?

The odd notion refused to dissipate even after I returned to the inn and packed for the airport. The colors of the world were flimsy. Things skittered in the corners of my eyes. They vanished in the murmuring fog when I looked at them. Whatever this new state was, it wasn't disconcerting. I felt warmer than I had in years.

The plane bucked as it lifted, startling the passengers. They looked at one another and laughed. They'd been worried about being grounded because of weather. I stared at the ground falling away, away, the white layers of Lahore undulating atop one another, like a pile of rugs.

My chin was scratchy, my flesh crept, as I brought the hammer down and smashed the pieces of the cup.

I leaned against the plane window. My forehead was hot. Was I coming down with something? Bereavement, PTSD, post-party blues? But I *had* been through hell. I should expect strange, melancholic moods.

The flame twitched in my hand. The smell of gasoline strong in my nose. At my feet the carpet lay limp like a terrified animal.

"Coffee, sir?" said the stewardess. She was young and had an angular face like a chalice. She smiled at me, flashing teeth that would look wonderful dangling from a hemp string.

"No," I said, horrified by the idea, and my voice was harsher than I'd intended. Startled, she stepped back. I tried to smile, but she turned and hurried away.

I wiped my sweaty face with a paper napkin and breathed. Weird images, but I felt more in control, and the feeling that the world was losing shape had diminished. I unzipped my carry-on and pulled out Gramps's journal. So strange he'd left without saying goodbye.

That ghost in the glass was just a fragment of Gramps's memories, I told myself. *It wasn't him.*

Wasn't it? We are our memories. This mist that falls so vast and brooding can erase so much, but not the man. Will I remember Gramps? Will I remember *me* and what befell me in this strange land midway between the Old World and the New?

That is a question more difficult to answer, for, you see, about ten hours ago, when I changed planes in Manchester, I realized I am beginning to forget. Bits and pieces, but they are disappearing irrevocably. I have already forgotten the name of the street where Gramps and the princess once lived. I've even forgotten what the rug shop looked like. What was its name?

Karavan Kilim! An appropriate name, that. The word is the etymologic root for *caravan*. A convoy, or a party of pilgrims.

At first, it was terrifying, losing memories like that. But as I pondered the phenomenon, it occurred to me that the erasure of my journey to Old Lahore is so important the rest of my life likely depends on it. I have come to believe that the colorlessness of the world, the canting of things, the jagged movements of shadows is the peeling of the onionskin which separates men from the worlds of jinn. An unfractured reality from the Great Unseen. If the osmosis persisted, it would drive me mad, see?

That was when I decided I would write my testament while I could. I have been writing in this notebook for hours now and my fingers are hurting. The process has been cathartic. I feel more anchored to our world. Soon, I will stop writing and put a reminder in the notebook telling myself to seal it in an envelope along with Gramps's journal when I get home. I will place them in a deposit box at my bank. I will also prepare a set of instructions for my lawyer that, upon my death, the envelope and its contents be delivered to my grandson who should then read it and decide accordingly.

Decide what? You might say. There's no more choice to make. Didn't I destroy the carpet and the cup and the jinn with my own hands? Those are about the few memories left in my head from this experience. I remember destroying the rug and its contents. So vivid those memories, as if someone painted them inside my head. I remember my conversation with the jinn; he was delighted to be banished forever.

Wasn't he?

This is making me think of the vision I had in—what did the jinn call it?—the Eternum.

The root *J-N-N* has so many derivatives. *Jannah*, paradise, is the hidden garden. *Majnoon* is a crazy person whose intellect has been hidden. My favorite, though, is *janin*.

The embryo hidden inside the mother.

The jinn are not gone from our world, you see. They've just donned new clothes.

My beloved Terry, I saw your face printed in a primordial's flesh. I know you, my grandson, before you will know yourself. I also saw your father, my son, in his mother's womb. He is so beautiful. Sara doesn't know yet, but Neil will be tall and black-haired like me. Even now, his peanut-sized mass is drinking his mother's fluids. She will get migraines throughout the pregnancy, but that's him borrowing from his mom. He will return the kindness when he's all grown up. Sara's kidneys will fail and my fine boy will give his mother one, smiling and saying she'll never be able to tell him to piss off again because *her* piss will be formed through his gift.

My Mughal children, my pauper princes, you and your mother are why I made my decision. The Old World is gone, let it rest. The primordials and other denizens of the Unseen are obsolete. If memory of their days threatens the world, if mere mention of it upsets the order of creation, it's too dangerous to be left to chance. For another to find.

So I destroyed it.

The historian and the bookkeeper in me wept, but I'd do it a thousand times again if it means the survival of our species. Our children. No use mourning what's passed. We need to preserve our future.

Soon, I will land in the US of A. I will embrace the love of my life, kiss her, take her to meet my family. They're wary, but such is the nature of love. It protects us from what is unseen. I will teach my parents to love my wife. They will come to know what I already know. That the new world is not hostile, just different. My parents are afraid and that is okay. Someday I too will despise your girlfriends (and fear them), for that's how the song goes, doesn't it?

Meanwhile, I'm grateful. I was witness to the passing of the Great Unseen. I saw the anatomy of the phantastique. I saw the pilgrimage of the primordials. Some of their magic still lingers in the corners of our lives, wrapped in breathless shadow, and that is enough. We shall glimpse it in our dreams, taste it in the occasional startling vision, hear it in a night bird's song. And we will believe for a moment, even if we dismiss these fancies in the morning.

We will believe. And, just like this timeless gold stud that will soon adorn my wife's nose, the glamour of such belief will endure forever.

ABOUT THE EDITOR
Jacob Weisman

Jacob Weisman is the publisher at Tachyon Publications, which he founded in 1995. He is a three-time World Fantasy Award nominee and is the series editor of Tachyon's critically acclaimed, award-winning novella line, including the Hugo Award–winning *The Emperor's Soul* by Brandon Sanderson and the Nebula and Shirley Jackson Award–winning *We Are All Completely Fine* by Daryl Gregory. Weisman has edited the anthologies *Invaders: 22 Tales from the Outer Limits of Literature*, *The Sword & Sorcery Anthology* (with David G. Hartwell), and *The Treasury of the Fantastic* (with David M. Sandner). He lives in San Francisco.

ABOUT THE EDITOR
Peter S. Beagle

Peter Soyer Beagle is the internationally best-selling and much-beloved author of numerous classic fantasy novels and collections, including *The Last Unicorn, Tamsin, The Line Between, Sleight of Hand, Summerlong,* and *In Calabria.* He is the editor of *The Secret History of Fantasy* and the co-editor of *The Urban Fantasy Anthology.*

Born in Manhattan and raised in the Bronx, Beagle began to receive attention for his artistic ability even before he received a scholarship to the University of Pittsburgh. Exceeding his early promise, he published his first novel, *A Fine & Private Place,* at nineteen, while still completing his degree in creative writing. Beagle's follow-up, *The Last Unicorn,* is widely considered one of the great works of fantasy. It has been made into a feature-length animated film, a stage play, and a graphic novel.

Beagle went on to publish an extensive body of acclaimed works of fiction and nonfiction. He has written widely for both stage and screen, including the screenplay adaptations for *The Last Unicorn* and the animated film of *The Lord of the Rings* and the well-known "Sarek" episode of *Star Trek.*

As one of the fantasy genre's most-lauded authors, Beagle has been the recipient of the Hugo, Nebula, Mythopoeic, and Locus awards as well as the Grand Prix de l'Imaginaire. He has also been honored with the World Fantasy Life Achievement Award and the Inkpot

Award from the Comic-Con convention, given for major contributions to fantasy and science fiction.

Beagle lives in Richmond, California, where he is working on too many projects to even begin to name.